OUTCAST ISLAND

Freedom's Last Stand

James Keena

Book II in The Pathless Land Series

Outcast Island
Copyright © 2024 by James Keena

All rights reserved. No part of this book may be reproduced in any form or by any means—whether electronic, digital, mechanical, or otherwise—without permission in writing from the publisher, except by a reviewer, who may quote brief passages in a review.

The views and opinions expressed in this book are those of the author and do not necessarily reflect the official policy or position of Illumify Media Global.

Published by
Illumify Media Global
www.IllumifyMedia.com
"Let's bring your book to life!"

Library of Congress Control Number: 2024905487

Paperback ISBN: 979-8-218-09919-0

Cover design by Debbie Lewis

Printed in the United States of America

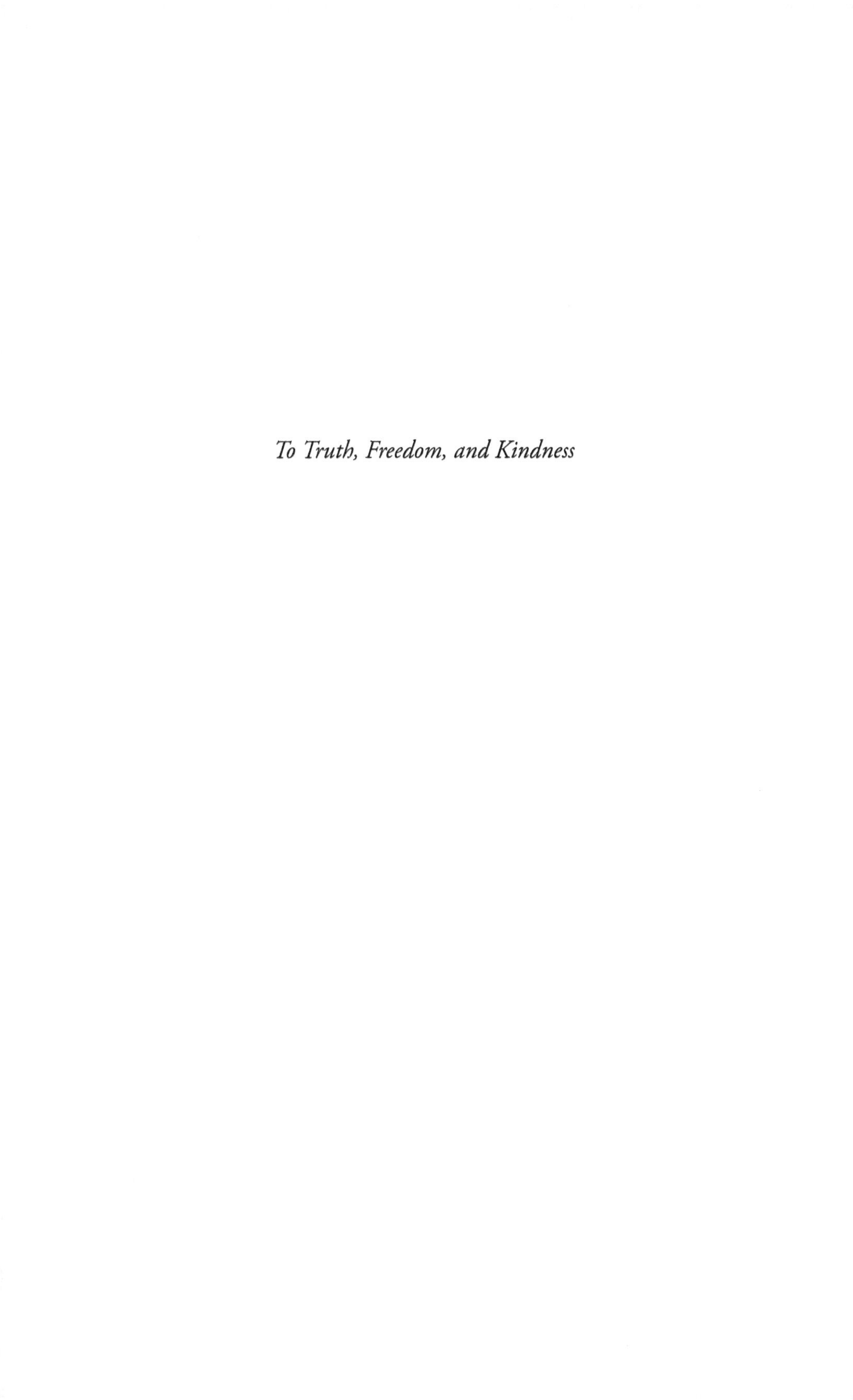

To Truth, Freedom, and Kindness

1

____

GOODBYE

John had just seen his wife, Mary, for the last time.

Their final goodbyes had nearly stolen his breath away with grief. Her wondrous lavender scent from their final hug still lingered on his clothing, and he inhaled deeply to sear it into his memory.

At his writing desk in their dank basement, he sat mesmerized by a faded sepia-colored picture of her that was set in a wood frame he'd handcrafted long ago. Tears formed in the corners of his eyes as his shoulders slumped. He and Mary had worked hard to raise their two children on their Kansas farm, overcoming daunting odds and facing countless dangers together. But after today, she would have to carry on without him. He dropped his head into his hands.

Their ranch was surrounded by a few acres of oxen-tilled farmland and endless miles of prairie. There were few people in the area who would be able help her. The nearest town, a village named Independence, was ten miles away. There were no phones, no police, no utilities, and no motorized vehicles—absolutely no societal structure in the entire region. Ever since the civil war had begun in 2057, people referred to these chronic deprivations as the Darkness.

After today, their younger son, James, would be Mary's only

companion. John's gaze shifted to a faded picture of James taken years ago when he was just a frolicsome boy. Now seventeen, he would have to become a man whether he was ready to or not.

John regretted the way he and James had parted just moments ago. His son was curt and impudent during an awkward discussion, laden with the edginess of teenage angst. James had sensed that dire things were afoot and therefore challenged his father to cease his dangerous involvement with the rebels and to instead focus on their family. John gruffly brushed off his son's remonstrations, hoping to trigger an angry response. His goal was to keep James out of harm's way. To his satisfaction, James left their home in a huff to sulk with his girlfriend, Audrey. John silently forgave him for his anger because his son was unaware he would never see his father again. Though he'd chosen not to reveal that sad fact, John now feared he would regret that decision for the rest of his life.

His thoughts drifted to his older son, Kieran, who had moved to the capital in Washington, DC, to join with the Elites. John had burned every picture that remained of him. Intentional betrayal by a child is almost as painful to a parent as the death of a child. He silently cursed his traitorous son because it was he who had summoned the armed agents converging on their farm. Their imminent arrival would rip their family apart. John kept an empty picture frame on his desk as a constant reminder of his son's treachery. A familiar surge of disgust washed over him as he glared at it.

John noticed his evanescent reflection in the smudged glass of the empty frame, but it soon became blurred by the tears welling in his eyes. His accumulating years were marked by some wrinkles and dark splotches on his sun-burnished face. His shoulder-length hair was a mix of gray and black, matching his trimmed salt-and-pepper beard. But his emerald eyes raged in stark contrast to his fading youth. He saw in them the depth of his own resolve to rectify his cowardice. Precious years were slipping away though.

John snapped out of his morose reverie. There was no time to reminisce, despite his desperate urge to cling to a life that was about to evaporate. His last remaining task was to pack the gray metal container that would store his meager personal treasures. He had delayed this effort partly because of a forlorn dread that it was pointless, and partly because it would entomb what remained of his past.

The first item he placed in the container was the black leather journal in which he had scribbled his deepest thoughts during the past three years. He whispered a bitter goodbye to a trove of wisdom and memories that would now be forever hidden.

He then placed seven small gold bars atop the journal. The gleaming metal rectangles were his family's life savings. The gold was carefully hoarded during twenty years of hard work on the farm and from black-market trading with the few remaining people in Independence. It was a small fortune by today's standard, especially since paper money was worth little in the year 2057, but the gold would be useless to him now. He had offered the bars to Mary, but she was deathly afraid that possessing such contraband would draw the unwelcome attention of covetous people.

Next, John placed a cigar box laden with bullets atop the gold bars. The ammunition was used for warding off starving itinerants intending to pilfer grain from their silo. It was also used for scattering the famished packs of feral dogs that threatened their farm animals. But the nomads and the wild animals weren't the most dangerous predators. He recalled the horrific day when he shot the two government agents who had come to their ranch with a warrant to apprehend his mother, who had committed the crime of turning seventy years old, which meant she was officially an unproductive burden on scarce societal resources. He'd spirited her away to live with his aunt in the survivalist enclave that used to be Montana and never heard from her again because long-distance communication was impossible now. Daily, he wondered if she was still alive.

The next personal treasure John chose was a desiccated white rose snipped from his carefully tended bushes. The roses were among his most sacred possessions. The white rose symbolized everything he believed in and everything he was about to pay a terrible price for. With reverence, he placed it into the container.

The final item he stashed was a pistol. Mary didn't want it, despite the dangers lurking in the Darkness. The Elites had outlawed private gun ownership for everyone except their bodyguards, and whoever was caught with one was punished. She feared the Elites more than she feared anything else in the Darkness because they were the cause of it. John was terrified by Mary's decision to face her dire future without guns or gold, but she was a tough, stubborn woman who could endure almost anything—except perhaps her persistent cough. She was tormented by chronic pneumonia. As if on cue, he heard her hacking up phlegm upstairs.

"Damn!" John blurted. She was supposed to be hiding quietly in a closet until the imminent crisis ended one way or another.

He closed the cover of the metal container as if shutting the lid to a coffin, then cradled it in his hands while an unspoken eulogy flashed through his brain. After placing it in a cavity he had chiseled in the foundation of the basement, he positioned some bricks to conceal the hole, then stacked dusty boxes of forbidden books in front of the concealment. The rest of his forbidden books were hidden in a cache under the basement floor.

More tears formed in John's eyes, and he wiped them away. His collection of illicit books was another of his sacred possessions. When TV, radio, and the internet were cut off for everyone west of the Appalachians, his books became his sole intellectual fuel and only source of entertainment. He also used them to homeschool his sons. He shook his head somberly, doubtful that James had absorbed the true potency of his outlawed education. He knew for certain that Kieran had not, simply because he had rejected it all by defecting to the Elites.

John jumped, startled by a violent pounding on the front door upstairs even though he had been expecting the unwelcome intrusion.

"Homeland Security! Open up!" The shouts reverberated down to the basement. A much louder smash against the door followed, which John guessed was the handiwork of a battering ram. He rose from his chair as he heard the splintering of wood. The door had given way to repeated assaults.

His heart raced, knowing he had instigated this crisis by making speeches in the town square of Independence and by distributing controversial pamphlets that railed against the country's leaders. The

Elites had abandoned America's traditional governance in favor of totalitarian control and suppression of all resistance. John's brazen calls for insurrection were impossible for his prodigal son, Kieran, and his network of spies to overlook. But even though John had purposely put himself in harm's way, the brutal reality of his sedition crashed down upon him. He started for the stairs in response to the incessant shouting from above, then retreated to his desk. Picking up Mary's picture, he gave her image a final kiss, then bounded up the stairs, his heart aflame with a strange mixture of sadness, dread, and excitement.

It was in that explosive mental state where John's worst fears and life's deepest truths were being realized. He was transitioning from a man once ashamed of himself to the man he'd always wished himself to be. It had taken him years to realize that no one should have to live on their knees. He had finally chosen the right path instead of the easy path, and now he was going to take a stand, even if it cost him everything. Today marked the end of his cowardice.

He heard heavy footsteps rampaging through the house and then furniture being tossed around. Just before he opened the stairwell door to reveal himself to the agents, he bowed his head. *Fear doesn't stop evil; it emboldens it,* John thought, assuring himself as he swung open the basement door.

His sudden appearance startled two Homeland Security agents, who leveled their guns at him. They were wearing black-shirted uniforms, each with a royal-purple logo just below the neckline, offset to the left. The logo depicted the world cradled in the hands of some unseen but presumably powerful person and bore no inscription.

Three other agents rushed to swarm John, who quickly raised his hands in surrender.

"John Paine?" a brawny agent barked.

"That's the name red-flagged in your surveillance databases," John said with a smirk.

The agent glared at him, then lifted his rifle and swung it with full force at his taller adversary. The butt collided against the side of John's head with an awful thud, causing John to stagger backward.

As his ears roared, confused images danced wildly in his brain. He felt warm rivulets of blood seeping down his face.

"By order of Kieran Paine, you're under arrest for sedition," the agent snarled.

"Did the bastard get his thirty pieces of silver?" John spat out.

Another agent kicked John in the abdomen with his jackboot. "Shut up and submit!"

John doubled over from the blow and gritted his teeth, refusing to cry out in pain. "If forced to choose between submission and rebellion, I'll choose rebellion," he grunted.

"You'll pay dearly for that," an agent replied, then signaled to his companions. "Secure him."

Two men grappled with John until they pinned his muscular arms behind his broad back. After they immobilized him, they searched him and applied handcuffs. Then they pulled a black executioner's hood over his head. John felt a heavy rope slide over his head down to his neck. An agent tightened the noose so that it would choke him if he resisted, and a chain was clasped to his ankles.

John said nothing while they manhandled him. He knew it was useless to argue with politically intoxicated people. In the old days, only criminals were punished. Now everyone who refused to comply with the Elites was punished. Laws and due process had become ancient artifacts of a collapsed society, leaving no safe place for anyone outside the cult.

Besides, everything was going as he intended.

2

———

OUTCASTS

John was shackled to a rotting bench in the bowels of a rust-bucket ship. He was among scores of other captives who were packed under the deck like sardines. They were assaulted by the accumulated stench of thousands of other prisoners who had previously been transported in the dank hellhole. The fetid bilge water, the feces and urine, and the unwashed prisoners produced a toxic air that burned their lungs. An open hatchway above their heads let in feeble wisps of oxygen, but it did little to ease the suffocation. They were given no food or water during their many hours of confinement.

The hold was dimly lit by two bare bulbs that flickered when waves shuddered the ship. In the cavernous dusk, John took stock of his fellow outcasts. Sweat streamed down their faces and bodies, soiling their ragged clothing. Most had long, unkempt hair that hung in sodden, tangled clumps. The unhealthiest of them gasped for breath. Everyone seemed to moan and curse. Some ranted forlorn pleas to their gods. Many had been beaten during their capture. The wretched men looked as if they were on the verge of surrendering their humanity. John wondered if he looked like that too.

The creaking ship tossed in the heavy weather, popping a few rusted rivets with each lurch. Before it departed Miami, a black-shirted guard on the wharf snickered that it was still hurricane season. He said a nasty storm was on its way, then expressed his hope that the prisoners would be brutalized by the rough transit across the Florida Straits to Outcast Island. He punctuated his hope with a guttural laugh.

The snickering guard was prescient. With each roll of the ship, storm-driven waves crested onto the deck. Sea water poured through the open hatch, blending with the sickening sewage in the hold to compound the misery of the prisoners. The cantankerous engines strained against the waves and the wind. Metallic clanging and grinding echoed eerily.

Seasickness swept through their ranks. Men retched violently, their puke blending into the rancid bilge water. John numbly realized that his harsh journey in captivity from Kansas to the docks in Miami was no longer the most soul-searing experience of his life. Even though that two-week trek included starvation, beatings, and bone-jarring jaunts across crumbling roads, it now seemed like heaven to him.

John suspected that things would get worse when they reached Outcast Island though. The ship was likely filled with felons, rebels, dissidents, and other social misfits. The ungoverned destination that awaited them was already crowded with such miscreants. For years, dictators around the world had deported their undesirables to Outcast Island, which used to be called Cuba before it collapsed into anarchy. John envisioned it as a devil's island of the world's worst criminals and rogues, a lawless land of unimaginable danger.

Wild rumors abounded about the wretched conditions on Outcast Island. It was said that savage gangs fought to the death for scarce food and dominion over others. Slavery and torture were commonplace. The outcasts spoke different languages, believed different creeds, and came from different classes and cultures. Their only commonality was that they would never see their home countries again.

The World Order maintained a naval cordon around Outcast

Island to prevent any escapes. They didn't care whether the abandoned outcasts lived or died after being dumped there. Their sole concern was making sure that the undesirables couldn't return to civilization to agitate the already unstable populations around the world.

The greatest fear of the World Order was an uprising by the proles, which is why they banished those who might spark a rebellion. They had learned that killing the outcasts in their native countries enraged people and elevated the slaughtered miscreants to martyrdom. So now the outcasts simply vanished from public consciousness to an utterly isolated island.

A violent roll of the ship caused John to lurch against the man sitting to his right. "Sorry," he muttered.

"I forgive you, *señor*," the Hispanic man replied in a tone so calm that John wondered if he was oblivious to their desperate situation.

John studied him. He had long, dark brown hair, a mustache and beard, and a dark complexion. His calloused hands evidenced a lifetime of hard work. A plaid shirt and denim pants covered his tall frame. The sandals on his feet were soaked from the noxious slurry in the hold. But what John noticed most was the incongruous look of peace on his face.

"Why are you in this godforsaken boat?" John asked.

"God forsakes nothing," the Hispanic man replied. "The Elites arrested me because I spoke the truth. They hate the truth. Many people do."

John raised an eyebrow, sensing a potential ally. "What did you do for a living?"

"I was a carpenter and a teacher."

John's face brightened a bit. "I homeschooled my two sons. And we're going to need a carpenter when we get to Outcast Island." He extended his hand. "Name's John. Yours?"

His neighbor grasped John's hand firmly with both of his. "It's not *mi nombre* that matters, but what I do. Please, call me the Carpenter."

"Then I should have introduced myself as the Farmer. But I prefer John."

"Why are you here, Farmer John?"

"Karma," he replied. "I wasted years being afraid to face dangers that eventually proved inescapable. I finally learned that cowardice never deters wolves that are on the hunt. So now I'm going to kill the wolves."

The Carpenter looked puzzled. "Does that mean you *chose* to be on this awful boat?"

A few heads within earshot turned toward John, wondering if a bizarre admission was in the offing.

"Yes," John said resolutely. "I wanted to be exiled from the insanity in America. It has no hope for redemption. Outcast Island is the world's best opportunity for a fresh start. It has no privileged Elites, only millions of desperate souls yearning for a better life. I intend to spark the rise of a new society there."

The eavesdroppers reacted with derision. John overheard mumbled judgments like "idiot" and "fool." The Carpenter, however, studied John with heightened interest.

One of the eavesdroppers nudged the Carpenter gruffly. "Ignore the suicidal lunatic."

The Carpenter smiled at the interloper. "I understand Farmer John's mission completely. The hated, the poor, and the marginalized are my people too."

John nodded in silent appreciation. "Rough crew we have here," he observed. "Probably some thieves and killers. And a whole bunch of rebels, I hope."

"Ignore their appearances and forgive their histories," the Carpenter replied. "All that matters is what they choose to do from this day forward."

John felt a finger jab his left arm. The wispy man on his other side was seeking his attention. John turned to eye the stranger. He did a double take because this short, wiry Asian looked so out of place wearing the simple brown robe of a monk. His head was completely bald, and his ears protruded awkwardly. His dark, serene eyes dominated his face and spoke of a wisdom acquired from many years of contemplation. It was hard to tell his age though.

"What do you want?" John asked.

"I want nothing," the Monk replied. "But I'm intrigued that you spoke of karma."

John shook his head in dismay. "This isn't the right time . . ."

"We're going to be tested beyond endurance," his seatmate persisted. "We own nothing now except the actions we're about to take. We can't escape their consequences. Isn't that what you meant by karma?"

"Something like that," John muttered. He glanced up at the ceiling because a torrential downpour was dumping rainwater through the open hatch, adding to their periodic dousing from the cresting waves. He wiped briny droplets from his face. "I'll say it differently. Working hard at the wrong things counts for nothing. That was my mistake. Working hard at the right things is what matters."

"Yes, yes!" the Monk cried, drawing annoyed glares from others around them. "We must not ignore our hardships. Instead, we must face them directly."

Heavy footsteps resounded on the decking above near the open hatch. "I think we're about to embrace a whole shitload of hardships," John said.

There was a loud metallic clatter as several keychains were tossed down the open hatchway by a deckhand. He shouted above the storm, "Pass the keys around! Unlock your shackles, then climb up to the deck one by one with your arms raised!" He paused, and then added some motivation. "Last one out gets shot." He thrust a rickety ladder down the hatch to aid their exit.

A mad scramble ensued. Men shouted, grabbed, and cursed, frantically unlocking their shackles when they got their hands on a set of keys. When keys finally were passed to John's bench, the Monk took them first. He hesitated, then handed them to John without unlocking his shackles. John was shaken by the significance of this.

"What the hell are you thinking?"

The Monk smiled serenely. "When I look at a sea of fire, I see a lotus instead. I shall go last."

They locked eyes. In that instant, John sensed that this unusual man might have been another ally, except he wasn't going to make it to the island. John sighed, unlocked his own shackles, and passed the keys to the Carpenter.

John and the Carpenter edged into the panicked queue that was scrambling to ascend the ladder. After some persistent jostling, they climbed up, then breached the hatchway and were assaulted by heavy rain and gusting wind. John took great gulps of fresh sea air to cleanse his lungs. Lightning slashed the darkness all around them like a celestial strobe. Guards nudged them with their rifles toward the aft of the ship where the other outcasts who had already ascended were huddled against the storm.

The cresting waves and the tossing ship made for treacherous footing on the deck. John slipped and fell while making his way aft. The Carpenter, who seemed to balance effortlessly on the watery sheen, grabbed John's arm to prevent him from sliding across the pitched deck into the railing.

More outcasts emerged from the hatchway and staggered to join their compatriots. When men stopped coming from below, a guard shouted to the last man who had climbed out. "Are you the last one?" He raised his rifle and aimed it at the straggler.

"Stop!" came a shout from the hatchway. The bald head of the Monk protruded above the deck. "I am the last, not him."

The guard waved his intended victim to the aft of the ship, gesturing for the Monk to stand alone in the middle of the deck. The Monk complied, standing erect in front of his executioner. The guard was taken aback by his stoic demeanor.

"You're not afraid to die?"

"I do not live in the past or the future," the Monk shouted above the storm. "Every moment of the present contains both joy and suffering. I always choose joy."

The guard hesitated as a flash of doubt washed across his face. Then he aimed his rifle and fingered the trigger. Before he could pull it, though, a massive wave smashed against the hull of the ship and flooded the deck. Its watery momentum swept the elfin Monk off his feet and slammed him against the railing. The burly guard lost his balance and dropped to one knee. Amid the darkness and the perilous rolling of the ship, he struggled to aim at the Monk, who now lay crumpled in a heap.

The Carpenter broke ranks from the outcasts and dashed across the deck toward the Monk. He threw his body over him to shield him from the shooter.

"Stand down!" the captain of the ship shouted, who had descended from the bridge to speed up their progress. "The storm's getting worse. No time for games. We need to hurry back to safe harbor in Miami. Toss the bastards and their rafts into the sea. Let's get the hell out of here!"

The guard reluctantly lowered his rifle. "Why don't we just shoot 'em all, Captain?"

"Because we'd still have to throw their bodies overboard, then clean up the bloody mess on the deck. Besides, these misfits deserve the terror of the sea rather than a merciful bullet to the head."

The captain turned his attention to the outcasts. "We normally jettison our prisoners near the sandy beaches!" he explained, his distaste for the men obvious. "But tonight, we're dumping you near the rocks as a hurricane approaches. Kieran Paine ordered us to abandon you into the worst possible conditions." The captain paused and pointed directly at John. "Because of him."

John was stunned. His backstabbing son had committed a final act of treachery by making sure the captain publicly defamed him. John was now marked as the cause of the outcasts' imminent terror in the sea. This would sow great animosity among his fellow exiles and maybe even poison his future ambitions. If he had a future. He hated Kieran more than he ever thought possible. How had he raised such a monster?

Men around him grumbled, but there was no time for John to fume over this new dilemma. Winches began lowering flimsy wooden rafts into the roiling sea. He counted them and estimated their capacity, figuring there were roughly a hundred outcasts on the ship. His grim math indicated there weren't enough rafts for everyone.

"Outcast Island is that way!" the captain shouted into the gale. He pointed, although no land could be seen in the stormy darkness.

"Whoever doesn't jump overboard within sixty seconds will be shot. It's your choice whether you enter the sea dead or alive. The sharks won't care."

"We outnumber the sailors!" one of the outcasts yelled. "Let's rush them and take the ship!"

There was a deathly stillness for several precious seconds as the outcasts considered this challenge. John counted seven leering guards arrayed around them, each armed with automatic rifles. The guards surely had more bullets than the outcasts had numbers.

"Don't!" he shouted to the conspirators. "They'll slaughter us!"

Seconds ticked away as muffled discussions swirled among the ranks. Suddenly, three men charged toward the nearest guard. Shots rang out instantly, and the three foolish men crumpled to the deck, their blood mixing with the salty foam sloshing around their inert bodies.

The bloody carnage shocked the rest of the outcasts from their stupor. They dashed pell-mell for the railing. They jumped overboard with insane abandon into the full fury of the rising hurricane.

John leapt with the rest. In the brief moment between his jump from the deck and his impact with the churning water, he yelled out a goodbye to Mary one last time.

3

———

STORM

J ohn plunged feet first into the dark cauldron. His momentum carried him deep under water, but his feet didn't touch the bottom. The sudden cold shocked his body and numbed his limbs. Sea water filled his sinuses. It felt like the entire ocean was pressing against his eardrums. He opened his eyes but saw nothing.

He scissor-kicked his legs and paddled madly with his arms, but the weight of his soaked clothes worked against him. So did the flailing and thrashing of other panicked castoffs nearby. There was pandemonium in the water, like when a school of fish senses an approaching shark.

John held his breath despite the desperate urge to suck air into his lungs. It struck him that it was easy to overlook the simple glory of breathing until he was unable to do so. His body was gyrated by the waves and the undertow, completely disorienting him. His heart pounded in his ears, and his muscles cramped.

After what seemed like an eternity, his head finally broke the surface. He sucked in great gulps of air mixed with sea spray. Unseen hands grabbed his legs, then slipped away into the churning nether below. He blindly snagged someone's arm, but a wave wrenched his grip loose. The howling wind lashed sea foam and rainwater sideways, pelting his face like sleet in a blizzard.

He bobbed up and down on the crests and in the valleys of enormous waves. Each harrowing descent into a steep trough left him fearing it would be his last until the swell of the next wave heaved him upward again. Lightning flashes briefly illuminated the seascape, but even then, the deluge was so intense that he couldn't see much.

Something bumped his shoulder. A shark? His panic rose another notch. When it bumped him again, he realized it was one of the rafts—a shabby wooden platform with two buoyant barrels underneath. It was a poor excuse for a vessel, John thought, which seemed a fitting farewell gesture from the fiends on the ship. He hoisted himself aboard with what little remained of his strength.

John sprawled on his belly with his fingers wedged between wooden slats. The rickety craft was perilously unstable in the maelstrom. Riding it was almost as terrifying as treading in the turbulent water. It had no oars or rudder, so John was going wherever the irresistible forces of nature took him. But at least aboard the raft he wouldn't sink to the sea bottom from exhaustion.

It dawned on him that his earlier concern about a raft shortage was pointless. Many men had likely already drowned or would never find a raft in the frenzied darkness. Or maybe the sharks had already devoured them.

He heard haunting cries for help but couldn't see anyone. He wriggled to the edge of the raft and tried to paddle toward the desperate pleas, but his awkward arm strokes were no match for the ferocity of the storm. The raft was pushed, pulled, lifted, plunged, and spun by wind and waves. He could only hope that the uncaring forces of nature were taking him toward the shore rather than out to sea.

John's raft bumped against a desperate man flailing in the water. John reached down and pulled him up with a mighty heave, nearly capsizing the raft in the process. The fellow castaway lay on the crude platform in near-death exhaustion, coughing up sea water. Another screaming, flailing man materialized nearby, like a ghost in the darkness. With a surge of adrenaline coursing through his veins, John hoisted him up too.

Their rudderless craft careened into another that was carrying four men clinging for dear life. That left four other rafts unaccounted for, along with roughly ninety missing men. John felt an overwhelming sense of helplessness and began screaming into the darkness, hoping his voice would be a beacon to attract survivors. The other raft-borne men joined his desperate chorus. There were no answering shouts.

A towering wave crested over John's raft, rocking it so violently that all three men were tossed overboard. When John plunged into the water, his feet struck a rock on the sea bottom. He planted them and propelled himself to the surface. All three men were able to climb back on board the bobbing platform. John felt a glimmer of hope because the contact with the rock implied they were approaching the shore.

Above the roar of the storm, John became aware of an even louder cacophony coming from the shoreline. He remembered the captain saying they were being jettisoned near the rockiest part of the coast. He heard massive storm-driven waves crashing with imponderable force against the rocks. Their raft was about to be sandwiched between the irresistible ocean and an immovable cliff face, and there was nothing he could do about it. Another wave broke over their heads. They clung desperately to the raft as each wave catapulted them closer to the deadly rocks.

John was struck by a stark realization that the remainder of his life was measured in minutes. Cherished memories flickered through his mind like an old movie, interspersed with deep regrets about the important things he had failed to do. The intensity of his regret triggered an even more intense yearning for survival. He wanted nothing more in this dreadful moment than another chance at life because he realized he had wasted his first.

Now delirious, as if in a dream, John imagined he had become one with the ocean, floating about like an insignificant iota in a vast and timeless body of creation. His own temporal existence was nearing an end, but the mighty ocean would go on forever. He was just part of another wave crashing on the shore, just another brief but unique arrangement of molecules that would soon slide back into the undertow of the great sea of eternity, swallowing any evidence he had ever existed. Millions of other waves would follow, all to crash upon this rocky shore and melt back into the vast oneness of the sea, just like him. The birth of each wave was simply the first step toward its inevitable demise. He had an eerie sensation of falling into an endless void with each descent into the trough of a wave. Total darkness beckoned.

He felt the very earth shudder as each wave exploded onto the rocky shore. He was doused by torrents of cold sea spray that were catapulted into the air by the titanic collisions of ocean against land.

In the flash of a lightning bolt, he saw rocks shockingly close, rising like watery black demons out of the dark sea. In the next instant, his raft smashed against one and exploded into pieces, throwing him into the eager arms of the unforgiving demons.

John was stunned for a few desperate seconds. When he regained his senses, he grasped madly for anything to hold on to. Water hammered him from all directions. Whitecapped waves boiled over the rocks with savage fury. The undertow tugged at him like a tentacled monster. Sea spray and rain poured from above. Wave after wave pummeled him like a ragdoll against the rocks, banging his head, his shoulders, his hips, and his knees. The rocks were covered with slimy polyps, yet his fingers were lacerated by sharp edges as he vainly tried to latch onto them.

A rogue wave bigger than the rest flung him upward onto a rocky ledge. When the water receded, he was able to gain a grip on the slick surface. Blessedly, the next few waves didn't quite reach his elevation. He blindly climbed the slippery rocks above him to escape any remaining attempts by the ocean to snatch him into oblivion.

When he reached another ledge safely above the turbulent sea, he could go no farther. Breathless, beaten, and bleeding, he lay down. A horrendous grinding sounded out, followed by the smashing of something massive against the rocks below, but John couldn't summon the energy to see what had happened. Exhausted and battered, he slid into unconsciousness.

4

SHIPWRECK

John felt someone shake his shoulder.

He opened his eyes to a world that had been radically transformed since he had fallen into the impenetrable sleep of exhaustion. A glorious sun was rising into a cloudless sky. The rain had stopped, and the wind had calmed to a refreshing tropical breeze.

He heard voices.

Rolling over on the ledge upon which he had collapsed the night before, he groaned in agony, bruised and lacerated by countless collisions with jagged rocks during his waved-tossed landfall. He gingerly moved his arms and legs to test them. Everything hurt, but his limbs still worked.

Rising to his hands and knees, his stomach suddenly convulsed. He vomited sea water and bile. Through teary eyes, he finally noticed that it was the Carpenter who had awakened him.

"You're alive!" John exclaimed. He sat up and shielded his eyes from the glare of the morning sun. "How many others survived?"

The Carpenter sighed heavily. "Thirty-eight, counting you, Farmer John. Mutilated corpses have been washing up on the rocks below. The sharks are feeding just beyond the breakers."

"Any of the survivors badly injured?"

"*Sí*, some broken bones and lots of cuts. One of our shipmates is a paramedic. He made splints from vines and pieces of driftwood. He also made bandages out of strips of clothing. Nothing can be done for their pain except to offer prayers."

John scanned their surroundings. He spied the dorsal fins of sharks circling in the sea below, drawn by the human chum. To his left was an imposing jumble of rocks and steep cliffs, interspersed with dwarf palms that had somehow found root. Above his perch, men were staring down from a plateau roughly fifty feet above where he sat now. When he looked to his right, he did a double take and pointed.

"What the hell is that?"

"A marooned sailboat," the Carpenter said. "It crashed on the rocks during the storm last night."

John studied the damaged craft. It was wedged aloft between boulders now that the tide and the storm surge had receded. Its mast and furled sails dangled below the boat, attached only by tangled rigging. The hull had a gaping gash. The boat would likely never sail again.

"That must have been the source of the loud crashing noises I heard just before I blacked out," John speculated. "I thought I was hallucinating."

The Carpenter nodded. "By the grace of God, the skipper survived. Our men are helping him up the cliff. Let's join the others above, Farmer John. Decisions need to be made."

He helped John to his feet, and they climbed up the cliff face via a treacherous zigzag path others had blazed. When they neared the edge of the plateau, many hands reached down to pull them atop.

John took stock of the surviving castaways. Most of their clothes were tattered and splotched with blood. They had abrasions and bruises on their exposed skin, and their hair hung in tangled mops. Looking exhausted and defeated, many had that dissociated, thousand-yard stare that often precedes desperate action. Under these circumstances, John knew that men were more likely to be beasts than saints. Everyone needed to be quickly organized into a cohesive team before they opted for savagery.

The Monk joined the Carpenter and John by the edge of the cliff, who quickly noticed that the wiry Asian was naked.

"Where's your robe?" John asked.

"Life never offers perfect choices," the Monk replied solemnly. "During my struggle in the sea, I shed the robe instead of drowning under the weight of my pride."

They were interrupted by the arrival of the sailor of the wrecked sailboat. He was built like a lumberjack and towered over everyone. His short, curly hair was bleached blond from his journey on the open seas, and his skin was ruddy from exposure to sun and wind.

Staring in bewilderment at the bedraggled survivors standing like zombies on the barren plateau, he eyed the naked Monk with suspicion.

"Where the hell am I?" he boomed.

"Outcast Island," John said darkly.

"Damn!" The sailor's massive shoulders sagged upon hearing the worst possible answer.

"What's your name?" John asked.

The sailor squinted at him. "I'd rather not say. I'm a fugitive. My friends call me Hammer because I'm a blacksmith. Who are you?"

"Name's John. I'm a farmer. Where were you headed before crashing?"

Hammer spit on the rocky ground. "I was fleeing America. I sailed from Nantucket several weeks ago in the dark of night. I was hoping to reach a sparsely populated Caribbean island to start a new life. The storm blew me way off course." He paused, looking around to further assess his grim situation. "Man, this is a disaster!"

"Yup," John said. "But you won't find much sympathy here."

"I spent five years secretly building my sailboat and preparing to escape, only to end up stranded on an island full of misfits and criminals. I went from the frying pan into the fire."

"This is our first day in the fire too," John said. "You at least had the luxury of crashing by boat. We body-surfed onto those rocks down there."

The Monk, who had been eavesdropping, sidled closer to them. Hammer took a step backward.

"Most people waste their lives searching for a gem that's already in their pocket," the Monk said. "Do your eyes not see the glorious sunrise this morning? Do your feet not feel the solid land that we safely stand on now? The richest people are those who can find happiness in the present moment."

Hammer eyed the Monk disdainfully. "That man is crazy. Why is he naked?"

"The Monk speaks the truth," the Carpenter said. "We may be destitute and hungry now, but if we do the right things, we'll earn our salvation. Even here on Outcast Island."

Hammer scowled. "He's crazy too."

"Then so am I," John replied. "Like you, I wanted to escape America's dysfunctional society. I chose to come here. It's my opportunity to start a new society."

A tall, slender man with a shock of dark, curly hair and black-rimmed glasses that were comically bent stepped forward. He had dark caterpillar eyebrows, a pock-marked face, and a slightly manic look in his eyes.

"I'm Nicolai, an electrical engineer," he announced. "Sorry to interrupt. We're strangers on the thin edge of survival, so we're potential threats to each other. We need to organize ourselves or else we'll fight over what little food and shelter we might find."

"Are you volunteering to lead us?" Hammer said, sneering. He eyed Nicolai with the same disdain as he did the Monk.

"No. I'm volunteering him." Nicolai pointed at John.

"Him?" Hammer exclaimed. "He just admitted he's crazy. He *chose* to come here."

"Maybe that means he has bigger balls than the rest of us. He wisely warned us not to charge the guards on our prison ship. It would have been suicidal. And just before we were thrown overboard, the captain singled him out as the reason for our brutal treatment. That means the Elites hate him. Or maybe they fear him. Either way, I'm willing to follow a man like that."

"At least he's wearing clothes," Hammer said grudgingly.

"I have no interest in being a dictator," John interjected. "Our tasks right now are obvious. We need to get organized and be productive. Some need to find water. Some need to collect food. Others need to gather firewood and make shelter."

John saw heads nodding as he made these simple suggestions. He realized that this was his first opportunity to test his leadership aptitude.

"I'm willing to lead for a few days," John declared. "But what we need most is collaboration. None of us are going to survive on our own here. We must work together, protect each other, take advantage of our combined skills, and build trust."

"How the hell can we trust each other?" someone shouted. "We're strangers who were crammed together on a prison ship. I'm guessing there aren't many saints here."

John gestured toward the Carpenter. "This man told me it's not important what we did before. It only matters what we do going forward. Our survival depends on strong bonds. It's trust or bust!"

This elicited a wave of murmuring and nodding. John interpreted this as assent, thin though it was.

"Time's wasting!" John barked. "Form into five groups. Each one will pick a task that must be done by nightfall. Find drinking water, forage for food, collect firewood, make shelter, and strip everything of value from Hammer's boat. Each group should pick its own leader. This will be our first test of self-organization. Go!"

The men scrambled on his command. At first, their efforts were a frenzied jumble of shouting and jostling, but the five groups eventually coalesced. Then there was a flurry of discussion as each group picked a leader. The whole process took about ten minutes, during which John never spoke. He noticed, however, that Hammer had stood the entire time amidst his chosen group with his arms crossed and his brow furrowed, clearly agitated.

Four of the groups hustled off to execute their tasks. The fifth group, which was assigned to scavenge Hammer's boat, stood paralyzed. They all stared nervously at Hammer. The burly blacksmith strode over to confront John.

"Who authorized you to give my stuff away? I spent years gathering those supplies and tools. I did it to start a better life for me, not them." He gestured angrily toward the other men.

John had spent decades as a rugged farmer, but Hammer was taller, stronger, and in a foul mood. Undaunted, he lifted his head to lock eyes with the mountain of a man.

"Our lives are all intertwined now," John explained calmly. "Unless you have a flying carpet stashed in your ruined boat, you're stuck here with us."

"So you're just going to steal my shit?"

John shook his head. "I apologize, Hammer. In our urgency, I got ahead of myself. I should have consulted with you first, but the path forward in our desperate situation seemed obvious. I assure you that I consider private property sacred, and I won't tolerate anyone lusting for the unearned. If you wish, return to your boat and horde your stuff. We'll find a way without you."

Hammer's face turned ashen. "I can't survive alone here! It's a jungle full of cutthroats. I just want to be compensated for my property."

"With what? Coconuts?" John gave a weak laugh. "We have nothing to offer each other right now but teamwork. What payment do you expect from castaways who haven't yet secured drinking water?"

"Don't you realize how much hard work and gold it took to—"

"Hammer, you have an opportunity to earn the greatest possible payment," John interrupted. "Gifting your supplies to the others will earn you a priceless karmic reward. Someday our community will begin trading value for value, but for now our goal is to survive until tomorrow. Have you seen the desperation in the men's eyes? Your generosity will put them forever in your debt, and they will reward you with esteem and companionship. Or you can horde your stash alone. But someday it will run out, and then surviving on your own will be impossible."

Hammer glared at John for a tense moment, then scanned the hostile island that was now their permanent home. He relaxed his combative posture, turned to his teammates, and shouted in a husky voice, "Let's go, boys!"

As Hammer's team rushed toward his boat, John realized he hadn't assigned himself a task yet. It dawned on him that they knew nothing about their surroundings, so he decided to scout their perimeter. The most obvious starting point was the steep hill that rose above their plateau. He began climbing to get a panoramic view.

When he reached the summit, the view took his breath away. From their limited perspective on the plateau below, the island appeared as a rocky and desolate place. But from his new vantage point, he saw a tropical paradise. Looking toward the sea, he was dazzled by the infinite indigo ocean. Above them was an azure sky aflame with a shimmering sun. To their right were glittering beaches of white sand caressed by foamy whitecaps.

Looking inland, he saw a riotously colored jungle. Palm fronds on stately coconut trees whispered in the ocean breeze. The broad leaves of banana trees danced beneath the palms. Under the arboreal canopy was a flamboyant montage of bird-of-paradise, hibiscus, bougainvillea, and giant crotons. Exotic birds soared in the thermals rising from the humid jungle.

A terrible beauty, John thought.

As he marveled at the view, the strategic implications of their landing site became apparent. Their barren plateau would be difficult to attack from the sea, which they had learned from brutal experience. But the jungle on this side of the hill was a problem. An enemy could sneak through the dense vegetation to the top of the hill until they were almost upon his defenseless group. He concluded they needed to gain command of the high ground.

John spotted a well-worn trail running from the jungle toward the summit of the hill. Curious, he followed the path down the hill until he came to the edge of the jungle. Then his heart skipped a beat.

The transition into the jungle was marked by a line of desiccated human skulls mounted on stakes. He crept deeper into the jungle, shoving aside vines and ferns. The line of skulls ran perhaps one hundred feet and then ended abruptly near a jumbled pile of whitened human bones.

John was sweating now. Perhaps it was from the withering jungle heat. Perhaps it was from the effort of navigating the steep hillside and the dense foliage. Or maybe it was because he had an eerie feeling that he was being watched. By whom? The question haunted him as he ascended the trail back to the summit.

He sat down to strategize. Several hours went by as he considered their location, their limited resources, and the potential dangers that lurked on Outcast Island. The sun was descending when he stood and took a final look across the vast jungle. On a larger hill perhaps a mile away, he spied wisps of smoke. Another ominous sign.

With heavy foreboding, he rejoined the men on the plateau, hoping that progress had been made by the five groups because the shadows from the setting sun were lengthening. He summoned the team leaders to report on their efforts.

The first to report was Nicolai, the electrical engineer. He was selected as leader of the water team. "We found a stream cascading down the rocks near here where the water is clear and cool. We drank some with no ill effects. We're now carving a path to make the stream more accessible. We also collected some coconuts and hollowed them out. We'll use them as drinking vessels until we craft something better."

"Nicely done," John said. "Food team?"

The paramedic stepped forward. The young man looked like an athletic surfer with long blond hair straggling across his tanned face. His cheery blue eyes hinted at a wisdom beyond his years. He had been studying to be a doctor before the civil war disrupted his plans. He was drafted into the army by the Elites to serve as a medic, but he was a free spirit, ill-suited for following orders. His stubborn recalcitrance led to his exile.

"My friends call me Doc. Someday, I hope to finish becoming one."

"Thanks for attending to the injured men," John replied. "Food status?"

"Grim so far. We collected the meat from the coconuts the water team gathered, then harvested some bananas, which was difficult without tools. We scavenged some clams from the shore. There's wild game nearby—probably goats or pigs based on the fecal droppings we saw on their runs. We haven't figured out how to trap them yet. I'm sure there are edible fruits in the jungle behind the big hill, but we haven't ventured there yet."

Disappointment registered on John's face. "It's a start," he said coolly. "But we have a lot of men to feed. Every day."

Doc nodded somberly.

"Firewood team?" John invited the next team leader to speak.

A bespectacled Black man with long, graying dreadlocks and a narrow scholarly face stepped forward. Of average height and build, he had been a chemist for many years until he was forced to work in a munitions lab. The work was repugnant to him, so he fled into the underground. Homeland Security eventually tracked him down and deported him.

"I'm Newton. We gathered a lot of wood, but most of it is still wet from the storm. We found some dry wood in a big hollow to the left of our plateau. Someone must have stashed it before we got here. Unfortunately, we haven't been able to start a fire yet."

More disappointment registered on John's face. He also pondered the implications of prior occupants on the plateau. Did they contribute to the line of skulls on the other side of the hill?

"Hopefully, the shelter team has better news," John said.

The Carpenter sighed. "The hollow in the hillside that the firewood team discovered is big enough for all of us to crowd into. It will keep us dry until we can build shelter. There are plenty of trees nearby that can be worked into building materials. Unfortunately, we have no tools. There are many vines to use for binding, but they're hard to cut with just sharp rocks. There are also plenty of grasses, palm fronds, and banana tree leaves that can be woven into sleeping mats and thatching for roofs. My team is trying to make some mats, but we have nothing to cut and trim with."

"So we're sleeping on the ground in a cave tonight," John summarized dryly.

"*Sí*, Farmer John."

John shook his head in dismay, then looked over at Hammer

who was preening with a bittersweet smile in front of a jumble of crates and barrels.

"Hammer, I hope those containers mean your team has salvaged some useful stuff from your broken boat."

"Let me show you!" He led John over to his stash. "Here's my metal-working equipment: bellows, anvils, hammers, and molds. We just need to build a forge and we're in business." He took a few steps to showcase his belongings. "Here's my weaponry: four rifles, six pistols, thousands of bullets, and gunpowder. I also have hunting knives and machetes. There was more, but the sea claimed the rest." He walked a few steps to the left. "Here are the tools that survived the crash: saws, axes, picks, shovels, and a big tool kit." Walking to another pile, he proudly said, "Here are ropes, tarps, matches, kerosene lamps, candles, water jugs, canteens, a compass, and fishing gear." Reaching the end of his stash, he noticed smiles from the hungry men. "Here are my cooking utensils, along with food staples that weren't contaminated by sea water: rice, flour, salted beef, and jerky. Oh, and I've got some spare clothing." He grabbed a shirt and a pair of trousers and threw them to Monk, who was still naked. "They're too big, but do us all a favor and put them on anyway."

Laughter erupted, followed by volleys of thanks to Hammer for his beneficence. The mood of the castaways improved palpably.

John waved to get their attention. "Let's lug these treasures into the hollow to keep them dry."

Reinvigorated, the men swarmed the containers and began carrying them. As the pile dwindled, John noticed other materials that were behind them. "What's that stuff?" he asked Hammer.

Hammer bowed his head. "It broke my heart, but I told my team to strip the boat of everything. We salvaged the mast, the spars, the sails, a lot of tangled rigging, all the gears, pulleys, and winches, some furniture, as much planking as we could tear off, and a lot of cabling. The hulk that's left down there on the rocks can hardly be called a boat now."

"I can't thank you enough!"

Hammer shrugged his shoulders. "That boat was my ticket to a new life somewhere, but that hope was dashed against the rocks."

"I think your hope will be fulfilled in a different way," John replied. "You're starting a new life here with thirty-eight new friends who would probably do anything for you now."

"We'll see. Excuse me while I recruit a few guys to convert sails into tents. I don't want to sleep in a cave tonight."

Later that evening, as dusk settled over the plateau, John gathered his newly formed leadership team. They sat around one of several campfires that had been started by the firewood team with Hammer's matches, roasting salted beef. He was grateful for a cooked meal and hoped the fires would keep predators away.

John had let his leadership team form by osmosis. Since each of the five teams had appointed their own leader, John took this as an early indication that the selected men had leadership qualities and some peer approval. He decided to retain them as his lieutenants until they were tested further. Thus, the Carpenter, Nicolai, Newton, Doc, and Hammer became the inaugural members of his Council of Sages. John also included the Monk because he was well-liked and had a calming influence.

Conversation flowed freely as his team basked beside the fire. They were experiencing a range of emotions: relief that they had survived the grim trip from Miami, trepidation about Outcast Island's reputation for savagery and violence, and sorrow for their fellow outcasts who had died the night before.

John gazed at the clear black sky sprinkled with millions of twinkling stars. It reminded him of those perfect autumn nights on his farm in Kansas. He felt a sudden jolt of longing for Mary and James. To redirect his thoughts, he asked the Council, "What should we do now?"

"Make a path by walking," the Monk said.

"What?" Doc exclaimed. "Translate, please."

"Here's what I think the Monk means," the Carpenter interjected. "Leaders with a vision and the courage to see it through can be a powerful force. Each step they take will naturally create a path. Over time, the path will become clearer and easier for others to follow as more people embrace the vision."

"I like that interpretation," John said. "I've been a rebel without a plan for too long. It's time to stop talking and start walking."

The Monk smiled.

"There are many obstacles in our way," Newton observed.

"The good news is that we have many clever men in our group," John replied. "Our ability to adapt to a capricious and dangerous environment will be a great resource."

"And the bad news?" the Carpenter asked.

"The natural environment isn't our biggest threat here. The greater danger will be the people we haven't encountered yet. It's likely that this is a lawless realm of gangs and apex predators who are addicted to using force. And perhaps the greatest threat lurks within our own team. We'll learn a lot more about each other as we get tested—"

"I think we're about to get tested right now!" Hammer interrupted, then stood up abruptly and pointed toward the shore. "There's a long line of torches down there. Whoever is carrying them is heading our way."

"We should put out our fires," Doc suggested. "Maybe they won't notice us."

"Too late," John replied. "If we can see their torches, they can see our campfires. We should do the opposite. Let's start more campfires. It'll create the illusion that we're a bigger force than we really are."

There was a murmur of agreement.

"You guys work on that," Hammer said. "I'm going to take some men to the hollow to uncrate my guns and ammo. If the campfires don't scare those intruders off, we need to be ready with plan B."

"Good idea," John said as he studied the sinewy line of torches snaking toward them. "And judging by their numbers, we may need plan C."

5

―――――

REMNANT

John eyed the line of torchbearers marching toward them below. His team had ignited twenty more campfires on their plateau. The fires lit up the night, but they weren't dissuading the oncoming intruders.

Hammer was frantically preparing plan B. His men opened the crates containing his stash of firearms. There weren't enough guns for everyone, so he asked for volunteers who were experienced hunters or marksmen. He selected the ten ablest men and distributed his four rifles and six pistols among them. He passed out his meager collection of hunting knives and machetes to others, keeping a machete for himself. That left eighteen men on the plateau unarmed, except for the hammers, crowbars, and axes they were given as pseudo weapons.

"We're ready!" Hammer announced to John.

"Not quite," John replied. He had been formulating plan C while studying the approaching intruders. "Send the four riflemen to the top of the hill. They'll have clear shots if things go awry. Tell them to hold their fire until my command. Position the men with pistols, knives, and machetes near the edge of our plateau to be ready to confront the intruders if they attack. Gather everyone else behind them. Let's create the illusion that we're all well-armed. The goal is to make it hard for them to count our manpower."

The men scrambled into position. John and Hammer stood in front of their ragged garrison to face the approaching danger. Hammer's machete looked like a toy compared to his Bunyanesque frame. John was unarmed.

"You want a weapon?" Hammer asked.

"No. I want them to think I'm not afraid."

Hammer nodded. "Brave man."

"I'm scared shitless."

They steeled themselves when the torchbearers began ascending the cliff face. The first head soon peeked above the edge of the plateau. In the intruder's flickering torchlight, John saw that it was a woman.

She vaulted atop the plateau with catlike agility. A steady procession of other torch-bearing women followed her. In short order, there were at least one hundred armed females on the plateau. A long train of torchbearers were still zigzagging up the cliff face behind them.

John and Hammer backed up a few steps to make room for the growing army opposing them. John held his arm up as a signal for his team to stand down.

A tall Valkyrie stepped in front of her assembled militants. John moved forward to confront her. They eyed each other as a heavy silence fell over the scene. The tall woman was an exotic blend of fearsome warrior and statuesque beauty. She had sun-bleached blonde hair that was tightly braided. Her torchlight flickered shadows across her prominent cheekbones and danced in her stunning blue-grey eyes. Her skin was bronzed from the sun, and her sinewy frame suggested an unusual athleticism. She was dressed in crude pants, a loose khaki shirt, and leather moccasins. A ferocious eagle was tattooed on her right forearm. She brandished a spear tipped with serrated metal. The women arrayed behind her were similarly dressed and armed. Most appeared to be Hispanic.

"My name is Olga," the leader announced with a Slavic accent. "Do you speak English?"

"Yes. I'm John."

"Welcome to the Bay of Death." Olga's eyes twinkled with mischievous sarcasm, which was followed by a flash of concern as she eyed the imposing physique of Hammer towering behind John.

Confusion washed over John's face. "Bay of Death?"

"We have nicknames for the most notorious spots on Outcast Island. This bay is where the World Order drops off their most incorrigible outcasts. If the rocks and the sharks don't kill the arriving prisoners, the gangs usually do. Perhaps you noticed the line of skulls on the other side of this hill."

"Are you gangsters?" John asked. "I'm warning you that we have guns, some of which are already aimed at you from up there." He pointed to the top of the hill behind them.

"We're not gangsters, but we're clearly much cleverer than you," Olga replied. "While you were distracted by our procession of torches, our best warriors surrounded you." She whistled a haunting signal. Within seconds, people clambered down from the hilltop. John turned toward the commotion, stunned to see his four riflemen with arms raised above their heads marching sheepishly without their weapons. Behind them trailed a squadron of women armed with spears, carrying the captured firearms.

John nodded grimly to Olga. "*Touché*. Who are you, if not gangsters?"

"The Remnant."

John looked puzzled. "Remnant of what?"

"Those who cling to the hope of a rational society despite the barbarism that reigns here. Our women escaped grotesque abuse by the vile men who control most of the island."

John waved an arm toward the phalanx of men behind him. "I assure you that I won't let anyone from my team harm your tribe. Unless we're provoked."

Olga eyed John's disheveled crew with a hint of amusement. "I give you equal assurance that we won't take any chances. This island is hell for women. La Habana, where I once lived, is ruled by lecherous men intoxicated by debauchery. It's full of obscene, jeering outlaws who treated our women as subhuman. In their eyes, we were merely breeders of new warriors for their gangs, and servants who deserved only leftovers for food. Rape was as common as the rising sun. When battles broke out between factions, we were used as human shields to protect our male masters from opposing fire."

"That's monstrous!" John exclaimed.

"They're Neanderthal swine. Many of us fled la Habana and formed a tribe of female mutineers. Our population keeps growing as more women who want to be in control of their own lives seek our sanctuary. It's vital to find people you can trust when civilization itself is untrustworthy."

"I agree," John replied. "I've explained the importance of trust to my new team."

"I don't care," Olga said disdainfully. "You may trust each other, but we'll never trust men again. Not on this awful island. We've forsaken them, even if it means never having children. This hellhole would be an awful place to raise them anyway."

John decided to change the subject from hatred of men. "What can you tell us about this island?"

Olga flashed a mercurial smile. Her personality seemed to be as fluid as the conversation. "Murderers, thieves, and rapists are everywhere. There are frequent skirmishes between gangs and factions. This place is a cauldron of violence where you're either the hunted or the hunters. Passivity will get you enslaved to a despot or consigned to a gulag. Everyone is armed, even if with just cudgels and spears."

"So not exactly a tropical spa?" John deadpanned.

Olga's mercurial smile evaporated. "Gallows humor is for those who've lost hope. We intend to survive."

John's face hardened. "So do we. Who are the main factions besides yours?"

"There's a band of runaway slaves called the Maroons led by a fierce warrior named Spartacus. They distrust everyone. There's a gang of narco-terrorists called the Jackals led by Pablo Guzman. They're thugs whose moral code is 'might makes right.' The Proletariat is a Stalinist group that rules Outcast Island as much as anyone can claim to. They're led by a heartless tyrant named Vlad. There's a band of pirates led by an enigmatic adventurer named François le Clerc. He's a duplicitous bastard I've learned to despise."

"Which faction is the most dangerous?"

"The most lethal one is never seen on the island, but its ghostly presence is always felt. They're responsible for the systemic oppression of common people across the globe. I was exiled here because of them. And so were you, whether you realize it or not."

"The Elites?"

Olga smirked. "No. They're mere puppets of other chess masters who live in the shadows yet pull the economic and political strings of the world. If I ever get off this island, I'm going to unmask them and hunt them to their graves."

"We have that in common then," John replied. "I also intend to hunt some wolves to the ends of the earth. I think we can be allies."

Olga laughed, but with a cynical edge. "How presumptuous! We know nothing about you. And your team has little to offer, judging by your haggard condition and inept tactics."

John reddened. "That's true. But I sense our worldviews are aligned. I believe that initiating force is the root of all social evil. I believe that coercion is the only form of villainy and that the role of leaders is to eliminate all forms of coercion. My enemies are not people of other genders, races, or creeds. My enemies are those who try to control my thoughts and actions for their own benefit."

Olga raised an eyebrow. "Interesting. Does the rest of your team believe that too?"

John shrugged his shoulders. "I don't know. I met them all yesterday."

Olga shrugged her shoulders in return. "If your whole team embraces that vision, I'll consider an alliance. Until then, we'll keep our distance."

"Time will tell," John replied. "But no matter what, we mean the Remnant no harm." He decided to end the encounter on a friendly note. "Do I detect a Slavic accent?"

Olga squared her shoulders, raised her chin proudly, and flashed the Polish eagle tattooed on her arm. "Yes, I was exiled from Poland years ago. My full name is Olga Kozlowski. The Elites despised me enough to dump me into the Bay of Death. Just like you."

"Why did they despise you?"

"My great-grandfather was a revolutionary who challenged Soviet fascists long ago. You've probably never heard of him. His name was Lech Walesa. But the fascists never forgot. They hold families accountable for insurrection, even across generations. I added fuel to their hatred by following in Lech's footsteps."

John nodded. "I'm here because of my family too. My son Kieran is one of the fascist Elites in America. He ratted me out as a rebel."

Olga bowed her head slightly. "I'm sorry for you. But ruing your past is meaningless here. Save your energy for the storm that will blow your way on this island."

"The island should prepare for the storm I'm going to unleash."

Olga frowned. "That would sound threatening if it wasn't so preposterous. But you've done us no harm yet. If that changes, beware. In the meantime, as a show of good faith, we'll return your rifles to you. Take better care of them next time." She turned and whistled another haunting signal to her team. The women holding the captured rifles dropped them to the ground, then Olga's warriors disappeared over the edge of the plateau in a disciplined retreat.

The men dispersed to finish preparing for nighttime. A tropical moon flooded the plateau with a silvery light. As exotic creatures chattered eerily in the darkness beyond, the men made jerry-rigged tents out of Hammer's sails using slats of wood, sections of mast, and oars from his dismantled sailboat as structural components.

After this work was done, John and the Council of Sages resumed their discussion around a campfire. Hammer summarized his impression of the Remnant's visit. "Olga made it clear that we need to prepare to fight to the death on this island."

"We all need to be warriors," Newton agreed. "This is no place for cowards."

"There's never a place for cowards," John said. "Freedom and bravery have always been inseparable. People who want freedom must be brave enough to accept its risks. And they must be brave enough to defend it against those who want to take it away. I wonder how many of our men are mentally and physically prepared for battle?"

"A few have broken bones," Doc reminded him. "Almost all are exhausted. And I suspect some are pacifists." He looked pointedly at the Monk.

The Monk bowed his bald head, then smiled serenely. "I do indeed desire peace. And this beautiful garden of an island begs a return to the peacefulness of Eden. But my martial arts sensei taught me that it is better to be a warrior in a garden than a gardener in a war. I will do what's necessary if the time comes."

Nicolai nudged the Carpenter's knee. "How about you? You don't strike me as a warrior."

"It's not my first instinct, *amigo*. Violence and morality rarely intersect. But if moral laws are violated without a price being paid, more violations will follow until the day comes when the price to be paid is beyond reach and societal collapse is inevitable. If conflict is necessary to secure the freedom people need to follow their moral convictions, then I shall be a warrior."

Hammer looked around at his compatriots, seeing grim resolve on every face. "Our Council of Sages seems aligned. How do we rally the rest of the men to follow us?"

John tossed a stick into the fire. "We explain that this is a chance for a fresh start, no matter what has happened in the past. It's like the opportunity the Founding Fathers had in America—a new continent with a blank slate and a chance to shed the deadweight of political oppression. Each of us has been exiled by our overbearing leaders, leaving us free to create any society we please."

"What shall we call our fledgling society?" Doc asked.

John thought for a moment. "Pathless Land," he said finally.

"Earlier we discussed *making* paths," Doc said.

"Sort of," John replied. "Each person should be free to blaze their own path in life, which includes being responsible for their actions. But that can't happen if tyrants are going to force everyone down the same narrow path, which they've done since the beginning of time. So our challenge is to create a voluntary society, a blank slate for the artistry of each individual life. In other words, a pathless land."

"That sounds noble," Newton said. "It also sounds impossible. Especially here and now."

"*Sí*," said the Carpenter. "But if heaven was easy, life would be meaningless."

"We make the path by walking," the Monk reminded. "And making a path toward a pathless land seems like a wonderful vision."

"We need to be warriors, and our vision is to create a free society called Pathless Land," Nicolai summarized. "So let's call ourselves Warriors of Pathless Land."

"Indeed, that's what we are," John agreed. He looked around at his team. "Everybody in?"

They studied each other in silence. Then Hammer stood up and extended his powerful arm with a clenched fist. One by one, each man stood and placed a hand atop his. "We pledge our lives and our sacred honor," John declared, finalizing the pact.

Hammer abruptly pulled his massive hand away and pointed toward the sea. All heads swiveled in that direction. They saw the lights of a ship off their shore.

"Looks like we've got more company coming to the Bay of Death."

6

———

MILITIA

The men from Pathless Land scrambled down the craggy cliff, guided by moonlight and Hammer's lanterns. They carried ropes, empty water jugs, first aid supplies, and sheets of canvas and wood poles for making stretchers. They knew there would be casualties if the ship idling offshore was disgorging outcasts into the Bay of Death.

At the shore, they heard desperate pleas for help above the roar of the breakers crashing on the rocks. John's men threw ropes tied to empty water jugs into the frothing sea. The imperiled swimmers latched onto the makeshift life preservers as the men on shore hauled in the ropes until the castaways were within arm's reach. Then they were pulled to safety.

It was treacherous, exhausting work. The waves pounded against the rocks with earth-shaking ferocity. They exploded into giant plumes of sea spray that saturated the seaweed and polyps covering the rocks, yielding a gooey mess that defied foothold. The waves, the slippery conditions, the darkness, the tangled ropes, and the panic of the survivors resulted in mayhem.

After two hours of mortal struggle, there were no more cries for help from the ocean. John assigned five men to stay at the bottom of the cliff in case more survivors were swept toward the shore. The others began assisting the exhausted newcomers up the cliff face. Four of the survivors were so injured that they couldn't walk. Crude stretchers were assembled to secure them. Hammer and other strong men standing atop the plateau hoisted the gurneys up with ropes.

It was dawn by the time the last survivors were safely on the plateau. Campfires were stoked to warm them and to dry their clothes. Food and water were dispensed. Doc worked feverishly to treat injuries with the meager supplies at his disposal. He was helped by a new arrival who was also a former medic in the military.

John noticed that a stocky man with a brush cut and wearing khaki fatigues was crisscrossing the plateau, offering solace to survivors. He also noticed that many survivors were wearing similar fatigues and were responding to the stocky man with deference.

John deduced that he must be a leader, so he strode over and extended his hand. "Name's John. Welcome to the Bay of Death Resort at Outcast Island."

The man returned the handshake with an iron grip. He had the neck and jawline of a prize fighter. His square, leathery face showed hints of middle age. His intense brown eyes bored directly into John's. "I'm Captain Mallory." He gestured toward the survivors sprawled around the plateau. "Thank you. I didn't expect any help, given the reputation here."

John nodded. "When we were dumped here two nights ago, our welcoming committee was a hurricane and some hungry sharks. Only thirty-eight out of one hundred survived. I saw you making the rounds. Did you do a head count?"

Mallory's powerful shoulders sagged. "There's seventy-eight of us left. There were ninety-seven when we embarked in Miami."

John put a consoling hand on his shoulder. "Maybe more survivors will make it to shore. We left a small crew there just in case."

"Yeah. Maybe." Mallory wiped his face of lingering seawater, and perhaps a tear.

"I see a lot of uniforms in your group. You're all military?"

Mallory nodded. "Most of us are militia. Part of the rebel underground in Alabama. There were some civilian dissidents and criminals on the prison ship too."

"Why were you exiled?"

Mallory frowned. "A traitor ratted out my unit to the Elites. We were captured in a surprise raid just north of Huntsville by Homeland Security. There were no trials. They just hauled us off to Miami, then shipped us here."

"A traitor ratted on me too," John said. "My own son."

"Jesus!"

John waved a dismissive hand. "I wanted to come here." He noticed the medals pinned to the captain's chest. One in particular caught his attention in the glint of the rising sun. It was embossed with the image of a rose. "Do you believe in fate, Captain?"

Mallory flashed a puzzled look. "If I did, this isn't the fate I would have hoped for."

John smiled. "Don't be so sure. I grew white roses on my farm in Kansas and distributed them to fellow rebels as a symbol of our rebellion. You and I might have a lot in common."

"Yeah," Mallory replied. "Our sedition got us both exiled to Outcast Island. Quite a dismal end to my career."

"No, it's a beginning," John countered. "That's why I wanted to come here. We're starting a bold new society."

Mallory looked around and smirked. "Are you the delusional tinpot dictator of this plateau?"

John shook his head vigorously. "Dictators are my mortal enemies. They surrender their humanity, and their subjects surrender their freedom. I've volunteered to lead until we can stabilize our budding society."

Mallory gave him a withering glare. "Temporary leaders have a nasty habit of making themselves permanent. Are you suggesting my men and I should follow you? I know nothing about your principles."

"Fair enough," John replied. "Quick summary. Every person owns their own life, along with the natural right to take the actions necessary to optimize it. This requires a voluntarist society committed to defending everyone's life and property from aggression. Our new society here is called Pathless Land."

Mallory looked at him with surprise. "My men and I share your views! That's why we deserted from the Elites." He extended his hand, which John grasped with enthusiasm. "I'll tell my team we're aligned," Mallory said. "Then let's gather everyone together."

After Mallory briefed his team, everyone on the plateau gathered for a meeting. John and Mallory climbed atop a large boulder to address them.

John studied the disheveled men as they closed ranks. Most were clad in the same clothes as when they were apprehended in America. They were emaciated, and their muscles were starting to atrophy.

John began his oration. "Gentlemen, this is the most important discussion we'll ever have on this island. Listen with your ears and your hearts.

"We have many things in common. The Elites exiled us because they hate us and fear us. We're tired, famished, and beaten down. Life as we knew it is gone forever. Our hardships on this island have just begun. We can expect no mercy from anyone except each other going forward.

"Our grim situation will expose the darkness in our hearts. Life will be reduced to its most barbaric core. We will be tempted to abandon every decency in the fight to stay alive. We'll have to choose between civilization or savagery.

"I'm imploring you to choose civilization. Captain Mallory and I believe that our cruel circumstances can be transformed into a thriving society. We each want peace, security, and happiness. The moral purpose of our new society is to ensure that everyone has the freedom to strive for a better life. That new society is called Pathless Land.

"We must all unite to promote that vision. If instead we each act in isolation, we'll become savages battling each other over scraps. Alone, we will each be powerless against the deadly factions that terrorize this island. Even though we are each sovereign individuals, none of us are self-sufficient. Individual survival, the most selfish motive, requires trading our talents with each other and joining together for mutual protection. Our answer to the chaos of the jungle must be voluntary cooperation.

"Since we're joining forces during desperate circumstances, we'll start by sharing our scarce food and limited resources with each other. Our long-term task, however, is to rise from destitution to abundance. The institutions for guiding this renaissance will evolve as our society stabilizes and grows, and they will be consistent with our vision of individual sovereignty. For now, we will share freely so we can prepare ourselves to fight clear and present dangers.

"Be assured that I will never become a dictator. No leader is omniscient or perfect. No one knows better than you how to live your own life. To wait for an elitist leader to authorize every action is to paralyze a society.

"We each despise it when others try to control our lives. That's probably why we've found our individual paths to this island. Nobody wants to be ruled, indoctrinated, spied on, censored, or coerced. I swear upon the sanctity of life that I will never commit such crimes against humanity.

"We've learned that the surest way to appreciate the value of personal freedom is to lose it. So now we must fight to regain it. If we fall prey to our tribal urges for political, religious, or cultural conflict, we'll end up killing each other. The world's pixie-dust ideologies have lured us into that trap throughout history. It's time to break free of it.

"In time, as we build our new society, we'll realize that we're in heaven on this island. We'll experience the joy of warm sun, soft sand, scented breezes, and good friends, in addition to lives that are full of hope and promise. We'll know the blessings of peace, freedom, and prosperity. But until then, we'll be tested in ways we can't imagine."

John paused and glanced at Mallory. "Want to add anything, Captain?"

"I want to speak as a career soldier." He turned to the audience. "Fate has given us this opportunity to start new lives and to establish a rational society. Fortune favors the bold. Our only obstacle is fear.

Our choice is between victory or death." He paused, then shouted the motto of the Army Rangers, "Rangers, lead the way!"

"Hooah!" Mallory's men shouted.

John clapped him on the back. "I admire your brevity and spirit, Captain. Well said."

John addressed the audience again. "I'll close with this. If you're unwilling to embrace the vision of Pathless Land, then you should opt out today. Let the Captain or me know by nightfall if you intend to leave us. There will be no recriminations."

John signaled an end to the assembly, then convened his Council of Sages, which now included Captain Mallory. They decided what the team leaders and their men should do next. The Carpenter would continue building shelters. Hammer would build a simple forge for fabricating tools and weapons from scrap metals. Captain Mallory would assess Pathless Land's military readiness. Nicolai and Newton would make crude explosives from Hammer's store of gunpowder. Doc would work with Mallory's medic to continue treating the injured men. The Monk would gather more food, and John assigned himself to dig latrines.

Even though everyone was exhausted from a sleepless night spent rescuing and being rescued, they knew that sleep was a luxury they couldn't afford. There were many primal needs that had to be addressed, so the teams worked hard throughout the hot, steamy day.

As John dug latrine trenches, he monitored the activity around the plateau, pleased with the energy and collaboration. *A good start*, he thought. But he was troubled that no one had come forward to say they wanted to leave their new society. Their group was too big for everyone to miraculously be of like mind. He worried that some malcontents would quietly stay only to stir up trouble later.

When night fell, fires were lit and food was distributed. John invited Mallory to sit with him by a fire. The two men chatted privately until they heard footsteps approaching behind them. Mallory turned and was surprised to see the concerned face of Sergeant Brown, his second-in-command, in the flickering firelight.

The visitor saluted. "Permission to speak freely, sir?"

Mallory returned the salute. "Granted. At ease. Have a seat."

Sergeant Brown shuffled his feet uncomfortably. "I'd rather stand, sir. I have bad news."

"You're leaving us?" Mallory asked with sudden concern.

"No, sir!" Sergeant Brown insisted. "I'm loyal to you, as are most of the men. But some aren't."

"Elaborate, Sergeant."

"Eleven men snuck out of camp when darkness fell. Five of our Rangers, three civilians from our shipload, and three people from John's team. Scuttlebutt says that they want nothing to do with John's flowery vision. They prefer conquest and looting and intend to find outcasts elsewhere on the island who prefer such things too. They've also heard there's a tribe of women nearby. They've gone in search of them to steal food and weapons."

"Damn it!" John exclaimed. "I had an eerie feeling that things were too quiet. This will end badly."

Mallory stood and paced. "This is indeed bad news, Sergeant." Turning to John, he said, "The five deserters from my outfit are among the best-trained fighters in the world. They'll be sorely missed."

John stood and grabbed Mallory's arm. "You're worrying about the wrong problem. Those clever women are armed, familiar with the terrain, and hate all men. And there's hundreds of them against the eleven deserters."

"There are none tougher than those five Rangers," Mallory insisted. "I'm certain the conflict will end badly for the women, not for my men."

John shook his head. "I don't care what happens to the deserters. I'm afraid that their aggression is going to end badly for the rest of us here."

"How so?"

"Those women call themselves the Remnant. They visited us last night. We made a tenuous peace with them. I shared my vision with Olga Kozlowski, their leader. She agreed that if our entire team embraced it, she'd consider an alliance. And now her tribe is going to be attacked by eleven of our men. She'll see that as pure treachery.

It'll confirm her belief that all men are untrustworthy. Our hope for an alliance is now gone."

Mallory shrugged his shoulders. "So we move on without our eleven deserters and without an alliance with the Remnant," he reasoned.

John shook his head grimly. "If I understand Olga's mindset, tomorrow we will be at war with the Remnant."

7

OLGA

John couldn't sleep.

His insomnia wasn't because his blanket was a giant banana tree leaf or because the rocky ground was an unforgiving mattress. It was because he dreaded how Olga would retaliate if the eleven deserters wreaked havoc in the Remnant's camp. This worry kept him awake for hours until it was replaced by a more visceral dread. He heard drumbeats in the jungle coming from several locations. There could be only one reason for such orchestrated signaling during this particular night. The Remnant was calling their warriors to arms.

He jumped to his feet and stumbled around camp in the starlight to find Mallory, then shook him awake.

"Captain, we've got big trouble."

Mallory sprang into a sitting position, got his bearings, then nodded after comprehending the meaning of the persistent drumming. "Wake the men now! We must prepare for battle."

"I'll trust you to do that while I'm gone," John replied.

Mallory did a double take. "You're leaving? Now?"

"I'm going to take a stab at peace."

Mallory shook his head in confusion. "What the hell are you talking about?"

"I'm going to meet with Olga before more tragedy occurs."

"You're going to stroll into the Remnant's camp while they're banging war drums, likely because of the treachery of our men? Do you have a death wish?"

"No, and neither do they," John replied. "At least that's what I'm counting on. They may be furious with us, but they also know we're armed, and I'm sure their spies have already discovered we have a lot more fighters today than yesterday."

"It's kill or be killed on this island," Mallory warned.

"At some point, that cycle has to be broken. We can't kill everyone. People can't live forever in separate factions whose only commonality is hatred and fear of the others. We need to be able to trade. We need allies. I still hope that the Remnant can be one of them."

"You're going to hike through the jungle in the dark of night by yourself to talk sense into them?"

"No. I'm taking the Monk and the Carpenter with me. They're insightful and nonthreatening. You stay here and prepare for the worst if we fail."

"You just lectured the team about loyalty and unity," Mallory persisted. "And now you're running off on your own?"

"There can be no greater proof of my loyalty to the principles of Pathless Land than the personal risk I'm about to take."

Mallory considered this for a moment. "Fair enough," he said grudgingly. "But how are you going to find their camp?"

"The same way the eleven deserters did. The Remnant marched up here last night—hundreds of them. Then they marched back to their camp. If I can't follow the trail of hundreds of warriors by the light of Hammer's lanterns, then I have much bigger problems." He turned and abruptly ended the conversation.

John wakened the Monk and the Carpenter. After he explained the situation, they embraced his strategy to avoid mortal conflict between the two tribes. The three hastily prepared for a hike, and John put a pistol in his waistband.

They climbed down the cliff and picked up the Remnant's trail on the sandy beach, following the footprints for a mile and then veering into the jungle. The swath cut by the Remnant through the ferns and thickets was unmistakable. However, it was slow going as the three men stumbled over roots, rocks, and fallen tree trunks in the thin light of their lanterns.

The Monk took the lead. He was smaller and nimbler and therefore adept at navigating the obstacles and pointing them out to his followers. Some of the hazards were alive. At one point, the Monk raised his lantern toward a branch arching over the trail. Upon closer inspection, they saw a boa constrictor coiled around it. At other times, they heard animals crashing through the jungle, likely spooked by the dancing lanterns and the scent of humans. The eerie howling of wild creatures served as the backdrop for their trek.

The Monk froze and put a finger to his lips. The jungle had fallen strangely silent. They waited a few minutes, motionless. John gave the Monk a questioning look, who simply replied with a shrug of his shoulders and then turned to proceed forward.

Before he could take another step, a birdlike trill broke the silence, and the jungle exploded to life. Barbed spears were pointed at them from all directions. In the lantern light they saw the eerie painted faces of warriors who materialized out of thin air like ghosts. There were at least fifteen scowling women, all with long braided hair.

John slowly extracted his pistol, dropped it to the ground, and raised his arms in surrender. The Monk and the Carpenter dropped their machetes and raised their arms too. One woman noiselessly scooped up the weapons. Another stepped onto the path in front of the three men. "Follow me," she commanded with a Cuban accent. "Do nothing foolish."

The men trod in her footsteps, shadowed by the rest of the armed entourage. They marched in lockstep for two miles until a hint of dawn appeared in the eastern sky when they came upon the main camp of the Remnant.

The leader of their entourage whistled a staccato burst of birdlike trills. At this signal, women poured out of wood-framed wattle huts that were roofed with thatched palm fronds. They hastened to a common area dimly lit by the glowing embers of a dying bonfire and the first rays of the rising sun. Olga was among them. She moved to the center of the commons and whistled a command to the escorting warriors.

The warriors prodded the men into the commons. John strode in front of Olga and bowed slightly at the waist, then gestured toward the women who had marched them at spearpoint.

"Thanks for the escorts. We've come to offer an apology and to make amends."

"My instinct was to slaughter your tribe," Olga replied coldly. "But now my rational side sees that you're not a coward and you're willing to take responsibility. You may be useful despite what happened last night."

John was stunned. He had expected fierce anger. "What happened?"

"Your men killed two of our women, kidnapped four others, and stole food and weapons. Three of the attackers were killed in the fracas, and one was captured. The rest got away. We've interrogated the captive. I'm curious to hear if your explanation of this assault matches his. It will be a test of your honesty about the treachery of your men."

"I don't know what he said," John replied. "Here's what I do know. Another shipload of outcasts was dumped in the Bay of Death. Most were military men. I bonded with their leader, Captain Mallory. We held a joint meeting with all our castaways to establish the vision for Pathless Land that I shared with you earlier. The eleven defectors who attacked your camp didn't embrace that vision."

"That mostly agrees with what the captive confessed," Olga said. "Except that he called you a starry-eyed philosopher who was perverting his captain into a weak-kneed pacifist. We killed him, for what it's worth."

John's face reddened. "This starry-eyed philosopher apologizes on behalf of that asshole for the atrocities he and his fellow deserters committed. But now that they've self-selected out of our tribe, the rest of us remain committed to peace with the Remnant. I still wish to make an alliance of mutual defense and trade."

"That remains to be seen. Apologies are mere words. You must make amends for the atrocities."

John continued to be surprised by Olga's stoicism. He reasoned that her muted reaction meant she also saw value in an alliance but was craftily negotiating. *Let the negotiations begin*, he thought.

"What amends?" John asked.

"First, you must rescue our women and kill the raiders who kidnapped them. The only way we'll consider an alliance with a group of men is if they value us enough to risk their own lives on our behalf. The captive we interrogated gave us a clue about where the kidnappers are headed. We'll share that with you."

"And then?"

"If you kill the kidnappers and rescue our women, we wish to do a joint military operation with your team. It's a dangerous one, but it's an opportunity to judge if we can work together in treacherous circumstances."

John raised an eyebrow. "What kind of operation?"

"I won't share the details until you rescue our women. I need to know whether I can trust you or not."

John shook his head. "You have to tell me something so that I can convince our team to take on these challenges. If you're considering a suicidal assault on Vlad's headquarters in la Habana, we're not ready for that."

"We're not suicidal," Olga replied, "but we do want to get our hands on better weapons. And there are other Remnant women who need to be rescued. The target is an old Spanish fort on Skull Ridge that Vlad is using as a key outpost. It has a stash of weapons and ammunition. It also has cannons. We can't conquer it with just spears and arrows, and our fighting skills are better suited for jungle warfare than for storming forts. But victory may be possible with the help of your trained military men. We can provide them information that our spies obtained about the fort."

John rubbed his bearded chin. Like Olga, he was anxious to increase the firepower of his team. He was also anxious to make an alliance with the Remnant. But he was leery of a risky dice roll with a team of exhausted men who barely knew each other.

The Carpenter broke the uncomfortable silence. "Farmer John, do not surrender to fear. Life entails risks. They can't be avoided if we hope to achieve the goodness of Pathless Land."

"That's a big leap of faith in our battered crew," John replied.

"Faith is both powerful and dangerous," the Carpenter replied. "The key is what you have faith in. Striking at a tyrant like Vlad is *bueno*. Acquiring what our people need to protect themselves is *muy bueno*."

John nodded respectfully. "Monk, what do you think?"

The Monk bowed his head respectfully. "We are children of the past. But more importantly, we are parents of the future. To give birth to Pathless Land, we must be bold parents willing to take on these challenges."

"Thanks." John turned to Olga. "It seems fate has steered us together."

"That's because there are no other tribes on this island worth collaborating with."

John smiled. "You're an unusual woman, Olga Kozlowski."

"Unusual times give rise to unusual people. You must know that yourself, John, since you chose to come to this island."

"It was a bold move," he acknowledged. "But the pain from leaving my family behind in Kansas is so brutal that not even sleep can hide it. And it's made worse by the betrayal of my own son."

Olga looked at him with surprise. "Your wife is still in Kansas?"

John nodded somberly. "I hope so. She was alive when I was exiled, but she suffers from chronic pneumonia. Who knows what's happened to her?"

Olga's face softened. "It appears tragic either way because you will never see her again."

John shook his head. "I feel Mary in my heart every day, no matter where I am."

"Why did your son betray you?"

"I started my own rebel cell and blasphemed the Elites in the local town square."

"I did much the same in Poland," Olga said. "But why did that lead to betrayal by your son?"

"In his warped view, the value of our relationship paled in comparison to the grand delusions that the collectivists infected his brain with. I became just another human sacrifice to abet his lust for power and prestige."

"Betrayal is something we have in common," Olga replied. "The only man I ever loved betrayed me. For gold."

"At least you and I left our traitors behind in our home countries."

Olga stared into the distance. "No. I met mine here. He's the pirate who calls himself François le Clerc. And I'm going to kill him."

8

———

SIX

Cosimo squinted at the opaque shadow where his boss lurked. The man known as Six was one of the ten numbered but otherwise anonymous leaders of the Deka, the group of reclusive oligarchs who led the Syndicate—a worldwide confederacy of financiers who controlled most of the world's dwindling wealth. It was a private organization that manipulated the puppet strings of almost every government and public institution in the world. The Syndicate was hidden inside a complex, shadowy web that most people would never understand or see.

Six never appeared in public. Even his private meetings, such as today's discussion with Cosimo, were shrouded in secrecy. Cosimo could see the vague silhouette of Six's gaunt figure seated across the room. He had never seen Six's face, but his resonant voice and heavy Slavic accent were unmistakable. Even though his boss was usually a man of few words, his utterances were laden with both import and peril. If he spoke a lot, then danger was at hand.

Cosimo was an apprentice Centurion in the Syndicate. Each of the ten numbered leaders in the Deka had ten Centurions who reported to them and carried out their commands. Thus, there were a hundred people like Cosimo in the confederation. The Centurions were collectively known as the Golden Hundred.

Cosimo was a tall, lithe, dark-complected man. His well-coiffed black hair was slicked back like that of movie stars in the silent film era. He was dressed in his usual immaculate suit. His only jewelry was an ostentatious ring that featured a snake encircling the globe. His manicured appearance gave him an aristocratic aura of wealth despite his relative youth.

The two men were seated in a secure room in an underground complex beneath one of the hills outside of Rome. It was rare for Cosimo to be summoned to the private bunker of his reclusive boss. These summonses never portended well, although Cosimo felt safe today because he believed he was succeeding in his training assignment to keep Outcast Island in chaos.

"I'm concerned," Six began, customarily avoiding small talk. The temperature in the room seemed to drop with his utterance. Cosimo was struck by the ability of his boss to say just two words that could darkly frame an entire conversation.

A chill ran down Cosimo's spine, but he maintained his well-practiced composure. Six had the power of a god who held life-and-death dominion over his ten Centurions. He hated being inconvenienced or disappointed. But Cosimo knew that he was one of Six's favored young lieutenants. He also knew that his boss appreciated the value of a competent and ruthless yet loyal operative.

Cosimo tilted his head submissively. "Your Excellency, I assure you that the unrest I've instigated on Outcast Island is accomplishing everything you desire. The Proletariat, the Jackals, the Maroons, the Pirates, and the Remnant will soon be at each other's throats. Vlad is under the delusion that his faction dominates the island, but he's a marionette who dances to my tune. The proles in every faction are fighting, bleeding, and dying under their opposing banners of futility, grinding themselves into dust. Outcast Island will never be a threat to the supremacy of the Syndicate."

"Perhaps," Six muttered. "But every week fresh outcasts arrive at the island who might refuse to bend to your manipulations."

"Your Excellency, the misfits who've been deported to Outcast

Island are safely quarantined by the World Order's naval forces. The Order flies their espionage drones to monitor the island on our behalf. Our Influencers on the island feed us information. Everything is under control."

"I was informed that one of your Influencers was captured," Six said darkly. "What if he talks?"

Cosimo lit a cigarette. "I recently planted that Influencer there among a shipload of exiles. His mission was to imperil his fellow outcasts upon landing. He organized a reckless raid on the Remnant, but he was captured and then killed. Such men are expendable, and he knew nothing about the Syndicate. He blindly served our needs because he was paid a few gold coins for his troubles. I have a stable of more reliable Influencers who've been on the island for some time and who've performed admirably."

"Like whom?"

"François le Clerc."

Six's dark silhouette nodded. "The pirate who calls himself the Avenging Angel."

Cosimo blew a smoke ring. "The savages on Outcast Island can't tell whether he's a demon or a saint, which helps me sow chaos. He's a reliable chess piece that I can maneuver at will. He'll continue to demonstrate his loyalty and trustworthiness."

"What makes you so confident?"

"Gold, Your Excellency. He's proven his willingness to commit any crime and to betray any person for the gold I supply him with. He even betrayed the love of his life for a few bars. He's a pirate, after all."

"As are we, but we sit atop the pinnacle of civilization and have cemented our institutionalized piracy with dazzling illusions."

Cosimo nodded his appreciation of another of Six's astute assessments. "Le Clerc knows that. He once said to me that there are only two differences between his piracy and ours: he steals a little bit of wealth, whereas we're attempting to steal most of it. And he's liable to be hanged someday, whereas we'll never be caught. He calls the Syndicate a vast criminal enterprise without a soul to be damned."

"You think such irreverence makes him trustworthy?" Six asked with a tone drenched in acid. "Our immunity from retribution is threatened only by independent thinkers and renegades. They tip over chess boards rather than obey the rules of our game. And pirates are among the worst renegades."

"Your Excellency, are you really afraid that those anarchic savages on Outcast Island will somehow rise up to threaten our gilded position in the world?"

"I fear any unruly group that operates outside the Syndicate's masterful control. If they somehow spark a rebellion that spreads around the world, it could undo centuries of our work to disarm the proles, numb them with dogma, mollify them with handouts, and lie to them about everything. Chaos is our friend if we instigate it from above, but it's our enemy if the proles start it spontaneously from below."

Cosimo scoffed. "Those barbarians on Outcast Island are incapable of building a military that can break through the World Order quarantine."

"And it was unlikely that some backwoods rebels in America would defeat the mighty British Empire in the eighteenth century. But they did."

"Your Excellency, what is your point?"

"Your role as an apprentice Centurion is to learn how to ensure the Syndicate's eternal prosperity," Six declared. "There are three classes of people in the world: We, who exist to rule the world; fools, who exist to be ruled; and renegades, who are too independent to rule or be ruled. The success of your apprenticeship will be measured solely by your ability to exterminate the renegades. The Golden Hundred are the ultimate predators on the planet."

"Of course," Cosimo replied. "I assure you that the desired carnage will happen on Outcast Island. They will never organize themselves into a force that can oppose us."

"I'm not so certain," Six said. "The Soviets supplied Cuba with weaponry for decades. Many of those weapons are still floating around the island. Someday they may be used against our interests."

"Your Excellency, I have the situation under control."

Silence followed as Cosimo squirmed uncomfortably. Finally, Six spoke. "That island has always been difficult to control. The Spanish conquistadors slaughtered the indigenous Taino Indians. Spanish colonialism succumbed to American imperialism under the Monroe Doctrine. American imperialism evolved into plundering by the mafiosi and their casinos. Then came Castro, Guevara, and Soviet communism. Communism collapsed into the chaos of poverty. And then the World Order began dumping its outcasts there. The island has a long legacy of slave revolts, corruption, guerilla warfare, organized crime, populist revolutions, and piracy, all led by incorrigible renegades who refused to follow the rules. We can be certain of only one thing: something unpredictable is going to happen in that cauldron of anarchy. That's why I called this meeting."

Cosimo struggled to hide his exasperation. "What do you wish me to do, Your Excellency?"

Six sighed heavily. "I shouldn't have to manage these details. Help a compliant faction become dominant, and then coerce them to wipe out every renegade on Outcast Island."

"Which faction should I pick?"

"The one that can crush dissent and control the food supply of the proles," Six replied. "Power over people's spirits and stomachs equals power over their wills."

"That will make Vlad and his collectivists happy. Crushing spirits and rationing food is in their DNA."

"I don't care if anyone else in the world is happy," Six snapped. "I only care that the Syndicate is."

Cosimo extinguished his cigarette. "Just one more clarification, Your Excellency. The renegades were deported to Outcast Island because the spineless leaders around the world didn't want to kill them in their home countries for fear that their martyrdom would arouse even more rebellion. Am I to understand that I now have your approval to kill at will?"

Six's silhouette stood up, signaling an end to the discussion. "Yes. Our power must be absolute and unchallenged. There are no rules."

9

———

ALLIANCE

John was surprised by the strength of Olga's arms as she embraced him.

"Thank you!" Olga exclaimed after releasing her bear hug. She was rejoicing at the return of her four kidnapped warriors to the Remnant camp. Bloodied and exhausted, they bore the devastated looks of violated women on their haggard faces. But at least they were alive.

John gestured toward Mallory. "The captain and his commandos were the real heroes."

Olga bounded over to Mallory and gave him an even more enthusiastic hug. He accepted it stiffly without reciprocating. Then she rushed into the arms of her four rescued companions for an emotional reunion.

She wiped a tear from her cheek when she returned to John and Mallory. "Tell me about the rescue!"

"My men were Army Rangers before our unit defected," Mallory began. "We plan meticulously, and we execute flawlessly. The kidnappers were careless. They probably didn't expect us to hunt them down, since they know us to be exhausted. We tracked them to the foothills of the mountains and quietly surrounded their bivouac. They lit a campfire, which was a fatal mistake. It gave our snipers enough light to identify targets and to line up kill shots. We killed four of them with our first salvo and the remaining three with the second. We couldn't carry their bodies back here as proof, but we brought their severed heads." He pointed to a bloody burlap sack that his men had dumped behind the four rescued women. It looked like it was bulging with soccer balls.

"Your skill and determination are remarkable!" Olga said to Mallory. Then she turned to John. "If you still wish for an alliance, I am willing."

John extended his hand to ratify their agreement, but Olga left his arm dangling in midair. She whistled to an aide, who hustled into one of the wattle huts and returned with a crude metal lancet.

"An alliance with the Remnant must include a blood oath." Olga took the lancet and jabbed the palm of her hand. Blood oozed from the wound. She handed the sullied instrument to John.

"Your turn."

John blanched, then jabbed his own palm. The pain was sharp, but a surprising charge of adrenaline followed.

Olga extended her bloodied hand. "To the death!" she proclaimed.

John gripped her wounded hand. "To the death!" he echoed. The intimacy of their handshake sent a chill up his spine.

"Did you do this with François le Clerc?" he asked.

"Yes. But he failed to honor our pact."

"And yet you're choosing to trust me anyway?"

Olga hesitated. "Your team has done more for the Remnant in one day than he did in his lifetime. And remember that I intend to kill him for his betrayal. Don't make the same mistake he did." She glared at him, then changed the subject. "Let's discuss the joint mission I mentioned at our last meeting."

"Against one of Vlad's outposts?"

"Yes," Olga replied. "He controls an old Spanish fort that's called the Rock. It sits atop Skull Ridge. He has many such outposts around the island."

"Why attack this one?" Mallory asked.

"They use it as a base to subdue people in our region. We expect to be targeted soon. It's filled with weapons and other useful items, including bicycles, horses, oxen, and carts."

"John told me you had information about the fort," Mallory added. "Please, share it so we can formulate a plan of attack."

Olga whistled. A wispy Hispanic women advanced noiselessly on bare feet from the crowd of women. She had a pretty but inscrutable face with penetrating dark eyes that appeared intent on seeing what others could not. Her skin was dark brown, and her wiry, athletic frame seemed to float where she stood.

Olga introduced her. "This is Maria. She leads our intelligence network. Her team of native Cubanos are very resourceful, and they're as brave as your Rangers. They've studied the fort in detail. Two of them have even infiltrated it. She will brief you."

Maria smiled politely, but her manner was businesslike. Her proficient English had a Hispanic lilt. "Gentlemen, here are the key points from our surveillance. The fort has two stone walls that are each six feet thick. The outer wall is fifteen feet high, and the inner wall is twenty-five feet high. The fort is surrounded by a moat that is eight feet deep and thirty feet wide with sharpened stakes implanted on the bottom. Outside the moat are trenches and barbed wire. The only access to the fort is across a drawbridge leading to the gatehouse. There are cannons on the battlements, but we don't know if they work. They have old Russian firearms, which we know work. There are turrets on the four corners that give their lookouts an unobstructed view of all approaches." She paused to assess their reactions. "Any questions?"

"How many soldiers are inside?" Mallory asked.

"There are about fifty capable fighters who are loyal to Vlad. In total, there are about two hundred fifty people inside, but most are infirm, imprisoned, or not loyal enough to be trusted with weapons."

"How do they get their food and water?"

"Their water comes from deep wells inside the fort. But food is a problem for them. They've already plundered the surrounding farms, so that option is gone for them now. We Cubanos learned long ago that when the communists urged the workers of the world to unite, they had no rational plan for encouraging production."

"Can we exploit their hunger?"

"Yes," Maria replied. "They're malnourished and miserable. Most have skin rashes, missing teeth, and atrophied muscles."

"Sometimes human weaknesses are easier to exploit than physical barriers," Mallory observed. "Are there any gaps in the fort's defenses?"

"A glaring one," Maria replied. "There's a maze of underground tunnels running beneath the perimeter defenses and the walls. They were dug long ago, perhaps during sieges or by escaping prisoners. We've mapped the entire network. Some of the passages are booby-trapped, and some are caved in. There are two tunnels that can be made viable. We've been secretly rehabilitating them for months. We don't believe Vlad's soldiers are aware of that."

"Where do they lead?" Mallory asked.

"One ends under the barracks where the soldiers live. The other ends under the jail cells where their prisoners are kept."

"Interesting," Mallory said. "Both options have military potential."

"There's one more situation that may have military potential," Maria said. "Two of our spies are inside the fort. They volunteered to infiltrate it. That's how we learned much of this information. They've sketched maps of the interior. We'll share those with you."

Mallory's jaw dropped. "How did they get in?"

Maria's demeanor suddenly became grim. "They allowed themselves to be captured during a Proletariat raid of a local village. Vlad's men are always hunting for sex slaves. He permits his thugs to commit any vulgarity. It distracts them from their otherwise shitty lives that are mired in poverty and tormented by secret police."

"That's an awful sacrifice for those two women to make," Mallory observed.

Maria lifted her chin in defiance. "Their reward will be the deaths of their tormentors."

"The Remnant was born of abuse by men, especially Vlad's

men," Olga interjected. "We'll get our revenge, even if the price is high. Failure on this mission could be catastrophic."

"How so?" John asked.

Olga looked at him with sorrowful eyes. "Our spies have witnessed Vlad's men make gruesome examples out of traitors and dissenters. They scourge them with barbed whips, tear their limbs off on the rack, and then behead them. Sometimes dissidents are drawn and quartered while still alive. If any of my women are captured during the upcoming battle for the fort, they might opt for suicide."

"Failure is never an option for my unit," Mallory declared. "Any military action must be decisive. We won't waste blood or treasure if the outcome is uncertain or unimportant."

"Are you up for this?" Olga asked.

"Yes," Mallory replied with a firm set of his jaw. "I'm intrigued by the challenge of storming a castle and capturing some cannons. But we need time to strategize and prepare."

"How much time?" Olga asked. "My spies in the fort are stuck in Dante's lowest circle of hell. A good day is when they're merely spit and pissed on. They're in grave danger. Initially, they were able to pass us messages through a narrow gap in one of the tunnels, but that has since caved in. They have no possibility of escape at the moment."

Mallory rubbed his stubbled chin. "I have to consult with my men, some of whom spent time in the Army Corp of Engineers. John has some clever men, too, including a metalworker, a carpenter, and a chemist. We also have firearms and gunpowder. I'm sure we can concoct a plan to breach the fort."

"Can you be ready in a week?"

"Yes. If nothing else, we'll resort to Irish Democracy."

Olga looked puzzled. "I'm from Poland. I don't know what that means."

"The Proletariat has better weapons and more resources than we do, like the British Empire did against the Irish, so we'll counter with cleverness, surprise, and speed. Sharp minds can overcome brute force, especially when freedom is at stake."

"Ah!" Olga exclaimed. "I understand. Poland was sandwiched

between Germany and Russia. We were always oppressed underdogs, but we managed to survive. My warriors and I will come to your camp one week from today. We'll bring the firearms that we captured in skirmishes with rogue factions, although we have no ammunition, and none of us are trained in their use. The Rock is a two-day march from your camp. Maria's spies will provide reconnaissance. Our archers could be useful if you can fit them into your battle plan. We can light our arrows on fire or poison the tips with pufferfish venom."

"You have firearms?" Mallory asked with surprise. "And archers?"

"Don't get too excited," Olga warned. "Two factions have already failed to conquer the Rock since Vlad took control of it. It's a bitch to attack."

"Which factions?"

"The first failed attempt was by a band of outcasts, much like yours. The Rock sits on Skull Ridge, which is so named because cannibals long ago staked the decapitated skulls of their victims along the ridge as trophies. Most of the newer skulls are from the outcasts who were slaughtered during the attack on the fort. Vlad likes to display trophies too."

"What other faction failed to take the Rock?" John asked.

Olga looked down at the ground. "The Remnant."

John put a hand on her shoulder. "My God! What happened?"

"François le Clerc happened," Olga replied, lifting her eyes to meet his. "He was my lover at the time and promised that his fellow pirates would help the Remnant take the fort. We showed up for the battle, but they didn't. Vlad's soldiers were forewarned that we were coming. They ambushed us. Over fifty of my warriors died that day, and many more were captured. I've pledged my honor to rescue them. That's another urgency for capturing the Rock."

John's face went pale. "Why did le Clerc betray his blood oath with you?"

"He sent an insulting note to me later saying that the only thing in the world more beautiful than me was the stack of gold bars paid to him by someone named Cosimo. He begged for forgiveness and predicted that I would understand someday."

"I take it you don't understand," John said.

Rage glittered like diamonds from Olga's blue-gray eyes, and she flashed the Polish eagle tattooed on her forearm.

"I will kill him someday or die in the attempt."

10

____

THE ROCK

The march toward the Rock was tortuous.

Maria and her nimble scouts led the way. There were three hundred warriors from Pathless Land and the Remnant trailing behind them. It was slow going. The native Cubanos were jungle-savvy, but the path they blazed was better suited for a squadron than an army. If there had ever been civilization in this area, the jungle now concealed it.

John trudged alongside Olga, Mallory, the Carpenter, and the Monk. They were silent for long stretches as they navigated the jungle obstacles and steeled themselves for the upcoming assault on the Rock.

Birds screeched overhead, and unseen animals crashed through the ferns. Whizzing insects harassed the warriors despite the tobacco juice they had spread on their skin as repellent. Snakes with demonic slit eyes were coiled in branches overhead. Giant centipedes and spiders lurked everywhere. The warriors forded several swollen streams and mucked through swamp after swamp. By the second day of the march, their bodies were covered with welts, sweat, and grime.

Despite his years of farming in Kansas, John was ill prepared for such hellish misery. Brief rain showers brought some respite from the oppressive heat, but they also brought more humidity and turned the ground into a slurry. His exposed skin was blistered from sunburn, and his lips were dry and cracked. He had a constant sensation that insects had infested his filthy clothes, which caused him to scratch patches of his skin raw.

Morbid thoughts crawled through his brain like the bugs on his skin. He knew that the impending clash required heroes, not cowards. Would he pass the test? He had severe doubts. John knew, however, that if nothing was worth dying for, then nothing was worth living for. He had come to Outcast Island to face such challenges.

They were beginning to climb the steep foothills of Skull Ridge upon which the Rock stood. The climb and the exhaustion from their long march left John short of breath. Or perhaps his lungs were constricting from his rising fear.

Their joint army carried an assortment of weaponry. Some of the men toted the firearms from Hammer's boat and the Remnant's captured stash. Olga's archers shouldered bows and quivers of arrows. Everyone else bore machetes, axes, spears, daggers, and crude shields made from fire-hardened wood. Muscular men lugged the tools and explosives that Hammer, Newton, and Mallory's army engineers had prepared for the assault on the fort.

John noticed that the Carpenter showed no signs of fear or fatigue. He was clad in a white linen robe that Hammer had gifted him, cinched with a leather belt. His only weapon was a stout staff, which he used for steadying himself on unstable terrain. The aura from his quiet presence was comforting.

"I hope this miserable day isn't our last on Earth," John mused, breaking a long silence. "I'm not ready to die."

The Carpenter smiled serenely. "Farmer John, it's better to think about how to live than to worry about death. Have faith, *amigo*."

"If we execute our plan, we'll be victorious," Mallory interjected. "The Remnant finishing the rehabilitation of the two tunnels was critical. And Olga says her scouts can use their clever whistling system to synchronize our attack."

"It took years to refine our clandestine system," Olga chimed in.

"Our coded whistles are indistinguishable from the calls of native birds."

John turned to the Monk. "My friend, you volunteered for the most dangerous part of this mission. How are your nerves?"

The Monk steepled his hands and bowed slightly. "The capacity to feel at peace everywhere yields a positive energy. The urge to run away does not. Fearlessness underlies all happiness."

John cocked his head. "But you'll be exposed and defenseless in full view of the Proletariat at the gate of the Rock!"

"Such is life," the Monk replied softly. "The nature of our existence is to face risk, then we eventually die. Today is no different than any other day."

John nodded. "Your wisdom is unusual but calming."

The Monk shook his head vigorously. "It's not my wisdom. My teaching is like a finger pointing at the moon. Do not mistake my finger for the moon. A teacher can open your eyes to the truth of existence, but he can never *be* the truth. The universe is the truth."

The group fell silent, walking in pensive contemplation. Finally, they arrived at their planned staging area just out of sight of the Rock. Mallory coordinated the stealthy deployment of their resources. Maria's guides led each squadron to their assigned location where they would wait for a signal. A synchronized attack was vital to the success of the mission.

Mallory's men were assigned to snipe the guards on the battlements and in the towers and to strategically deploy the explosives fabricated by Newton. Hammer's unit would attack through the tunnel leading to the penitentiary. Olga and her archers would launch flaming arrows into the interior of the fort and poisoned arrows at any enemies attempting to flee. Maria's scouts would enter the fort once it was breached and then lower the drawbridge over the moat. John's unit would storm the interior of the fort after crossing the drawbridge.

Birdlike whistles chirped from many directions informing Olga that all units were in position. She nodded to Mallory, who surveyed the battle scene one last time from their hidden command post. He returned a somber nod to her.

Olga whistled a mesmerizing sound, which was echoed by a symphony of birdlike calls that swirled around the fort. The battle was on.

On cue, the Monk emerged from his jungle seclusion across from the gatehouse of the Rock. His naked body was smeared with mud. He carried aloft a white flag as he walked slowly toward the Rock. Then he stopped at the edge of the moat, collapsed to his knees, waved his white flag above his head, and shouted gibberish in his native Vietnamese.

His distraction had the intended effect. Shouts reverberated inside the fort in reaction to the bizarre apparition that had materialized outside the gatehouse. The guards on the battlements ran to the section that cantilevered over the gatehouse. The sentries in all four towers trained their eyes in the Monk's direction. They peered deep into the jungle from where he had emerged to see if a malevolent faction was poised to attack.

Simultaneously, at the end of the tunnel beneath the soldiers' barracks, Mallory's engineers placed explosives where most of the dirt and rock had been quietly excavated from beneath the flooring above by Olga's advance miners. The engineers then retreated to a safe distance.

At the end of the tunnel beneath the jail cells, Hammer and his men were positioned with axes, crowbars, and picks. Most of the dirt and rock had been excavated away there too. They stared upward at the underside of the wooden flooring, waiting for the next signal.

Outside the fort, the Remnant's hidden archers lit their flaming arrows. When they were ready, Olga's whistle triggered another wave of whistles to swirl around the fort.

Mallory's snipers fired at the exposed guards, who were keeping watch inside the Rock. Flaming arrows soared in graceful arcs over the walls. The explosives under the barracks detonated. Hammer and his men began chopping a large hole in the wooden floor of the penitentiary.

The guards shot by the snipers plunged from the battlements and towers to the ground below. The ancient wooden roofs of the buildings started to burn, kindled by the flaming arrows. The thunderous explosion under the barracks killed half of the soldiers who were idling inside. The survivors suffered a horrific assortment of burns, shrapnel wounds, and broken bones.

Hammer's armed warriors poured upward through a jagged hole in the penitentiary floor like giant subterranean cockroaches. Hammer hoisted them up one by one, then hauled himself up. A gun battle erupted with the surprised prison guards. The fierce exchange sprayed bullets around the tight quarters, and two of Hammer's men fell to the ground. The prisoners sought any cover they could find, but several were shot. Hammer leapt over his fallen mates and charged at the last two surviving guards. They fired recklessly in his direction as they turned to flee in terror from the onrushing giant. He crashed into them like a human bowling ball, knocking them like pins to the ground. He shot both in the head at close range, their blood and gore splattering his face and shirt.

It wasn't until then that Hammer realized one of their bullets had struck his abdomen and passed completely through. He took a moment to assess his wound, shook it off, then scrambled to locate the keys to the jail cells. He found them and tossed them to his surviving men, who immediately began releasing the shocked prisoners from dank pens that smelled like zoo cages.

Once the gunfire ceased, Maria and her spies followed Hammer's men through the hole in the penitentiary floor and sprinted into the interior of the fort. Under cover of the growing chaos, they snatched guns from fallen guards, sprinted across the courtyard, and shot their way into the gatehouse. In the process, Maria was hit in the arm by return fire, and one of her spies was fatally wounded. Several women pulled the levers of the drawbridge to lower it toward the Monk, who had remained kneeling by the moat with his head bowed.

Before the drawbridge could fully descend, the gears jammed. The bridge had lowered to six feet above the ground on the other side of the moat. John's team was already pouring from their hiding places in the jungle and were halfway to it. When John saw the malfunctioning bridge, he raised his arm to halt his men. Gunshots came from the few remaining guards who were watching them from the battlement. John's men hunkered down behind their wooden shields while John studied their predicament.

Then arrows filled the sky from Olga's archers, raining down on the guards inside the fort. At the same time, Mallory's snipers began picking off any guards who exposed themselves. John waved his men forward now that they had cover. When they reached the drawbridge, they leapt to clamber onto it. The Monk had already scrambled atop, so he reached out to help John's men. One of them was shot and plummeted into the moat. The rest of John's squadron mounted the bridge and sprinted through the gatehouse into the fort.

Pandemonium was now raging inside the Rock. Acrid smoke from the flaming roofs billowed everywhere, burning lungs and stinging eyes while reducing visibility. The prisoners fleeing their jail cells ran pell-mell. John's soldiers spread out inside the complex. The fort was engulfed by a cacophony of screams, shouts, gunfire, roaring flames, and collapsing roofs. Some Proletariat soldiers fled the mayhem across the drawbridge toward the jungle, but most of them were slaughtered by poisoned arrows from Olga's archers. The few survivors were shot from close range by Mallory's Rangers, who had abandoned their sniping nests and were now rampaging into the fort.

Mallory met up with John inside the fort. They and a few other soldiers sprinted through the mayhem toward the headquarters of the fort, the location of which they had memorized from Maria's maps. When they neared the building, Mallory tossed a crude grenade at the front door. The explosion blew a gaping hole in the wall. The men dashed up the steps and into the smoking structure.

There was no resistance as they opened doors and secured the building room by room. When they got to the end of the main hall, which was constructed of stone walls that were damp from humidity and smeared with black mold, they saw a door marked "Comandante," but it was locked. Mallory splintered it with a vicious kick. A man inside screamed and raised his arms as soldiers charged in. The markings on his uniform confirmed his rank as the Rock's commander.

Mallory aimed his rifle at his heart. "Do you speak English?" he demanded.

"*Sí*, don't shoot!" The Hispanic man was clad in a rumpled, ill-fitting uniform and sported a scruffy black beard and mustache. Thick, dark-rimmed glasses balanced on his bulbous nose. His dark, wide eyes flitted nervously, revealing his fear and guilt.

"I'm taking you hostage," Mallory barked. "I won't kill you unless you disobey my orders or Vlad refuses to pay your ransom."

Relief flashed across the *comandante's* face. "And my soldiers?"

"Most are already dead, which you would know if you weren't cowering in here," Mallory sneered.

A Ranger tied the captive's hands behind his back, then Mallory grabbed him by his collar and shoved him toward the door. With their hostage in tow, they sprinted across the smoking fort and then jumped down from the drawbridge and headed to a planned staging area where Olga was waiting.

"Quick battle assessment?" she asked.

"As good as could be expected," Mallory spat out between gasps for fresh air. "Prisoners are released. Barracks are destroyed. Most of their soldiers are dead." He gestured toward his trembling hostage, who had landed awkwardly on the ground after being tossed off the drawbridge. "And we captured the commander."

Olga nodded. "Then it's time for triage. Clear everyone out of the Rock. Move the rescued women from the Remnant over there, where Maria's scouts will attend to them." She pointed to a clearing on her right. "Move the noncombatants and the other released prisoners over there, where Sergeant Brown and his medic will attend to them." She pointed to a clearing on her left. "Send our warriors here after the fort is cleared. Doc will assess them for injuries and treat them."

"And the surviving enemy soldiers?" Mallory asked. "Shall we proceed as planned?"

Olga nodded grimly. "They must pay the ultimate price for the crimes they've committed against my women and the local villagers. Search everywhere. Leave no stone unturned. Show no mercy."

Mallory and John reentered the fort to execute Olga's

commands. Several hours later, the compound was completely evacuated, and the survivors were sorted into the groupings specified by Olga. Doc and the Ranger medic treated the wounded, which included Maria and Hammer. John, Olga, and Mallory separated from the others to discuss the next steps.

John noticed that Olga was gritting her teeth and her fists were balled. "What's wrong?" he asked.

She glared at the smoldering fort. "Forty-three of my women were captured in the Remnant's first raid, plus the two who later volunteered as spies." She waved her arm disconsolately toward the small group of surviving women huddled in the clearing. "There are only eleven left. Look at their terrible condition! They look dehumanized and so much older than they are." She turned to Mallory. "I hope the Proletariat soldiers all met the fate they deserved."

Mallory nodded. "All are dead except for our one hostage."

Olga's eyes shot lightning bolts. "That bastard allowed his men to abuse and kill our women! And now he trembles like a coward. I don't know whether I hate him or François le Clerc more!" Then she calmed herself, realizing that more lives were risked in this battle than just the women of the Remnant. "And our losses?"

"The enemy was unprepared and no match for our Rangers," Mallory replied. "Our foes were malnourished, demoralized, and led by an incompetent commander. Our planning was superb, and our execution was excellent. By my reckoning, just six of our warriors were killed, and a few more were seriously wounded."

John put his hand on Mallory's shoulder. "Every loss is a horror, Captain. But you and the warriors accomplished a vital mission." He turned to Olga. "My heart also aches for the grim condition of your colleagues. There is some good news, however."

Olga looked at him with watery eyes. "Yes?"

"The fort is well stocked, just as your spies reported. Most of their stuff survived our attack. We've found firearms, ammunition, bicycles, carts, and lots of tools. There's a corral with horses, burros, and oxen that seem better fed than the people. And there's an intriguing bone pile of old electronics and communications devices. I'm hoping that Nicolai can scavenge enough parts to make something useful. There's also a large electric generator in disrepair. Maybe Nicolai can work a miracle with that too."

Olga studied the damaged fort. "It just occurred to me that we never discussed what to do with the Rock once we captured it. I assumed we would just rescue our women, take the Proletariat's belongings, kill their soldiers, and return to our separate camps. But now I see possibilities . . ."

Mallory nodded. "Maybe we're thinking the same thing. Let's make the Rock the base of operations for our new alliance. It needs some repairs, and those tunnels must be sealed, but once my engineers and the Carpenter's workers tackle those challenges, it'll be hard for Vlad—or anyone else—to take it from us. Especially if we get those cannons working."

"That's a brilliant idea," John agreed. "I was dreading a two-day return march to our camps. And the reward for our fighters was going to be more nights sleeping on the ground."

"Here's a sobering question," Olga said. "How soon do you think Vlad will seek revenge?"

"He may not hear about this assault for a while," Mallory reasoned. "We killed all their soldiers, and I don't believe they have any electronic communications. However, there might be regular horseback messengers between la Habana and the Rock."

"Vlad does indeed run messengers to and from his outlying posts," Olga replied. "Maria's scouts can monitor that threat and eliminate it. We should delay demanding a ransom from Vlad for the commander we captured. Maybe then it will take a while before he realizes something is amiss here."

"I had no intention of demanding a ransom," Mallory said. "That man isn't worth a damn. I lied to him about the ransom so that he had a glimmer of hope. I intend to interrogate him and then dispose of him."

Mallory abruptly glanced over Olga's shoulder. "Sergeant Brown is heading this way with one of the prisoners we freed from the jail cells."

John and Olga turned. Trudging behind Brown was an old man who looked like a walking corpse. His malnourished body had sticks for appendages. His hair and beard were gray and straggly. His face and arms were covered with sores, scars, and strange swellings. His reddened eyes were sunk into his skull. Many of his teeth were missing. His body shook with tremors. Overall, he had the deranged look of a man who saw some horror no one else could see, or who knew some dark humor that no one else perceived. When he neared, his stench struck them like a physical blow.

"This man's a lunatic," the sergeant announced. "He says he knows you, John."

John scrutinized the derelict and then shook his head. He didn't recognize him. Besides, it was impossible that he would know someone atop Skull Ridge on Outcast Island.

The shoulders of the trembling man drooped. "John, it's me. Jed. I recognized you when you ran through the Rock."

John's confusion mounted. The mumbled voice was familiar. "Jed?"

The man's mournful eyes bored into John's. "Jed Starnes. From Kansas."

John's jaw dropped. "Dear God . . ." Recognition triggered a tidal wave of memories. He embraced Jed despite his appalling odor and deathly afflictions. "I assumed you died years ago. You look so awful I didn't recognize you!"

"Life's been hard here, John."

"You know this man?" Olga asked incredulously.

"Yes! Jed was my best friend in Kansas. He founded a rebel cell, then was captured by the Elites in 2054. He is the bravest man I know because he was one of the few rebels who refused to carve out his SIN chip or to adopt a pseudonym to hide his identity."

"Sergeant, why did you call this man a lunatic?" Mallory asked.

Brown looked sheepishly at his commander. "Sir, he claimed to know John, and he was ranting that he knew the location of a huge treasure."

"What's this about a treasure, Starnes?" Mallory asked curtly.

"It's a secret I kept from the Proletariat, despite two years of torture. I know where the famous buccaneer Henry Morgan hid his chests full of gold pieces that he stole from Panama in the seventeenth century."

Olga gasped. "That's rumored to be the biggest hoard of Spanish gold ever amassed. Le Clerc has been trying to find it for years."

"How can you possibly know where it is?" John asked.

Jed attempted a toothless grin. "I came into possession of a map drawn by Morgan's own hand. If the map is correct, the gold is in a cave not far from here. But legend says that anyone who attempts to retrieve it will die a horrible death."

"You have the map?" John asked breathlessly. "Where is it?"

Jed nodded weakly and jabbed a skeletal finger against the side of his mangy head. "Right here. I memorized it, then burned it before I was captured."

"How good is your memory?" John asked. He eyed the physical wreck standing before him with skepticism.

"My memories are the only things of value I have left," Jed replied.

11

———

SOUL

Pathless Land and the Remnant immediately began rehabilitating the Rock and adapting it to their needs. Teams were formed to repair the fire-damaged structures, rebuild the demolished barracks, seal the tunnels, and transport everything of value from the old camps of both factions to their new home. While Maria was treated for her wounded arm, her scouts patrolled the perimeter outside the moat and maintained watch from the four towers. Some scouts were posted along a well-worn trail that ran toward la Habana so they could intercept Vlad's horseback messengers.

Now that the two factions were joined, the leadership structure was modified. Pathless Land's original Council of Sages had too many of John's shipmates, some of whom had personalities and aptitudes better suited to doing rather than leading. The new Council included Olga, John, Mallory, Maria, the Carpenter, and the Monk. They insisted that John be the first leader of the consolidated group, although the potential for rotating leadership among them was left open. The Carpenter and the Monk were included because their calm wisdom was a much-needed counterbalance to the brashness of the others.

On the evening of the Rock's conquest, the new council sat around a campfire just inside the gatehouse. The captured commander of the fort was with them. His hands were bound and his ankles were shackled as his interrogation was about to begin. His face registered great anxiety, and his leg muscles twitched nervously.

"Your name?" Mallory began. He toyed with a crude branding iron crafted by Hammer despite his wounded abdomen. The business end of the iron was red hot in the coals of the fire.

"Capitán Garcia." The prisoner scanned the faces of his adversaries with jittery eyes. "Are you going to torture me?"

"That depends," Mallory replied. "Are you going to cooperate?"

Garcia stared morosely at the ominous device in Mallory's hand.

"*Sí*," Garcia grumbled.

"Where were you born?" Mallory asked.

"Santiago de Cuba."

"Why did you join the Proletariat?"

Garcia dropped his head. "I joined during the great chaos in Cuba when the World Order started dumping outcasts here. People were hungry. There was violence everywhere and no structure to tame it. Vlad promised order and safety if we obeyed him. We Cubanos were already conditioned to submit under Castro and his successors, so embracing Vlad's socialism was a familiar path."

"Why did you stay with them?" Mallory asked. "Life looked hellish at the Rock. Your troops were demoralized, your civilians were starving, and your prisoners were treated worse than your animals. And it appears that you maintained order with a heavy hand." Mallory pointed to two morbid structures in the center of the Rock's yard. "We will dismantle your guillotine and your gallows tomorrow."

Shame washed over Garcia's face. "What other option did I have? If I refused Vlad's orders, it would be the gallows or the guillotine for me. It was better to conform than to resist. Now that the nightmare has ended, I see the situation in a clear light. All I can say is that I was intoxicated."

"Intoxicated by what?"

Garcia shrugged. "The lure of power and prestige, especially when I was given more authority. There's something addictive about giving orders to people, knowing that their obedience is a matter of life and death settled by a mere nod of my head. It was easy for me to rationalize that my power was being exercised for the common good. And Vlad himself is intoxicating despite his other shortcomings. He can convince people of the rightness of his mission and of the necessity to use force to achieve it. He assured us that a wondrous Utopia would emerge once the difficult transition to communism was completed. His sugary dishonesty held our faith despite famine, shortages, and oppression. He preached that each setback was just a minor detour from our great journey."

John rolled his eyes. "The glory of socialism is always in the future and never in the present. We learned that lesson the hard way in America. We held a Constitutional Convention in 2041 that neutered our individual rights and ushered in a society based on group rights. After that, our currency collapsed, everything was in short supply, the groups were constantly fighting each other, Homeland Security hunted down dissidents, and the bureaucrats took control of everything. You Cubanos should have learned the lesson, too, especially after the collapse of your Soviet mentors."

Garcia nodded sadly. "It's true that we're starving and oppressed now. But we were always starving and oppressed. At least Vlad gave us hope, even though it turned out to be a lie. Our leaders pretended to feed us, and we pretended to work. Then Vlad's grand philosophy morphed from 'From each according to his ability' into 'Those who do not obey shall not eat.' A police state with its guillotines and gallows soon followed. The only incentives to produce food were threats, whips, and executions."

"Interesting," Mallory observed. He wondered if Garcia's answers were sincere, or if he was just mouthing platitudes to appease his interrogators. "That might explain why we encountered little resistance during our attack. Do all of Vlad's compounds suffer from this lack of personal responsibility?"

Garcia nodded. "It defines socialism, which entices people into its embrace like a dreamy Siren, but in reality, it is a venal witch who is impossible to escape from once you're in her clutches."

"I was wondering specifically about Vlad's forces in la Habana," Mallory pressed. "Are they paper tigers like your soldiers at the Rock?"

"The elite Palace Guards protecting Vlad are well fed and very capable," Garcia replied. "Despite your clever assault on the Rock, don't be overconfident. Vlad preaches equality and brotherhood but practices self-preservation at the expense of everyone else."

"It seems you did the same," Mallory judged. "How much of Outcast Island does Vlad control?"

"Most of it. The Jackals are ruthless and fearless, but they don't control much territory. They steal from peasants who live on the fringes of Vlad's domain. The Pirates don't control much either because they're marauders. They steal from the Proletariat and the Jackals but leave the peasants alone. Spartacus and his Maroons hide in the mountains near Sancti Spiritus, a rugged terrain that Vlad has no interest in. The Remnant was a minor nuisance—until today."

"Which faction does Vlad fear the most?"

Garcia smirked. "You're trying to decide who might be good allies against him?"

"I'll ask the questions," Mallory replied curtly. He rotated the branding iron slowly in the fire, then held the glowing menace up in the air to admire it.

Garcia's smirk evaporated. "Everyone is dangerous to the Proletariat simply because Vlad is dangerous to everyone else. Le Clerc makes him the most nervous. His pirates occasionally raid Vlad's remote outposts, although they never attack la Habana. And le Clerc is so enigmatic that Vlad is confused whether he's friend or foe."

Olga threw a stick into the fire so hard that sparks flew into the air. "Le Clerc is always a friend until he's a foe," she said bitterly.

"So le Clerc is Vlad's greatest enemy?" John asked.

"He's a thorn," Garcia said. "But the ugly truth is that Vlad's own people are his biggest concern here on the island because he knows that he can never fulfill his promises of food and safety. He worries that revolution will come when enough of his proles regain their sanity."

Mallory raised an eyebrow. "Why did you say, 'here on the island'? Is Vlad afraid of someone who's not here?"

Garcia fell silent for a moment. "I believe there are forces in the world who are unspeakably dangerous."

Mallory stoked the hot coals in the fire with his branding iron. "Do tell."

Garcia's face twitched. "Nobody knows anything for sure. That's by design, I suppose. But there is an invisible evil that's stoking the turmoil on the island. Common people like me are pawns, but even powerful men like Vlad, le Clerc, and Guzman don't rank much higher. They're all being manipulated by the unseen hand of a chess master."

John changed the subject. "Do you think Vlad will pay a ransom for you?"

Garcia's shoulders slumped. He didn't reply.

"Of course he won't," Mallory said. "You lost one of his forts, which he'll never get back. You're just a soulless cog in his machine. A pawn, as you put it. You're disposable now because you're no longer useful to him, nor to us. Unless you can convince me otherwise."

Garcia looked desperately around the campfire. Shadows flickered across grim faces. The realization that he had nothing to barter for his life hit him like a sledgehammer. He was going to be killed, just like his soldiers. He suddenly understood that he was *always* going to be killed, that the life he had chosen with the Proletariat was not actually life but merely a mortal clock ticking down to his demise, whether in the form of execution, starvation, or other such damnation. The only meaningful question about his hijacked life was the day and time of his death. What an idiotic, gullible fool he had been! He looked up into the abysmal darkness of the night, realizing his entire life was a self-deception.

The Carpenter stood up abruptly. He had been watching the contorted emotions scud across the condemned man's face. "Captain Mallory, this *hombre* has a soul, despite his years of collectivist conditioning to the contrary. All people do, and most are redeemable."

"What are you saying?" John asked.

"Farmer John, there's nothing to be gained by killing this man now. We've already captured his fort and rescued our prisoners. I'm disturbed by the harsh retribution taken out on Vlad's soldiers at the Rock earlier today. I understand that was done during the irrational frenzy of battle, but that crisis is over." He turned his attention to Garcia. "I'm giving you a chance to save yourself. Enough talk about politics and factions. Let's address the deeper issues. Who owns your soul, the essence that is uniquely you?"

Garcia was bewildered by the bizarre turn orchestrated by the bearded man in the white robe. He looked imploringly at the Carpenter, trying to tease the real meaning of his question out of the wisps of smoke rising from the campfire.

"Who are you?" Garcia asked the Carpenter with wonderment.

"I am who I am," the Carpenter replied. "Like you, I once faced torture and was condemned to die. Now think hard. Who owns your soul? Vlad? The Proletariat? Mallory?"

A revelation welled up in Garcia, and his face lit up. It was now clear where the Carpenter was leading him. "Not them," he answered.

The Carpenter smiled. "Then who?"

Something that had been simmering inside him for decades, a spirit that had been nearly coerced into complete submission, suddenly erupted. "Me!" Garcia exclaimed.

"*Sí!*" agreed the Carpenter. "No one can claim ownership of another's soul, not even the strongest man nor the most powerful group. A soul is a wonderfully exclusive jewel that came to each person with the gift of free will."

Garcia was puzzled. "If I own my own soul and have free will, then why is the world full of people who want to control my life?"

"Many people struggle with that moral confusion. It's only the individual who hopes, thinks, feels, values, chooses, and acts. The reason you hid in your office when we stormed the Rock was to preserve your own life, which means your unique identity. That is the animating force of all living creatures. And since only you can rightfully lay claim to your own soul, it's a terrible sin for someone else to claim to it. But too many people want to take shortcuts in life. They want to control others for their own benefit. They don't want to be responsible for themselves or for their own choices. So here's another question for you. Who owns the consequences of your actions, for better or for worse?"

"*Dios mio!* There can only be one answer," Garcia responded immediately. "I do."

"And that's the only basis upon which you'll be judged," the Carpenter replied. "Such is the true nature of justice." He turned to John. "I believe this man is redeemable, and it would be wrong to kill him. However, justice demands that he pay a severe penalty for his past transgressions."

Olga jumped up. "Didn't you see what his demons did to our women?" she raged. "The only penalty should be death!"

"*Señorita* Olga, I have seen more inhumanity than I can bear to carry on my shoulders," the Carpenter replied calmly. "Is our mission to add to the inhumanity or to put an end to it? It's my judgment that killing Garcia in his current state of mind would add to it."

"What do you propose to do with this fiend?" Olga demanded. "Let him slither back to our enemy so he can spill our secrets? Let him loose here among our women whom his men have already abused?"

"Neither. If John allows it, I'll invite *Señor* Garcia to join me on the carpentry team. I'll be his mentor. His punishment will be to make restitution. I propose that for the next ten years he split his workdays into two halves. One half will be dedicated to doing works of kindness for the women of the Remnant. The other half will be dedicated to working for free as a carpenter to benefit our community. In that way, the good within Garcia becomes the good of others. That's my definition of love." He looked expectantly at John.

Olga glared at John in a way that suggested there would be an awful price to pay if he sided with the Carpenter. John worried that their blood oath might not survive the week.

Garcia looked at John with eyes filled with piteous hope. "If it will make your decision easier, I have useful information," he pleaded.

"This is your last chance," John said, grateful that an opportunity might arise to make a Solomonic decision. "Your information better be good."

"It's priceless. The freed prisoner named Jed isn't the only one who knows the location of Morgan's treasure."

"How is that priceless? We don't need *two* people who know."

"What if Jed doesn't tell you? He never told us, despite our . . . methods. But even if he does reveal the location, your faction might not be the first to find the treasure. It may already be gone."

"What the hell are you talking about?" John exclaimed. "Who would get there before us?"

"A messenger delivered a cryptic note from Vlad two days ago. It said that le Clerc and his pirates would be moving through my area, and I was not to interfere with them. The purpose of le Clerc's venture was to collect an enormous payment in the form of buried gold for services he had rendered to the Syndicate."

"How does that help us?" John asked.

A sly grin creased Garcia's face. "I took the liberty of assigning some men to quietly follow le Clerc as he passed through our area. I know exactly where he's heading. I also learned the vulnerabilities of his team."

Olga put her hand on John's shoulder. A strange fire blazed in her eyes. "Let Garcia live, John, at least for a while. He might be useful to us after all."

12

PIRACY

"Not bad for a day's work of digging in a dark cave," François le Clerc boasted to his parrot Merlin. He inhaled luxuriantly on a cigar, reveling in his success.

The two were mesmerized by a cornucopia of treasure. Le Clerc's men had broken open the locked chests that once belonged to the buccaneer Henry Morgan. The chests contained not only the fabled gold pieces Morgan had heisted from Panama, but also silver bars, exquisite jewelry, and a cascade of diamonds, pearls, and other precious gems.

Le Clerc ogled the Midas-worthy hoard like he would a cherished lover. For years he doubted the rumors of its existence, even after Cosimo had given him the centuries-old map of its location written in the very hand of Morgan. He believed that if there was such a hidden treasure, someone would have unearthed it long ago. But as a pirate, he was unable to resist the siren song of greed and adventure.

And now the treasure lay miraculously before him. His mental recollection of Morgan's map, which had been stolen from him a couple of years ago by Jed Starnes, led him to a hilly region known as the Caves of Despair. There were hundreds of caves penetrating the hillsides surrounding this valley, which would have made it a frustrating search for anyone. But with recent help from Cosimo, he had decoded the obtuse clues on the map and knew the landmarks that singled out which cave to explore. Cosimo's assistance was an advance payment for future services to be rendered. Given the value of the treasure, le Clerc knew that the required services would be of great importance.

Le Clerc rubbed his bearded chin in glorious contemplation of his windfall. As a thirty-year-old Arab thrown into the steaming cauldron of chaos on Outcast Island, he was ecstatic with his good fortune. Growing up in the poverty and turmoil of Egypt, he had often despaired that his life would amount to nothing. He was a scrawny, sickly orphan who scratched and clawed a wretched existence in the seedy back alleys of Cairo. His one personal treasure was a relentless, unforgiving passion to rise above those who made his life miserable.

He had matured from the sickly waif into a tall, muscular adult who commanded the respect of most men and the hypnotic attraction of most women. His mane of wavy black hair, mysterious dark eyes, a manicured beard, and an alluring smile inspired heart-stopping admiration in all who beheld his immaculate face. His Arabic attire, with loose trousers and a long belted cloak, was topped off with a red-and-white checkered keffiyeh. He had the exotic look of a sculpted Bedouin sheik.

His exile from Egypt to Outcast Island many years ago was liberating. It allowed him to escape the dark undercurrents of the medieval, theocratic Egyptian oligarchy. The tyrants and bureaucrats who held sway there tormented him and others like him. His heretical outbursts and rebellious antics threatened those in power, so he was arrested. He escaped from his captors and stowed away on the first ship he saw moored in the Nile River. It was full of misfits bound for Outcast Island.

Once on board, le Clerc felt at home for the first time. He experienced a profound metamorphosis during the difficult ocean crossing to Outcast Island and swore a personal oath to never again be abused. He vowed to assert his own will and submit to no one because if he didn't think of himself and for himself, no one would. He aspired to become fearsome and invincible.

Lacking a surname because he was abandoned at birth in a mosque in Cairo, he had grown up known only as Ammon, which meant "hidden one." Because his ship of misfits was destined for a Caribbean Island, he adopted the pseudonym François le Clerc in honor of the dreaded sixteenth-century pirate who raided the islands. His swashbuckling namesake was famous for brazenly boarding enemy ships and engaging in hand-to-hand combat.

Outcast Island was even more chaotic than Egypt when he arrived, but it was a chaos that allowed him to blossom rather than suffocate under the dead weight of centuries of rigid theocratic tradition. He quickly grew in stature, courage, and wealth as he emulated his Arabic ancestors, the Barbary pirates, who had pillaged the Mediterranean region for centuries. Behind his pseudonym le Clerc, he became the bold pillager of Outcast Island. He relentlessly pursued his vision of liberation, beholden to no dogma, creed, or nation.

Le Clerc dipped his hand into a tarnished oak chest filled with jewels, reveling in the emotional electricity that shot up his arm and jolted his heart. He was overcome by a heady spiritual intoxication. He didn't need the celebratory rum his fellow pirates were chugging as they fantasized about spending their cut of the loot. Le Clerc eyed with satisfaction the men sprawled around him as they lazed in exhausted bliss. He admired his small army of cutthroats and rebels, and they loved him for his fearlessness and unbreakable loyalty.

"Sinbad!" Merlin squawked. Le Clerc stroked the radiant blue feathers of his gold-breasted pet. He looked in the direction that Merlin was pointing with his black beak. Sinbad, le Clerc's second-in-command, was running toward them. He was a swarthy, stout Arab born in Baghdad who had adopted his pseudonym in honor of the mythic hero of the Seven Voyages. He was a shipmate of le Clerc on the journey from Cairo to Outcast Island. His large bald head was beaded with sweat, and his dark eyes, which hinted at a trace of Mongol ancestry, were wide with alarm.

"Go away!" Merlin squawked. Le Clerc put a finger to his own lips to silence his pet. He was often amused by the seeming jealousy between Merlin and Sinbad. He turned to his lieutenant. "You look troubled, Sinbad. Too many riches to spend in one lifetime?"

"An army's coming!" Sinbad blurted between gasps for air. "I spied them moving through the jungle from my lookout on the ridge."

Le Clerc's brow furrowed. He should have known that danger would haunt their good fortune, especially since legends warned that Morgan's treasure was cursed. His mind raced as he considered the implications of Sinbad's ominous news. The army couldn't be a patrol from the Rock because he was assured that the local commander would ignore his trespass into their territory. Besides, there were rumors that the Rock had been sacked by another faction. It couldn't be a raid by the Jackals because they had stopped venturing into this region in deference to Vlad. That left only the Remnant as a local faction large enough to be described as an army. It might even have been the Remnant who captured the Rock. If so, their second attempt had gone better than their first. His heart pounded in his chest, partly from a surge of guilt for his betrayal of Olga during their first assault and partly from anticipation of an encounter with her.

"Go away!" Merlin squawked again, interrupting le Clerc's introspection.

"That damn bird thinks he's second-in-command," Sinbad said with disgust.

"That's ridiculous," le Clerc replied. "I'm certain Merlin thinks he's first in command. Maybe he's simply warning us to flee from the approaching army. You take his commentary too personally, my trusted friend. Let's climb to your lookout on the ridge."

The two men made the difficult ascent to the summit. Sinbad pointed toward the northwest, and Le Clerc squinted in that direction. He frowned and then pulled a telescope from his belt, focusing it as he scanned the area.

"I'll be damned!" le Clerc exclaimed, pulling the telescope away from his eye.

"What did you see?" Sinbad asked anxiously.

"It's clearly the Remnant headed our way. I spotted Olga and Maria leading them. But there's something odd."

"What?"

"Olga's companions," le Clerc replied. "Most of them are men. And there are lots of them—with guns."

"But Olga and the Remnant despise men!"

Le Clerc nodded. "There's something even odder. I recognize one of the men marching alongside Olga and Maria."

Sinbad raised an eyebrow. "Who?"

"Jed Starnes."

Sinbad gasped. "The American who stole Henry Morgan's map from you?"

"Aye," le Clerc replied. "I heard he was captured by the Proletariat two years ago. I assumed they killed him."

More sweat dappled Sinbad's brow. "That implies many things . . . and all of them are bad."

"You are wise, my friend. It implies the rumors are true that the Rock was sacked, because Starnes is now a free man. That means Vlad can no longer guarantee us safe passage in this area. It also means that it's no coincidence Starnes is leading the Remnant to the Caves of Despair, because he knows the location of Morgan's treasure. And if the Remnant was able to capture the Rock despite their prior failure, the men marching with them are very capable fighters. If they find us here with the treasure—"

"They will surely try to kill us," Sinbad finished. "No one hates you more than Jed and Olga."

The two men fell silent. Le Clerc felt a strange juxtaposition of emotions. First and foremost was grave concern for his men. A well-armed force was bearing down on them, and there was too much bad blood for a peaceful encounter. There was also a gargantuan treasure at stake, and neither side would be willing to yield the riches to the other. He would have to choose between a harrowing escape burdened by tons of treasure on a plodding mule train or mortal combat with a capable enemy that had just conquered the Rock.

Complicating matters was the fact that the person leading the encroaching army was the woman he loved. Olga was the only person who had ever loved him. His parents had abandoned him at birth, and he grew up adrift in a hostile realm. But his betrayal of her during the Remnant's first tragic attack on the Rock was something she would never forgive him for, no matter how necessary he rationalized his treachery to be.

Despite the unlikelihood of a reconciliation with Olga, thoughts of the strange man walking alongside her tore at his heart. He raised the powerful telescope to his eye, driven to feel once again a surprising pang of jealousy that until now had receded into a dim, almost alien emotion. He studied the magnified image of her companion. It pained him that he was tall, handsome, and muscular. It pained him even more that he appeared to be chatting with her in a friendly and familiar fashion. What pained him most, though, was the smile on her face.

Le Clerc lowered his telescope and reminded himself why his treachery had been necessary. Maudlin sentiment would only cloud his judgment. Anger and jealousy were toxic emotions, and their poison would diminish his usual cunning and courage. He glanced down to the bottom of the hill where their Jolly Roger flag whipped in the tropical breeze. His team had planted it victoriously near the entrance of the cave that once hid Morgan's treasure. The skull and crossbones reminded him that he was a pirate and ought to act like one.

Le Clerc believed that love, power, and hunger were the deepest urges. Growing up, he had been deprived of love and power and knew only hunger. The wealth he had commandeered today would eliminate hunger and facilitate power, but it couldn't bring him love. Perhaps that was always the devil's bargain. Like with all brigands, his spiritual scale tipped toward plunder and away from intimacy.

Another sharp pang jolted his conscience more than his jealousy. His turbulent childhood had conditioned him to believe that good and bad were equal parts of nature, and that the choice between them was one of expedience. He often chose "bad" because it seemed as though the meek, the good, and the rule-followers were always downtrodden. He had vowed to never be a victim again.

Le Clerc rationalized that his chosen path was less destructive than most. He was a pirate, but even though he stole things, he left his victims otherwise alone. That was more than could be said for most bullies and political oppressors. And unlike the political oppressors of the world, he made no pretense that he was stealing from his victims for their own benefit and protection.

But his moral dilemma today was more immediate. Should he take his treasure and run, or set up an ambush in the valley to kill Olga and her newfound allies? He wasn't a coward, but he feared that if he extinguished the one flickering flame of love he had ever experienced, it would be the same as fully extinguishing his own darkened soul.

13

GOLD

John shook his head in disbelief. "You stole the map to Morgan's treasure from a pirate?" he asked Jed.

"Aye," Jed replied. "It's one of the few things I'm proud of." He was invited to sit at the campfire with the Council of Sages after they had interrogated Captain Garcia, who had revealed the bombshell news that François le Clerc was likely heading to the purported site of Morgan's treasure. They were anxious to learn what Jed really knew about it.

"You were one of bravest men I knew in Kansas," John said to Jed, although the sight of his broken condition blurred John's recollection. "You have an opportunity to be a hero again."

"There's a fine line between bravery and lunacy," Jed replied. "But I haven't learned exactly where it is. What brought you to Outcast Island, John? I thought you were laying low in Kansas to protect your family."

"I can't tell bravery from lunacy either. I finally realized that I couldn't protect my family by hiding from the wolf. I had to kill the wolf. So I became more active in the rebel underground. Kieran used that against me to make his bones with the Elites. Then I volunteered to come here, aided by his treachery. It's all part of my plan."

Jed rolled his eyes. "That's some plan you got there."

"It's coming together," John said with a wry smile. "I've found some great allies here. We've started a new society called Pathless Land. We captured the Rock to serve as our base of operations. We rescued you and many others. And now you're going to help us race against le Clerc to find a fortune in gold."

"Le Clerc's a terror," Jed cautioned. "After we stole Morgan's map, his pirates chased me and my partners across the island. They caught my cohorts and killed them. The only thing that saved me was being captured by the Proletariat instead. Not that being their prisoner was a picnic, as you can see from my somewhat disheveled appearance."

"What possessed you to steal the map?"

"Le Clerc pissed me off," Jed replied. "After I was dumped into the Bay of Death, I joined his pirates, partly for protection and partly because he boasted he was going to bring down the powerful on Outcast Island. It reminded me of our mission in Kansas. He's a persuasive man who mesmerizes like a swaying cobra. However, after roving with him for a while, it became clear that he was just another bandit pillaging others and enriching himself. When he confided in me about the map that someone named Cosimo had given him, I decided to steal it."

"How much do you remember of the map?"

"I know what you're thinking, John. I assure you I'm the same man I was in Kansas—harder to kill than a cockroach. I mentally rehashed every detail of the map a thousand times. It was the only thing that kept me sane while the Proletariat tortured me. The map says the treasure is buried in the Caves of Despair. I even figured out some of the riddles that hint at which cave it's hidden in."

John gestured toward Garcia, who had been sitting quietly in the shadows, hoping not to be noticed by Jed.

"I think you know this man," he said to Jed. "He claims to know where le Clerc is headed and how the Pirates might be vulnerable to attack."

Jed glared at Garcia as if his former tormentor was a rattlesnake. "I don't care what he knows. I say kill him right now."

"I share your anger, Jed," Olga said. "But the team convinced me that he can be useful, at least for a while. It's possible he knows some of the riddles about the exact location. And it's also likely that we're going to have to fight the Pirates."

Jed kept glaring at Garcia but said nothing.

"How long of a march is it to the Caves of Despair?" Mallory asked Maria.

"If we start tonight, we can reach them by morning the day after tomorrow," Maria replied.

"Mallory, you've inventoried the Rock's armory," John said. "Do we have enough firepower in case we encounter le Clerc's pirates?"

"Yes. Between the stash from Hammer's boat, the unused weapons that Olga's team hoarded, and what we captured today at the Rock, we can arm everyone. The Proletariat had an assortment of pistols, old AK-47 rifles, and a few ancient Kalashnikov light machine guns. They're all Russian made, but we'll figure out how to use them."

The Carpenter cleared his throat. "Farmer John?"

"Yes, my friend?"

"I support your vision of Pathless Land, but why this obsession with hunting down a treasure and perhaps killing to obtain it?"

The blunt question jolted John. He thought the need for money was obvious, but it was also true that the lust for gold had inspired tragedy throughout history.

"The love of money can lead to evil, but money itself is not evil," John replied, breaking an awkward silence. "Civilized society must be based on free trade. Efficient trade requires money, or else people would face the absurdity of bartering a house for loaves of bread. Gold is the most reliable form of money."

The Monk raised an eyebrow. "You're not tempted by material splendor?"

"I'm human, so of course I'm tempted," John replied. "But being human also means I can put things into rational perspective. My highest ideal is a society where everyone can freely pursue their own desires. That requires commerce and therefore money. The free pursuit of individual satisfaction is the real source of meaning, not chests full of gleaming metals and gems. I intend to earn my happiness just as everyone should. I'm not a pirate."

"But you and the Pirates are chasing after the same treasure," the Carpenter said.

"True. But if a man works hard to earn his rewards, is that the same thing as a man stealing rewards?"

"No," the Carpenter concluded. "One is just; the other is unjust. But you're not earning Morgan's treasure. You're intending to take it, Farmer John. Just like the pirate."

John sighed. "That's also true. But Morgan is long dead, and we have no way of finding his heirs. The treasure has been handed back to nature but will soon belong to the first person who is industrious enough to unearth it."

"Both you and le Clerc intend to do so," the Monk challenged. "How are you two different from each other?"

"I don't know the pirate, except by legend. But I assure you I'm not seeking Morgan's treasure for personal gain," John defended. "Judge me harshly if my words prove to be false. I'm seeking the treasure to seed our new society with money. Everyone in Pathless Land will get a cut. Trade on the island will never be effective using shells, shark's teeth, or opium as money."

"You will indeed be held to account," the Carpenter said. "All leaders should be. But why did you ask Mallory about the status of our weaponry? Do you intend to kill to obtain Morgan's treasure?"

"I intend to beat le Clerc to it. If he finds it first, we won't steal it from him. But I have no assurance that he'll accord us the same justice. His avarice may drive him to attack us."

Olga glared at John. "You're not going to kill le Clerc if there's an opportunity? His villainy has nothing to do with Morgan's gold and everything to do with his deadly betrayal of the Remnant!"

The two locked eyes. "Olga, your pain and anger are justified," John replied. "But I won't order our forces into combat against a powerful enemy just to punish past treachery against your tribe. We justified that when taking the Rock, but only because your innocent comrades were being held captive. A day will come when we can administer justice to le Clerc properly without risking the lives of hundreds of our people."

Olga turned her head and looked away. John could tell by her rigid posture that more emotional distance had come between them. He felt a gnawing pang from her chilly demeanor and sighed.

"Time's wasting!" Jed interjected. "If we're going to beat the pirates to the Caves of Despair, we must leave now. Le Clerc is relentless when he sets his mind to something."

John ordered everyone into action. Mallory rallied his troops. Maria picked the brains of Jed and Garcia to convert their knowledge of the treasure's location into a set of directions that she and her scouts could use to lead the expeditionary force. John met with the Carpenter and the Monk to plan the next few days of reconstruction at the Rock while the treasure hunters were away.

The expeditionary force set forth under a cloudless sky. Maria and her scouts fanned out to mark the path and to detect any threats. Mallory marched with his troops. Olga marched with a squad of archers she had selected for this mission. John trudged alongside Jed, using it as an opportunity to reconnect with his old friend from Kansas.

The two men chatted as the hours went by. Their iron-clad friendship warmed John's heart once again, but he felt an awful dread about Jed's physical condition. John had lost him once in Kansas to the predation of the Elites, and he feared losing him again, this time to the predators on Outcast Island.

Dawn broke on the second day of their march as they ascended a steep hill near the Caves of Despair. John and Jed had gradually lagged to the rear of their fellow marchers. Jed was struggling more and more with each step up the incline, and his limp was growing more pronounced.

"Are you going to make it?" John asked.

"I've been through worse," Jed grumbled. "Doc gave me some coca leaves to chew on. Cuts the pain. Keeps me awake. Takes my mind off stuff."

"What the hell did they do to you in the Rock?"

"They tried everything," Jed said with a faraway look in his eyes. "They fed me rancid bread and thin gruel to keep me alive, but just barely. They stretched my limbs on a rack. They lashed me with a whip woven with barbed wire. They broke one of my legs with an iron bar. They even prepared to hang me once, although they stopped at the last second."

"Dear God, what did you do to deserve all that?"

"The short answer is nothing," Jed replied. "Nobody deserves such barbaric punishment. But that doesn't deter people who believe others are mere tools for fulfilling their desires."

"What did they want from you?"

"They wanted to know where Morgan's treasure was. Le Clerc was so pissed that I stole the map that he sent a messenger to Vlad informing him I knew Morgan's secret," Jed explained. "The bastard knew what Vlad would do to me then. He was determined to extract the secret from me, and I was equally determined to take it to my grave. Hence some of the torture."

"Some? What was the rest for?"

"I'm not a good follower of orders," Jed admitted. "I've always thumbed my nose at those in power, as you well know."

"Yeah, that's what got you exiled to Outcast Island."

"Yup, and my disobedience at the Rock earned me some extra torture, much of it done in public. The thugs wanted the other proles to see what happens to nonconformers. I was kept in an open cage in the yard, like an animal in a zoo. I laughed at my torturers, which confused the proles and frustrated their leaders."

John shook his head. "You're a madman."

"It's a mad world. But I refused to submit. I hoped that the timid proles watching me would be inspired to revolt, but they didn't. It must take people a long time to realize that they're not being forced to conform for their own good but rather to sustain the privileged lives of their overlords."

"You thought laughing in the face of torture would inspire a revolt?"

"It would have worked if I had more time," Jed said. "But you cut my plan short by rescuing me."

Olga interrupted their conversation. She had quietly fallen into step beside them without their notice. "Pick up the pace!" she admonished. "We need to join Maria and Mallory at the front of our army. We're nearing the Caves. We might encounter le Clerc at any moment."

Her surreptitious approach reminded John of the remarkable stealth that the women of the Remnant were capable of.

"We're on speaking terms again?" John asked.

She avoided his eyes. "John, you were right. I let my personal animosity toward le Clerc cloud my judgment."

John stopped and faced her. She lifted her eyes to meet his. "Olga, I swear that when the time is right, I'll help you avenge le Clerc's treachery against the Remnant. I'll hunt down anyone who initiates aggression against innocent people I care about. It's the very reason I came to Outcast Island."

Jed, Olga, and John moved to the front of their army, which had stopped marching to wait for further direction, and joined Mallory and Maria. After a quick discussion, they decided to send Maria ahead to examine the situation at the purported cave where Morgan's treasure awaited discovery.

The wait for Maria's return was agonizing because every moment of delay gave a greater advantage to their adversary. After nearly an hour, Maria suddenly crashed through the ferns, heedless of stealth and her injured arm.

"I made it to the cave where Morgan's treasure was!"

"Was?" Olga asked with a sharp intake of breath.

"The Jolly Roger was planted outside the cave entrance," Maria said between pants. "The rock sealing it had been rolled away. The cave was empty."

"Damn it!" Jed swore. "I endured years of torture for this?"

"There's more," Maria said darkly. "I saw a lot of boot prints and hoof prints heading away from the cave. I presume they're from le Clerc's men fleeing with the loot. But I was surprised to see other prints made by lots of bare feet overlaid on theirs. We're apparently the third group of prospectors to arrive on the scene. Some other tribe is already trailing the pirates."

John looked skyward. "This is surreal!"

Maria nodded. "There's something even more surreal. A note was pinned to the Jolly Roger. It's addressed to Olga."

She handed it to Olga and cast her eyes to the ground.

14

VLAD

Vladimir Lenin Sokolov admired the imposing metal frame of the guillotine. It dazzled in the pinkish rays of the sun that was setting over the massive western wall of El Morro Castle, the old Spanish fortress that had guarded the entrance to la Habana harbor for centuries.

Vlad had commandeered the castle for use as his headquarters many years ago. The fort's iconic lighthouse was once the proud symbol of a dynamic city on a resplendent Caribbean Island. Now, a blood-stained guillotine looming in a courtyard was the castle's iconic symbol. The castle no longer protected people from marauders and brutes attacking from without. It protected marauders and brutes sheltering within.

Vlad's main military complex, which included El Morro Castle and the adjacent San Carlos de la Cabana Fortress, covered nearly twenty-five acres. It was a city within a city. During its long existence, it had served as a naval facility, a prison, and a bastion for the original communist leaders of Cuba, Che Guevara and Fidel Castro.

Waves thundered against the rocky peninsula upon which the mighty walls of the castle were built. Each concussive wave that pounded the shore felt to Vlad like a physical exclamation point celebrating his transcendent power as the leader of the Proletariat.

While standing on the balcony of his private residence inside the fortress, his favorite concubine, Benita, kept him company. She was a majestic blend of African, Spanish, and native Taino ancestry. Her lustrous black hair hung past her shoulders, and her dark, smoldering eyes contrasted perfectly with her impish girl-next-door smile. With a flawless brown complexion and an attractive figure, Vlad could hardly ask for more. But what he loved most was her sharp, incisive wit, which she delivered with a polyglot accent. It revealed a deep-rooted wisdom that both challenged and intoxicated him. Other women in his harem were more beautiful than Benita, but they were all diminished by plebian intellect and interests. Despite being the leader of the island's biggest faction, and despite his role as the curator of a collectivist society, he felt desperately alone, except when he was with her. He adored her and needed her.

Vlad often wondered why Benita reciprocated his affection. Even though he was a man of great power and relative wealth on a destitute island, his physical appearance ashamed him. First off, he was shorter than Benita. Next, he was overweight, partly because eating and drinking were among his favorite indulgences, and partly because he considered physical effort to be something people who were less equal should do on his behalf. His graying brown hair covered less than half of his pate, and his scraggly beard obscured a pasty face that rarely saw the tropical sun. Adding insult to injury, he suffered from periodic eruptions of strange rashes. And his crumpled army fatigues never retained their crispness, no matter how often they were starched. They had perpetual sweat stains.

He was an intelligent man, though, and a prolific student of human nature. Much of his study was channeled toward exploiting the weaknesses of both friends and foes. His manipulative skill and his heartless lack of compassion abetted his power.

Vlad's lust for power was generational. His great-grandfather was a lofty Soviet KGB officer who helped Castro and Guevara establish communism on the island. Vlad's grandfather and father followed in their forebears' footsteps, playing pivotal roles after the death of the

Castro brothers to continue the tradition of communism in Cuba. It was a wasted effort because the Cuban society collapsed on the watch of Vlad's father.

In the wake of the collapse, the Cubanos resorted to riding horses and then to eating them. Pets mysteriously disappeared. Still, Vlad remained true to his Marxist roots. He continued to preach the gospel of class warfare, although it was never clear which classes should battle which. In the anarchy of Outcast Island, everyone was at war with everyone else. But the one thing Vlad had learned from his autocratic Soviet ancestors was that one class always rises above the others, no matter what form a society takes. The ascendant class is always comprised of elitist leaders who are addicted to placing the burdens of effort and risk onto everyone else.

Vlad put his arm around Benita's narrow waist as he stared out over the courtyard from their palatial balcony. Sunset was the usual time for the daily executions. A tattered red flag with a hammer and sickle flapped in the ocean breeze. The sullen proles who were gathering in the courtyard ignored the flag. They also ignored Vlad and his concubine. And they especially ignored the screaming prisoner being dragged by the police toward the guillotine. But they were required to attend, so they did.

A policeman signaled to Vlad. The dictator raised his arm in an awkward salute to initiate the grim proceeding. The prisoner was manhandled to the platform of the killing machine. Guards held his arms and legs with iron grips and positioned his neck into the curved slot. The heavy metal blade, gleaming blood-red in the rays of the setting sun, was cranked upward. Then it was released. The victim's final scream was cut short by the brutal efficiency of the plummeting blade. The scream became a surreal gurgle that faded into stark silence. His head dropped into a basket with a thud, and the decapitated body twitched grotesquely.

Vlad smiled triumphantly and turned to Benita. She looked away from him and from the carnage in the courtyard below. Disappointed, he dropped his arm from her waist and retreated into his residence.

"Come," he instructed, holding open the door. She followed him but not because she wanted to.

Vlad snitched a muscovado sugar cookie from a gilded platter on a teakwood credenza, then poured himself a glass of rich golden rum. He nibbled on the cookie, reveling in the delicious thought that the proles festering in the courtyard below would never taste such a delight. Light strains of calypso music floated from hidden speakers in his receiving room. Two golden-skinned girls with flowers in their hair lounged on a leather couch, waiting indolently for his summons. A gentle breeze wafted from a large fan suspended from the vaulted ceiling.

He ignored the two temptresses and entered his study. Benita followed him without acknowledging the existence of the other women, slamming the study door behind her.

Vlad lit a cigar and offered one to Benita, but she waved her hand in disgust.

"What the hell's wrong with you?" he asked.

"You know I despise your executions," Benita snapped. "Especially of Black men."

"He was one of Spartacus's Maroons. We conscripted him into our military. Those rebels are dangerous and unpredictable. He was being taught a lesson."

"Why must Black men be taught such lessons?" Benita asked.

"I don't discriminate, if that's what you're insinuating. Proles of every race must be taught that they're subordinate to their masters. That's why I require everyone to watch the daily executions."

"What do they learn from watching?" Benita asked. "Other than to despise you and to despair of their awful lives? Such punishment merely forces anger underground."

"They learn that their lives aren't as miserable as that of the Maroon who just lost his head. And they learn that antisocial behavior won't be tolerated. Anarchy is the worst form of society. We must enforce complete order."

"Why was that particular Black man executed?" Benita questioned.

"He was caught illegally obtaining food," Vlad replied. "He's been sneaking outside the fort at night to gather shellfish without sharing them with the collective. Our people are hungry. We must all face hunger equally."

"You don't share your muscovado cookies."

"Ah, my delightful little treasure," Vlad said with a malignant leer. "You're so sexy when you're feisty. But surely you realize that some people are born to command and the rest are to merely obey. The world has always been divided up that way. Are you suggesting that all of history has been wrong?"

"Yes. Because truth is always the victim of mythology and power."

"But that merely proves my point," Vlad persisted patiently. "Here you are, my delicious but stubborn little pet, living a pampered life solely for my satisfaction, and yet you harbor such insubordinate thoughts. Imagine what the proles must be harboring in their barren souls and how little of a spark could trigger an insurrection. Such sparks can burn down a whole city. They can destroy an empire. They must be stamped out!"

"You're of Russian descent," Benita observed. "You must know then the absurdity of your pretense. It is no different than the Tsarina Catherine's Potemkin villages. You dictators will always lie about the glory of your elitism."

"It is neither lying nor pretense. We are simply making sure the shepherds continue to be shepherds and the sheep continue to be sheep. That's how order is maintained in the world."

"Perhaps in your truthless world," Benita sneered. "Doesn't it concern you that so many of your subjects consider you a black-hearted villain? The other girls in your harem whisper that not even God could forgive a man like you."

Vlad snickered. "Castro once said of the historical necessity of communism, 'Condemn me. It doesn't matter. History will absolve me.' My actions aren't driven by morality or truth, but by a future that can't be stopped. Good is that which moves the world toward communism, and bad is that which gets in the way." Vlad paused and eyed Benita. "What does concern me is the sharpness of your tongue today. Your words no longer seem playful."

"I'm still here with you."

"Because you choose to be, or because you must?"

"I always have a choice," Benita asserted with a strange fire in her eyes. "Everyone does. But one must weigh the costs of everything. Don't assume that I'm your kept woman because I approve of it. It's not in anyone's nature to be a slave forever."

Vlad laughed. "There's no such thing as human nature. As the great Russian scientists like Pavlov taught us, human nature is infinitely malleable. We will create the kinds of people necessary for socialism to succeed—people who prefer dependency, even at the price of sacrificing their freedom and personal ambitions."

Benita sneered. "Perhaps your great scientists weren't so great."

Vlad fell silent. An insistent knock on the door interrupted his struggle to summon a clever riposte to Benita's insult of Mother Russia. "Who is it?" he barked.

"Leon. I have urgent news."

Leon was Vlad's second-in-command. He was a career ideologue who chose to believe rather than to know, which made him the perfect lieutenant. He was tall, thin, white-haired, and perpetually officious and aspired to be Vlad's successor, which sometimes made his boss nervous.

"Come in!"

Leon entered and did a stiff salute.

"Report!" Vlad commanded.

"Sir, our courier to the Rock hasn't returned."

Vlad waved a dismissive hand. "Then send another."

"He was the third to disappear. Perhaps the rumors are true."

Vlad scowled. There were rumblings that the Rock had been captured by unknown assailants, but the notion seemed so unlikely that he ignored it. The Remnant had tried to take the Rock once before, but the betrayal of Olga Kozlowski by one of his double agents had turned her assault into a wondrous victory for the Proletariat. He swallowed hard. What if le Clerc had changed sides once again? Cosimo had sent instructions recently to let the pirates pass through Vlad's territory with assurances that le Clerc posed no threat. But whose side was Cosimo really on? Whose side was anyone really on? Even Benita seemed more combative than usual this evening.

Leon interrupted Vlad's dour musings. "Shall I send a division of the Red Army to the Rock, sir?"

Vlad shook his head. "Why? A division of the Red Army was *guarding* it! You and I will go with hand-picked men. I want to see the situation for myself. I trust no one now."

Leon was crestfallen.

"Except you," Vlad reassured. "I still trust you."

"Sir, it may not be safe for us to go. My informants say the Cubanos in la Habana are spreading rumors. Those stupid proles are irrational and superstitious, but they talk of a bold new band of men on the island. They say these men must have black magic and great voodoo if they conquered the Rock."

"How would such a force get to Outcast Island?" Vlad asked.

"Ships from around the world are always dumping fresh outcasts here. Perhaps a nastier bunch than usual arrived. The Cubano rumors suggest that this mysterious new force is allied with the Remnant."

"That's doubtful," Vlad replied. "Le Clerc told me long ago that Olga despises all men. If there's a new force on the island, I wish to meet their leader. A fresh rival invigorates me. We will either come to terms as allies, or I'll annihilate him."

"The rumors suggest the situation is very complicated, sir."

"How so?" Vlad asked.

"It's said that Olga and the mysterious men are hot on the trail of le Clerc, who is moving through our territory."

Leon noticed the unholy grin that was spreading across Vlad's face. "Sir, why does this news please you?"

"War pleases me. The fear of outside invaders makes the proles forget their fear of their own leaders. With le Clerc, the Remnant, and the mysterious new arrivals on the prowl, we don't even have to invent enemies to quiet our proles."

15

SPARTACUS

Spartacus scanned the valley from his perch on Skull Ridge. He studied François le Clerc's sinuous line of mules trudging along the slope opposite the Caves of Despair. The loaded mules indicated that the pirates had indeed found Morgan's legendary treasure. It explained why the Jolly Roger flag had been planted triumphantly near the entrance to an empty cave.

Spartacus was travelling with a contingent of Maroons, a faction of rebellious slave descendants whose forebears were imported long ago from Western Africa by Europeans to harvest sugarcane and tobacco on the great Cuban plantations. For centuries the colonial powers fought each other for the right to claim the slaves as their property.

The slave importation began in the sixteenth century and continued for three hundred years. At one point, Cuba had almost four hundred thousand human chattel. Slavery in Cuba was abolished by Spain in 1886, but the former slaves maintained their aversion to Europeans. Generations of Maroons continued to hide in their strongholds in the Cuban mountains.

The ranks of the Maroons recently swelled when a new epidemic of slavery infested Outcast Island after Cuban society collapsed.

During the chaos, various factions on the island scrambled to enslave marginalized people. Blacks in particular were hunted, captured, and sold to the highest bidders in flesh markets, just as their ancestors were hundreds of years ago. To avoid capture by brutish masters who no longer had civil authority to fear, many refugees fled to the mountains, joined the Maroons, and learned to hate everyone else.

Spartacus and his Maroons had tracked le Clerc westward after the pirates raided the main Maroon stronghold in the mountains near Sancti Spiritus. The Maroons not only wanted revenge against le Clerc, they were also intrigued by the possibility of getting their hands on Morgan's gold. Le Clerc, in his usual braggadocious manner, declared during his pillaging of Sancti Spiritus that he was going after the mythic treasure in the Caves of Despair next.

Spartacus now had le Clerc and Morgan's gold in sight, but the situation was complicated. While tracking the pirates, Maroon scouts discovered other threats in the vicinity of Skull Ridge. There were rumors from the locals that the Rock had been conquered by a powerful new military force. The locals believed that Vlad would soon send an army from la Habana to retake the Rock. The scouts also discovered that they themselves were being tracked by a tribe of female warriors called the Remnant. The women were accompanied by a group of well-armed men. Spartacus mused that everyone seemed to be chasing everyone else, which was perhaps the abridged version of human history.

A warm tropical rain fell as Spartacus reflected on how he had arrived at this inflection point in his life. He was a handsome forty-two-year-old Black man with long salt-and-pepper dreadlocks and a scruffy, untrimmed beard. His body and mind had been honed by a hardscrabble life and constant danger. His skin was leathered from sun and wind, and his bare feet were calloused from hiking countless miles through the mountains and jungles of Outcast Island. His six-foot, six-inch frame, his Samson-like physique, his penetrating gaze, his gregarious smile, and his indomitable will afforded him a commanding presence among the Maroons.

The fearless exploits of Spartacus were legendary. He had been shot by bullets, gashed by machetes, and pierced by an arrow. He wore his battle scars as badges of honor because he considered submission to any faction as intolerable as the submission of his ancestors to colonial masters. He had long ago learned that a slave was anyone who labored against their will to satisfy others, whether it was for a commune, a plantation owner, a gangster, or a charismatic leader.

The Maroons struggled for years to acquire their meager wealth. They weren't tyrants like Vlad who taxed others. They weren't sociopaths like the Jackals who trafficked in narcotics, women, and children. They weren't pirates like le Clerc who stole from living people. They were grave robbers who disinterred bodies to scavenge gold teeth, jewelry, or other valuables that were buried with the deceased. It was hard, gruesome work, but over the decades they had accumulated a small fortune.

Le Clerc had gotten wind of their small fortune from Cosimo, who persuaded him to steal it. So he raided the Maroons' compound in the mountains, stole their meager treasure, and killed dozens. This brutal affront convinced Spartacus that hiding in the mountains was no longer a viable strategy for the Maroons. They would never be able to run from their history or avoid their tormentors. The aggressors on the island—colonialists, Proletariats, pirates, and Jackals— had already stolen most of what the Maroons owned over the centuries. Spartacus was sure that what little else they owned was coveted too.

As the rain intensified, Spartacus reflected on the Maroons' difficult trek from their mountain stronghold. For many weeks, they plodded through the jungle, wondering if rogues lurked beyond each hill or in the depths of each forest. They dreaded the nights, fearing that treacherous forces were approaching in the dark. They had no shelter from the sun or the rain, but they pressed on because hatred for le Clerc roiled their blood.

Spartacus scowled as jagged bolts of lightning flashed across the darkening sky and the rain intensified. "Damn!" he mumbled to himself. It would be impossible to attack le Clerc's mule train in such foul weather. He fumed at this temporary setback imposed by the uncaring forces of nature. He decided to descend from his vantage point and instruct his men to hunker down until the storm blew over.

Before he could take a step, he heard a twig snap, and then a knife was at his throat. The soundless attacker had used the cover of thunder and rain to sneak up behind him. His heart sank to his toes, and he immediately regretted his decision to climb the hillside alone to spy on le Clerc's progress.

"Don't resist or we'll kill you!" instructed the knife-wielder in a firm but feminine voice. Several other women materialized like ghosts from the sodden jungle to surround Spartacus, armed with spears and knives.

"Who are you?" Spartacus demanded in a thunderous voice.

"My name is Olga," the voice behind him snarled. "We are the Remnant. We've been tracking your Maroons. You must be Spartacus."

"I am. And my fighters will slaughter you all if any harm comes to me."

"No, they won't," Olga said confidently. "The Warriors of Pathless Land have surrounded your men in the ravine below. Why are you following le Clerc?"

"To make him repay the fortune he stole from us in Sancti Spiritus," Spartacus replied, blinking the rain from his eyes. "And then we'll kill him."

"You'll have to wait your turn." Olga withdrew her knife from Spartacus's throat and stepped back. She gestured to her team, who prodded their captive down the muddy incline to where the Warriors of Pathless Land had corralled the other Maroons. At the bottom, John and Mallory were huddled near the captives.

Olga eyed the Maroons, who had been disarmed of their machetes, spears, and sugarcane knives. Their faces and bare torsos were adorned with war paint. Their bodies bore telltale signs of many battles, including gruesome scars, missing limbs, and a smattering of eye patches.

Olga approached John and Mallory with her imposing hostage in tow. "This is Spartacus, the leader of the Maroons."

They nodded. "I'm John, the leader of Pathless Land, and this is Mallory, my military commander. Your reputation precedes you."

Spartacus sneered. "I have not been treated honorably. A knife was put to my throat, and you're holding my men captive."

"An unfortunate but necessary precaution," John replied. "This area is teeming with danger. Le Clerc and his pirates are fleeing with Morgan's treasure, your Maroons are hunting them down, and Vlad is mustering an army to retake the Rock from us. All hell is going to break loose. We need to understand your intentions simply as a matter of self-preservation."

Spartacus glared at John with paralyzing fury. "Who the hell are you to hold us hostage? You assume that we've been conditioned for centuries by abusive overlords to meekly submit?"

John shook his head vigorously. "You couldn't be more wrong! Our new society is hungry for allies who've learned to *hate* submission. I suspect that your Maroons would fit in perfectly. We're just trying to sort out friend from foe right now."

"We're not looking to fit into anyone else's society," Spartacus snapped. "That always ends badly for us. We'll be foes if you don't immediately set us free. We don't have much left to call our own, but freedom will always be our prized possession."

"Then we're completely aligned," John replied. "Everyone must choose between living their life according to their own will or living according to the wills of others. In Pathless Land, we're committed to mutually protecting our sacred freedom to live as we please."

"We can do that without joining your society!" Spartacus said. "Your impending battles with the other factions are not our battles. Our fight is with le Clerc."

"Bigger conflicts are coming," John replied. "Everything is coming to a head. The day for making difficult decisions is upon us all."

"Are you suggesting that our only choice is to join Pathless Land?"

"I'm suggesting that the worst way to live is to forever wonder which faction is going to unleash the hunting dogs on you next. The world is full of human predators trying to enslave others for their own purposes. Hiding in the mountains is no solution. The tyrants, gangsters, and warlords will eventually find you. There will always be a le Clerc who wants to steal your gold, a Vlad who wants to collectivize you, or a colonialist who wants you to labor on his behalf. It's always been the great empires, the dominant races, the exalted religions, or the aristocratic classes against the common people. Which side do you want to be on?"

"None!" Spartacus replied. "We just want to be free, even though that desire seems to trigger much hate. Why should we join another society when every society in history has rejected us?"

"It's indeed absurd that some people are allowed to be free but not others," John replied. "Let's join forces to bury that notion forever! If a person isn't free to act, to produce, to trade, or to own property, then their existence is entirely at the mercy of others. That realization will underlie everything in our new society."

Spartacus looked down at his body. "Look at my scars! It's hard for me to believe that your vision is possible."

"Pathless Land refuses to kowtow to any masters!" John exclaimed.

Maria jabbed John's shoulder with her good arm to get his attention. "What is it?" he asked with a touch of annoyance.

"John, I just received two messages from my scouts."

"Bad news?"

Maria nodded. "A contingent of the Red Army just left El Morro, led by Vlad and Leon. They're heading toward the Rock. They must have finally figured out why three of their couriers between El Morro and the Rock have disappeared."

"That was expected," John replied somberly. "And the other bad news?"

"There's trouble at the Rock. Garcia has been lecturing our people. He's convinced some of them that everything in Pathless Land must be collectivized. Things are unraveling fast in our new society while its leaders are away."

John looked over at Olga and Mallory. "We must return to the Rock. Now!"

Olga's jaw dropped. "Damn it, John! We have le Clerc nearly in our grasp! Are you forgetting what you promised me?"

"I promised to administer justice to le Clerc when the time was right. This isn't the right time. Vlad has the Rock in his gunsights, and Garcia is working to undermine it from within."

Spartacus, who had been pondering Maria's grim news in the hopes of finding an opportunity, had a sudden inspiration after seeing the tension between Olga and John. "John, I have a proposal."

"I'm all ears," John replied.

"Let me and my Maroons go. We'll hunt down le Clerc, snatch Morgan's gold, and deliver justice to him."

"And then what?" John asked.

Spartacus smiled in a way that charmed friend and foe alike. "We'll decide if we're going to join with Pathless Land or not."

"We're to just let you go and take the treasure we were hunting for too?" Olga asked incredulously. Her efforts to detain the burly rebel now seemed a waste of time. She had a growing belief that John was coming unhinged and that their blood oath was a mistake.

Spartacus nodded and continued smiling. "I thought you folks were all about freedom. This is your chance to prove it."

"You're right," John replied. "My intent was to seed an alliance with you, not to violate your personal sovereignty. And you have every right to take Morgan's gold from le Clerc because his pirates pillaged your compound."

"I don't know if my Maroons will choose to join your new society or not," Spartacus said. "But your words weren't lost on me."

"And your courage isn't lost on me," John said. "I believe our futures lie together. I'll leave you with this paradox. The only way to unite all the races, creeds, and affiliations is to guarantee the rights and freedom of each person as a *person*, no matter their race, creed, or affiliation."

16

____

CARPENTER

John and his team hustled through the two-day march back to the Rock after the dire warnings from Maria. When they arrived, John immediately noticed the tension that had arisen during the excursion to find Morgan's treasure.

Some of the tension was due to the arrival of a shipload of outcasts who had been dumped onto a safer beach south of the Bay of Death. The castaways were men and women from Eastern Europe who had stumbled upon the Rock while exploring the jungle. In John's absence, the Carpenter and the Monk welcomed the refugees into Pathless Land out of sympathy for their plight. John couldn't quibble with the mercy shown by his lieutenants, but the addition of the strangers, with their own language and culture, destabilized their fledgling society.

The rest of the tension was from the mountain of work that needed to be done at the Rock. It was difficult to organize complete strangers to labor collaboratively in the jungle heat. The community had an eclectic mix of people. There were survivors from the Rock's prison, women from the Remnant, men from John and Mallory's two shiploads, the new Eastern European outcasts, and some stray Cubanos who had been granted refuge. Without the decisive leadership of John, Olga, and Mallory, and without Mallory's Rangers and the Remnant's warriors, efforts to organize the strangers at the Rock to do productive work had languished.

John immersed himself in the community to better understand the tension. He spent the next few days talking with people, getting to know their problems, and studying the dynamics that had derailed their fledgling society so easily.

His assessment was grim. Little progress had been made with repairs inside the Rock, and not enough food was being scavenged to feed their growing community. John blamed himself. Until now, he had relied upon the desperation of their situation and the adrenaline surge of their attack on the Rock to energize cooperation and work ethic. These motivations had waned, partly from exhaustion, partly from lack of leadership, partly from the arrival of more strangers, and partly from negative influences. He had not yet established a self-sustaining system for organizing and incentivizing work. That would take time, but he had not even begun.

The biggest negative influence was former *comandante* Garcia. He had abused his sheltered status as the Carpenter's apprentice by lecturing the newcomers about the traditional economic system on the island. Socialism was implemented in Cuba long ago with the help of the Soviets. Vlad maintained this collectivist tradition even after the island had collapsed into chaos. Garcia had never known another way to organize economic activity, so he decided to publicly share his experiences. He hated Vlad's authoritarianism and brutality but loved the concept of economic equity. He hadn't learned one of the great lessons of history yet: a society can have liberty, or it can have equality of outcomes. But it can never have both.

John had intended to teach new arrivals to Pathless Land the basic elements of his philosophy, but he had been caught up in emergent events. Now too few knew his philosophy, and too many were ensnared in Garcia's collectivist leanings. This contributed to the disarray in the fort and was exposing the community to the threat of starvation.

John resolved to get Pathless Land back on a rational course. He noted to himself that Garcia was very persuasive, and the lure of food without effort always tempted destitute people. Garcia had leveraged his divisive views into an informal leadership role among the recently arrived Cubanos and Eastern Europeans, which made John angry. Entrusting him to the Carpenter, who was distracted by his own efforts to repair the Rock, had been a mistake.

John summoned the Council of Sages to a campfire meeting so they could hold Garcia accountable for his disruptive efforts. The Carpenter, Olga, the Monk, and Maria sat across from Garcia. Mallory was away preparing for the Rock's defense against the expected counterattack by Vlad's Red Army.

"You've been publicly advocating a social organization that's contrary to the ideal of liberty and to the justice of self-responsibility," John addressed Garcia. "Now there's tension in the Rock and a growing unwillingness to work. Explain yourself."

Garcia shrugged his shoulders. "People are hungry, and more are arriving each day. We must share our scarce resources, regardless of who does what. That's what decent people do."

"Resources aren't scarce," John observed. "The jungle is full of potential food. What's becoming scarce are people willing to go get the food. When things are shared regardless of effort, there's no incentive to do anything. People naturally prefer better rather than worse, and 'better' in a collectivist society means working as little as possible while continuing to consume."

"But we're all in this together!" Garcia protested. "If we let the strong have their way, they'll hoard the food for themselves. They'll eat while the others go hungry."

"You're a fool!" John exclaimed. "Common sense says to let those who are good at hunting and gathering do so. Then they can freely trade their abundance with others who are good at different tasks, such as sewing clothes, building shelter, shaping iron, and making weapons. That motivates each person to work hard and to hone their unique talents. Each is better off that way, and so is the entire society."

"But people working for their own benefit is selfish," Garcia said. "It's immoral!"

"Selfish?" John shouted. "Why is it selfish for workers to keep or trade what they produce, but it isn't selfish for idlers to demand that things be given to them without effort? 'To each according to his need' is the ultimate expression of greed because it ignores the effort required to create things in the first place, as if they come from some mysterious source. A society that makes it preferable to take rather than to produce is doomed. To hell with that kind of morality!"

The Carpenter suddenly arose and strode toward Garcia. On the way he said, "Farmer John, let me handle this. You're too angry, and I'm failing as Garcia's mentor. Since he's made this a moral debate, I want to redeem myself by resolving his confusion. I'll focus on timeless and universal concerns."

"He's all yours," John said. "I should have heeded Olga's advice to kill him."

The Carpenter turned to Garcia. In the glow of the campfire, and with the darkness of the night as a backdrop, his robe seemed whiter than white, and his smile radiated an inner peace that was in stark contrast to John's anger and Garcia's rising fear.

"You've ignored my mentoring, *mi amigo*. Perhaps you can't bear to hear my words. Are you open to my wisdom, or are you going to cling to incoherent dogma that you've been conditioned to believe your whole life?"

Garcia knew that in light of John's urge to kill him, his future would be determined by the sincerity of his answers to the Carpenter. "My heart and mind are open to you," he replied softly.

"Then why are you preaching envy of what other people produce? Envy is one of the seven deadly sins, yet you glorify it. People should count their own blessings, not the blessings of others! Staking a claim to what others have earned will not help your moral accounting. Envy rots to the bone and leads only to conflict."

"But shouldn't people be charitable?" Garcia asked.

"*Sí.* But the virtue of charity evaporates when it's forced. Charity is a voluntary act inspired by each person's own compassion. But to be generous, a person must first have earned something to be generous with. Taking from some to give to others may be inspired by sympathy, but it injures those from whom something was taken. Moral charlatans take, then give. Charitable people earn, then give. That was the lesson of the Good Samaritan."

"Who?"

"*Mio Dios!* What were you Cubanos taught? The Good Samaritan acted out of compassion with his own resources to aid a foreign traveler who was assaulted. He bound the man's wounds and soothed him with his own oil and wine. He carried him on his own animal to an inn where he paid the keeper to care for him. The Samaritan didn't leave the fate of the traveler to the bureaucrats of the realm. He didn't force other travelers to help him. He took the burden upon his own shoulders. He taught us that the real virtue of helping others requires making the effort yourself, not taking from some to give to others as a mere pretense of virtue. The Samaritan's personal responsibility and voluntarism were just as important to the essence of the parable as was his charity. Do you know why?"

Garcia stared at him blankly. "No. I lived in a society where responsibility was collectivized and nothing was voluntary."

"I'll explain. You're always being judged, but only for what you personally do."

"Judged by whom?" Garcia asked with a hint of a sneer. "You?"

"Everyone. All judgment is karmic."

Garcia shook his head. "I don't understand."

"You're judged in three ways. First, you judge yourself because you're the sum of all your decisions. Every version of you in the future will judge every choice you've made in the past. Second, your choices affect your personal relationships. Your companions care how your actions affect them. And you care that they care, or else there would be no relationship. Your personal relationships are continual exercises in mutual scrutiny and judgment. Third, every stranger you trade with judges you because everyone is both a producer and a consumer. You are rewarded or shunned based on how much value you contribute to society as you seek value in return."

"What does that have to do with our discussion?" Garcia asked.

"It explains why collectivism is morally bankrupt," the Carpenter replied. "You can only demonstrate personal value and achieve moral redemption through your own acts. Your success in life, and your value to society, depend on accepting the burden of individual responsibility and its consequences."

"That sounds rather daunting . . ."

"Because life itself is daunting! Morality is neither kind nor merciful. The universe keeps perpetual score of either your moral courage or your moral cowardice. It's unforgiving in its accounting and its justice. As Emerson pointed out, cause and effect are the chancellors of God."

Garcia dropped his head into his hands. "Is there any virtue at all in collective action?"

"Only if those involved are acting voluntarily. The Ten Commandments are individual mandates, not collective ones. Only individuals can be saved or damned. Free will is a glorious gift, but it requires every individual to be self-responsible. To wish away the consequences of your choices is to wish away free will. To wish away free will is to wish for slavery. To wish for slavery is to wish away the sacredness of each individual life. That's always the causal chain in forced collectivism. It tears a person spiritually in two, tempting their heart with empathy and altruism, but its coercive methods blacken their soul."

"That's easy for you to believe," Garcia said. "But you've never known the hunger and deprivation that we've known in Cuba."

The Carpenter laughed. "Cuba didn't know hunger until it adopted totalitarianism under Batista and then communism under Castro. My family was brutally poor. I was born in a cave. My parents fled our hometown to save me from government agents. My hands are calloused from working with stone and wood all my life. I've wandered far and wide with merely the shirt on my back and the tools of my trade. I've been hunted and tormented by those in power. They consider me a dangerous rebel."

The approach of Mallory interrupted the discussion. He addressed John, panting. "Vlad's forces are positioning in the jungle around the Rock. And they have cannons."

John became rigid. "When do you expect them to attack?"

"At sunrise is my guess."

"Are we prepared?"

Mallory nodded. "It's much easier to defend a fort than to attack one. We have some surprises in store for them. But we must all move to battle stations now, just in case."

"Thanks," John replied. "Carpenter, what should we do with Garcia?"

The Carpenter glanced at Garcia, who stared back with wide-eyed trepidation. "Everyone was born with free will, Farmer John. So everyone must choose their own path. If Garcia wishes to continue down Vlad's immoral path, he should rejoin him and receive his karmic fate there."

"You're more merciful than I," John replied. He turned his attention to Garcia. "If you wish to leave, I'll escort you to the Rock's gate and shove you toward the hell you came from. If you want to remain here, you must heed the words of the Carpenter and embrace the vision of Pathless Land. A society can either be based on voluntarism or coercion. It's time for you to choose. Fair warning: I'll kill you if you stay here and attempt to subvert our society again."

17

ASSAULT

Vlad was knocked off his feet by the explosion. He lay on the
ground in shock as a scorching tsunami of heat washed over
him, his ears ringing.

After his senses recovered, he raised his head to assess his injuries.
He saw small blotches of blood spreading on his uniform, yet the
shrapnel wounds didn't seem serious. He tested his arms and legs.
They responded, though the pain was intense.

Someone hefted him to his feet, causing him to groan in agony.

"Are you okay?" Leon asked with trepidation.

The two men were near the Rock at the head of their Red Army
contingent. Their oxen had been towing heavy cannons through the
jungle into a clearing. A cannon wheel had triggered a land mine
planted by Mallory's team. The deadly device was crafted by Newton
and Hammer from gunpowder and spare parts they had scavenged
from the fort.

"I'm fine," Vlad snarled. Leon's impertinent question implied it
was possible for him to be harmed. "What happened?"

"A land mine. We lost a cannon. And a couple of men," Leon
added as an afterthought.

"Perhaps we should move to the rear of the troops," Vlad said.

"We're supposed to be leading them. But there are probably more mines out here. I suggest standing still until other soldiers march ahead of us," Leon noted.

There was a violent thrashing in the jungle to their left, accompanied by harrowing screams. Two soldiers had plummeted into a camouflaged pit, impaled by jagged wooden stakes.

"I'm not moving from this spot," Vlad said as the death throes of the impaled soldiers echoed hauntingly. "Order the men to advance on the fort!"

Leon signaled his lieutenants to attack. Meanwhile, Vlad fumed. What devil dogs had conquered his fort? Were the local voodoo-obsessed Cubanos right that the mysterious conquerors possessed powerful juju? Who was the audacious leader challenging the historical inevitability of the Proletariat? He vowed to kill the vile heretic. Only the strong survived on Outcast Island, and Vlad was going to prove to every wretched soul that he was the baddest animal in the jungle—as long as he didn't have to move from his spot.

Leon suddenly rammed his shoulder into Vlad, toppling him into a patch of ferns. A barrage of arrows swished through the air above them. Vlad crawled out of the ferns and arose on unsteady legs, then pumped his fist at the Rock.

"I'll punish you bastards for your treason!"

Leon extricated himself from the ferns and brushed off his impeccable uniform. He yanked Vlad's arm down and maneuvered him out of the fort's line of sight.

"Why did you knock me down?" Vlad barked. "I was just about to duck from those arrows. Order our cannons into firing position!"

Leon sighed and waved another signal to his lieutenants. Oxen grunted and crashed through foliage as they tugged the heavy weapons into position. Leon had a rare flash of doubt while overseeing this activity.

"Sir, has it occurred to you that the result of war is usually a lot of dead proles? Violence always begets violence. This may come back to haunt us."

Vlad shot a questioning look at his second-in-command. "The

proles exist merely to produce for their masters and to fight their wars. That truth is as old as civilization itself."

Leon clicked his boot heels together and saluted. "The cannons are in position and ready to support your vision, sir."

"Order them to fire."

Leon sighed again but gave the signal. Orange flames erupted from the cannons, followed by prodigious billows of smoke. A cacophony of exploding ordnance rent the humid jungle air. Vlad spun toward the Rock to view the devastation wrought by his fusillade and smiled vaingloriously. Cannonballs had smashed into the façade of the Rock, blasting away large chunks of stone and mortar.

Vlad's smile quickly morphed into a grimace of fear. He didn't notice the enemy cannons positioned on the parapet of the fort until he saw them belch great bursts of flame and smoke. A second later, he heard the rolling thunder of the defenders' return volley.

The answering fusillade tore through their position at the edge of the jungle. Explosions erupted all around them. Men screamed in agony, and frightened oxen tore against their restraints. Three precious cannons were obliterated. Miraculously, Vlad and Leon were unharmed. They dashed deeper into the dense jungle, oblivious to the risk of land mines.

Another volley of shells was launched from the fort, wreaking more havoc on Vlad's forces. He sensed the terror rising in his unstable troops, fearing that at any moment they would drop their weapons and flee. They were better suited for bullying defenseless proles in the safe confines of El Morro than fighting trained soldiers hunkered down in a hostile fort.

The violent retaliation by the rebels reminded Vlad of a lesson from his father, who told him it was imperative for a domineering state to disarm its subjects. The state must not only be stronger than a few rogue criminals, it must be stronger than *everyone*. To be a fate that no one can escape, there must be no way for the proles to fight back.

"Look!" Leon exclaimed, pointing at a banner fluttering above the rim of the fort. "They've hoisted a flag!"

Vlad squinted into the distance. There was indeed a flag flapping in the tropical breeze above the fort. It was a crude banner, but it filled his soul with dread. It wasn't the brash Jolly Roger of the pirates, nor was it the ominous sickle and hammer of the Proletariat. This flag was covered with brilliant stars of random sizes and colors, overlaid on a faint background of blue, red, and purple stripes. Such a flag wasn't hoisted by mere troublemakers. It was hoisted by people establishing a new society. Vlad had no idea what kind of society it was, but he knew that they had stolen his fort and were now firing cannons at him. His world was being turned upside down.

~

Benita reined her stallion when she saw Spartacus emerge from the jungle at their appointed meeting spot. She dismounted expertly and plunged into his waiting arms.

After an intimate kiss, Spartacus put his massive hands on her delicate brown shoulders.

"Does he know you're away?"

"No," she replied. "He and Leon are off fighting another battle. I'm sure more innocent people are dying somewhere. I heard him say that the Rock had been captured by demons."

"They're not demons," Spartacus said. "I've met them. I'm glad our Cubano messenger got through to you. I need your advice."

"I love giving advice," Benita said. "But I hate when you ignore it."

Spartacus flashed his legendary smile. "You're the only person I fully trust. But it's a complicated world. I can't always do what you suggest."

"I've never been wrong."

"Then why are you still with Vlad? Our people need you." Spartacus paused. "I need you."

Benita's dark eyes met his. "I'm serving you and our people by being with that disgusting man. I'm repulsed by what he does to me. But the information that he spills is priceless. I wear my physical humiliation as a badge of honor. Someday, you and I will revel together in our triumph." She changed the subject. "What advice do you need?"

"Whether to kill a man or not."

"You usually resolve that question yourself. He must be a very unusual man."

Spartacus nodded. "François le Clerc."

Benita flinched, then fell silent for a moment. "Why kill him? He can be useful to us."

Spartacus's posture stiffened, and his mood darkened. "Maybe he's been somehow useful to you in the games that you must play, but not to me. Le Clerc raided Sancti Spiritus. He stole from us and killed some of our people. Then he found Morgan's gold in the Caves of Despair. Our Maroons are tracking him. We intend to kill him and take Morgan's treasure."

Spartacus watched uneasily as a mélange of emotions flashed in Benita's dark, mysterious eyes.

"I'm sorry for the terrible things he's done to our people," Benita said finally. "But you can't kill him."

Spartacus couldn't fathom her motives. He felt a crack in his once-immutable trust in her. "You must explain."

"We have Vlad isolated. He has enemies on all sides now. His own proles hate him. The demons stole the Rock from him. Pablo Guzman and his Jackals are rumored to be venturing back into his territory. And Vlad trembles when he speaks of an invisible force in the world called the Syndicate. Le Clerc despises Vlad, too, although the buffoon is oblivious to that. This isn't the time for Vlad's enemies to fight each other. We have a common goal. We can finally rid the island of his oppressive regime!"

"But surely we don't need le Clerc in an alliance," Spartacus replied, his deep voice laden with skepticism. "Whose side is he on today? Whose side will he be on tomorrow? I know the answer. He is always on his own side. And he caused the Maroons great harm!"

"He has friends in the highest places," Benita persisted. "I'm certain that le Clerc is a double agent and that the Syndicate is paying him handsomely. Angering the Syndicate is a dangerous strategy. It might be a tragic mistake to kill le Clerc now."

Spartacus fumed, knowing that le Clerc was so near physically, yet so far away strategically—at least according to his beloved. "So do I just bide my time? I'm not a patient man . . ."

"I'm part Taino. Time means nothing to an Indian."

"You're also part African," Spartacus said a little louder than he intended. "Have you forgotten the rapes, the enslavement, and the slaughters of our people? It's time for revenge!"

"I've forgotten nothing, and I'm committed to fixing everything!" Benita snapped. "I'm also part Spanish. I'm stuck in the middle of everything by heritage and by strategy."

Spartacus felt the moorings of their relationship loosening. "In the middle of what? You told me your role has always been to fool Vlad into thinking you're his trusted concubine. Is there more?"

Benita's dark eyes bored into his. She held her head high and said nothing.

"Who gave you that beautiful Arabian horse?" Spartacus demanded.

Benita looked off into the distance.

"Why don't you answer me?"

"People dread two things," she replied softly. "Death and truth. And perhaps truth is the most fearsome."

"I fear nothing," Spartacus huffed. "Tell me the truth."

"Truth may not inspire fear in you, but surely it will inspire hate. It has that effect on people. The last thing I want is for you to hate me. Everything I do is for you, the Maroons, and Cuba."

Benita spun away from him and mounted her horse like she was born to ride. She spurred it into a gallop toward la Habana, her black hair whipping in the tropical breeze.

Spartacus clenched his fists in silent rage as he watched her depart on the splendid Arabian, wondering if le Clerc's treachery against him involved more than just the attack on Sancti Spiritus.

John, Mallory, and Olga stared out from the battlements of the Rock, stunned by what they were seeing. After the fourth volley from the fort's cannons, Vlad's forces retreated in panic. Many had dropped their weapons to lighten their loads and speed their flight. They abandoned their cannons and their oxen. They left their wounded to die terrified and alone.

"What do you make of this?" John asked Mallory.

"I'm not surprised. Bullies fear opponents who fight back. And soldiers led by someone pursuing a degenerate cause rarely fight with courage."

"I didn't think it would be this easy," Olga said.

"It'll be much harder when the day comes to attack la Habana," Mallory replied. "Then the Proletariat soldiers will be fighting to save their lives, their families, and their homes. Desperation can turn dispirited fighters into heroes. That's how the Soviets held off Hitler's Wehrmacht at Stalingrad."

"True," Olga replied. "But le Clerc's note implied today's battle would be more difficult."

Mallory looked at her in surprise. "The note that Maria found at the Caves of Despair? What did it say?"

"That Vlad is to be feared, not because of his own competence, but because of the hidden forces who are now supporting his conquest of the island," Olga explained. "He warned that no one will be able to stand against them."

Mallory threw his hands up. "So even though we humiliated Vlad today, more storm clouds are gathering on the horizon? Why didn't you warn us earlier?"

Olga looked away as a hint of shame tarnished her perfect Slavic face. "I never know whether to believe le Clerc or not. And the rest of the note was very personal."

John gripped the edge of the parapet harder as he listened to Olga's words. Confused questions tumbled through his head. Who really were their enemies on this island? Who was behind this hidden force that kept coming up in conversations? More to the point of Olga's note, was le Clerc an avenging angel or a conniving devil? And was she still secretly in love with him? He felt a cloying twinge of jealousy, followed by a sharp pang of guilt.

A similar jumble swirled in Vlad's head as he and Leon trudged back to la Habana behind their surviving proles. Were the reports from his spies true that Benita often left El Morro on horseback when he was away? Where would she get such a horse? Why did his soldiers flee today's battle so readily? Why did Cosimo really instruct him to let le Clerc run free through his territory?

Vlad began to wonder if he was living in a purely imagined world spawned by his own megalomania.

The chief collectivist felt very alone.

18

COSIMO

Cosimo and Six met once again in a secure room in an underground complex in the hills outside of Rome. It was the second time in the past month that Cosimo had been summoned to his boss's private bunker, and he hoped it would be the last. He fussed nervously with his well-coiffed, pomade-slicked hair. The only sound in the subterranean stillness was the hum of the ventilation system.

Six remained silent as both men stared at a luminous but blank television screen on the wall. The dim grey pixels were the only light in the room. Six's gaunt figure remained hidden in the shadows, as was his custom. Cosimo fiddled with the ring on his right hand, drawing comfort from the tactile sensuality of its adornment, a snake encircling the globe. He wondered what unpleasant images Six intended to display. He waited for his boss to speak first because that was the protocol.

The television screen flashed to life, showing an aerial view of a jungle battlefield. Cosimo recognized the uniforms of the Proletariat soldiers who were sprawled in their death poses. He also recognized the Rock. *Shit*, he swore to himself.

"These are images from drones flown by the World Order ships surrounding Outcast Island," Six pronounced in his heavy Slavic accent. "The Syndicate has access to their surveillance data. It's useful for monitoring your performance. Hence today's meeting."

Cosimo swallowed hard.

"In our last meeting, you agreed to help Vlad gain control of the island," Six resumed. "I authorized you to use them as our proxies to kill any renegade forces posing a threat to the Syndicate. And yet on the screen, I see dead Proletariat soldiers and no dead rebels. Am I mistaken?"

Cosimo knew it would be unwise to say yes. Besides, the video evidence was clear.

"A minor setback," Cosimo conceded. "But I've lured other factions into the area to destabilize the rebels, despite their capture of the Rock. The Proletariat, the pirates, and the Maroons are all in the vicinity of Skull Ridge spoiling for a fight. Greed and enmity will lead to war. The upstarts at the Rock will get drawn into the conflict."

Cosimo heard a faint click. Another image flashed on the screen showing an unusual flag flying above the Rock's battlements.

"The rebels have their own flag," Six said darkly. "The Syndicate establishes and destroys societies. Are you relinquishing our role to some filthy rabble?"

"Your Eminence, I'm committed to eliminating all opposition to the Syndicate."

Another faint click. Another fresh image. It was a close-up of two men and a woman standing on the battlements of the Rock.

"Then why are these people still alive? One is a former US Army Ranger, judging by his sullied uniform. That might explain their conquest of the Rock. Another is Olga Kozlowski, a descendent of a notorious Polish rebel who annoyed the Syndicate long ago. She's the troublemaking leader of the Remnant. The tall man with the salt-and-pepper beard is the leader of the new rebel faction." Another click triggered a grainy close-up of John's face. "Get familiar with him. I predict he'll be a thorn in your side."

"He'll never warrant a mention in a history book," Cosimo huffed.

"I applaud your bravado," Six said from his opaque shadow. "But examine the next image."

A new picture splashed onto the screen. John, Olga, and Mallory were standing around the imposing figure of Spartacus on a hillside in a rain-soaked jungle.

"That's Spartacus, the leader of the Maroons," Six said. "He's conversing with the three rebels from the Rock. An alliance between those four would be dangerous to us. It would include two historically abused factions: the Black Maroons and the female Remnant. They would naturally want retribution against their perceived oppressors."

"Their alliance would still be no match for the Proletariat," Cosimo replied. "If necessary, I'll enlist military support from the World Order."

"Here's another image," Six said.

The screen flashed an aerial view of the Rock.

"It's a fort," Cosimo said dismissively. "I'll help Vlad take it back."

"I'll bring some ominous points to your attention," Six said. "The gallows and the guillotine that formerly stood in the courtyard have been dismantled. This implies their new society has a much different culture than the Proletariat. They're building a windmill near the old generator, which means they intend to produce electricity from the tropical breezes atop Skull Ridge. They've already built a crude smith, which means they can fabricate weaponry."

Cosimo's bravado waned. "How many more pictures do you have?"

"That's the last, but only because the rebels shot down the drone, which means they have skilled sharpshooters. But that's not the most ominous news."

Cosimo fidgeted with his ring. "What is?"

"Before the drone was destroyed, it picked up radio signals coming from inside the Rock. The rebels must have some technical wizards who were able to scavenge parts to make a functioning transmitter."

Cosimo frowned. "Hmm. The only thing worse for the Syndicate than proles armed with weapons is proles armed with information. The World Order's strategy of exiling rebellious engineers and technicians to Outcast Island may haunt us."

Cosimo saw Six's silhouette nod in the shadows. "You've been authorized to exterminate the misfit geniuses on Outcast Island," his boss reminded him.

"Why don't you just order the World Order ships to bombard the whole island and be done with it?" Cosimo asked.

Six snorted. "You have much to learn in your apprenticeship as a Centurion. Our mission isn't to kill everyone, only the troublemakers. We need bodies to operate our supply chains. What good is our wealth if there's nothing to buy? On Outcast Island in particular, we need the Proletariat alive and intact to control the island. Without a strong dictatorial presence, chaos will reign, especially if we destabilize everything with indiscriminate bombing. If chaos reigns, rebels will take control. When rebels take control, the Syndicate is threatened. America in 1776 is a perfect example."

"Your Eminence, the drone images are concerning. But I assure you I have the situation well in hand."

"I don't share your optimism! You're clever and talented, but you foolishly think of Outcast Island as a barbaric hellhole incapable of threatening us. In reality, it's a breeding ground for revolutionaries, especially if there are no autocrats strong enough to quell their fervor. You think the factions on the island will fight each other to the death. I think some are forming an alliance that will eventually destroy the Proletariat. If that happens, it will not bode well for your apprenticeship."

"Your Eminence, Vlad will vanquish the rebels. There may be an awkward period of chaos and confusion, but it will be contained entirely on the island. The World Order's naval quarantine will prevent the mayhem from spilling over to the rest of the world."

"You're naïve," Six grumbled. "I have more information than you, as always. Don't expect the naval quarantine to go on forever. The countries of the World Order are nearly bankrupt because of the Darkness we instigated, along with the spate of civil wars around the globe. The Syndicate has become richer at the expense of everyone else, but the cost of our success will be a period of worldwide turbulence. We must navigate it wisely."

"Cuba is a small island," Cosimo replied. "Surely there are bigger fish to fry."

"The bite of the smallest snake can be deadly if its venom is potent enough," Six said. "Cuba is almost as big as Florida. If the rebels establish a viable society there, they could export their subversive ideas to a broader alliance throughout the Caribbean. Such an alliance would have enough resources to threaten the US mainland, especially since the American Elites are immersed in a civil war against the Caliphate, the Jackals, and their own rebels. The Straits of Florida are only ninety miles wide."

Cosimo laughed. "That's absurd! An invasion of America will never happen!"

Six slammed his fist onto a table in the shadows. "We can't allow it to happen! If a rebellion succeeds in one society, the blueprint for it will spread like wildfire everywhere! The mythos we need to maintain is simple: nations are more important than individuals, and the Syndicate is more important than nations."

Cosimo realized it was time to humbly acquiesce to the greater wisdom of his mentor. "Your Eminence, what advice do you have for me?"

Six's anger subsided. "You must help Vlad build a strong enough alliance to crush the budding rebel alliance. I have no faith that he'll succeed on his own. Consider coercing the narco-terrorist Jackals to join with him. Pablo Guzman is no fool. He knows that an alliance between the Maroons, the Remnant, and the rebels would threaten his livelihood. His modus operandi includes violence and pillaging, just like Vlad's but without a powerful state and its altruistic charades. His gang members have no moral restraints on their brutality. And they've already cowed much of the population into submission with their mafia-like tactics."

"What about le Clerc and his pirates?" Cosimo asked. "He's also fond of violence and pillaging. And he's already made a connection or two inside Vlad's inner circle."

Six scoffed. "You believe you have le Clerc in your pocket, but my intuition tells me that he's irredeemably self-interested. However, the pirates may be useful in the short term."

"Yes," Cosimo agreed. "Everyone hates le Clerc. Hatred is something I can leverage. And he loves gold, the universal elixir for men with unbounded egos. That gives me an even more powerful lever."

Six fell silent in his shadow.

Cosimo gulped, realizing that he had just insulted his boss, so he changed the subject. "Your Eminence, what else should I do in addition to reinforcing Vlad's alliance?"

Six thought for a moment, then growled in a low, foreboding voice, "Explore your darkest brutalities! If bodies need to hang from gibbets everywhere, so be it. If entire villages need to be burned to the ground, so be it. Mass burials influence people more than logic does. The body counts in the Soviet Union and Maoist China were the greatest propaganda weapons of the tyrants there. The proles need to understand that the distance from today to a gulag is much shorter than they think."

Cosimo heard the scraping of Six's chair as his boss rose to leave, leaving him alone to ponder the full implication of the reference to gulags.

19

JACKALS

John leaned against his shovel under the scorching sun, physically exhausted from digging graves to bury the dead soldiers abandoned by Vlad. He was also emotionally exhausted from the visceral horror of death. Olga had suggested that they leave the dead bodies for the scavengers to feed on to save precious time and effort, but John felt that if he didn't honor the dead proles in this feeble way, their lives would have meant nothing. To him, a life with no meaning was the gravest sacrilege.

He glanced at the Monk, who had followed John's cue to rest from shoveling. "I'm learning something with each body we bury," John said. "People are born neither good nor bad, but their ideologies can turn them one way or the other. Sometimes to their death."

The Monk studied the carnage around them. "There's dark cruelty everywhere," he agreed. "A wise man once said that good people know about good and evil, but bad people know about neither."

John wiped his brow of sweat. "Jed says that rogues are roaming the countryside looking for people to rob or to conscript into their gangs. He thinks it's dangerous for us to be outside the fort. But we have no choice. Today, we must bury the dead and collect their weapons. We have to round up the oxen and cannons left behind by Vlad's army. And since we keep taking on new arrivals, we must begin growing food and constructing houses outside the Rock. The women of the Remnant and from the recent shiploads are warming to our men, and families will come from that someday. There are trees to cut, stumps to clear, and fields to till. I'm worried about how to protect everyone as we do that."

The Monk nodded. "A black cloud of entropy hangs over us. It will never go away. But we can choose where to focus our minds. That's what gives us agency. We must treasure what we have rather than worry about everything else. That's the only path to happiness."

John pondered the Monk's allegorical black cloud and looked around at the other men who were digging graves and clearing the jungle. They were as tired and filthy as he was. Their hair was long, unkempt, and sun-bleached, and their skin was blistered and peeling from sunburn. They were getting thinner too—some from malnutrition, some from dysentery, most from endless hard work. John itched from the lice in his hair, and a strange fungus had infested his armpits and crotch. Jungle rot, perhaps.

His worst torture, though, was his haunting separation from Mary. Life had been difficult in Kansas, but she had always been by his side to heal his wounds and mend his spirit. Despite the hardships on their farm, she was a relentless fount of hope and courage. Now she was thousands of miles away, and he would never see her again. Mary might even be dead, stricken by her chronic pneumonia or murdered by rogues.

Last night, John felt so despondent that he wrote a letter to her. He knew it was futile because it would never get delivered. The effort was born of gut-wrenching loneliness and the need for catharsis. He had no one on the island with whom to share his most intimate thoughts. The Monk and the Carpenter were good sounding boards, but Mary had always been his best friend. He missed her desperately.

Dark thoughts continued to haunt John. He had sworn an unwavering oath to pursue his vision of Pathless Land, but last night he nearly fled the Rock in a fit of madness. An absurd notion came to him, and he wondered if he could somehow repair Hammer's boat and sail across the Straits of Florida to the mainland. He over-came the madness because he knew that Mary would never forgive him if he abandoned the mission they were both committed to. Then he wept like a child in the anonymity of the night.

When he finally fell asleep, he dreamt that he was reunited with Mary and James at their ranch in Kansas. The Darkness was over. They babbled giddily about their wondrous future on the farm. The dream was so lucid it prompted the deepest love and the most profound sense of peace he had ever experienced. Every minute of his dreamtime was as vivid and tactile as actual reality. Mary's lavender scent still intoxicated him. Every word she uttered was precisely what he longed to hear. Every caress felt heavenly. Her lips were so warm and tender when they kissed, it absorbed him into a sensual paradise.

Then he awoke. His dream evaporated into a confused ether of fragmented imagery. He was crushed by the sudden, unwelcome return of loneliness. The pain from the abrupt end to his beatific dream was worse than from his actual parting from Mary. He wanted to never dream again.

John noticed that the Monk was eyeing him with concern during his morose recollection of last night's dream. He suddenly realized he had been crying and wiped his cheeks with the back of his toilworn hand, leaving dark smudges on his face. "I'm okay," he muttered to his companion. He resumed digging with a fury that made it clear he wasn't.

"What troubles you, my friend?" the Monk asked.

John dared not share his real feelings. It was likely that everyone at the Rock was suffering from similar distress. As their leader, he had to be a source of strength, not a trigger for widespread despon-dence. "There'll be reprisals against us for these dead Proletarians," John grumbled instead.

"There have been reprisals since the beginning of time," the Monk replied. "That's human nature. But the best way to prepare for a dangerous future is to act wisely in the present. That includes taking care of yourself."

John nodded, suspecting that the Monk had seen through his

diversion. Before he could reply, shouts arose from the men working to clear the jungle. Gunshots rang out like mini thunderclaps. There was a violent thrashing of ferns and branches. Bandits mounted on powerful stallions and brandishing guns stampeded from the jungle into their clearing.

John's heart filled with dread. He reached for the pistol in his waistband, but a fearsome array of rifles were immediately aimed at him. He froze. One of the bandits prodded his mount to the fore.

"Are you John?" he asked with a malignant leer that seemed permanently etched on his scarred face.

"I am. Who are you?"

"Pablo Guzman." The attacker said nothing more, certain that his infamy preceded him.

John's mind raced with dire thoughts. Jed had told him gruesome stories about the leader of the Jackal faction. Right and wrong for the bandit were determined solely by whoever could wield the most vicious force. Today, that was Guzman and his Jackals.

"How do you know my name?"

Guzman's smile was born of bloodlust rather than mirth. "I asked one of your lumberjacks who his leader was. He identified you, then I shot him."

John reached for his pistol again, driven by anger and instinct. One of the Jackals fired his rifle in quick response, kicking up stones near John's feet. John raised his arms, though his body still trembled with fury. He reminded himself that the lawful world had disappeared.

"You'll pay dearly for murdering one of my men," John said through clenched teeth and pursed lips.

Guzman shrugged. "On this island of the damned, the strong prosper and the weak pay dearly. Today, that's you."

John studied his adversary in the glare of the noonday sun. Guzman was a Cubano built like a baby bull with powerful shoulders connected directly to the base of his skull. His roundish head and face were defined by harsh features, and his ears protruded awkwardly on each side. His small eyes were narrowly spaced and topped with jagged eyebrows that framed a perpetual scowl. A goatee jutted aggressively from his chin, and his hair was cropped short. Guzman looked exactly like who he was, a triumphant warlord leading cutthroat desperados who thrived on intimidating victims.

"What do you want?" John asked.

"I was sent here," Guzman said.

"By whom?"

A scowl darkened Guzman's face. "A bigger den of thieves."

John surmised that Guzman was referring to the Syndicate, although why the bandit was entangled with that mysterious confederacy was a puzzle. "Why did they send you here?"

"Cosimo offers no explanations. Perhaps he feels threatened by you, although I don't see why. He paid me to deal with you, since Vlad failed."

"So you've been hired to kill us?" John was stalling for time, hoping that the sentries in the Rock's towers had heard the shots, seen the intruders, and were now mustering fighters to pour across the drawbridge.

"Killing all of you would eliminate a revenue opportunity," Guzman replied. "Instead, I'm going to tax your pathetic society. Frequently. I told Cosimo that today's tax collection will go to Vlad as reparations for you murdering his soldiers. He liked that idea."

John glanced imperceptibly at the drawbridge. No activity. "Governments tax. Gangs steal," he said.

Guzman smirked. "The only difference between a gang and a government is that people foolishly believe a government is not a gang."

John stalled for more time. "Suppose I paid this tax. What services would your gang provide in return?"

"We'll promise not to kill any more of your people. It's called *protection*."

John shook his head in dismay. "So every time you want money from us, you'll renew your promise not to kill us? If we submit to this tax once, you'll always tax us. And each time you'll demand more and more. We don't intend to live that way."

"I don't care how you live. I only care that you pay your taxes.

Your new role in life is to subsidize my Jackals in this tropical wasteland."

"Fuck you!" John swore. "We'll determine the purpose of our lives. We intend to work hard, build a robust community, and pursue happiness." John glanced uneasily toward the Rock. Nothing was stirring.

"You must be new here," Guzman replied with exaggerated patience. "Barbarism reigns on this island. Power is the only useful virtue. And we are the most powerful."

"In Pathless Land, we seek control of nature's bounty, which is the true source of prosperity. You Jackals want control of other people's bounty."

Guzman raised a jagged eyebrow. "Owning you and stealing your labor is the most efficient way for me to live."

John's arms ached from being raised overhead. Where were his rescuers? "I own myself," he replied. "So I own what my hands and mind produce. They can't be claimed by anyone else. Including you."

"You're wrong!" Guzman exclaimed with a guttural laugh. "The way I see it, mastering you is easier than mastering nature."

"We're not your beasts of burden! A society should be based on reason and collaboration, not force."

"My rifles say otherwise!" Guzman snapped. "They say that you'll plead on your knees for a mercy that will never come."

John glanced again at the Rock. He saw Maria on the rampart, gesturing in his direction. He felt a surge of hope that the tide was about to turn in this standoff, but he needed a bit more time.

"You probably think I have two choices right now," John said. "Submit or be killed. But there's only one choice for me. And it's not submission."

"Have it your way!" Guzman barked, leveling his rifle. John tensed as he watched Guzman cast a dark eye down the barrel sights with a lecherous grin. He could see his thick finger start to pull the trigger. John closed his eyes, then heard two chilling sounds almost simultaneously: the swoosh of an arrow and the thunderclap of a gunshot.

The arrow pierced Guzman's horse in the neck, barely missing the bandit. The horse lurched violently just as Guzman pulled the trigger. His shot went slightly off its mark, slamming the bullet into John's left shoulder rather than his heart.

John spun from the stunning force of the impact. He fell to the ground in a fetal position, writhing in agony. The bullet had smashed through bone and made a gruesome exit wound. A warm stream of blood seeped down his back, and his brain glazed over from shock. As if in a nightmare, he was unable to move or shout. He heard a garbled cacophony of frantic sounds from deep within a psychic well. People screamed, more arrows whizzed past, and more gunshots rang out. Hooves pounded the ground.

Even though John's left arm was paralyzed, he somehow rose to his knees and retched violently, frothing at the mouth. The sudden loss of blood weakened every fiber of his being. Through blurred eyes he saw the archers of the Remnant rushing from the drawbridge, releasing volleys of arrows. A Jackal sped to Guzman, who was using his collapsed horse as a barricade while he fired at the archers. The speeding Jackal swooped Guzman up onto his mount. The surviving bandits galloped away from the scene, firing wild shots as they fled.

John heard a woman frantically calling his name. From the depths of his delirium, he groaned, "Mary, I'm here." He collapsed to the ground again. His addled brain imagined his wife cradling him in his arms, whispering soothing words to guide him peacefully to the other side of death.

Olga, sweating and distraught, bent over his prone body. She felt his neck for a pulse and breathed a sigh of relief. "Doc!" she shouted. "Over here!"

Doc sprinted to her side, tore open John's shirt, and began ministering to the gaping wound at the back of his shoulder. He put a coca leaf under John's tongue so that his saliva could digest the mild narcotic.

Doc lifted John's head and dribbled some rum into his mouth, which caused John to open his eyes. He looked up at Olga, surprised to see her rather than Mary leaning over him. A surge of warmth coursed through his veins, perhaps from the rum.

"You're going to be okay," Olga consoled, stroking his grimy forehead.

"And the others?" John croaked.

"Three of our men were killed," Olga replied somberly. "And one was taken hostage by the fleeing Jackals."

John's heart sank. He blamed himself for their lack of defensive preparations. "Who?"

Olga paused. "Jed."

Tears formed in John's eyes. Jed had already suffered years of captivity by the Proletariat. And now he was a pawn in the hands of the fleeing Jackals. John imagined him shackled by the ankles with his hands tied behind his back. Perhaps they were dragging his haggard body behind a horse. John was certain that Guzman would seek retribution for today's skirmish in a heinous manner. Would he dump Jed's mutilated body outside the Rock's drawbridge? Would he cut off Jed's ear or finger and send it with an outrageous ransom demand?

The warmth of Olga's consolations turned frigid in his veins, and he shivered uncontrollably.

20

JOHN

Three weeks had passed since Guzman shot John.

Doc had fabricated a makeshift harness to immobilize John's wounded shoulder. Now that John was unable to share in the physical work of their expanding society, he spent much of his time contemplating the structure of it. The effort rekindled his love of philosophy and other intellectual pursuits. With his good arm he began composing a second journal. He had abandoned his first journal in Kansas.

His journal entries, however, unleashed an overwhelming sadness that had been lurking deep within. But the sadness wasn't due to a lack of progress at the Rock.

During the past three weeks, John's lieutenants led the growing population of Pathless Land to accomplish wonders. Hammer had improved his smith, and he and several apprentices were now manufacturing a wide variety of products from metal. The Carpenter and his team finished the repairs to the Rock and were now constructing crude homes and defensive barriers outside the fort. Maria set up surveillance outposts around the fort to avoid any more surprise intrusions. Mallory was training everyone in the use of firearms. The Monk provided martial arts training. Nicolai and Newton, along with their team of outcast engineers, continued to add technologies to the community. Garcia, under the watchful tutelage of the Carpenter, coordinated the allocation of plots of land outside the fort to homesteaders who wished to begin farms, families, or cottage industries. The foundations of a healthy trading economy were being laid.

John's sadness wasn't simply due to his yearning to reunite with Mary. During his recovery, he often reminisced about his old life with her. But in every memory, every dream, and every imagined conversation, her ethereal message to him was identical to her actual parting words months ago. She was proud of the dangerous mission he had chosen, and she was determined to carry on without him in Kansas. Her reward was knowing that his vision of a rational society would come to fruition for the entire world someday.

Even Olga's tireless help during John's recovery couldn't dispel his sadness. She was a dynamo of compassion. She changed cold compresses when he was feverish, read him to sleep at night, prepared his meals, and assisted with his rehabilitation exercises. They chatted for hours about their difficult pasts, their current challenges, and the dangers lurking in the future.

He was deeply moved by Olga's support. After he'd been shot, she swore she would do whatever it took to help him recover. She saw John as the catalyst for a brighter future for her, for the women of the Remnant, and for most people on the island. During the past three weeks, she had fully honored her oath to stand by his side.

On a sultry tropical night, John was seated around a campfire with Olga, the Monk, and the Carpenter. The three had become his spiritual physicians, each trying to dispel the strange ennui that had sapped his characteristic hope and optimism. Olga sat beside him, and the other two sat facing them.

The Carpenter eyed John with concern. "Farmer John, each day I hope I'll see a genuine smile grace your face again. Are you still in pain?"

"Not much. Doc has worked miracles with his limited resources. Olga has made life tolerable for me. And you and the Monk have become my good friends."

"Then what are you struggling with?" Olga asked. She paused. "Mary?"

John saw discomfort in her body language. "No. I've accepted my permanent separation from her."

"Share your troubles with us, *por favor*," the Carpenter pleaded. "We desperately want your passion to be rekindled."

John studied their imploring faces. He hated to show weakness as a leader, but he knew he owed them some insight.

"I dread that I've bitten off more than I can chew," John admitted. "I worry that everyone around me will suffer the consequences of my poor decisions. Including you, my dear friends. Including Jed, who's enduring another awful fate he doesn't deserve. Including everyone else who has suffered under my leadership already."

"It's best to face your fears directly," the Monk stated. "Say them aloud to us."

John sighed heavily. "The list is long. Retribution by Vlad. Reprisal by Guzman. Betrayal by Spartacus. Robbery by le Clerc." He shook his head dismally. "And I'm sure our struggles on this desolate island have only just begun. Everything seems pointed toward disaster."

Olga nudged his good shoulder. "I'm surprised."

John looked at her with a raised eyebrow.

Her stunning eyes twinkled in the firelight. "Here's how I see you. You captured the Rock from Vlad. You showed Spartacus you had enough faith in your vision to let him go free. You stared down Guzman's gun while choosing liberty. And you walked unarmed into the Remnant camp to face me after our women were kidnapped."

"Farmer John," the Carpenter interjected. "I agree with Olga. You're wrong to doubt yourself. You've acted bravely thus far during awful circumstances. You must believe in yourself!"

John sat transfixed by the dancing flames of the fire.

"Achieving good always comes with risk," the Carpenter continued. "If you want to get warm, you must stand near the burning fire. If you want to cool off, you must jump into the dangerous water. Good and bad exist side by side. To protect those you love, you must be willing to challenge the lion and tread on the serpent."

"There are many lions and serpents on this island," John mused.

"The right things to do are usually the most difficult," the Carpenter observed. "Every person must carry that cross. But if you've built your moral foundation upon bedrock, nothing can deter you from your mission."

John hung his head. "Sometimes the struggle seems pointless. Everything ends in darkness anyway."

"Darkness is certainly all around," the Carpenter replied. "But we are each a drop of light who can illuminate the world if we choose to. We just need a motive. We need to be committed to something positive, however glorious or humble, for as long as we're alive. This leads to the most important question every person must answer."

John looked up at him.

"Why do you want to go on living?" the Carpenter asked.

The question stunned John. The Carpenter seemed eerily tuned to his deepest struggles.

"Let me turn the question on you," John countered. "What's the meaning of life?"

"Why are you asking me, Farmer John? It's your life! The meaning of your life is to give your life meaning. You were born with incredible gifts. You have senses, you have reason, you have instincts for love and companionship. You have free will in a world full of infinite possibilities. Open your eyes and your heart! Meaning is all around you. It's so near that you can reach out and touch it every day."

"Lao Tzu pointed the way on this," the Monk interjected. "He said that being deeply loved by someone gives you strength, while loving someone deeply gives you courage. Meaning lies in both."

Something stirred in John's heart. A collage of images flashed through his mind. He thought of his dear Mary and the promise he had made to her. He thought of his loyal son, James, growing into manhood without a father. He thought of his brave mother, who had raised him during horrific circumstances, only to be spirited off into the netherworld of Montana to avoid a dire fate. He thought of Olga, who had nurtured him back to health despite her deep-rooted distrust of men. He thought of the Carpenter and the Monk, who cared enough about him to delve into his deepest concerns. He thought of the rest of the men and women in Pathless Land who were looking for leadership in desperate times.

It became clearer what the Carpenter and the Monk meant. The meaning of life wasn't to be found in navel-gazing or holding up a mirror in morose self-examination. It was to be found by being a mirror for those he loved, and they for him, each affirming the value and beauty of the other.

"Okay, I get your point," John replied to his spiritual mentors. "But there's so much to be fixed in this shitty world that everything I do seems futile. Or maybe *pitiful* is a better description."

The Carpenter smiled serenely. "Farmer John, think of your efforts as being like planting a mustard seed. It's a tiny seed, but once it takes root, it grows into the greatest of shrubs and spreads wildly. You're planting a mustard seed called Pathless Land. It will spread across Earth with the help of those you inspire. That's why I call you Farmer John, even though you roll your eyes when I do. You're growing something priceless."

John smirked. "Some people will help it to grow. Others will poison it, labeling it a vile weed. Hence all the violence in the world."

"There are certainly villains who want to steal, destroy, and kill," the Carpenter replied. "The awful man who put a bullet through your shoulder is one. But doesn't that amplify the meaning of your life?"

"How so?"

"You stand opposed to the envy and violence of those who rule and plunder. You're offering a vision of abundant life for sovereign individuals seeking a just and peaceful world where they can exercise their free will. Can there be any greater purpose under the heavens? Can there be any greater gift for those you love and for their future generations? You're the first candle that is lighting the second that will light the third, until eventually the whole world is illuminated by your vision."

The Monk arose and put a hand on John's good shoulder.

"There's an old Chinese proverb that says no snowflake in an avalanche ever feels responsible. You're the exceptional snowflake who's taking responsibility. I believe you'll transform the avalanche of totalitarianism into a tidal wave of freedom and justice. You may be afraid today, but the powermongers are the ones who should be quivering."

John furrowed his brow, then reached into his pocket and pulled something out.

"What's that?" Olga asked.

"The Carpenter spoke of mustard seeds," John replied. "This is a packet of white rose seeds. It's the only thing I brought with me from Kansas into exile. Our discussion reminded me that I need to plant them here in Pathless Land."

"They were that important to you?" Olga inquired.

"Yes. Tonight's discussion confirmed it. White roses are the symbol of our rebellion in America. They represent purity in the face of evil—"

John was interrupted by Maria's sudden appearance at their campfire. "Sir, you need to see this. I didn't think it could wait," she said as she approached the group.

In the flickering firelight John saw that Maria held a rock in one hand and a piece of paper in the other. "What's going on?"

"A scout brought me this rock. It was thrown into an outpost on our perimeter. This note was wrapped around it. It's addressed to you." Maria handed it to him.

John took it and angled it toward the fire to see the handwritten scrawl.

"Read it aloud," Olga said. "There should be no secrets among us."

"It's from Guzman. It says, 'John, you disrespected me, a man of great stature. I've been considering how to fix this problem. You have three choices. One: submit to the taxation that I demanded just before I shot you. Two: Hand over Olga Kozlowski to me. She's the most desirable woman on the island, and she could be a valuable bargaining chip in the shifting alliances. Three: watch helplessly as your tribe is slaughtered by my Jackals and our new allies. I'm sending your friend Jed Starnes to retrieve your decision for me. If he fails to return your answer to me within twenty-four hours, I'll assume you've chosen the third option.'"

John looked up and waved the note in the air like a white flag of surrender. "This is worse than anything I feared."

Olga stood up. "John, the answer is simple. You can't agree to Guzman's extortion. Once a society surrenders its freedom that way, it's almost impossible to get it back. And our small society can't withstand a united attack by whatever alliance he has now. At least not yet."

It took John a moment to digest the stunning implication of Olga's assessment, then a look of horror washed over his face.

"I forbid you to sacrifice yourself!" John declared.

"You can forbid me nothing!" Olga retorted.

21

———

SINALOA

"Olga's lost her mind," Jed said.

"Or maybe she's very brave," John replied.

The two men were marching at the vanguard of Pathless Land's army toward Guzman's camp. The jungle raged with tropical noises as they trudged along. Jed had been released from captivity by the Jackals to obtain John's response to Guzman's ultimatum. When Jed arrived at the Rock, he was surprised there was no debate among the Council of Sages about how they should respond. No one supported being taxed by the Jackals. No one supported girding for an attack by Guzman and his allies. Olga had buried all debate with a stunning offer to sacrifice herself.

"How rough was it in Sinaloa?" John asked Jed. Sinaloa was the name the Jackals had given to their headquarters located deep in the jungle fifty miles southeast of la Habana. The name was a reference to the birthplace of the Mexican and Central American narcoculture. The Jackals had no political structure beyond gangland rules. Theft, drugs, and human trafficking were how the merciless cutthroats acquired wealth and hedonistic delights.

"My three weeks as Guzman's captive were rougher than my two years as Vlad's captive," Jed replied flatly.

John studied the bedraggled, beaten body of his best friend and shook his head in dismay. Jed looked like one of those relentlessly staggering zombies in Caribbean folklore that terrified Cubano children.

"What did they do you?"

"The Jackals are atavistic killing machines," Jed replied. "When you're their prisoner, you wish they *would* kill you. I was held in an underground dungeon along with other prisoners. Muddy water flooded the dungeon whenever it rained. Slime dripped from the ceiling onto our heads. Guards opened a small grill in the door once a day to toss in pitiful rations of rancid bread. We had rotted planks to sleep on and leaky pails to piss and shit in. The stench was so horrific that after a few days I couldn't smell anything. I may never smell anything again."

"Did they torture you?"

Jed shrugged his shoulders. "Of course. It was an opportunity for them to convince the others in their soulless gang that disobedience was a poor life choice. I was tortured in public in the middle of their camp. They bullwhipped me and pissed on my open wounds afterward. They manicured my fingers and pedicured my toes." He spread his hands to display some missing fingernails. "And then they covered me with a concoction that attracted fire ants. Fire ants will make anyone welcome death."

"Aren't you afraid of more torture when you deliver our answer to Guzman?"

They heard footsteps behind them. They turned and saw Olga approaching.

"That won't be necessary," she said, indicating she had overheard part of their conversation.

Jed looked at her quizzically. "I don't understand."

"Since I'm surrendering myself to Guzman, my arrival in Sinaloa will be the answer to his ultimatum. There's no need for you to return there."

Jed shook his head. "You don't owe me anything, Olga."

"You're right," she replied. "But I owe something to the Remnant spies who infiltrated the Rock after our failed assault. A leader should show at least as much courage as her followers."

"Guzman will abuse you in horrific ways," Jed warned. "He's a heartless psychopath."

"Jed, I have faith in myself. I also have faith in John and Mallory. Guzman will be destabilized by my unexpected surrender. I'll do whatever I can to keep him distracted and to give him a false sense of security. That way Mallory will have the element of surprise when our fighters attack Sinaloa."

"Olga's made up her mind," John interjected. "We'll rescue her before Guzman can abuse her."

"How are you going to do that?" Jed asked wryly.

"Mallory's working on a plan," John said. "Maria's scouts are surveilling up ahead, but they haven't reported back yet. The distraction of Olga's surprise appearance might be our only advantage."

"I can tell you a few things about Sinaloa," Jed said. "I spent some time on display in the middle of their camp. I observe and listen well, even when I'm being brutalized. It's one of my superpowers."

John stopped and waved a signal to Mallory, who was trailing behind them but quickly caught up. "I want you to hear Jed's report about Sinaloa," John said. "The information might help with your plan."

"I already have a plan," Mallory said stiffly. "But I'll listen to Jed's briefing."

"Sinaloa is more a nest of gangsters than a military base," Jed began. "Most of the Jackals are career criminals: pickpockets, robbers, and killers. They're not trained fighting men, but they're vicious and fearless, so don't underestimate them. None of them believe murder is a crime unless they're the victim. They eat well because they steal well, but they're weakened by alcoholism, drug addiction, and sexual disease."

Mallory nodded. "Describe their compound."

"It's a third-world slum. Except for Guzman's lavish quarters, which are protected by capable guards. The dirt roads in the compound become quagmires when it rains. The homes of the common bandits are wattle huts with rusted tin roofs. They get their water from a dirty stream running through the compound, close to where their latrines are dug. There's a stone tavern that serves rum, ganja, and hallucinogens. Most of the women are there against their will, and unspeakable things are done to them."

"When's the best time to attack them?"

"After midnight. By then, they're either intoxicated or sleeping off their excesses."

John noticed that Olga was trying to catch his eye. His heart thumped because they hadn't had really spoken since she scolded him back at the Rock. He nodded to her in understanding, then instructed Jed and Mallory to continue their debriefing. He and Olga slowed their pace to fall behind the two men.

"John," Olga began when privacy was possible. "I'm sorry. I was wrong to snap at you earlier. There's a fine line between chivalry and being patronizing, and I mistook your intentions. You're an honorable man."

John was mesmerized by her eyes, which seemed more alive than usual. She was charged with emotion, perhaps because she was about to place her fate into the hands of a barbarian. Or maybe there was something else.

"No need to apologize," John replied. "We all have our dark moments on this island."

Olga sighed. "I've been worrying about my fate. I'm haunted by those who've already died here because of hatred and violence. Walking on the ground of Outcast Island is like treading on a giant cemetery. Soon, others may be walking on *my* grave."

"That's pretty dark," John replied. "I wrestle with my own darkness. It seems like we're all engaged in a futile struggle in an endless funeral called life. If it wasn't for your support and the support of the Monk and the Carpenter, I might have quit the struggle."

Olga turned to face him, then put her hands on his shoulders, taking care not to jostle the injured one. "I may only have a handful of hours left. Something in my heart tells me that I need to live an eternity right now. The Monk once told me that the present moment contains every moment. I'm very glad you're here with me in this moment."

"Olga, I'll move heaven and earth to rescue—"

She put her finger to his lips, cutting off his words. He saw both desperation and longing in her eyes. She wrapped her arms around him. The distance between their faces closed.

Suddenly, there was a violent thrashing of foliage to their left. Their intimacy evaporated as they jumped away from the commotion. They were stunned to see a giant of a man emerge from the jungle. His muscular torso dripped with sweat. He clenched an oversized machete in his powerful right hand and was scowling.

"Spartacus!" John exclaimed. "What are you doing here? I thought you were tracking le Clerc to get Morgan's treasure."

"This is the second time you Pathless Land people interrupted my hunt," Spartacus growled.

"What are you talking about?" John asked.

"We finally had le Clerc and his pirates in a vulnerable position yesterday. They had no idea they were surrounded. We were planning to attack last night, but one of his couriers slipped through our cordon. The messenger must have delivered some unsettling news to le Clerc because the pirates suddenly broke camp. There was a brief skirmish as they forced their way through our perimeter and escaped. We were taken by surprise with their sudden flight."

"What does that have to do with Pathless Land?" John asked.

"The pirates raced in this direction as fast as their mules and horses could take them. They're less than a mile from your left flank. That can't be a coincidence on this big island. It must have something to do with you Pathless Landers."

"Spartacus, I swear on my life that we know nothing about le Clerc's maneuvers." John looked at Olga. "I'm surprised that Maria and her scouts didn't know the pirates were this close to us. Or that the Maroons were too."

Olga paled. "Le Clerc is a master of stealth. We should be very concerned. His motives are always mysterious."

Spartacus glared at them both. "What are *you* people doing here?"

John decided to share everything because he still hoped for an alliance with the Maroons. He pointed to his slinged arm and explained that Guzman had wounded him. He described the ultimatum that was going to be resolved by Olga's surrender and revealed that their army was then going to execute a surprise attack on Sinaloa to rescue her.

"So your presence here has nothing to do with me or that devil le Clerc?" Spartacus asked.

"Your pursuit of le Clerc is the last thing on our minds right now."

"Of course," Spartacus sneered. "Who are we to you?"

"People we hope will join Pathless Land," John replied. "You Maroons have fought for liberty for centuries. True appreciation for freedom usually comes from those who've lost it. People who've never been enslaved fall into a complacent stupor. They think slavery can't happen to them, so they let charlatans and thugs slowly erode their freedoms, like a frog being boiled alive. The vision of Pathless Land is to restore liberty for everyone on Outcast Island. I'm certain your people will do anything to be free."

"Do you think you can vanquish the oppressors of the world?"

"Those who rule by force will die by force," John said. "We're looking for brave people to help finish them off."

Spartacus held John's gaze. "Why should we Maroons join in your cause?"

"Acquiescing to tyranny is the worst way to live," John replied. "I didn't make this world, but I'm willing to risk my life to remake it."

"Your words *seem* sincere."

"They are. But pay more attention to my actions, which are the true measure of character. I allowed myself to be exiled to Outcast Island. I left my wife and son behind. I will never see them again. I may die today trying to rescue Olga. My actions are inspired by a belief that freedom is sacred because each human life is sacred."

"We've never lived in a society that believed such things," Spartacus replied. "Within a few miles of us are four factions flexing their muscles: us Maroons, le Clerc's pirates, your warriors, and Guzman's Jackals. I don't know friend from foe anymore. Even the woman I trusted my life with has become mysterious in her motives. For some reason, she's being protective of le Clerc. She made me promise to let him flee with Morgan's gold. I stewed over that for a few weeks, then broke my word with her and restarted my pursuit of the pirates."

"So what are you going to do now?" John asked.

"Le Clerc and Guzman make my blood run cold, so I'm willing to align with Pathless Land for the next few days while all the factions circle one another. If you remain true to your lofty words, I'll consider a more permanent arrangement."

"John," Olga interjected. "I'm leaving . . . now! Guzman's deadline is almost up." She dashed abruptly into the ferns.

Stunned by her sudden departure, John hastily bade Spartacus farewell and then plunged into the jungle to catch up to her. Heavy thoughts raced through his mind as he leapt over obstacles and plowed through vines and creepers. *Why had she gone so pale at the mention of le Clerc? Did the nearness of the pirate cast a terrible shadow over her soul?*

John tripped over a root and tumbled to the ground, landing brutally on his wounded shoulder. Paralyzing pain shot through him like a lightning bolt. His pain and the impersonal coldness of Olga's hasty flight cast a heavy shadow over his own soul. As he lay in shock, he wondered about the mysterious machinations of everyone on the island. He recalled Spartacus's worry about his most trusted ally with regard to le Clerc. Was it a coincidence that Olga was sacrificing herself and separating from Pathless Land at the very same time that le Clerc had materialized in the area?

Then an uglier question arose. Was she running to surrender to Guzman, or was she running toward le Clerc?

22

____

REVENGE

"John!" an urgent shout came through the handheld radio.

John pushed a button on one of the radios that Nicolai, the electronics wizard, had pieced together from the dust-covered bone pile in the Rock.

"John here. Do you see the fire too?"

A blaze had erupted in Sinaloa—Guzman's compound. It was almost midnight. The Warriors of Pathless Land had approached to within one hundred yards of the compound perimeter, which was surrounded by dense jungle. In five minutes, the Warriors, aided by the Maroons, were going to execute Mallory's plan to swoop in, extract Olga from captivity, and do a surprise attack on the Jackals.

"Yes, I see it," Mallory replied. "What the hell?" A massive explosion erupted in Sinaloa, sending skyward a giant ball of orange flame that lit up the jungle.

"Did your guys jump the gun?" John shouted into his radio.

"No! That's not our doing!" Mallory screamed. "We don't announce surprise hostage extractions with giant explosions."

"Are they blowing up their own camp?" John asked. "This makes no sense!"

"John, we've lost control of our operation and we haven't even started it yet! We have two choices. We can stand down and monitor the situation, or we can scuttle our original plan and go in guns blazing. Your call."

John swore to himself. Maria reported that Olga had made it to Guzman's camp, but almost half a day had elapsed since then because Mallory was adamant that they wait until midnight to attack. John was deathly afraid of what might be happening to Olga, so if they stood down now, it would seem like a betrayal. But if they charged in recklessly, Olga might die anyway, along with many of her rescuers.

"John!" the voice on the other radio snapped.

John thought of Olga being exposed to the horrific conditions that Jed had described. Then he thought of the bullet wound in his own shoulder. He didn't need to think any further. He hated Guzman, and he hated a world in which such brutes had power over others. "Go! Go! Go!" he commanded.

Mallory relayed the command across their radio network. The night erupted with gunfire. Hundreds of shadowy figures poured from the jungle into the compound. Crude incendiary devices lit up the battlefield. Shouts filled the humid air.

John rushed in as fast as his wounded shoulder would allow. He was stunned when he saw the results of the first minutes of their blitzkrieg. Nobody was fighting back. It was as if the Jackals had abandoned everything and fled into the jungle. The maze of ramshackle huts were eerily deserted.

Mallory saw John and sprinted over to him. "This is too easy. There's something else going on here."

John's mind was reeling. "Like what? Black magic? A trap?"

"Don't have a clue," Mallory replied. "Let's head to Guzman's quarters and see what we find. Maybe that will help unravel this mystery."

Mallory ordered several platoons to sweep the compound to clear the huts of any hidden threats. John directed Maria and her scouts to pick up the trail of Guzman's forces, who seemed to have simply vanished. Then the two men headed to Guzman's quarters, flanked by veteran Rangers.

Guzman's palatial quarters were a monument to excess. The bandit clearly took advantage of his exalted station in the gang. Whereas the common criminals among the Jackals lived in shacks with dirt floors, Guzman lived in an ornate tropical spa. It had a diesel generator, slate roofs, adobe walls, stained glass windows, a meandering swimming pool, intricate stone walkways, and sculpted landscaping. It was protected by a high stone wall, concrete barricades, and a heavy metal gate.

There were dead bodies splayed near the gateway, presumably some of Guzman's elite guards. The gate was blown off its hinges, leaving the entrance to the estate exposed. Mallory peeked inside the stone wall, then waved the rest of his men in.

More bodies lay in their death poses along the pathway leading to the building's front entrance. The Rangers stepped over the cadavers and approached the gaping doorway, which had also been demolished with explosives. They encountered no resistance. One by one, they slipped inside Guzman's private quarters, covering each other as they advanced.

The Rangers fanned out to inspect each room in the villa. The smashing of doors and shouts of "clear" echoed throughout the building. John and Mallory remained in the great hall near the entrance, pondering the mysteries of who had attacked the complex and where Guzman's survivors had disappeared to. John's heart was heavy with concern for Olga. Was she lying dead somewhere in the wreckage of Sinaloa? Had Guzman fled with her? Was she a prisoner of someone else now? He recalled from Guzman's ransom note that the bandit thought she might be useful as a bargaining chip with other factions. Had that bargaining gone horribly awry?

There was movement behind a lavish couch near a marble fireplace. John and Mallory spun toward the sound. Mallory levelled his weapon.

"Show yourself!" Mallory barked. "Arms up!"

A pair of delicate hands inched above the back of the couch. A bloodied woman arose with arms raised toward the ceiling. She was a beautiful Cubano whose dark hair, brown face, and flowered dress were matted with blood that was still trickling from where a bullet had grazed her head.

"Who are you?" Mallory demanded.

"Isabella." Her voice conveyed great pain, but she held her head high as her obsidian eyes blazed with anger. "I'm Pablo Guzman's wife. One of many."

John was taken aback. The bandit fled the compound but left one of his wounded wives behind? That did not portend well for Olga.

"Where's Guzman?" Mallory asked.

"He ran," Isabella replied, "with the rest of the survivors. Like all bullies, they're really cowards. They left me here to die."

John waved his good arm around the damaged villa. "Who did this?"

"Le Clerc and his pirates."

John's jaw dropped. The pirates had detoured from transporting Morgan's treasure to their home base to race over to Sinaloa and ransack it? There must have been something even more valuable here.

"What did they take?" John asked.

A derisive laugh escaped Isabella's pained grimace. "All they took was Guzman's new whore, the tall blonde with eyes like diamonds."

John's knees nearly buckled. The pirates took Olga! His head spun with the implications. Why would le Clerc risk everything to rescue her? How did he even know she was here? Was Olga a prisoner of le Clerc now . . . or something more? Was she going to be used as collateral to extort Pathless Land? Where were the pirates heading? Were Guzman and his surviving cutthroats chasing them with murderous revenge on their minds?

John knew one thing for certain. The pain in his heart from Olga's peril was surprisingly sharp.

Mallory saw the distress etched on John's haggard face. "John, we need to make some quick decisions. Maria should be back any minute with reconnaissance. Let's find Spartacus and strategize."

John and Mallory sprinted from Guzman's palace to the center of the compound. Spartacus was there directing the efforts to secure the compound. Ten bandits, all of them injured, were bound and under guard. Also under guard were thirty frightened women who had hidden during le Clerc's attack.

Maria was standing beside Spartacus. Her torn clothing, bedraggled hair, and bloody lacerations suggested her reconnaissance effort had been hasty and reckless.

"What did you discover, Maria?" John asked.

"Less than I hoped," she sighed. "There's a trampled trail running toward the east. Hundreds of people must have been chasing each other. Some were Guzman's Jackals, a few of whom had collapsed along the trail from their injuries. They refused to answer questions. I don't know which faction was chasing them."

"It was le Clerc's," John said. "One of Guzman's wives was wounded and left behind. She was angry enough to spill her guts. The pirates took Olga—but nothing else."

The color washed out of Maria's face. She shivered, shocked by the impressive espionage capabilities of le Clerc. She wondered how he knew that Olga had been captured by Guzman.

"What should we do?" Maria asked weakly.

"First things first," John replied. "Mallory, who's your most trusted lieutenant?"

"Sergeant Brown," Mallory answered without hesitation.

"Spartacus, who's yours?" John asked.

"Abah," he replied. "He's a fearless warrior who has been by my side for years. I trust him with my life."

"Maria, aside from you, who would Olga trust most as a lieutenant?"

"She trusts everyone in the Remnant. Our bonds have been forged in hell. But the most capable is Martina."

"Your lieutenants are about to get very busy," John revealed. "Mallory, instruct Sergeant Brown and his men to reduce Sinaloa to rubble. Burn everything that can burn. Make it uninhabitable. Obliterate Guzman's palace. We must eradicate criminal organizations like the Jackals. Destroying their Sodom and Gomorrah of a home base is a start. Leave the bandits nothing to come back to."

Mallory suppressed a smile as he nodded.

"Maria, instruct Martina and her team to explain to the Sinaloa survivors who are still here Pathless Land's vision for this island. If any are genuinely willing to commit to our principles, even if they've violated them in the past, offer them refuge with us. If not, abandon them to the jungle and the cruel fate that awaits them."

Maria nodded.

"Spartacus, in appreciation of your support tonight, your Maroons can have Sinaloa's spoils. Your people have been forever robbed and abused. Instruct Abah and his men to collect everything of value from this compound before Sergeant Brown destroys it. Gather every weapon, animal, bicycle, and tool. Take the clothing and jewelry too. I presume that it was all stolen by Guzman and his thugs. Since we have no way to identify the true owners, I'm declaring it all yours. Consider it your karmic reward."

Spartacus straightened, making himself appear even taller. He lifted his head proudly. "I am now convinced that your actions match your words. Thank you, my friend."

"You're welcome. No one should accept a lesser station in life imposed upon them by others. I will never tolerate that in Pathless Land. I refuse to leave this fight to future generations."

"We will join your fight," Spartacus declared. "And we will never shrink from the challenge. We've learned that if we're complacent, we get abused. It's better to die fighting back than to do nothing."

John extended his hand to Spartacus. The leader of the Maroons squeezed it with vigor. John winced.

Mallory jockeyed for John's attention. "Time's wasting! The trail of the pirates and Jackals is getting colder."

John nodded. "Maria, Spartacus, and Mallory, quickly organize your lieutenants to execute their assignments. Then gather everyone else to meet here in five minutes."

When the three of them reported back to John with their remaining warriors, Maria took the lead with her scouts to begin the pursuit of le Clerc and Guzman. John, Mallory, and Jed marched together, chatting as they trudged through the dark jungle.

"I'm not sure who we're hunting," Jed observed.

John looked at him quizzically. "We're hunting le Clerc to rescue

Olga, and we're hunting Guzman to finish off his gang. If the Jackals are hot on the heels of the pirates, we can nab two birds with one stone."

"John, we've been together a long time. Even back in Kansas, things were never quite what they seemed with the factions in America. Who was really in control? What were their motives? The strings seemed to be pulled from far away for unknown reasons. I'm convinced there's a subterranean force in the world that's like a fog on a moonless night. You can't touch it, yet it's everywhere, haunting us. I'm getting that feeling right now."

"What the hell are you talking about?" Mallory asked.

"Can't you sense it? The only way to understand the bizarre behavior of the factions on this island is to realize that they're all puppets on a string. How did le Clerc know that Olga was a prisoner at Sinaloa? How did he get safe passage through Vlad's territory to get to Morgan's treasure? Why was Guzman ordered to shoot John? You could ask a hundred such questions and puzzle endlessly over the answers, but to no avail. Yet there must be a common thread, one that's strong enough to connect all the pieces."

"Enough riddles!" Mallory snapped. "What's the common thread?"

"It's got to be the Syndicate!" Jed replied. "The whole world is being plundered by that invisible aristocracy. When the confounding layers of politics and history are peeled away, I'm certain the Syndicate will be at the core."

"You realize what that implies, don't you?" John asked.

"Yes," Jed replied. "The leaders of the factions are all willing to sell their souls to the highest bidder, and the highest bidder is always the Syndicate."

"Not all leaders," John said testily. "You may be right about the Syndicate, or it may all just be balderdash. Either way, we can't fight shadowy ghosts. We can only fight enemies who are here among us, whatever their motives. This is the same debate we had in Kansas countless times."

"That's right," Jed agreed. "But it still feels like we're poodles being led on a rope."

"I'm doing the leading," John snapped. He waved his good arm in the darkness. "Look! No strings!"

"I'm not saying you're corrupted, John. But don't you wonder if you're being misdirected somehow? In the darkness of the cells where I've spent most of my years on this island, I've seen mysterious green eyes staring at me from hidden depths. I'm sure I was hallucinating, but even hallucinations are born of something we fear deep inside."

"What do you fear?" John asked.

"We're less in control of events than we think. Let me ask you something, John. I mentioned earlier that I was surprised le Clerc knew Olga was Guzman's prisoner. Hell, I was even surprised she was willing to surrender herself to Guzman. What if Olga volunteered to surrender because she knew le Clerc would rescue her?"

John stopped in his tracks. The implications of the question staggered him. "Are you suggesting that Olga's loyalty lies elsewhere on this island? She was at my bedside for three weeks helping me recover from a gunshot wound! I know her better than you do."

"Three weeks?" Jed scoffed. "How long did you know Mary? Thirty years? You can't possibly think you've reached a level of trust with Olga worthy of betting your life on."

"How could she communicate with other groups?" John asked. "There are no phones! There's nothing!"

"There's Maria's network of scouts and spies. That's more than nothing. Way more. What do you really know about the Remnant other than their reputation for hating men, of which you are one? Don't forget le Clerc left a message for Olga at the Caves of Despair. Mallory said Olga admitted it contained something very personal. What if there were other messages you don't know about? Maybe messages were going both ways."

A pall of darkness came over John, leaving him lightheaded. He unconsciously touched the scar on his palm from the blood oath he took with Olga and began to doubt everything.

23

———————

CONTROL

"Pirate!" Merlin squawked. The parrot tightened its claws on François le Clerc's shoulder.

Cosimo had just sat down across from le Clerc. "Is that obnoxious bird referring to me or you?" the Syndicate's Centurion asked.

Le Clerc stroked the radiant blue and gold feathers of his preening pet. "It must be you because he calls me *sir.*"

Cosimo glared at Merlin, then le Clerc. "I'll not be insulted by a mindless creature!"

"I don't think Merlin meant it as an insult," le Clerc soothed. "I'm a pirate too. And he's not mindless. He's campaigning to be my second-in-command."

Cosimo and le Clerc sat beneath a canopy of palm trees a safe distance from Sinaloa. Le Clerc wore a red-and-white checkered kaffiyeh bound by a black cord on his head and beige khakis. Cosimo wore an expensive black suit that was out of place in the tropical climate. He wasn't planning to stay long.

"Your insolence will get you killed," Cosimo snapped.

"That's what the mullahs told me when I was an incorrigible orphan in Egypt," le Clerc replied. "But here I am."

Cosimo grunted.

"How did you get here?" le Clerc asked. "Outcast Island isn't the tourist destination that Cuba used to be."

"I can go anywhere I desire. The Syndicate controls the World Order. The World Order controls every military. I flew in a jet from Rome to an aircraft carrier stationed in the Caribbean. Then I took a helicopter from the carrier to here."

"Just to visit me?" le Clerc asked with a seditious smile. "Am I that important?"

Cosimo shuffled his feet uncomfortably, perhaps because his Italian leather shoes were unsuited for the Cuban jungle. "My boss thinks you're untrustworthy. I'm here to make sure our relationship is still on solid ground."

"Well, is it?"

"That's what I'm here to verify," Cosimo repeated stiffly. "I also have a proposition for you, if we are indeed still aligned."

"We pirates like to steal things, too, if that's what you mean by aligned."

"You impugn my character," Cosimo said gruffly. "I meant that you're naturally amoral and you love gold."

Le Clerc nodded but said nothing.

"I'm going to describe what it means to be a Centurion in the Syndicate," Cosimo said. "I'll explain why shortly."

"I am indeed curious," le Clerc replied.

"My assignment, even though I'm still an apprentice, is like that of all Centurions around the world. Sow chaos and fan hysteria. Set the factions against each other. Spawn class warfare, race warfare, gender warfare, and terrorism. Instigate epidemics, famines, power grid failures, financial crises, and wars. Then, when the world is completely shaken and ablaze, the proles will be desperate for security and order. They'll give great power to the governments that created all the problems in the first place. They'll clamor for their own governments to delegate even more power to the World Order, who will thus acquire more authority to tax everyone, police everyone, make and enforce laws, censor information, manipulate currencies, control supply chains, indoctrinate new generations, and claim eminent domain over the global commons."

"To what end?" le Clerc interrupted.

"To our end! Behind the scenes, the Syndicate controls the World Order by controlling the finances of every government and the funding of every politician. Elections mean nothing in this arrangement because politicians no longer represent their constituents; they're agents of our banking cartel. The most heinous crimes in the world can be committed with impunity by politicians. One criminal will be hanged for a murder, but political leaders are lionized for murdering millions during wars. One thief will be imprisoned for a bank heist, but politicians who manipulate the entire banking system to their advantage live in grandeur. Politicians always go unpunished unless the Syndicate decides that punishment is necessary. For example, Kennedy insulted the Syndicate by calling us the Gnomes of Zurich. Then he was killed. As one of the Rothschilds put it, it doesn't matter who writes the laws; it only matters who controls the money. The end result is that our small band of financial marauders reap the riches and rewards of our masterful control over everyone and everything."

Le Clerc nodded studiously. "As I said, you like to steal things too. You and I are still on solid ground. Per your instructions, I have faithfully sown chaos around Outcast Island. The Maroons are chasing me because I attacked their home base and stole their meager riches. We ransacked the Jackals' headquarters, so they're chasing me too. I kidnapped Olga Kozlowski, the leader of the Remnant. The rebels who call themselves the Warriors of Pathless Land are utterly confused, and their leader is wounded. Everyone is on the verge of killing everyone else. And with your generous contributions, I'm getting fabulously rich. Thank you again for the clues to the location of Morgan's treasure."

"Indeed," Cosimo conceded. "But are the factions on this island as quarrelsome as you think, or are they beginning to align with the upstarts from Pathless Land?"

Le Clerc studied Cosimo's stoic appearance. He was struck by how circumspect, merciless, and deadly calm the Centurion looked. Even though his dark eyes seemed barely alive, it was clear that he saw everything and filtered his observations through a private calculus that was somewhere beyond good and evil. His aura was that of the wickedest man on Earth, though le Clerc knew he was subordinate to other secretive, deadly men who were probably worse. Le Clerc steepled his hands in front of his chest, unsure of what the Centurion wanted him to say. He decided to go with his favorite standby.

"I'm as loyal as a beagle, Your Excellency. What's good for the Syndicate is good for François le Clerc."

"Don't think you can fool me," Cosimo replied. "You won't survive it because you're in too deep. It's impossible to resign from our service, and it's fatal to cross us. We're like the Mafia in that regard, but unlike the Mafia, there's no greater power on Earth than the Syndicate."

"Aren't you afraid to be here?" le Clerc asked. "This island is full of uncivilized brutes with bad intentions. Like me."

"If any harm came to me, indescribable things would happen to the perpetrators and to every person they've ever loved. Remember that."

"You said you had a proposition . . ." le Clerc prompted.

"It's an offer you can't refuse. I was recruited by the Syndicate to be an apprentice to my boss. I hope to become a full-fledged Centurion soon. In a few years, I want to be promoted to the Deka, so I'll need to begin developing my own reliable apprentice. I've selected you for that role."

"And if I refuse?"

"Nobody refuses," Cosimo sneered. "You misunderstood the Syndicate's definition of the word *proposition*."

"Will I get to meet your boss?" le Clerc asked. "Not that I don't enjoy your company, but you're a mere apprentice. I just want to know what kind of men I'd be working for."

"You will neither meet the Syndicate's leaders nor hear their names spoken until you are fully indoctrinated into the organization. They're the ten most powerful people on Earth, known only by reference to their numbered aliases."

"Pirates!" Merlin squawked again.

Cosimo scowled. Le Clerc smiled.

"I need to know a bit more," le Clerc pressed the Centurion. "What kind of political structure does the Syndicate prefer for the world?"

"Surely you've figured it out," Cosimo scoffed. "We desire a world with no freedom, no autonomy, and no ownership for anyone but the Syndicate. We desire compliant serfs who labor mindlessly in a system designed to enrich us. And if we sense any discontent among them, we start wars. Wars distract the proles and frighten them with churning cauldrons of death. The Syndicate always comes out ahead during wars because we cleverly support both sides, and most of the money funneled into the wars gets laundered into our own coffers. The supposed protectors of the proles are their worst enemies."

"So you're a socialist? Like Vlad?"

"You insult me more than that filthy bird!" Cosimo exclaimed. "I'm nothing like Vlad, that imbecilic puppet. The Syndicate has no political ideology. We do, however, make good use of those who *are* ideological. We gain when capitalists believe they run things. We gain when socialists believe they run things. However, socialism has a practical advantage over capitalism in our calculus. When we allow socialists to be in charge, the proles are much easier to mystify and manipulate. They surrender their minds and their freedom to their imposturous leaders who are mere puppets of the Syndicate. They surrender ownership of their property, which leaves them at the mercy of the collective for everything. They sacrifice meritocracy in favor of party affiliation and loyalty to leaders. They are conned into believing they're getting their cake and eating it, too, when in fact they're baking our cake and starving. Socialism is a wonderful weapon for us to use against the rest of humanity. Its bonds are harder to escape than the manacles of chattel slavery."

"Doesn't it bother you it always yields dead bodies and destroyed civilizations?" le Clerc asked.

"You're a slow learner, pirate. The Syndicate cares nothing about such drivel. We who rule the world have always been hostile to those we rule. Fortunately, very few people know the true predicament of humanity. Even if more knew, they wouldn't have the fortitude to resolve it. Handouts and hedonism are sufficient for them."

"I'm surprised you're sharing this so candidly with me," le Clerc replied. "What if I spill the beans on the Syndicate?"

"Traitor!" Merlin squawked.

Le Clerc stroked his parrot. "Don't mind my pet. He barely understands English."

There was an ominous pause. "It doesn't matter at this point if you or anyone else tries to expose us," Cosimo said resolutely. "Truth is the one thing that will never be embraced, because those who tell the truth will be destroyed. Besides, who would believe such an outlandish tale from a pirate?"

"Then continue sharing," le Clerc said dryly. "It's clarifying my thoughts."

Cosimo smiled like a crocodile. "Everything the national governments say are lies. Everything they have is stolen. To properly understand history and politics, you must realize that central governments are vast criminal enterprises used by the Syndicate to forcibly extract wealth from their subjects. They're part of an unbreakable cycle wherein political power creates enormous wealth, and enormous wealth controls political power."

"You mentioned the Mafia earlier," le Clerc observed. "Are you Italian?"

"My heritage isn't your concern," Cosimo replied. "I am of the world, not a nation. It's a world that the Syndicate is shaping according to its own desires. When all power eventually becomes vested in our single authority, who can stop us? When our shadow government looms over every nation, there will be no place to flee to. Everyone will be at our mercy. Unwittingly, Woodrow Wilson, in *The New Freedom*, described us perfectly when he said that there's a power that is so organized, so pervasive, so subtle, so watchful, so interlocked, so complete that those who condemn it had better not speak above their breath."

"How can you corrupt an entire planet? Surely there must be millions who see troubling signs of your subterranean influence."

Cosimo cracked a sly smile. "We don't corrupt anyone. People corrupt themselves. If you put food in the proles' bellies, give them a roof over their heads, and create the illusion of security, they will see nothing, hear nothing, and say nothing. A dog gnawing on a bone ignores everything else. And if perchance someone stumbles upon our secrets, it is always their last forlorn step."

The roar of a descending helicopter interrupted their conversation. "And now I must go," Cosimo announced. "You've been faithful to me thus far. But if you cross me . . ." His sentence trailed off ominously.

Le Clerc skipped saying a pleasant goodbye because another thought occurred to him. "How far from the shores of Outcast Island are the World Order ships?" he asked Cosimo.

The Centurion looked at him quizzically, then boarded the helicopter without replying.

"Pirate!" Merlin squawked.

"Shh," le Clerc admonished.

24

ESCAPE

Olga was mesmerized by le Clerc's dark, unrepentant eyes. Seeing him in person after all these years roiled her emotions. Old feelings she thought she had safely sequestered long ago rushed in. Her hatred of him melted into the background as warning signals flashed in her head.

"Why did your pirates stop to set up camp this morning?" Olga asked. "You're being chased by people drunk with murderous revenge. And you're still a long march away from your sanctuary on the eastern end of the island."

"I had an important meeting. Attendance was mandatory."

"With Cosimo, I presume," Olga said. There was only one person who could make such an imposition on him, and it wasn't her. "What was it about?"

"The prickly Centurion was concerned about my trustworthiness."

Olga laughed sharply. "Isn't everybody?"

Le Clerc looked away.

"Did you set his larcenous mind at ease?" she asked.

"I pandered to him."

"Did he threaten you?"

Le Clerc shrugged. "He's a threat to everyone. He simply reminded me that he holds my life, and the lives of those I love, in his greedy hands."

"What does he want from you?"

"The same thing he's wanted all along," le Clerc replied. "He wants me to stir up trouble so that the factions are at each other's throats. When they're killing each other, they aren't paying attention to their puppet masters."

"That's all?"

"That's all I was willing to agree to."

"So what are you going to do?"

"I'm a pirate. I'm going to take stuff and betray people." He paused, then added ominously, "Including Cosimo."

Olga eyed him with a mixture of surprise and concern. "He'll kill you. And me. And Sinbad."

"And Merlin," le Clerc added. "Cosimo hates my second-in-command."

"And you care nothing about any of us?" Olga shook her head in disgust. She had just been lumped with a parrot in le Clerc's circle of concern. She had been put in her place once again.

Le Clerc studied her face in his penetrating way that always made her feel spiritually naked. "I care more deeply than you'll ever give me credit for. But how much longer can the world let this insanity go on? The villains who run it are liars and thieves. They want us to play a game in which they're the rule makers and the referees, which means they'll always be the winners. We can either genuflect to them or defy them. That's why I'm going to play a different game."

"But you're getting rich from their game," Olga said with a smirk. "Cosimo pays you well."

"That's part of *my* game. I'm merely one pirate stealing from another. But I'll never make a whore of my soul."

Olga's eyes blazed with fury. "You already have!"

"That's not true!" le Clerc snapped. "I rescued you from Guzman, didn't I? At great risk to me and my men!"

"You abandoned me when the Remnant attacked the Rock! At great cost to me and my tribe! For a few bars of gold!"

"I never abandoned you in my heart. The Syndicate doesn't suspect I'm playing a different game. My betrayal of you at the Rock was a chess move, a ploy to gain their trust."

"And lose mine?"

Le Clerc sighed. "Every decision has a price. But I intend to win everything in the end." He locked eyes with her. "Everything."

"Against the Syndicate? Against all the other factions? Despite your own deceitfulness?" Olga flailed her arms in exasperation. "How are you going to do that?" She was exhausted once again by the absurdity of his ambitions and by being reminded that she was merely a pawn in his masterful game. "If what you told me before is true, the Syndicate is pulling all of the puppet strings!"

"I will win one bloody step at a time," le Clerc replied. "Another reason my pirates stopped and made camp is that we're going let the Jackals catch up to us. Then we'll ambush them."

"Why?" Olga began to suspect that he had succumbed to his basest instincts.

"I just explained that I intend to win everything. The Jackals are an obstacle."

"So you're just a cold-blooded killer now?"

Le Clerc's eyes flashed like glinting knives. "Guzman was going to abuse you. He'll die for that. His Jackals raped and pillaged this island for decades. They will die for that. We pirates are renegades, but we have our own code of justice, and it's merciless. Are we thieves? In the eyes of some, yes. Although we usually steal from those who have stolen from others. Are we killers? In the eyes of some, yes. Although we usually kill those who deserve to die. The Jackals, on the other hand, are indiscriminate thieves and killers. No society can survive with such anarchists in their midst because they unleash the darkest impulses of humanity."

"They might kill you too," Olga observed.

"We pirates don't fear common criminals. They're thieves first and fighters last. Sinaloa was a filthy den of pickpockets, drug dealers, and human traffickers who drank cheap gin and grog. The last thing those cowardly bullies want is a pitched battle against seasoned fighters. They'd rather get howling drunk and abuse women than engage in mortal combat in the jungle."

"Cosimo will never forgive you," Olga warned. "You said he wants you to coerce the factions to fight each other. Instead, you're going to eliminate them. Fewer factions might lead to bigger alliances that could threaten the Syndicate."

"Fate forgives everything but weakness and cowardice," le Clerc replied. "But aren't you the pot calling the kettle black? Didn't you and Spartacus form an alliance with Pathless Land?"

Olga blushed. "Perhaps. But not to double-cross Cosimo."

"Then for what reason?"

"One that you wouldn't understand."

Le Clerc eyed her coldly. "Is the reason named John by any chance?"

Olga looked away. "Pathless Land has a vision. It's bigger than just the wild adventures of your rambunctious pirates."

"You danced around my question."

Olga turned to meet his eyes again. "I'll say it more directly. John is the first man I've met on this island who treats me with respect. He respects everyone on his team. It's more than just words with him. He demonstrates it by his actions and by his willingness to put his own life on the line."

"And I do not?"

"You abandoned me before!" Olga shouted. "And now you're holding me prisoner!"

A look of insincere surprise washed over le Clerc's dark face. "You're not chained to anything. You're free to leave if you wish."

"You'd release me alone into the jungle? That doesn't count as respect."

"Perhaps there's more than fear driving your reluctance to leave," le Clerc observed.

Olga's heart fluttered in her chest. Her brief reunion with le Clerc stoked long-suppressed feelings. He was still the handsome, powerful, and fearless hero that she had once admired and loved. She was still entranced by his beautiful but unforgiving face, his long, flowing black hair, and his sculpted physique. The temptation to stay was indeed more compelling than her fear of fleeing into the wild jungle.

But she also knew deep down that his dashing traits were corrupted by shattering flaws. His motives were mysterious. His zeal to achieve his ambitions was merciless and unforgiving. He wasn't driven by love but by an even hotter inner fire that she never understood. She just knew that his inner fire transcended her own needs and desires.

For now, though, she was exhausted, partly from the ordeals of the day, and partly from the emotional turmoil that had always haunted her relationship with le Clerc.

"Ammon," Olga said, "do what you will. I need to rest. And to think."

Le Clerc was momentarily speechless. Olga was the only person on the island who knew his real name. Her mention of it today expressed an intimacy that confused him.

He nodded politely. "If you need rest, Sinbad will escort you to a safe place in the jungle. Our bivouac here won't be safe. For now, though, I have important business to attend to." He abruptly turned his back and walked away.

"Of course," Olga grumbled to herself.

The slaughter of the Jackals was anticlimactic.

The pirates had crafted a masterful ruse. Their camp, which was set up in a clearing in the jungle, was made to appear occupied and vulnerable. Campfires with glowing embers hinted at recent meals. Horses and donkeys milled about. Pots, pans, and other detritus of daily life were strewn about as if in normal use. Clothes were hung out to dry. Tents were sealed as if the occupants were taking afternoon siestas.

The Jackals bumbled into the trap. As le Clerc suspected, Guzman's men were criminals, not warriors. They were thrilled that they had caught up to their enemies and ecstatic at their perceived element of surprise. They could taste the sweet joy of imminent revenge and blindly rushed into the camp, firing guns indiscriminately into the sealed tents.

But the pirates weren't napping in their tents. They were hiding in the surrounding jungle. The Jackals were so absorbed in the thrill of their assault that they were oblivious to any threats around them. When the pirates began firing from their blinds at the exposed Jackals, it was like shooting fish in a barrel. In a few minutes, gunfire from both factions ceased.

Le Clerc strutted into the camp, pleased at the sight of so many Jackal carcasses strewn on the ground. Groans of misery rose from the wounded above the stillness of the battle scene.

A surviving Jackal emerged from a hiding spot waving a white swatch of clothing. Le Clerc looked at the symbol of surrender, then locked eyes with the frightened man. He raised his pistol and fired a masterful shot at the bridge of his nose. The bandit collapsed to the ground in a lifeless heap.

"Kill the rest of the survivors!" he shouted to his fellow pirates. "These brigands don't deserve the mercy and protection of civilization. They lived in anarchy and they'll die in anarchy."

Le Clerc headed toward the jungle to find where Sinbad had hidden Olga, but an injured man on the ground caught his attention.

It was Pablo Guzman.

The eyes of the wounded kingpin pled for mercy as le Clerc slowly raised his pistol. "Please," Guzman groaned. "Spare me! Is there no honor among thieves?"

"Honor?" le Clerc echoed, then laughed sharply. "You were holding Olga Kozlowski captive. She's the love of my life. You gained your wealth by extorting innocent people and selling drugs to addicted victims. Your life has been nothing but hedonism, brutality, and disdain for civilization." Le Clerc fired his pistol.

The bullet ripped through Guzman's leg, splintering his femur. The bandit howled in agony. "Put me out of my misery!" he begged.

Le Clerc laughed heinously. "You don't even deserve that dubious honor. We'll drag you into the jungle and let nature do what it will. I hope it takes a long time for you to die. It would be poetic justice if a boa constrictor finished you off."

Le Clerc heard a noise behind him. He spun and saw Sinbad and Olga approaching from the jungle. It was obvious from their expressions that they had witnessed his brutal administration of pirate justice. Sinbad was smiling. Olga had a look of horror on her face.

"François!" Olga exclaimed. "You are your own worst enemy. You preen for me, but your actions define your character. And they're disturbing."

"Olga, you don't understand," he replied, noting that she didn't call him Ammon this time. "Everything is coming to a head. The demons are eating into our lives from all sides. They all must die. I'm told that you administered the same kind of justice at the Rock when you rescued your devastated women."

"I can't tell demons from angels anymore." She sighed, obliquely acknowledging the moral contradiction le Clerc had pointed out. "You abandoned the Remnant, you're betraying Cosimo, and you're pitting all the factions against each other. You lie to everyone while pretending to be their ally. I can't respect a man who says one thing but does another. What's next, François?"

"The Warriors of Pathless Land," he replied with grim resolve. "They're hot on the heels of the Jackals and will fall into the same trap."

Olga drew a sharp breath. "You're insane!" It suddenly dawned on her that le Clerc might be motivated more by eliminating a rival for her affection than by a rational strategy.

"Am I?" he asked. "My greatest enemies have joined with Pathless Land. The Remnant hates me because I betrayed them. The Maroons hate me because I raided their headquarters. And the Warriors of Pathless Land probably think I've kidnapped you. You're right that I promised Cosimo to sow chaos on the island, but that was always a lie. I sowed chaos when it suited my purposes. Now I need to eliminate rivals."

"Rivals for me, or rivals for supremacy over Outcast Island?"

"You presume too much, my dear," he replied.

"As do you, François. Slaughtering the Jackals was no accomplishment. What lies ahead will be a greater challenge. The Remnant is battle-tested. The Maroons' resolve is fueled by centuries of abuse. The Warriors of Pathless Land have a contingent of American Army Rangers. And most of all, they have passion for a vision. A real vision, unlike yours."

Le Clerc snickered. "All of that may be true, but I have Cosimo eating out of my hand now, and with that comes the ultimate advantage. The Syndicate controls everyone and everything."

"Not the Warriors of Pathless Land," Olga said. "And I guarantee that you won't take them by surprise like you did the Jackals."

Le Clerc raised an eyebrow. "A guarantee? Bold words, my dear. What's your plan?"

"I'm leaving!" Olga retorted. "Now. Unless you shoot me in the back as I run into the jungle. I will eventually stumble upon one of Maria's scouts when I retrace our path. Then the news of your planned ambush will quickly get to John and his men. Captain Mallory, his military commander, is a genius. You're picking a fight with the wrong faction. And you broke a blood oath with the wrong woman."

"Why are you telling me this?"

Olga hesitated. "Despite my anger, I no longer want you to be killed. My hope is that you and John can join forces someday. You're the only two men I know who have the courage to defy the agents of darkness."

She spun on her heels and headed for her escape. Le Clerc stared at her retreating figure in amazement. "Olga!" he shouted as she neared the edge of the jungle.

She stopped to take one last look at him and noticed that he was pointing his pistol in her direction. She steeled herself, expecting the worst.

"You'll need this!" le Clerc shouted. He tossed the pistol in her direction, and it landed on the ground at her feet. She stared at it like it was an evil talisman, then she picked it up and slipped it into her waistband.

She disappeared into the jungle.

25

MONK

Maria's sudden appearance surprised John.

She materialized out of the jungle as the Warriors of Pathless Land were pursuing the Jackals who had fled Sinaloa. Maria and her scouts had been deployed ahead of the Warriors to track the Jackals. Her sudden return suggested she had encountered something unexpected.

She rushed to him, her face ablaze with emotion and her chest heaving from exertion. "John! We must stop our pursuit. Now!"

John had learned to respect Maria's ability to assess dangerous situations calmly. Her emotionally charged manner today was not only out of character; it contradicted their mission to annihilate the surviving Jackals. "Maria, what happened?"

"Olga's alive! And she escaped from le Clerc!"

John was thrilled. But then a dark corner of his brain triggered alarms about her recent mysterious behavior. Why was she so quick to sacrifice herself to Guzman? How did le Clerc know she was at Sinaloa? And how did she "escape" from him? Doubts flooded his brain.

"Where is she?" John asked brusquely. "And why do we have to stop our pursuit?"

Maria hesitated. Her body language screamed discomfort. "She's nearby, but she sent me to speak with you first."

Maria's change in demeanor heightened John's suspicions. The two women were unbreakably loyal to each other. Maria seemed to be wearing Olga's emotions on her own sleeve by osmosis. He didn't like the feel of it.

"Why is that necessary?"

"Olga's afraid that you're skeptical about recent turns of events," Maria replied. "For example, you're probably wondering why she was able to escape from le Clerc, knowing their long history of animosity."

"Yes. I would have expected them to kill each other instead. I also wonder about other things."

"Of course," Maria replied. "Olga instructed me to tell you that she can explain everything. However, she knows that the situation is on a hair trigger, so I'm here to make sure nothing dire happens when she arrives."

John's head was spinning. "I ask you again, why does this require us to stop our pursuit?"

Maria snapped to her usual businesslike demeanor. "Olga shared shocking news. Some good, some terrible."

"The good news?" John asked.

"Le Clerc ambushed the Jackals, who were hot on his heels. They were all killed, including Guzman."

John's jaw dropped. "Guzman and his thugs are dead?" He paused for a moment. "What's the bad news?"

"Le Clerc intends to ambush the Warriors of Pathless Land next. That's why Olga wants you to stop your pursuit."

John pondered this dire revelation. His concerns about Olga's motives were redoubled. Was she trying to save the Warriors of Pathless Land or trying to save le Clerc? He recalled her demands for the Warriors to kill le Clerc on other occasions. So what changed?

"Thanks for the heads up," John replied coolly. I'll tell Mallory to prepare for an ambush. But we'll continue our pursuit of le Clerc."

Maria nodded, but her eyes showed disappointment. "What should I tell Olga in the meantime?"

"That I need some time to think."

"For what it's worth, I trust her with my life," Maria replied. "Her behavior has been strange, but I think that's because she's confused, not because she's untrustworthy. She's been mired in evil and violence her whole life, to the point where good is sometimes indistinguishable from bad."

"Our lives hang in the balance," John replied. "It won't matter to others whether she's untrustworthy or merely confused. The net result is that she's unreliable."

Maria became stoic again. "I'll tell her you're thrilled that she's alive, but before she returns you must consider how the entire team will react."

"Very diplomatic," John replied. "Pass that message on to her, then return here before sundown to get my decision."

"Yes sir," Maria said, then paused. "John, I don't mean this as a threat in any way, but you must understand that if Olga isn't allowed to return, I'll follow her, not you. I believe that most of the Remnant will react the same way. We have a long history together." She smiled thinly and then bounded back into the jungle as silent and mysterious as a fog on a moonless night.

John's head ached from trying to unravel the twists and turns of his relationship with Olga. After an hour of intense contemplation, he was still in a muddle and decided to seek counsel from the Monk.

He found the Monk sitting cross-legged on the ground. "May I join you?" John asked.

"I've been expecting you," the Monk replied. "Please, sit down."

John did a double take. *I was expected?* He pretzeled his long legs and joined the Monk on the ground.

The Monk offered him a coconut husk filled with manioc. "The body needs nourishment as much as the heart and soul." Then he offered some rum. "Life requires nectar as much as it requires effort. It's important to find time to refresh ourselves in mindfulness."

John nodded, and some of his tension eased. The monk's demeanor was always calming.

"How is your wounded shoulder?" the Monk asked. "More importantly, how's your wounded spirit?"

"Shoulder's healing fine. My spirit is not."

"To fully taste life, one must struggle sometimes," the Monk said. "What troubles your spirit?"

"Love."

"Ah . . ." the Monk replied knowingly. "Why does your budding love for Olga wound your spirit?"

"How did you know I was referring to Olga?"

"The same way that I knew you would be coming to see me. If one is observant enough, one becomes aware of almost everything."

John shook his head in wonderment. "I've been observing that Olga is smart, beautiful, and courageous."

"Then what's the problem?"

"She's also dangerous. And maybe untrustworthy."

"A paradox!" the Monk exclaimed with enthusiasm. "Beauty and danger are opposite sides of the same coin. What tempts you can also harm you. Such is the yin and yang of our existence."

"That's not helpful . . ." John's voice trailed off in confusion.

"Then let's get nearer to the truth," the Monk replied. "As a philosopher once put it, there are two ways to be fooled. One is to believe what is *not* true; the other is to refuse to believe what *is* true. Either way, you must move from the uncertainty of believing to the realm of knowing."

"Still not helpful," John muttered.

The Monk smiled tenderly. "Think of it this way: all suffering is born from wrong perception. Our perceptions are conditioned by our histories and mythologies, our hopes and fears, our misjudgments and confusions, and by the lies and deceits of those around us. The only way out of that trap is to comprehend reality directly."

"What does that have to do with Olga?"

"Everything! Never fall prey to blind faith in any person, even if the person is the wisest and most beautiful in your estimation. It's like trying to build a house on sand. You can't make a rational judgment by guessing what's inside another person's mind and heart."

"But shouldn't her character be obvious to me by now? I thought it was a week ago, but today she's a mystery to me."

"That's what makes life such a wonderful challenge!" the Monk replied. "Reality can't be cut into pieces that are isolated from each other. All things are connected, including your perceptions from a week ago and those from today. Karma is a vast matrix that links all of existence together. One thing is affected by all things, and all things are affected by one thing. Causes contain their effects, and their effects become causes."

"You're speaking in riddles!"

The Monk smiled again. "You're looking at reality solely from your perspective, as if that's the only valid slice of reality. Perhaps it's time to see it from hers. You may be right, and she may be wrong. She may be right, and you may be wrong. Perhaps the truth lies somewhere between or outside the two of you. Perhaps she's not untrustworthy but rather confused or entangled. You can either be angry with her as she fights through her dilemma, or you can help her. If you help her, you may also come to know what's really in her heart and mind. Then you can move beyond the uncertainty of believing into the realm of knowing. From there, the two of you can walk toward joy together."

"But what if I learn that her character is flawed and she's truly untrustworthy?"

"Even that knowledge is valuable," the Monk replied. "One can't offer the right medicine without knowing the patient's illness. If she truly suffers from flawed character, your path forward will be obvious."

"And if she objects to my path forward?"

"The hardest lesson for a person to learn is that they are only themselves," the Monk replied. "Be a lamp unto your own feet. No one should choose your path for you, and you shouldn't choose anyone else's path for them. It's a terrible mistake to confuse the two paths."

"Perhaps that's why the world is in such a mess."

The Monk smiled knowingly. "The thing that leads to sadness is the same thing that leads to happiness. That's free will. Without it, we would never know love or happiness, because the price for those is the risk of sadness or pain. All life is drama, and none of it is predestined because everyone has free will. Embrace the drama, but only while creating your own path."

John fell silent and sipped his rum as the Monk waited patiently. Finally, John said, "This conversation is why I hold you in high esteem. You've added another reason for our society to be called Pathless Land. Thank you."

The Monk steepled his hands and bowed slightly. "That is most satisfying to hear. I aspire only to help people find a peaceful path to deepest liberation." He paused. "And let me say that your vision of freedom is why I hold *you* in high esteem. Without free will, there can be no path to spiritual fulfillment. The Carpenter and I agree completely on that point."

John arose to leave, but the Monk gestured for him to stay. "One last thing," he said. "Our capacity to make peace with others depends on our capacity to make peace within ourselves. Those who mind other people's business usually neglect their own. You must take some quiet time to reflect. Find solitude. Do not strain to think. Just be still. Imagine the most peaceful scene, then wisdom will emerge."

The Monk waved him away. John thanked him for his counsel as he departed. He strolled numbly past everyone who meandered by and slipped into the jungle. He walked until he came upon a secluded opening where sunlight glinted through the canopy of trees like a beam from heaven.

John sat down in the glade and closed his eyes, clearing his mind of everything. Soon he noticed two powerful sensations. The sun warmed his body in a way that seemed life-giving rather than oppressive. And the sounds of the jungle became soothing music rather than warnings that danger lay everywhere.

Images of his ranch back in Kansas flooded his mind like an old cinema film. In a kind of out-of-body experience, he observed his dreamlike self from above. His imagined body was hunched over, tending his beloved patch of white roses on their farm. Cultivating the roses was his one escape from the drudgery and hardship of their spartan lifestyle during the American Civil War. The blossoms were the spiritual symbol of the underground resistance he had abetted before his exile.

John observed his dream-self sniffing a rose. He smelled its fragrance as if the image in his mind were real. He twitched when a thorn pricked his skin and then watched an aphid crawl across a gloriously white petal. The heat of the Kansas sun felt warm on his back. The morning dew from the stem of the rose wetted his fingers. He was magically transported to a different place and time.

He felt a gentle hand on his shoulder, which was now magically healed. He turned and looked up into Mary's angelic face. Her head was haloed by the sun. Their eyes met, and his heart thumped in his chest. She was a blessed vision that he thought he'd never see again. He had stepped through a looking glass into a timeless interlude where past, present, and future were blended together.

Mary's eyes passed an unspoken message directly into his soul. It was the most unexpected message he could imagine. It wasn't quite that he was being forgiven. And it wasn't quite that he was being given permission. It was more an affirmation that love bears all things, believes all things, and endures all things.

Her message was that she was content knowing that the possibility of intimacy with a woman was not a casualty of his permanent exile to Outcast Island.

A cloud blocked the sunlight that had been glinting into the glade, casting a scudding shadow. At the same moment, Mary vanished like an apparition from an interrupted dream.

He looked around at the riotously colored jungle that was alive with ominous foreboding. Three things were clear to him now: beauty and danger were indeed opposite sides of the same coin. Beauty was always more fleeting than one hoped. And danger was never as terrifying as one feared.

26

BENITA

"**I** don't want to die!" the prisoner shouted.

The hapless man was being tortured in a secret chamber inside El Morro, the Proletariat stronghold in la Habana.

Vlad laughed at the victim, then looked over his shoulder at Leon and Benita, who were witnessing the interrogation. Leon was studying the prisoner's dehumanized agony as if observing a scientific experiment. Benita's face was contorted with hatred, at least until she saw Vlad glance in her direction out of the corner of her eye. Then she summoned a thin smile, devoid of any emotion. Her eyes took on a blankness that Vlad always mistook as rapture, especially during their most private moments.

The prisoner was a young Cubano who had been arrested by Vlad's spies. They accused him of being a rogue agent. He was officially employed by the Proletariat's secret police but was suspected of passing sensitive information to other factions on the island. He was also suspected of leading a double life as one of Cosimo's informants.

"I don't want you to die either," Vlad replied with a leer. "You pay your taxes on time, but you haven't confessed to me. We're certain you know something. Answer my questions!"

"I swear I don't know how le Clerc found out Olga Kozlowski

was going to surrender to Guzman!" the prisoner grunted through clenched teeth. His face was contorted into a grimace, and his desperate eyes begged for mercy. Sweat oozed from every pore in his body. His arms and legs shook with palsy even though they were bound with straps.

"Liar!" Vlad shouted. He signaled to the torturer to spin the large wheel that turned the gears on the rack the prisoner was manacled to. The victim's arms and legs were stretched further by the medieval contraption. A gruesome snapping sound came from one of his knees as ligaments and cartilage gave way. A scream from the depths of hell followed. A stench filled the room from his loosened bowels.

Vlad turned and winked at Benita. "Your master always knows how to get the truth. Remember that."

Benita smiled thinly again, her dark eyes expressionless. "Your skill is admirable, my hero. You torture your opponents as efficiently as you murder the truth."

The Cubano's screaming waned to a guttural moan. Vlad leered at him and said, "There's an old adage that says, 'If you put your head into a lion's mouth, it might get bitten off.' I'm the lion. If you wish to save your head, tell me who you've been passing information to."

The victim's body suddenly relaxed into a deathly stillness. Vlad signaled to the torturer to spin the heinous wheel one more time.

"Sir, he's either unconscious or dead. More torture will accomplish nothing right now."

A wave of dejection washed over Vlad's face. "I hate it when my subjects disappoint me," he grumbled. He gestured to Leon and Benita to follow him. He led them from the torture chamber into his private sanctuary.

A servant brought them rum. Benita pretended to take a sip. "Why do you need to know how le Clerc found out about Olga?" she asked.

"Cosimo visited me. He said things aren't going well. Le Clerc betrayed him by slaughtering the Jackals. The Remnant, the Maroons, and the Pathless Land renegades are forming an alliance.

Cosimo says it's up to me to take control of Outcast Island with a heavy hand. I'm the only one he trusts to get the job done. That includes finding out who's spilling secrets."

Benita raised an eyebrow. "Cosimo trusts you? I'm not sure you trust yourself."

Leon burst out laughing, despite great effort to suppress his mirth. Vlad shot his lieutenant a withering glare. "Cosimo knows I'm the only capable leader left on this island."

This time Benita laughed sharply, though it cut with a serrated edge. "Because you lost the Rock to the upstarts from Pathless Land? Because they sent you scampering home with your tail between your legs when you tried to recapture it? Because your tortures are failing to reveal who the real spies are on this island?" She smiled conspiratorially.

Vlad's shoulders slumped. He loathed himself when Benita belittled him, especially since he couldn't bring himself to punish her, and even more so because she *knew* he couldn't. He felt a rash spreading across his fleshy face as his anxiety rose. He could command the services of any whore in la Habana, but he knew deep down that it was a miracle he had the companionship of a woman as smart, confident, and beautiful as Benita. Despite his practiced haughtiness as a dictator, he endured her pointed jabs with sanguine complacence as if they were part of the normal banter between lovers, even though they were nothing of the sort. It was one of his many self-delusions.

Benita knew from Vlad's sullen silence and reddening face that her jabs had hit home. She felt no remorse. To her, he was the worst kind of bully, one who deserved no sympathy for anything. But he was in a talkative mood today, perhaps fueled by the sadistic rush from torturing the Cubano, and she wanted him to keep talking. Knowledge was power for her because of how she had secretly positioned herself in the political struggles on the island. Things were moving fast, and dire events loomed on the horizon. She needed to know more from him.

"Why do you care so much what Cosimo wants you to do?" Benita asked.

"Why ask me?" Vlad blithered, still smarting from her jabs. He struggled to hide the pout on his face. "Leon, you explain it to her."

Leon was tired of these spats between the two people who ruled his life, but his options were limited. He didn't have the same protected status as Benita, so any insolence on his part would earn dire consequences. His unquestioning loyalty was his greatest value to Vlad. He wasn't going to undermine himself now.

"It's very simple," Leon said to Benita, whom he despised and distrusted. "The Syndicate and their Centurions control the World Order. The World Order controls the fate of every leader on the planet. Cosimo is the Centurion assigned to our part of the world. Perhaps you've noticed the warships encircling our island. Thus, we do what Cosimo desires."

"What would happen if you defied him?" Benita asked. "Not that you're brave enough." She knew that Leon was in an emotional box, so she took advantage of every opportunity to torment him. She was pitiless beneath her demure façade.

Leon looked down at the floor. "Watch what Cosimo does to le Clerc in retaliation for his betrayal, then you'll understand."

"But Cosimo will do nothing to le Clerc," Benita said. "That's precisely why he's imposing on us to do something. Cosimo's job is to live in luxury, not to die in wars. That's what we're for, isn't it?"

Leon's eyes shot daggers at her. "No, that's what the proles are for. Shit travels downstream. The financiers control the leaders, and the leaders rule the proles. Vlad and I have no intention of dying in a war either."

"What if the proles rise up and kill you?" she teased.

"They won't! They don't understand their true predicament."

"Or perhaps you don't understand the true nature of humankind," Benita shot back. "Do you think men like le Clerc and Spartacus are of a nature to meekly follow orders issued by you buffoons? Perhaps you should worry less about Cosimo and more about the desperate people under your thumb who harbor an anger that will swallow you whole someday."

"Why do you say such things?" Leon demanded. "Do you know something about le Clerc and Spartacus that we don't?"

Benita's smoldering eyes were no longer blank. "I'm a daughter of this island, a tropical paradise rich in soil and once rich in ambition," Benita began, avoiding a direct answer to his question. "But I'm also the offspring of a century of socialism. I've heard the sordid tales of my ancestors, of their hunger, of their fear, of their submission. I learned about Castro and his worthless philosophy. I learned of the show trials, the executions, the confiscations of farms and homes, and the prison camps. My parents bequeathed to me an unyielding desire for freedom. This passion is shared by most Cubanos, despite their feigned acquiescence to collectivism, the greatest con in the history of the world."

Leon was shocked by the vile narrative pouring from the mouth of Vlad's favorite concubine. "Don't you understand that strength comes through social unity? To seek individual freedom is to be a selfish criminal!"

"Peace!" Vlad exclaimed. "We're on the same team!" He was anguished by the tension between his only two reliable subordinates. He was also frightened by Benita's open rebelliousness. He began to wonder how much power he really had over her. He also wondered what she was capable of.

"How can there ever be peace when you torture and kill your subjects?" Benita asked.

"I don't want to kill them!" Vlad protested. "I love my people! We can't use them for the collective good if they're dead. However, if they resist doing their duty for society, they must be tortured or eliminated so that their insubordination doesn't become contagious."

"You don't love us," Benita replied. "You only love our obedience. We Cubanos will never be fooled by that difference again. Even though I'm your lowly slut, don't mistake my passivity for acceptance."

A look of horror washed over Vlad's reddened face. The urge to kill her suddenly filled his whole being. However, he knew he could never do such a thing because he was emotionally paralyzed. He lusted after her even when she tormented him with her insolence. So he resorted to his primal instinct.

"I don't care what you or the other Cubanos think," he huffed.

"My philosophy requires a leader with absolute power to achieve the common good."

"Wielding absolute power doesn't prove you're doing good," Benita replied. "It only proves that you're violent."

Vlad lit a cigar to calm his frazzled nerves. He puffed prodigiously, filling the room with aromatic smoke. "Even though the ruling class is greatly outnumbered, it never loses. It makes the rules, writes the textbooks, and invents the history that fills their pages."

"You lust for mastery over other people rather than mastery over your own character and talents," Benita admonished. "The Cubanos on this island learned the hard way about the life cycle of your Marxism. You start by promising a collective utopia. Then you steal from the productive people. Then you force everyone to work for pittances. Then we run out of food because no one wants to work. Then you lie that the starvation wasn't because of real Marxism. Then you double down with naked totalitarianism. The only thing that stops this deadly cycle is when people grab their pitchforks and revolt."

"Shut your mouth!" Vlad shouted. Immediately, he regretted his outburst, and his eyes became wide with fear. He reached for her hand as a gesture of penitence.

She spit on it, then turned for the door. "Thy will be done," Benita snarled without looking back at him, then slammed the door behind her.

Leon saw the stunned look on his master's face and realized that he needed to bring peace to El Morro before tragedy unfolded. He followed Benita out the door and caught up with her.

"Watch your back, you fool!" Leon barked at her. "It doesn't matter how much Vlad desires you. He wants something even more alluring, and he's playing for keeps."

Benita stopped in her tracks and stuck her face inches from his. "Hold tight to your own head, you traitor to the Cubano people. I know many warriors who are itching to lop it off. And I might be first in line."

27

―――

GENIES

Six months had elapsed since Sinaloa was sacked and the Jackals were slaughtered. The pirates had long since made it to the eastern end of the island with Morgan's treasure, and Olga had long since returned to Pathless Land.

Spartacus had become a respected member of the Council of Sages. Abah, his trusted lieutenant, had become a key leader in the Pathless Land military. Spartacus had finally heeded Benita's pleadings to stop chasing le Clerc and Morgan's treasure—partly because of the windfall John had granted the Maroons after sacking Sinaloa, and partly because John himself had been persuaded by Olga to call off the chase. Neither man was fully reconciled to letting le Clerc escape though. Both had lingering doubts about the motives of their lovers.

However, the cessation of hostilities against le Clerc led to a time of relative calm for Pathless Land. The community was expanding into the jungle well beyond the protective confines of the Rock. It was growing in territory, population, and productive might. The population was buttressed by shiploads of new outcasts who were guided inland to the Rock by Maria's scouts. Exiles from prior years continued to stumble across the Rock as they wandered the desolation of Outcast Island.

The Maroons became active investors and benefactors in the new community with their windfall from Sinaloa. The silver and gold coins that they "inherited" from the Jackals served as currency to grease Pathless Land's blossoming economy.

The jungle around the Rock was divided into parcels that were homesteaded to members of the growing community. Everyone who actively occupied a granted parcel for at least a year was promised title to it. They could build a home, farm the land, manufacture goods, or provide services to the community. A robust trading culture emerged, built around cottage industries and small shops. John and Olga were now a committed couple. They used their parcel of land to build a crude home. John obsessively tended a thriving patch of white roses there.

Hammer hired and trained several apprentices in his blacksmith trade. They scavenged raw material for smelting from old Russian-made Lada coupes, hulks of ancient tractors, and scrap metals from decrepit buildings. Hammer's team forged clever tools, weapons, and other metalworks that were in high demand. His business thrived, so he was now one of the wealthiest members of the community.

More exiled mechanics, engineers, and craftsmen poured into Pathless Land. They fueled an explosion in technology and automation. The community instinctively knew that machines were vital, partly to replace the drudgery of manual labor, and partly because their efficiency afforded greater wealth, safety, and convenience for all.

An abandoned tool-making shop was discovered three miles from the Rock. A team of technicians rehabilitated its presses, lathes, and drills that had sat idle for years. The refurbished equipment was used to transform the smelted metals from Hammer's forges into complex implements. The factory was powered by a diesel engine and a generator that were scavenged from a freighter that crashed in the Bay of Death during a violent storm. Newton developed a process to thermochemically refine biomass from jungle flora into fuel for the engine.

The Carpenter's woodworkers helped the homesteaders build crude homes. Most were constructed with thatched roofs and walls made from woven wattle and sun-hardened mud. The floors were made of sand-packed pebbles set with lime. The windows were simple framed openings covered by curtains made of goat leather.

The community now had plenty of food because the homesteaders were bringing their agricultural products to market. To create farmland and pastures, they felled trees, pulled stumps, and cleared vegetation. They harnessed oxen to plow the fields with tills manufactured by Hammer's blacksmiths. They grew sugar cane, manioc, sweet potatoes, and taro. They hunted agouti, wild hogs, pheasants, and turkeys. They raised chickens for their eggs and goats for their milk, meat, and hides.

One of John's biggest concerns was providing security for their growing society. Maria's spies had learned that Vlad was preparing a massive assault in retaliation for his prior humiliations at the Rock. Since the territory of Pathless Land was expanding outward, it was impossible to fortify a permanent perimeter. Instead, Nicolai's team of electrical engineers recommissioned World Order drones that had been shot down by Mallory's marksmen. The refurbished drones were used to continuously surveille the surrounding area. The devices occasionally detected rogue bandits probing their territory. Those were easily dealt with by the Rangers.

John and the Carpenter were walking on a glorious day along a new dirt road that bisected the homesteaded lands. John's shoulder had healed, his relationship with Olga was deepening, and his spirit was vibrant in a way he never thought possible after leaving Kansas.

A bicyclist trundled down the road, causing John and the Carpenter to sidestep. There were now hundreds of such bicycles used for transportation around the Rock. The bikes were decades-old discards that were repaired by enterprising mechanics in Pathless Land.

John gave the Carpenter a friendly backslap. "I'm impressed with your mentoring of our recovering Marxist Garcia. I wouldn't have predicted he would become the coordinator of our homesteading program and an organizer of our emerging markets. You're a miracle worker!"

The Carpenter smiled with a radiance that rivaled the tropical sun. A sparrow landed on his pristine white shawl, and he reached into his pocket to offer the bird some seeds. It ate out of his hand and chirped in contentment.

"*Gracias*, Farmer John," he replied. "There was indeed a miracle involved. I had to break through Señor Garcia's conditioned belief in magical genies. Like most in the Proletariat, he assumed manna fell from the heavens or grew on Edenic trees. I had to convince him that abundance comes from individual effort and creativity."

"How did you dispel his conditioned beliefs?" John asked.

"It required a deep moral journey. It's hard to separate a person's beliefs from their formative environment," the Carpenter replied.

"Please, describe the moral journey," said John invited. "It might help me explain things to new arrivals."

"It's just common sense. The nature of our universe is that every person must expend effort to stay alive," the Carpenter explained. "We each need to breathe, drink, eat, and protect ourselves. Some people are tempted to place the burden of this constant struggle onto other people. They wish for elves and genies, usually in the form of slavery or collectivized responsibility."

"Go deeper . . ."

"The life of each person is equally sacred with all others. The most immoral act is to force others to serve your interests because it diminishes the sanctity of their lives in favor of yours. It's the greatest sin of all because it's the source of all social evil. Every person is born with a unique and irreplaceable essence, and that essence can only survive and blossom if each person is treated as a sovereign being."

"So preserving the sanctity of each person is the highest moral ideal?" John questioned.

"It's been that way forever," the Carpenter replied. "Thou shalt not steal. Thou shalt not kill. Thou shalt not covet thy neighbor's goods. Do unto others as you would have them do unto you. It's a simple moral code, but it requires free will, freedom of action, and deep respect for others."

"Those in power have always tried to subordinate the individual to the collective," John said. "Does that mean resisting their coercion is a moral act?"

"Interesting question, Farmer John. Moses disobeyed King Ramses by protesting the abuse of Hebrews. Peter disobeyed Emperor Nero, who forced his Christians to act against their consciences. My own parents disobeyed the tyrannical ruler in their land. I, too, am a rebel. I have more respect for the outcasts of society than for its Elites and would rather befriend prostitutes and drunkards than aristocrats who use their power to coerce others. If leaders are allowed to trample individual sovereignty, then all social morality is rejected. My tutoring to Señor Garcia was quite simple. You own your own life, and you're responsible for its outcomes. We're all self-directed beings."

"Doesn't that breed a selfish civilization?" John asked.

The Carpenter laughed. "What an absurd question! Is a slave selfish for wanting to be free? What could be more selfish than forcing others to take care of you? Adaptation and collaboration are the great strengths of humans, not conformity and servitude."

"Your insights are very helpful," John observed.

The Carpenter winked mischievously. "I suspect you already knew much of them, Farmer John."

John blushed. "Perhaps. But I felt a need to hear the moral clarity in your own words."

The Carpenter laughed. "Most people run from my words! The right path is often the least popular."

They heard footsteps coming up behind them. Both men turned to see Spartacus jogging to catch up.

"John!" he spat out between gasps for air. "I have troubling information."

John waited for Spartacus to catch his breath. "Well?"

Spartacus squared his shoulders. "Cosimo has instructed Vlad to take control of the entire island. Pathless Land is considered the primary enemy. During the past six months, Vlad has been building a large army. An attack is now imminent."

"Maria has reported similar concerns," John said.

"It gets worse. Cosimo told Vlad that the World Order will use its military resources to help vanquish us."

"Damn!" John exclaimed.

"There's more," Spartacus continued. "In a bizarre twist, Vlad and le Clerc have joined forces. In combination, they have the wealth of Morgan's treasure, Vlad's conscripted foot soldiers, and the military resources of the World Order."

John blanched. "How do you know things that Maria's scouts don't?"

"My source is impeccable."

"How impeccable?" John asked.

"My information comes right from Vlad's bedroom, from a person who despises him and loves this island."

"And you believe this person?"

"I would die for her. And she for me."

Dire thoughts began to whirr in John's head. "I must find Mallory immediately," he declared.

28

DEFIANCE

"**I**s your Declaratory Act wise?" Benita asked Vlad. Her question was drenched with snark, but his megalomania clouded his ability to recognize it.

They were seated in Vlad's formal chambers in El Morro where he did official business as the dictator of the Proletariat. He was perched on a pretentiously ornate chair that would be described as a throne if he wasn't the leader of a Marxist society. Benita was seated on a smaller but equally ornate chair beside him. Four grim-faced palace guards lurked in the shadows behind them. Two beautiful Cubano women fanned Vlad and Benita with palm fronds. Vlad's eyes occasionally strayed to the lovely feminine forms attending to him.

Vlad and Benita were holding court, receiving representatives from each town and village in Outcast Island. The morose officials entered single file to humbly place their tax tributes at Vlad's feet. In return, the visitors received haughty stares from Vlad and sly winks from Benita.

The representatives were making their fiscal sojourns to la Habana under duress. Vlad had recently issued a decree called the Declaratory Act. In the wake of Cosimo's orders to take control of the entire island, Vlad printed thousands of copies, which were couriered to every town, village, and outpost.

The Act was blunt and broad. It declared that Vlad had unlimited authority to decide everything for everyone in all cases whatsoever. It also declared that he was empowered to impose taxes on everyone. Lastly, it declared that every able-bodied person was "required to volunteer" for military service when summoned. The justification for the Act was that the Proletariat was facing unprecedented threats from rebels, so the proles needed protection for their own good.

"The Act is brilliant," Vlad replied to Benita as another forlorn official dropped a small bag of silver coins at his feet. "Who would follow my orders if they weren't forced to? Who would fund the upcoming war if I didn't impose these taxes? Who would fight in that war if they weren't conscripted? The proles should appreciate my efforts to protect them from harm."

Benita rolled her eyes. "You've just described the grand paradox of politics. Governments rely on force, although force is what must be governed. Even though you don't allow elections, people can still vote with their feet. There's a reason why the exiles deported to Outcast Island end up at Pathless Land rather than la Habana. It's the same reason many of your soldiers are going AWOL in the dark of night. The jungle whispers the truth to everyone."

"That's why we have to attack Pathless Land now!" Vlad replied, oblivious to the gist of her jabs. "I must act before Pathless Land gets too powerful."

"Or before you get too weak," Benita countered.

"I've got the pirates on my side!" Vlad protested. "They slaughtered the Jackals! With them as allies, how can we lose?"

"You might be surprised. Le Clerc betrayed Cosimo. He also betrayed Olga Kozlowski. Why wouldn't he betray you?" Benita eyed him coldly from head to toe as if he was nothing compared to those two.

"Le Clerc will be the one who's surprised," Vlad declared, holding his head high while cautiously casting sidelong glances at her. "I'm going to betray him after he helps me destroy Pathless

Land. Cosimo assigned me to conquer everyone on the island. That will eventually include the pirates. I'll do whatever it takes."

"That's obvious," Benita replied. "The 'able-bodied' men you're conscripting are as young as ten and as old as seventy. The 'able-bodied' women you're conscripting are being abused as sex slaves to keep the men from deserting. You're releasing hardened criminals from your jails if they promise to fight in your army. You're dispensing free rum, ganja, and coca to mollify your terrified soldiers."

"Soldiering is dangerous work," Vlad reasoned. "There must be some rewards. Sex and intoxication are two of the best."

"You indulge in those, too, even though you're not doing any soldiering," Benita sneered. "And I've noticed that your high-placed friends are somehow also exempt from soldiering."

"They've done their duty," Vlad huffed.

"How? When?"

"They bribed destitute villagers to fight in their places."

Benita laughed. "Do you think you can beat the Warriors of Pathless Land with conscripts, criminals, and mercenaries marching with guns pointed at their backs?"

Vlad launched a wad of spittle in anger. It landed on the hunched back of an official who had just placed a tribute at Vlad's feet.

"Yes, I can beat them!" Vlad declared. "Their leader is just another Don Quixote jousting at windmills. My spies tell me his lieutenants are just credulous squires like Sancho Panza. A carpenter? A monk? A runaway slave? A woman we already defeated when she first attacked the Rock?"

"Have you looked in a mirror lately, my hero?" Benita asked acerbically.

Vlad subconsciously glanced at his bulging midriff that was stretching his vest. He squelched his embarrassment by haughtily eyeballing the next unkempt representative bowing before him. The poor commoner was missing teeth, his hair was a tangled mess of graying strands, and his skin was mottled with sores and rashes. He was shoeless and dressed in patched sackcloth. Vlad's resurgent superiority inspired him to engage the wretch in paternalistic conversation.

"My good fellow, how are things in your humble village?"

The decrepit man looked up at Vlad with fear in his eyes, wondering why he was being singled out for conversation with the great leader. "It's been an average year for us," he mumbled.

"How so?" Vlad inquired.

The villager eyed him darkly. "It's worse than last year, but probably better than next year."

"Wonderful!" Vlad exclaimed, oblivious to the man's sardonic wordplay.

The man shook his bedraggled head in despair and dropped a bag of silver at Vlad's feet. He looked perpetually resigned to being stepped on and then apologizing for getting in the way. As he limped away, Vlad checked the name of his village off the list of debtors.

Benita jumped up from her ornate chair, scooped up the bag of silver, and tossed it back to the limping official.

"Here's hoping your village has a better year next year," she said. She turned to Vlad. "How can you take money from these destitute people? You're a thief with no soul!"

Vlad was surprised by her insolence, the reality of which was slowly penetrating his stubborn defense mechanisms. "My dear," he blubbered. "The most delicious privilege is to live off other people's money. Don't you appreciate our lifestyle?" He swept his arms around their luxurious receiving room. "And some of the money will even be used to help the proles. I'm a genius, not a thief!"

Benita glared at him. "A word often used before *genius* is *evil*."

Vlad glared back, then softened his expression into a tight-lipped smile. She was the only person who ever seemed to show him affection, delusional though his perception was. "Benita," he entreated, "you and I are at the pinnacle of society on this island. We're living out the two fondest dreams of all people. Our power to tax is like having a genie, and we get to tell others what to do. For the good of all, of course."

"The power to tax is the power to ruin!" Benita snarled. "Look what it's doing to these stricken creatures groveling at your feet! It also gives tyrants like you the resources to wage war!"

The destitute officials queued in Vlad's chamber froze, astonished by the vitriol exchanged between their two overlords. They were even more astonished that Benita was sympathetic to their plight. Such sympathy had never before come from the leaders who imposed themselves on everyone else.

Vlad glanced around his chamber and noted the favorable nods that Benita was getting. "Perhaps I misspoke," he announced grandly. "The only reason I need absolute authority is to ensure that we all work together to usher in an era of prosperity and peace. Someone must lead the herd!"

"Rumor has it that you're planning a war," said one of the filthy proles, emboldened by the apparent solidarity between Benita and his fellow commoners. "Is that your way to prosperity and peace?"

Vlad was speechless in the face of this plebian impudence. It reminded him of some advice from his Russian father long ago: the educated person is the easiest to con. Common people assume that every bit of propaganda from the Elites is designed to keep them in their place, so they reject it all. Educated aspirants, on the other hand, assume that they are kindred spirits with the ruling Elites whom they wish to be among, so they assume that every bit of the elitist propaganda must be true. Therefore they are more easily drawn into the illusions.

"There will indeed be war!" Vlad pronounced into the awkward stillness. "But only against those who reject my authority. One leader must command everyone! How else can things be decided? Without complete conformity, society is just a brainless mob. Plato, the greatest of all philosophers, said that individuals are just transitory accidents of history, while the state is permanent. That's why we must defeat those selfish renegades from Pathless Land! They glorify the individual at the expense of our wondrous collective!"

Benita cocked her head. "If the Dictatorship of the Proletariat is such a great thing, why is so much force required to maintain it?"

"You are as simple as you are beautiful," Vlad chided. "All power is founded on fear, especially the fear by subjects of their own leaders."

"Does that power include a license to kill enemies and opponents?"

"It must!" Vlad exclaimed. "How can it be a crime to kill those who threaten the state? It's a normal act of self-preservation for the state, which is the grand protector of the collective. The harshest punishments are reserved for acts *against* the state, not acts *by* the state. Protesting, dissidence, treason, tax evasion, counterfeiting, desertion, and assassination are the true crimes that must be exposed and punished!"

"This island has a long history of subjugation by force," Benita persisted. "It's all my ancestors have known. There must be a better way, and I intend to find it. The true strength of a society isn't founded on force, but rather on its ability to administer objective justice and to generate abundance for its citizens. There's no other reason for people to support it."

Vlad stared at Benita as if seeing her for the first time. Or perhaps he was seeing a ghost who represented all the Cubanos and slaves who had been abused by powerful people on the island over the centuries. He shivered. It suddenly dawned on his sluggish brain that Benita might not be on his side.

"Why are you so disagreeable?" Vlad asked nervously. He was visibly hurt now. For the first time, he considered the possibility that she loved someone else. But who? Le Clerc?

"You pay me for sex and obedience!" Benita shot back. "That makes me a prostitute. I'll have to live with that shame, necessary as it was. But what would I be called if I supported a society that abused me and everyone I love? I don't think there's a word that adequately describes such treachery. If there is, I refuse to wear its mantle. And some day, I'll refuse to be your whore too."

Vlad's eyes grew wide with confusion and fear. "You can't run away!" he cried. "I'll catch you and imprison you!"

Benita smiled calmly. "Sometimes the freest person is the one trapped in the prison because they no longer have to hide their seditious thoughts."

Confusion overwhelmed Vlad. "I have power over you and everyone else!" he shouted. "After I defeat Pathless Land, I'll be invincible!"

"You'll never be invincible," Benita replied quietly. "No abuser ever can be."

"Who shall take me down?"

Benita sneered insolently. Then she spun and strutted out of the chamber.

Vlad stared in horror at her departing figure and shouted, "Guards!"

29

———————

BUCCANEERS

"Ship ahoy!" Merlin squawked, who was preening on le Clerc's shoulder.

Sinbad stared distastefully at his feathered rival. "That vile bird is wrong again," the swarthy lieutenant said to le Clerc, who was savoring an aromatic cigar. "I don't see a ship out there."

The three of them were on the shoreline of la Habana harbor, staring out at the vast ocean. The sun blazed down from an azure sky. Wavelets lapped gently at their feet. The imposing bulk of El Morro castle loomed over them.

"Merlin is never wrong," le Clerc replied. He lowered his telescope, offered it to Sinbad, and pointed. "Look there."

Annoyed, Sinbad grabbed the instrument and put it to his eye. He scanned the horizon, then spied the distant silhouette of a craft. "Aye," he admitted. "There's a ship out there. What kind?"

"It's a destroyer. Part of the flotilla quarantining Outcast Island. It's flying the rag of the World Order, but it'll soon be hoisting the Jolly Roger."

"You're going to capture a modern warship?" Sinbad asked incredulously.

"I already have."

Sinbad shook his head in disbelief. His boss was a clever adventurer, but this latest fish tale was unbelievable.

Le Clerc smiled at Sinbad's confusion. "Cosimo gave me the ship when I met with him last night."

Sinbad's jaw dropped. "Cosimo gave you a destroyer? Why?"

"Because I told him that it was unnatural for pirates to be without a ship."

"We've never had a ship," Sinbad replied.

"Exactly. And now we do."

Sinbad raised his palms in exasperation. "But why would a Centurion of the Syndicate give you a ship? Every time you try to explain Cosimo's shadowy motives, my head hurts."

"It was a trade. He wants us to support Vlad's mission to conquer Outcast Island. I told him we'd help the blubbery tyrant, but I wanted a ship in return. We haggled for a while. He agreed to give me a destroyer, but only if I gave him half of Morgan's treasure in addition to supporting Vlad. We shook hands, and now we pirates own a ship. I just have to figure out how to take possession of it."

"Damn you!" Sinbad exclaimed. "You made a deal with the devil and gave away half of my share of Morgan's treasure?"

Le Clerc waved his hand dismissively. "I didn't give it away. I traded it. Now you own a share in a destroyer." He slapped Sinbad on his muscled back. "You're a real pirate now!"

"What in hell are we going to do with a destroyer?"

Le Clerc shrugged his shoulders. "Destroy things."

"Like what?"

"I promised Cosimo I would bomb the Rock. But maybe our aim won't be so good." Le Clerc turned his sly gaze toward the stony bulwarks of El Morro.

Sinbad followed where le Clerc's eyes were focused. "You're mad! You're going to bomb Vlad's headquarters?"

"Why would I do that?" le Clerc asked, his palms upraised with feigned innocence. "Vlad's now my partner in crime."

"But his crime is to take over the whole island. That will eventually put us in his gunsights."

"You're beginning to connect the dots, my slow but faithful friend."

Sinbad shook his head to dislodge some mental cobwebs. "I see some holes in your plan, sir. Are you going to swim out to that ship? And who's going to be the crew? We flatter ourselves as pirates, but none of us have ever swabbed a deck, much less piloted a destroyer. Cosimo is taking you for a fool. He's got half of Morgan's treasure while you're staring at a ship you have no way to use."

"You're right about something," le Clerc replied. "Cosimo takes advantage of people, especially when the prize is gold. That's what his kind of pirates do."

"You didn't answer my questions."

Le Clerc sighed. "We'll use my connections to get real sailors and a method to transport them to the destroyer. I'm not the fool you or Cosimo may think I am."

"Do these connections have anything to do with Olga?"

"Everything has something to do with Olga," le Clerc said. "You should know that by now."

Sinbad grunted. He couldn't tell whether Merlin or Olga was his biggest rival for le Clerc's friendship. Sometimes he wondered if he had hitched his wagon to the wrong leader.

"Last I knew she fled from your captivity to return to her new lover," Sinbad said with some rancor.

"But I let her go and gave her a gun. We'll see what she does with it."

"I could never walk in your shoes." Sinbad sighed. "How can you live every day on the edge of a knife?"

"I decided not to fear living as much as I fear dying," le Clerc replied. "We're all destined for the Grim Reaper's scythe anyway, so why worry about taking risks along the way? Great men know that there's no reward for playing it safe, but there might be great rewards for risking the gallows. Great men also threaten those who don't wish to be threatened."

"I still don't understand what use that monstrous ship is to us," Sinbad said. "We live on an island!"

Le Clerc laughed uproariously. "Wouldn't people who live on an island be the ones most desperate for a ship?"

Sinbad grunted his assent to this logic. "But where in Neptune's Sea would we go with it?"

"I've been thinking . . . Perhaps we've set our sights too low. This is a poor island. We've already found Morgan's treasure, so what more is there for us here? But legends say that there are treasures buried on all the shores around here. Haiti's only fifty miles away. Jamaica is only ninety-two miles. Key West one hundred miles. There may be conquistador gold buried under every beach. Think of the plunder that awaits us around the rim of the Caribbean if we pirates had a navy! Even Cosimo would be jealous."

Sinbad stared apprehensively at his boss, wondering if the aspiring buccaneer had finally crossed the line separating genius from madness. "But you've already sold your loyalty to Cosimo!"

"My loyalty is indeed for sale. Until it's not."

"The Remnant learned that the hard way," Sinbad mused. "At what point will your loyalty no longer be for sale?"

"When it can no longer be bought," le Clerc replied cryptically.

Sinbad glared at him. "Sometimes not even I know who you really are."

Le Clerc nodded. "I wear many masks, but they are all me."

"I don't understand that riddle," Sinbad said. "Or any of your others."

"Then I'll make it simple for you," le Clerc replied. "Continue to trust me. I haven't failed you yet, and I never will."

Sinbad fell silent for a moment. "What makes you think you can pull this naval coup off?"

"I think I'm able; therefore I am able. Some call it the Law of Intention and Desire. I call it having giant brass balls. The result is an iron will."

"An iron will to do what?" Sinbad wondered. "Find treasure? Win the heart of an elusive woman? Get yourself killed?"

"This is a time of great consequence. It will decide which people really matter: the conniving octopi in the Syndicate, the tyrannical politicians who are their puppets, or the rest of us who are their prey —at least for now."

"More riddles," Sinbad fussed. "Why pretend you're a champion of the common man if you've promised to help tyrants like Cosimo and Vlad?"

"Tyrants can be unmade just as they're made. Benjamin Disraeli said the world is governed by very different people than imagined by most. I, François le Clerc, say there's a greater power than all of those. It's the man who is fearless and independent, the man who refuses to be tread on by masters. I refuse to bend to the unholy vermin who control the world."

"Intruder!" Merlin squawked with unusual agitation.

The two men followed the bird's beady eyes. A magnificent Arabian stallion was galloping along the beach toward them bearing a rider cloaked in a black shawl and a black hood. The intruder was whipping the horse to a frothing frenzy. Le Clerc and Sinbad studied the steadily approaching figure carefully. Sinbad reached for his pistol while Le Clerc did nothing.

"Avast!" Merlin squawked in alarm when the approaching rider neared them. The mysterious figure reined the horse and pulled back the hood.

Sinbad raised his pistol. Le Clerc smiled.

30

UNDERDOGS

"He's a narcissistic piece of shit!" Jed exclaimed, handing John a copy of Vlad's Declaratory Act. "From what I hear, the bastard posted this obscene proclamation in every village."

Jed, John, Mallory, Olga, and Spartacus sat around a campfire outside the Rock, mapping out a strategy to defend Pathless Land against the anticipated attack by Vlad and his allies.

John tilted the proclamation toward the campfire for illumination. "So the tyrant is claiming unlimited authority to decide everything. And he's planning to tax everyone for that privilege." He smirked. "Which of you granted these powers to Vlad?"

A chorus of "Not I" rang out in unison.

"But our approval doesn't matter to tyrants," Spartacus added. "We Maroons never granted authority over us to anyone, but others claimed it anyway."

"Aye," John said. "That's the abridged version of human history. So the endless battle between the Elites and everyone else is about to be fought once again."

"It's ironic that you and I were exiled from a civil war in America only to fight another one here on Outcast Island," Jed observed.

"Such wars will always be fought until a fundamental question is resolved," John replied.

"What question is that?" Olga asked.

"Do individuals own themselves, or are they owned by others?"

"I know the right answer," Spartacus muttered.

"I think we all do," Mallory said. "Which explains why we're here on Outcast Island."

"John, we may know the right answer to your question, but do you have any qualms about risking the lives of our people in a fight with Vlad over it?" Jed asked.

"Come on, Jed. Only a fool thinks that good and bad are equal. Vlad is initiating violence, so that's bad. We'll be resisting it, so that's good. I'm confident our people will embrace the challenge, because the most basic instinct of all living creatures is self-defense," John avowed.

"John's right," Spartacus said. "Passivity ends in slavery. My people have been abused forever by others. We'll fight against it!"

"Even if some Maroons get killed?" Jed asked.

"I want everyone to live in peace and prosperity," Spartacus replied. "But life is a cruel jest if you live at the mercy of others. If you don't defend your life or your property, what are you? A slave! An order taker! A coward!"

"I agree," John said. "I dread violence, but self-defense is the only option when civilization is broken. I want to hear details of our intelligence about the impending attack. Olga?"

"Maria reports that Vlad's troops are being trained and mobilized south of la Habana. He's conscripting soldiers from every village. His proclamation clearly states that he intends to take over the whole island. Pathless Land is the last bastion of real resistance. Everything seems poised for an imminent attack."

"What about the rumor that le Clerc has joined forces with Vlad?" John asked pointedly.

"I wouldn't trust any rumor about le Clerc," Olga said sharply. "He's supported lots of people over the years, only to stab them in the back. If I were Vlad, I'd sleep with one eye open."

John nodded. "Spartacus?"

"I'm certain that Vlad will attack," he said. "And I'm certain the pirates will be involved."

"How can you be sure?"

Spartacus glanced sidelong at Olga. "My information is unimpeachable." The powerful man fell silent, signaling he didn't intend to reveal anything more.

"Jed, what have you learned?"

"I've been chatting with the men who deserted from the Proletariat to Pathless Land," he replied. "They all believe an attack is imminent. And they didn't want to die for Vlad."

"Mallory?"

"John, the visual evidence is indisputable. We've flown some drones toward la Habana to do forward reconnaissance. Maria is correct. Vlad is massing large forces. Their positioning makes it clear that they'll target the Rock."

"So all evidence points to an imminent battle," John concluded. "Next question: How will they attack? Mallory?"

"Vlad will try to overwhelm us with waves of raw troops. He considers his proles to be disposable. We'll be outnumbered—by a lot."

"That's concerning," John replied.

"But it's not the biggest concern," Spartacus interjected. "My informant confirms that Vlad has Cosimo's support too. We can expect naval barrages from the World Order fleet."

"The biggest question is what le Clerc intends to do," Olga said. "His men are seasoned fighters. He values their lives and he's very clever, so he'll use them strategically in ways no one would expect. That's how he slaughtered Guzman's Jackals."

"So we'll be the underdogs," John concluded. "But hard times make hard people. Mallory, what's our defensive strategy?"

"One of our advantages is that all our able-bodied people own guns that we captured in our earlier battles. They're trained to use them. Most of Vlad's soldiers are recent conscripts who have little experience with guns. Our drones will give us real-time information on troop movements to aide our maneuvers. Maria's spies have mapped out the logical route Vlad's legions will take when they march on us. We've booby-trapped it. The attackers will then have to march through a narrow gorge to approach the Rock atop Skull Ridge. Maria's archers will be positioned on both sides of the gorge, ready to skewer them with arrows. Hammer's and Newton's teams have been working around the clock preparing the Rock's cannons and making shells. My growing cadre of Army Rangers and Navy Seals will be used for special operations and emergency backup."

"Spartacus, what about your Maroons?" John asked.

"We've been spreading the word to African descendants around the island that Vlad is no different than all the other leaders who've abused our people," Spartacus replied. "Even though many of them have since been conscripted into his army, I expect them to melt into the woods when the fighting starts. They won't kill us, and we won't have to kill them."

"That's brilliant," John affirmed. "Olga, what's the Remnant planning?"

"Maria's scouts have fanned out between here and la Habana. They're equipped with radios to give us immediate intel. We also have scouts positioned in village churches to use their bells as coded signals if the radios fail." She paused as her eyes betrayed some discomfort. "John, I have another strategy in mind, but I need some resources."

"What do you need?"

Olga swallowed hard. "I need Mallory to loan me some experienced divers and men who are familiar with modern warships."

Everyone fell silent. Alarm bells rang furiously in John's head. "Is that all?" he asked acerbically.

"No," Olga replied. "I want the loaned men to be entirely under my command. They're to follow my orders without question and to keep their assignment secret. From everyone."

"That's unacceptable!" Mallory barked. "You have no formal military training! And you want me to hand over my best soldiers? Without explaining your purpose?"

John put a hand on Mallory's rigid shoulder, then addressed Olga. "Your request is almost impossible to consider." He paused, knowing that her plea came not just as a member of the Council of

Sages, but also as the woman he had come to love. "Consider how your request looks to us. What could it possibly mean? We don't even have a navy."

"Not yet," Olga said confidently. "Which leads me to my final request. I need two seaworthy skiffs. The Carpenter and his team could fabricate them from wood. They only need to survive at sea for less than a day. They must be robust enough, however, to carry thirty men each, along with their equipment. The boats must be delivered to the la Habana harbor within two days."

John's jaw dropped. "What will Pathless Land get in return for this insane and mysterious commitment of resources?"

"John, I beg you to trust me!" Olga said. "I can't explain why this must be done, but the reason will become obvious during the battle. It'll be the Bay of Pigs redux."

John shook his head in dismay. "What does a fiasco from a century ago have to do with our situation today?"

"It's an enlightening lesson. The elegant plans made by attackers can collapse into a steaming pile of shit if they're betrayed."

"Hints of betrayal don't warm my heart," John said.

Olga sighed in exasperation. "What can I do to win your trust?"

"You must trust *me*," John snapped.

"I don't understand . . ."

"You said that no one can know your plan. You must make one exception. Tell it to me and trust me to keep it secret. Then I'll trust you." John looked at Jed, Spartacus, and Mallory. "You guys okay with that?"

"Yes," Jed replied. "I'd trust you with my life, John."

"Your actions have been trustworthy so far," Spartacus added.

John turned to Mallory. The grizzled Army Ranger was clearly disgruntled. "John, I trust you a lot, but my greatest trust lies with my own men. That's the way of a warrior. I'll agree to your arrangement, but you need to know that if we loan men to Olga, they'll be instructed to kill her if she betrays us." Mallory eyed Olga coldly, who returned his malevolent glare without flinching.

John stood up. "Olga, let's take a walk."

She arose and joined him. They wandered along a dark stretch of the moat, treading carefully by starlight. As they walked, Olga shared the details of her plan and explained its risks and benefits. John stopped in his tracks a couple of times to fully absorb the audacity of it. It was wild, brilliant, and dangerous. It had the potential to trigger a stunning reversal of fortune in the upcoming battle. It also had the potential to fail spectacularly. He loved the bold roll of the dice that it entailed, but it had one element that troubled him. But because they needed bold action, he decided to tuck that one discomfort into a dark place in his heart.

The two returned to the campfire and sat down together. The three others eyed them apprehensively.

"It's settled," John declared. "I'll instruct the Carpenter to build two wooden boats. It will take a miracle for him to finish them in time, but he's worked miracles before. Jed, organize some men to rig two carts so oxen can haul the finished boats to the harbor. Maria's team will blaze a navigable route to a designated spot on the beach. Mallory, transfer the military men and equipment Olga needs for her mission to her temporary command."

Mallory studied the ground, then raised his eyes to meet John's. "Yes, sir," he said, almost inaudibly.

"John, what do you think our chances are in this battle?" Jed asked.

John stared at the fire. "I like the chances of a free people better than the chances of a coerced people. But we must be vigilant. Our enemies are capable of anything. Vlad's lust for power knows no bounds."

"Does vigilance include blind trust in Olga?" Mallory grumbled.

"It's not blind," John protested. "Her strategy is brilliant. Its only flaw is that it relies on le Clerc to keep his word."

"Which word?" Mallory challenged. "The one he gave to Vlad, or the one he somehow gave to Olga?"

"He'll keep his word!" Olga declared.

"And our lives depend on that?" Mallory scoffed.

Their conversation was interrupted by a figure on horseback who burst from the jungle and galloped toward them. A breathless woman dismounted. Spartacus jumped up in surprise.

"Benita!"

He ran to her and dwarfed her with a massive hug. They kissed as the others around the campfire stared in amazement.

"That's Vlad's whore!" Jed exclaimed, who knew of her when he was a captive of the Proletariat.

Spartacus led Benita toward the fire. "She's not Vlad's whore! She's the bravest woman on Outcast Island. I would sacrifice anything for her."

"And I would sacrifice anything for Spartacus and for Cuba," Benita said. "I've sacrificed more than you can imagine already."

"My dear, why are you here?" Spartacus asked.

"Armageddon is nearly upon us. There was nothing more for me to do in la Habana. I want to be here with you when the final battle for Outcast Island begins. And I bring important news."

The group fell deathly still.

"Well?" Spartacus prodded.

"I met with le Clerc after I fled from Vlad at El Morro," Benita revealed. "My informants told me that the pirates were watching the World Order ships from the harbor."

"What a reckless thing to do!" Spartacus exclaimed. "That man can't be trusted!"

"I had to know!" Benita shot back.

"Know what?" Spartacus asked. He was surprised that Benita knew exactly where to find le Clerc. He wondered once again who had given her that fine Arabian horse.

"If it was true that le Clerc was really going to join forces with Vlad to attack Pathless Land, because then he would be attacking you and the Maroons. I pled with him to reconsider. I poured my soul out. I described Vlad's wickedness and the moral bankruptcy of the Proletariat. I explained to him what you recently convinced me of. That the only hope for a peaceful and prosperous Cuba is the rise of Pathless Land."

"What did he say?" Olga asked apprehensively.

Benita burst into tears. "He told me that I wasted my time! So I rode here as fast as I could."

John looked pointedly at Olga. The troubling thought that he had tucked into a dark corner of his heart erupted to the surface. How did Olga know what le Clerc needed for their secret mission? He recalled the private message le Clerc had left for her at the Caves of Despair. How many more messages had there been since then? What were they about?

"I don't know who to believe anymore," John said to Olga.

31

———

ARMADA

Olga stepped onto the sand of la Habana harbor around midnight. A harvest moon loomed over the sea like a celestial jack-o'-lantern. Its amber light rippled across the waves lapping onto the beach. Olga inhaled the sea air wafting on a gentle breeze. The alien smells of brine, fish, and seaweed were more invigorating than the fetid jungle air she was accustomed to.

Maria stood beside her, nervously scanning the beach. Behind them at the edge of the jungle were sixty of Mallory's finest Seals, Marines, and ship mechanics who had been exiled from America. Behind them were two crude wooden boats laden with equipment. They were mounted on large carts that had been towed by oxen through the jungle.

"Ahoy!" Merlin squawked, startling Olga and Maria. The parrot and le Clerc emerged from the jungle a mere fifty yards from where the women stood. Le Clerc was accompanied by several dark-clad figures.

The shadowy men approached. Olga raised her pistol.

"My dear!" le Clerc exclaimed amiably. "Is that the gun I tossed you when you fled from me? It wouldn't be sporting to shoot me with it."

"This is just business, François," Olga said sharply, though she was grateful she couldn't see le Clerc's alluring eyes in the darkness. "I've brought everything you asked for."

"Show me."

Olga waved her arm, then Mallory's men emerged from the shadows. The steaming oxen were led onto the beach with the two skiffs in tow.

Le Clerc strode confidently around the gathered men and the two crude boats, inspecting them like a practiced drill sergeant. He climbed into a boat and examined its cargo in the moonlight, nodding with satisfaction at the sight of the explosives. He jumped down onto the sand and went to Olga.

"Well done. Do these men know how to operate a destroyer and plant explosives underwater?"

"Captain Mallory, Pathless Land's military leader, vouches for their capabilities," Olga replied.

"I intend to make sure," le Clerc said. "Let me introduce you to Captain Anders, the senior officer of the *USS Comrade*, my new destroyer. He'll question your men to verify their skills." A tall, uniformed man with a manicured beard stepped forward and saluted with precision.

Olga noticed that Sinbad was jabbing a gun into Captain Anders's back. "It doesn't seem the captain is here willingly," she observed.

"Of course not!" le Clerc said, laughing. "What captain worth his salt wants to surrender command of his ship to pirates? But part of my deal with Cosimo is that the ship's senior officer would be delivered to me as a personal hostage until our men could board the ship and take command. Even commissioned officers would rather be keelhauled than say no to the leaders who heel to the Syndicate. But I'm sure his eyes will bleed when he sees the Jolly Roger run up the flagpole of his ship."

"Who will command the ship if not Anders?" Olga asked.

Le Clerc bowed at the waist with great flourish. "'Tis I. And now release your men to my command so that Captain Anders can question them."

Olga hesitated. She distrusted le Clerc, but she reminded herself that transferring the men to his command was the reason for this meeting. She signaled to Sergeant Brown, who Mallory had assigned to keep a watchful eye on these proceedings. Brown barked an order. The soldiers dutifully assembled around Captain Anders, who began questioning each man with Sinbad's pistol still firmly planted in his back.

Le Clerc motioned for Olga to walk with him along the beach. She did so but looked nervously over her shoulder to make sure no ambush was in the offing. Maria trailed a few steps behind her for the same reason.

"Olga, thank you for trusting me by delivering these vital resources."

Olga scoffed. "I don't trust you at all! But I'm gambling that your interests align with Pathless Land's, despite the rumors of your alliance with Vlad."

"That's quite a gamble," le Clerc replied nonchalantly.

"What choice do I have? My goal is to protect everyone in Pathless Land. If you align with Vlad, I admit we're in deep trouble. But I'm hoping you'll keep your promise to me and that our assistance helps torpedo Vlad's battle plans. I'm willing to take the risk."

Le Clerc rubbed his chin thoughtfully. "What you didn't say is that you still love me. But in my heart, I know it to be true. I believe that's why you're doing this."

"I don't care what's in your heart anymore."

"Liar!" Merlin squawked.

Le Clerc playfully slapped Merlin's beak. "Ah, Olga Kozlowski. Always playing hard to get. I admit it's effective. If I let my unrequited feelings for you get the better of me, life seems tragic. But if I keep a cool head, life is a comedy."

"There is nothing funny about the impending tragedy on this island," Olga snapped. "You laugh about things you shouldn't. You should be fighting for liberty instead."

"I can do that and laugh at the same time. If you think deeply enough about it, liberty and joy are two sides of the same coin."

"If only you were as trustworthy as you are brilliant," Olga sighed. "But who wants a man whose loyalty is for sale?"

"Despite appearances, my loyalty has never been compromised," le Clerc replied. "Ever since I was young boy who was abandoned and tormented in Egypt, I've been inscrutably loyal to myself. And someday you'll learn that includes being loyal to everyone I care about too."

"That makes it clear where I stand with you."

"Nothing is clear to anyone but me at the moment," le Clerc replied. "And that's exactly how I wish it to be."

Olga gazed at the harvest moon that was now blurred by fog rising from the warm ocean into the cool night air. The evanescent mist swirled like a mirage. The hazy scene was the perfect backdrop for the emotional turmoil in her heart and the confusing intrigues on the island. *Indeed*, she thought, *nothing is clear.*

"Clarify at least one thing for me," Olga said. "Are you going to use these men and resources as you promised? My life depends on it."

Le Clerc shrugged. "There are spies everywhere, as you well know. Whatever I intend to do must come as a brutal surprise."

"To me too?"

"You're a smart woman," le Clerc replied. "I learned more from you than anyone else. Those men you're lending me are very smart too. How do I know? Because they were exiled here as incorrigibles. The Elites fear smart people. Not politically astute people who operate in an imagined world of wishes and myths, but rational people who prefer facts and logic. They fear engineers, craftsmen, mechanics, and technicians. They fear rebellious Army Rangers and Navy Seals. Such men are going to be rowed out to my new destroyer. Destroyers destroy things."

"I'm to be reassured by that riddle?" Olga asked.

"Our world is on a razor's edge," le Clerc replied. "Reassuring you isn't on my priority list right now."

They both fell silent. Le Clerc sensed Olga's rising anger. "Here's a hint," he conceded. "Cuban history is filled with military intrigue. For example, in 1898, the *USS Maine* was blown up in Havana harbor, killing three hundred sailors. No one really knows why or who did it, but the result changed Cuban history."

"Damn you, François!" Olga exclaimed. "Enough with the riddles! Am I going to live or die?"

Le Clerc shrugged. "We're all going to die. You're special in many ways, but not in that regard."

"You're impossible!" Olga shrieked. She spun on her heels and stomped toward the soldiers, who were now boarding the two crude boats.

Maria followed close on her heels. "You're better off with John than that bastard," Maria consoled. "When I'm around John, I feel a sense of peace. When I'm around le Clerc, it feels like the Four Horsemen of the Apocalypse are lurking just around the corner."

"I used to think that le Clerc's aura of impending danger was attractive," Olga admitted. "But I now realize how destructive it is to me and to everyone around him."

Le Clerc rushed past them as if they didn't exist and jumped over the gunwale of one of the boats. The craft creaked and rolled as waves slapped against its hull. He sidled up behind Captain Anders and stuck his pistol into the officer's back, relieving Sinbad of his guard duty. Sinbad jumped out of the boat onto the sand and hastily herded the last few soldiers aboard. He waved to Sergeant Brown, who had lingered behind.

"Come aboard!" he shouted. "We have a date with destiny!"

Sergeant Brown unshouldered his rifle and levelled it. Sinbad instinctively raised his hands, but Brown spun and aimed the rifle at Olga.

"You're coming with us!" Brown shouted to her. "Captain Mallory ordered me not to let you out of my sight, which means you can't go back to the Rock. And if this adventure goes off the rails, I'm to kill you."

Olga froze. She looked desperately at le Clerc, whose attention was caught by the sudden drama on the beach. He motioned for a fellow pirate to guard Anders, then leapt back over the gunwale to the beach.

"What's the meaning of this, Sergeant Brown?" le Clerc barked.

"My men and I have been ordered to help with your mission. We'll comply because we're good soldiers. We've also been ordered to respond to treachery with extreme prejudice. Olga is our insurance policy against your treachery or hers. No quarter will be given if we're betrayed."

Maria jumped between Sergeant Brown and Olga as a shield. "François!" Maria shouted fiercely. "If you have any love left in your heart for this woman, you'll order Sergeant Brown to stand down and let her return to the Rock with me!"

Le Clerc froze. His eyes moved back and forth between the grim visage of Sergeant Brown and the supplicating eyes of Olga.

"Maria," le Clerc said evenly. "This isn't the time for love. Olga must come with us because that's the condition set by Pathless Land's military leader for this mission to proceed. Everyone will get their just rewards in the end."

Le Clerc winked at Olga and then turned toward the boats. "To the briny deep with our armada, my fellow pirates! It's time to destroy!"

"I hate you!" Olga screamed at his turned back. "If there is a God, I hope you rot in hell!"

Le Clerc paused, then spun to face her. "I've rotted in hell already, first in Egypt and now on Outcast Island. The only lesson I've learned from all that rotting is that every decision I ever make should be based on what I desire and nothing else. I own myself, and I will never sacrifice that ownership to anyone. And I will never lay the blame for my choices at anyone else's feet, including society, history, or God."

32

WISDOM

Dark clouds loomed ominously above Skull Ridge. It felt like dusk at noon.

John was strolling through his garden of white roses, to which he had added some lavender shrubs. It was his refuge from the stress of leadership and other deep concerns.

The Carpenter and the Monk walked alongside him. John had invited them to his spiritual sanctuary because he needed their wisdom. He paused to take a luxuriant whiff of lavender.

The Carpenter smiled. "Farmer John, what does that scent remind you of?"

John blushed. "My wife, Mary. Her lavender scent was my last experience of her. Our separation still torments me. It was impossible to fully anticipate the anguish of its permanence. I'm consumed by dread wondering if her chronic pneumonia has finally taken her life. Her days must be a daunting struggle for survival. Sometimes I wonder if I made the right decision to leave Kansas."

"You can't know the future when you're choosing a fork in the road," the Carpenter said.

"But we can remember the past," John replied. "My son's girlfriend, Audrey, asked me to search for her parents one awful night when the Elites were bombing our local village. I found the bodies of both her mom and dad. They were killed shopping for scarce food. I felt a bottomless pit of sorrow when I told Audrey the horrific news. I'll never forget her soul-churning torment that night. I should have realized I would feel the same anguish when I said goodbye to Mary forever."

The Carpenter nodded solemnly and put a gentle hand on John's shoulder.

A calmness came over John, but his sadness lingered. "I also wonder how my son James is doing. Just before I was arrested by Homeland Security, he and I argued. Those angry words were our very last. I'm haunted by regret."

"He may be maturing into a man you'd be proud of," the Carpenter consoled. "I'm certain you had a positive impact on his life."

"Who can know? I hope he and Audrey marry. I often dream that they did, and that I was reunited with them and met my grand-children. Such glorious moments in my sleep! Yet such a brutal reality when I awaken. It hammers home the truth that I'll never see them again nor be able to make amends."

"*Que será, será,*" the Carpenter said. "But when a door closes, another opens. I've seen your love for Olga."

John blushed again. "Can I confess something?"

"I'm always here for you, Farmer John."

"I want to have another child. One whom I won't fail this time. One who grows up to heal others and to protect life. A doctor, maybe?"

"I can relate to that," the Carpenter replied. "I have a love affair with life. It's the most sacred thing in the universe."

John nodded. He reached for a rose blossom and gently rubbed his nose against its soft petals. The Monk sidled up to him and admired a blossom too.

"I sense these roses have profound meaning for you," he said to John. "You're growing hundreds of them in a land already resplendent with beautiful foliage."

"You're quite perceptive."

"Only because I observe with a clear mind," the Monk revealed. "Please, tell me about your infatuation with these white roses."

"They symbolize my deepest commitment," John said.

The Monk bowed subtly. "As I suspected. Deep commitments are sacred. I wish to hear about yours."

John looked at the expectant faces of the Carpenter and the Monk. "The white rose represents purity in the face of evil. I want it to become the national symbol of Pathless Land. Our soldiers are each going to wear one on their uniforms in the upcoming battle."

"How does purity help against evil?" the Carpenter asked.

"The white rose is my reminder that the only way to remain pure is to fight against evil. To not do so is to be complicit. I'm inspired by five German students who exposed the Nazi horrors to the world. While the hypnotized adults around them acquiesced to the vile ideology of National Socialism, the five teenagers bravely distributed pamphlets, calling the fascists to account for their atrocities. They risked death with their public dissent against repression and genocide. They called themselves the White Rose Society."

"What happened to them?" the Monk asked.

"They were caught and executed," John replied grimly. "Just like we might be in the next few days. But their spirit lived on. The Allies captured some of the White Rose pamphlets and dropped millions of copies from airplanes all over Germany. The resistance of a handful of brave students became one of the daggers in the hearts of the tyrants."

The Carpenter gave John a puzzled look. "Isn't the goal of life to live rather than to die? It would be strange to think an omnipotent being created life with death as its celebrated ideal."

"Of course," John replied. "But it would be equally strange to think that life exists merely to live the unlivable. The failure to stand against evil is a form of death. It's a death of the spirit, enabling the oppressors of the world to suck the vitality out of people, turning them into empty shells. Every generation that follows will inherit the same spiritual malaise. The only escape from that grim spiral is to fight evil head-on. The five students in the White Rose Society died, but we must celebrate the spirit of life they bequeathed to those they helped escape from tyranny. That's the meaning of the white rose for me. That's why I'm here on Outcast Island instead of with my family in Kansas. That's why I'm giving birth to a society called Pathless Land."

The Carpenter smiled. "Let me say it differently. You walk alone with God because He gave you your own brain and your own free will. Only your noble and righteous actions matter when He is judging you. It's not sufficient to think good thoughts and to speak high-minded words. It's not sufficient to virtue signal like the Pharisees. It's not sufficient to bask in the glory of others. It only matters what *you do*. And sometimes that requires the ultimate sacrifice."

John nodded. "And what we do must be consistent with the truth of our existence."

"*Sí*," the Carpenter said. "The greatest religion is the love of truth and kindness. Those who exemplify both are the real priests of the world."

"I believe that. Unfortunately, I might be leading the people of Pathless Land to hell on Earth in the next few days," John admitted.

"You misjudge yourself, John," the Monk interjected. "Don't make the mistake of setting utopia as your goal. Outcast Island is a mess, but it's clearly better since your arrival here. People seeking refuge now have a place to come to. They have hope."

"Thanks," John replied. "I need some reassurance, especially with vengeful armies looming on the horizon. I always appreciate the guidance from you two."

"Perhaps our advice is helpful," the Monk replied. "But don't be mesmerized by it. Too many people look to theories and dogma rather than to reality. No ideology can ever be the completely truthful one because they're all abstractions of reality, which means they're prone to human error and poor judgment. Be skeptical of them. The right ideology is the disavowal of all ideologies because tyrants use them to engineer submission. Understand reality directly, without prejudices or self-deceptions. I sense that you realize this because it's consistent with your vision of Pathless Land."

"My vision might lead to the deaths of many Pathless Landers."

"If they die, it won't be because of you," the Monk assured. "It's not your fault that asteroids hit the earth. It's not your fault that hurricanes wreak havoc. It's not your fault that diseases infect us. And it's not your fault that evil people try to harm us. It would only be your fault if you failed to fight back."

John frowned. "I understand the righteousness of resistance. But is it moral for us to risk the lives of our entire community to battle the perpetrators?"

"A moral society must punish aggression," the Carpenter explained. "To paraphrase St. Paul, it is not our intent to strike against flesh and blood, but it's sometimes necessary against the minions of darkness. Peace and freedom must be defended with sword in hand. You're a slave to as many masters as you fear to confront."

"I agree," the Monk said. "When demons try to exterminate the lovers of peace and truth, then there's only one rational and moral response. At heart I'm a pacifist, except when pacifism becomes suicidal."

The Carpenter nodded. "Well said. The lambs must fight back against the wolves. A wicked person initiates aggression. An honorable person resists it."

John studied his mentors. "That's why the motto of Pathless Land is 'Neither coerce nor be coerced.'"

"It's a great summation, Farmer John," the Carpenter replied.

"Someone's coming!" the Monk said.

The three men peered into the gloom of the rising storm.

"It's Maria!" John declared.

They rushed to meet her as she jogged toward them. "John!" she cried. "They've taken Olga!"

John's heart sank to his toes. "Who has?"

"Mallory's men. They're heading out to sea with le Clerc in the two boats."

"Why would they take her?" the Monk asked.

"They said she's a hostage in case the loan of Mallory's men turns into treachery," Maria explained.

John blanched. He recalled that Mallory threatened to kill Olga if she betrayed Pathless Land. He should have realized that Mallory would ensure her fate with brutal certainty if things went awry. His rising anger toward Mallory rivalled his fear for Olga's safety. And then another concern struck him like a sledgehammer. Olga was once again with le Clerc, involved in something that was opaque to him.

A church bell rang in the distance. Maria looked toward the sound with alarm.

"What does that signal mean?" John asked.

"Vlad has begun his attack," she said grimly.

Suddenly, a thunderous explosion erupted a short distance from the Rock, shaking the ground like an earthquake. The four of them were knocked down by the concussion.

"They're shelling us!" Maria screamed as she scrambled on hands and knees for cover.

"The bastards must be firing at us from the ships in the harbor!" John shouted. Dark thoughts about Olga and le Clerc roiled his brain.

33

――――――――――――

DESTROYER

Le Clerc craned his neck under the looming hulk of the *USS Comrade*. His two crude skiffs bobbed precariously in the heaving swells of the harbor, rubbing against the steel hull of the destroyer. He swallowed hard, experiencing an uncharacteristic moment of hesitation in the shadow of the immense ship he was about to command. He was a pirate, but he wasn't a sailor.

"Captain Anders," le Clerc said, addressing his captive standing beside him in the boat. "I was assured by a very powerful person that we won't be ambushed when we board your ship. What say you?"

"If we were going to be ambushed, your two puny boats would have been destroyed when they shoved off from the beach," Anders replied.

"Ah, but if your men had done that, they would've killed you too," Le Clerc added. "What reception awaits us on deck?"

"You'll be pleasantly surprised. That gun your man Sinbad is jabbing into my ribs is unnecessary. You're correct in assuming that most of my men are loyal to me. You're wrong in thinking that most are loyal to the World Order. No honorable man should be. I certainly am not."

Anders whistled loudly through his fingers. Within seconds, rope ladders dropped from the deck above. He grabbed hold of the netting of one.

Le Clerc put a heavy hand on Anders's shoulder. "I'm going aboard first. If I encounter any hostility on deck, Sinbad and his men will feed you to the sharks."

The pirate grabbed the netting, swung himself upward, and began climbing. The ladder dangled precariously as the ship rolled in the swells, alternately slamming his body against the hull and then swinging him out over the sea. When he neared the deck, hands reached down for him. He locked wrists with them and was hoisted aboard.

"I'm your new commander, mates!" le Clerc announced. "Former Captain Anders will join me here shortly." The assembled sailors were all brandishing weapons in an awkward silence as they studied the incongruous appearance of the brazen Arab. Some of them chuckled. Most of them scoffed.

Le Clerc ignored their disdain. They hadn't swarmed him yet, he reasoned, so either Anders had already explained that something unusual was going to happen, or they were waiting for their captain to safely arrive on deck.

"Strike the colors of the World Order!" Le Clerc barked. He tossed them a flag that he had untied from around his waist. "Run these colors up instead."

An ensign picked up the flag, studied it briefly, and then glared at le Clerc. "You want me to fly the Jolly Roger above this ship?"

"I'm a pirate," le Clerc declared. "This is a test of your loyalty. Are you with the World Order, or are you with my brave men who are about to stab the Elites in the back? Captain Anders informs me that you're honorable men, so I'm giving you the benefit of the doubt . . . for now."

His words were greeted with stony silence. The armed men confronting him had been trained their entire lives, first as civilians and then as sailors, to submit to their leaders and to follow orders. The lobes of their brains responsible for considering alternatives to the established hierarchy were in deep hibernation. They stared in zombie-like disbelief at the outlaw who was ordering them to revolt against the only authority they'd ever known.

Le Clerc felt like a Christian in the Coliseum. "I'm not asking you to desert your stations," he persisted. "There's going to be a battle one way or another. I'm asking you to consider what side you're on. You operate a ship armed with lethal weapons. If you obey your current orders, you'll murder innocent people on the island who won't understand why your bombs are falling on them. You'll be doing so at the behest of vile men who care nothing about ordinary people, including you. To them, you sailors are all mindless human triggers that they can pull with mere words from their gilded tongues for opaque reasons they'll never explain. The Darkness in the world today isn't the fault of those destitute rebels on the island you've been ordered to annihilate. It's the fault of a handful of very rich people who orchestrate everything from within the shadows. They're demons who've set the rest of humanity against each other for their own unholy gain. I'm asking you to lay down your guns, at least until we can sort out whose side each of you are on."

"And that's an order!" Captain Anders shouted, whose head had just poked above the rim of the ship. He clambered onto the deck, followed closely by Sinbad and Sergeant Brown, whose guns were aimed at him. "I heard much of what the pirate said," Anders declared. "I don't like the methods of brigands, but le Clerc's words ring true. He's about to betray some of the vilest people on earth. He's asking you to do the same, and so am I. I've spoken with most of you privately over the years about our disdain for the Elites. It's time for our resistance to come out into the open. To hell with the consequences!"

An eerie silence was broken only by the squawks of seagulls. Then a grizzled sailor saluted Captain Anders smartly and placed his weapon on the deck. This was repeated by several other sailors. Within minutes, every sailor on the deck had laid down his weapon.

"Thank you," Anders said. "I appreciate your loyalty to me, but I'm most impressed by your loyalty to your own consciences."

Le Clerc walked over to Anders and shook his hand. "Captain, I was planning to formally relieve you of your command. I realize now that would be a mistake, partly because you're a man of conscience who has earned the loyalty of your men, and partly because I don't know how to sail this ship. I'd like to discuss our next steps with you and Sergeant Brown. In the meantime, order your men to battle stations. The next twenty-four hours are going to be hellacious."

"Ensign, sound battle stations," Anders barked.

"Aye, Captain," the ensign replied. "But am I really supposed to run this flag up the mast?" He flashed the Jolly Roger to Anders.

Anders nodded. "There isn't a better message to send to the world."

Sinbad coordinated the onboarding of the remaining crew from the two skiffs. Anders, le Clerc, and Sergeant Brown headed for the control room of the ship. Suddenly, a woman's voice pierced the night air.

"François!"

The three men spun toward the shout. "Who's that?" Anders asked.

Le Clerc realized he had forgotten about Olga in the heat of the moment. "Her name is Olga Kozlowski," he explained to Anders. "She's one of the rebel leaders you were about to bombard. She's Sergeant Brown's prisoner."

Anders looked at him quizzically. "Why is she here?"

"Long story." Le Clerc sighed. "For now, it might be to our advantage to include her in our discussions. She knows the island intimately."

Le Clerc waved Olga toward them. She rushed across the deck, glared at le Clerc and Brown, and extended her hand to Captain Anders.

"Olga Kozlowski," she announced. "I'm a prisoner, just like you."

"Greetings," Anders replied. "But I'm not a prisoner anymore."

"And Olga's hostage-taking was unnecessary too," le Clerc said while glaring at Brown. "Let's finish introductions, Anders. This is Sergeant Brown. According to Olga, he's one of the military leaders of Pathless Land. Olga was instrumental in arranging the assistance of his special forces. But enough formalities. We have much to do with little time."

"To the control room," Anders said curtly.

They bounded up a flight of metal steps and entered the operations center. It was alive with computer screens, blinking lights, and humming electronic equipment. The captain waved them into an adjacent room and closed the door. The technicians in the control room snuck curious peeks through the window.

"Share your plan," Anders barked to le Clerc. "If you want cooperation, I need to know everything."

"Ditto," Sergeant Brown said.

Le Clerc eyed them calmly. "This ship was traded to me by one of the most powerful men in the world. In return, I gave him half of Morgan's fabled treasure and also committed to do his bidding for the rest of time."

"Who is this person, and what is his bidding?" Anders asked.

"His name's Cosimo. That won't mean anything to you, but if you press the question high enough in your chain of command, someone will eventually get weak at the knees at the mere mention of it. You must already suspect something like that, based on the bizarre order I presume your superiors gave you to surrender this ship to me."

"Go on," Anders grunted.

"Cosimo assigned me to help the Proletariat attack Pathless Land, a bastion of rebels on the island. He believes that I'm preparing this ship to launch cruise missiles at Pathless Land's headquarters, a fort called the Rock. He also believes that the rest of my pirates are going to march with Vlad's army in a coordinated land attack. But that's no longer the plan."

"So you intend to betray this powerful puppet master even though he gave you a destroyer?" Sergeant Brown asked. "I might learn to like you."

"I remind you that I'm a pirate. I'm loyal only to myself."

"I can vouch for that," Olga said bitterly.

Le Clerc ignored her. "Cosimo is a worthy opponent who should be feared. But a day of reckoning always comes for tyrants. Here's the new plan. We'll indeed launch some missiles at the Rock, but they'll be slightly off target. The surrounding foothills and jungle can absorb a few errant bombs. The pyrotechnics will give Vlad's forces the false impression that he's getting the promised support from the World Order ships. Then he'll have no reason to doubt the loyalty of my pirates, who are supposed to be following behind his forces."

"That's the whole plan?" Anders asked incredulously. "The other World Order ships that are quarantining the island will be aware almost immediately that something is amiss, especially if they spot the Jolly Roger flying above ours at daybreak."

"By then, that problem will be resolved," le Clerc replied. "However, I have a question for you before I share the rest of the plan."

"Go on," Anders said, leaning forward.

"How well do you know the captains and crews of the other ships in the fleet? Are any others ready to turn against the World Order if you confide that an opportunity is at hand?"

Anders rubbed his chin in contemplation. "There are seven ships in our squadron, including the *USS Comrade*. Three guided-missile destroyers, two cruisers, and two littoral combat ships. You're correct that there's a great deal of hatred for the World Order in our squadron, but it's not universal."

"Think hard, Captain," le Clerc said. "Our lives will hang in the balance based on your assessment."

Anders removed his cap and scratched his head. "I'm certain that the crews of the other two destroyers and the two littoral combat ships will switch allegiance. They've been waiting for a spark like this. The timing of your audacity is exquisite."

"And the two cruisers?"

"Their captains are loyal to the Elites," Anders replied. "I wouldn't put our lives in their hands."

Le Clerc nodded. "Then here's the rest of the plan. Within the next two hours, you will personally communicate with the captains of the friendly crews. Confirm to me that they'll join us in this revolt against the World Order. Once we have their assurance, you'll work with them and Sergeant Brown's men to plan three events. The five ships loyal to us will sink the two opposing ships while it's still dark. We'll reprogram most of our missiles to bomb Vlad's headquarters at El Morro, except for the few that will be aimed to slightly miss the

Rock. And finally, the littoral combat ships will transport Sergeant Brown's special forces to launch an amphibious assault on El Morro. They'll be joined by the rest of my pirates, who will abandon their pretense of a coordinated march on the Rock and attack El Morro instead."

Anders' jaw dropped. Sergeant Brown smiled. Olga stared intently at le Clerc.

"Why are you doing this, François?" she asked. "Betraying Cosimo will make you the most hunted man on Earth. You could've lived in luxury with Morgan's treasure the rest of your life."

"I don't aspire for luxury. I aspire for justice. It's something I've never experienced."

Olga fell silent. She wondered where she fit in his concept of justice.

"There's a big problem we must resolve before we execute your plan," Anders interrupted.

"What's your concern?"

"Most of the men on this ship despise the Elites. But a handful are still loyal to them. Even now, I suspect they're plotting against me, especially with the skull and crossbones flapping above their heads. I assume they'll try to counter our mutiny."

"Do you know who they are?" Brown asked.

"Of course," Anders replied. "A good captain always knows the sentiment of his crew. It's hard to hide anything on a crowded ship."

"Then immediately organize your most loyal sailors to round up the potential plotters and escort them to the aft of the ship," le Clerc ordered. "Disarm them. Explain nothing."

"Then what?"

"We're at war now. We must separate friend from foe," le Clerc declared. "We have no choice but to be judge and jury. We may misjudge a few innocents in the process, but thousands more innocents will die in the next few hours if we fail at our mission. It's no different than the awful decision Truman had to make before Hiroshima. Line the suspected plotters along the deck railing and give them a choice. They can stand there and be shot, or they can jump into the harbor. Give them thirty seconds to choose. Then be merciless."

Anders blanched. "It'll be tough to do that to my own crew members. Can I lock the plotters in the brig instead?"

Le Clerc smirked. "And then what? You're an outlaw like me now. There's no other system of justice to turn them over to. They'll either die in the brig someday or keelhaul you if they escape from it. It's better to be rid of them now. There's an island full of innocent people living under a black cloud of impending death, and an entire world living in the Darkness. It's time for choosing sides and taking decisive action. I'm choosing the side of justice, no matter how brutal it seems."

Anders nodded. "I understand. War is hell, but surrendering to evil is worse. I'm on the side of justice too."

"Good," le Clerc replied. "One last thing. We need to impose radio silence immediately, except for your discreet calls to kindred commanders on the other ships. No outbound communications of any sort by anyone else."

"Already done," Anders replied. "I arranged it when I learned that I was compelled to turn the ship over to you. I had no idea what to expect, so I took every precaution."

"Then let's roll," le Clerc said. "We'll meet back here in two hours. We have much to do before dawn breaks."

"François?"

Le Clerc turned toward Olga. "Were my instructions not clear?"

"Perfectly. But I want to speak with you privately."

Le Clerc hesitated, then nodded. He waved the others out of the room. Sergeant Brown, however, planted himself inside the room by the door as if standing guard.

"You're dismissed, Sergeant Brown," le Clerc ordered.

"I take my orders from Captain Mallory," Brown replied with his shoulders squared and his head held high. "I'm not to let Olga Kozlowski out of my sight."

Le Clerc shook his head. "I admire your discipline, Brown, but you're going to leave this room now. The door has a window if you insist on watching her. I'll respect your orders if you respect our privacy."

It dawned on Brown that he was adrift in a world where all ranks and hierarchies were collapsing into a calamitous flux. Nothing was going to be the same from this night forward. He gave le Clerc the barest nod and exited the room.

"My dear," le Clerc said to Olga, "you're mixed up in a swamp full of angry factions and powerful forces."

"I'm not mixed up," Olga replied stiffly. "I want to go home to be with my team during these terrible times. Order Sergeant Brown to release me."

"Home?" Le Clerc snickered. "You've found such a place on Outcast Island?"

Olga blushed. She had unconsciously selected the word *home*, but his challenge made her realize that her life with the people at the Rock emotionally fit the bill. "Laugh if you want. That's where I belong."

"I can't allow that," le Clerc replied bluntly. "My order for radio silence applies to everyone. No one can leave this ship or communicate to the outside world until our plan is executed. Our advantage of surprise is the difference between life and death in this adventure."

"So I'm *your* prisoner now?"

"No, you're still Sergeant Brown's prisoner." Le Clerc waved playfully to Brown, who was observing them dutifully through the window. "Sergeant Brown, on the other hand, is my prisoner. He just hasn't fully absorbed that reality yet."

"Why are you really doing this, François?"

"Doing what?"

"Risking death. Squandering Morgan's fortune. Alienating me. It seems like you're throwing away everything you ever valued."

"I love life. I enjoy money. I treasure you. But surely you've figured out that there's something more important to me than all those things."

"I learned that when you abandoned me at the Rock long ago," Olga replied. "I just don't know what it is."

Le Clerc looked beyond her to a distant place that existed

outside of the ship, outside of la Habana harbor, and outside of Outcast Island.

"I've learned an important lesson in life. Human nature drives us to be committed to something bigger than ourselves. Without that, we become lost in profound meaninglessness. We sink into dark labyrinths of hedonism and destructive behavior. We stand arrogantly on quicksand and then flounder in it. That inevitably leads to self-loathing."

His answer shook Olga to her core. It contradicted every hateful thing she had ever thought about him. "What are you committed to?"

"I'm committed to a young boy in Egypt who was abandoned by his parents and then abused by criminals and tyrants. In a narrow sense, that boy was me, but in the broadest sense, that young boy represents every innocent person sucked into a miserable life by the tidal forces of powerful people who use everyone else as playthings to live extravagant, omnipotent lives. My enemies are the Elites. The rest of us have always been at war with them. I'm going to win that war, no matter what." He paused. "Even if it costs me your love, which I treasure."

Olga's heart skipped a beat. "Ammon, maybe—"

"Don't call me that name!" Le Clerc arose, flung open the door, and strode past a startled Sergeant Brown. "She's all yours."

Olga was shocked by le Clerc's abrupt departure. She felt like she was sinking into spiritual quicksand and dropped her head into her hands.

She cried for François. She cried for John. She cried for a choice she would have to make.

34

———

TRAP

"That one was close!" John shouted to Mallory above the din of battle.

A missile had just exploded near their foxhole. Clumps of dirt and debris rained down like a hailstorm. Their ears rang from the thunderous blast.

"You should be sheltered in the Rock," Mallory yelled back. "Not out here on the front lines. You're our leader!"

"That's exactly where a leader should be when his people are under fire."

Mallory nodded. It was the same reason he was at the vanguard of his troops. "Something's odd, John."

"Sure is. Every missile has missed the Rock. Most of them landed around our perimeter. Some landed on Vlad's front lines. The World Order guidance systems can't be that bad, can they?"

Before Mallory could reply, John's walkie-talkie buzzed. He pressed a button. "John here."

"Maria here. Got an update from our scout monitoring la Habana harbor. It's truly bizarre. Two major warships are on fire. Vlad's headquarters have been hit by missiles. Two World Order landing crafts ferried armed men to the shore near El Morro. Most are Sergeant Brown's. A few of them look like pirates."

Mallory overheard Maria's briefing. "That aligns with an odd report I got from one of my sentries," he told John. "There are scads of Proletariat soldiers marching our way, but none of le Clerc's pirates who were rumored to be marching with them." He paused. "Maybe Olga wasn't the turncoat that I feared."

"You misjudged badly taking her hostage," John said. "It was a huge breach of trust."

"I was wrong, John," Mallory replied brusquely. "I apologize."

"John!" Maria's voice blared over the radio. "Olga was spotted in one of the landing crafts with the pirates. It looks like she's involved in the attack on El Morro. Maybe Vlad doesn't have the World Order support he thought."

Church bells clanged in the distance. "Another signal!" Mallory barked. "The enemy is approaching our trap at the gorge. Time to attack!"

"Gotta go!" John snapped into his radio. Mallory leapt out of the foxhole and waved his arm to mobilize the soldiers behind them, then he sprinted toward the enemy. John followed close on his heels. He wasn't a warrior by nature, but the unavoidable moment was upon them. Some of their men might be maimed, captured, or killed. He was afraid for them and for himself. *Courage isn't the lack of fear, it's the ability to act in the face of fear*, he silently repeated. If he could manage that, then perhaps the frightened souls following him would be inspired.

Their assignment in the battle plan was simple. They had to funnel Vlad's onrushing troops into the gorge leading up Skull Ridge so they could be ambushed. John and Mallory's battalion would attack from one flank while Jed and Abah's battalion would attack from the other. This would leave Vlad's soldiers no option but to head directly into the trap.

Pathless Land soldiers poured out of their foxholes behind their leaders. Many of them were local Cubanos who had been drawn by word of mouth to the prospering community blossoming around the

Rock. John was surprised when they began bellowing a boisterous song in Spanish.

"What are they singing?" he asked one of Maria's scouts.

"'La Bayamesa.' It was Cuba's old national anthem. We Cubanos are a proud people who are exhausted by perpetual oppression and privation. We're finally getting a chance to strike a blow against our overlords."

When they neared the Proletariat soldiers, Mallory's men crouched into a firing line. On his signal, they launched a fusillade at their plodding adversaries. The thunderclaps of exploding ordnance were followed by a wave of unholy screaming as the bullets found their marks. Bodies dropped to the ground beneath a wafting mist of blood and gore. Those who survived the volley fled in panic. Some went toward the gorge, some went toward the rear of their army, and some went directly toward John and Mallory's unit.

"Hold your fire!" John shouted. He saw that the survivors running toward them were waving white rags of surrender.

"Are you nuts?" Mallory challenged. "It could be a ruse!"

"They're Cubanos. They've dropped their weapons. They must have heard their national anthem being sung by our Cubanos. I'm sure they don't want to die fighting for Vlad. They're not our enemies!"

Mallory glared at him but turned and shouted, "Stand down! Apprehend the POWs, search them, and put them under guard at our rear."

John eyed with sorrow the motley assortment of Cubano POWs who filed past him. The recent conscripts were dressed in crude uniforms scavenged from ragged remnants. Some of them hobbled on shoeless feet that had been lacerated during their hard march. They wore homemade body armor that offered little more than psychological protection. Some were emaciated from hunger and yellowed from disease.

John's sorrow deepened as his battalion marched through the killing field where their deadly volley had slaughtered scores of enemy soldiers. Some of the bloodied corpses had died with rifles in their hands, but most were armed with machetes, spears, and spiked clubs. Their predicament had been hopeless from the start, but that was nothing new. The dead were of all ages, laying bare Vlad's desperation to conscript anyone with a pulse.

John's dismay rose at the insanity of it all. His loathing of power politics hadn't prepared him for witnessing the barbarous carnage that follows naturally from it. Somehow, a small cadre of world leaders repeatedly convinced the masses to slaughter each other. They used a witch's brew of mythology and coercion to intoxicate the proles, derange their souls, kindle hatred in their hearts, and then propel them into a litany of cataclysmic conflicts. Millions of victims paid the ultimate price on behalf of apex predators who were enraptured by power, hedonism, and narcissism.

Mallory interrupted John's morose reverie. "Our side of the pincer movement has done well," he said. "Vlad's surviving soldiers are headed up the gorge. I hope Jed and Abah had similar success on the opposite flank."

"Should we be concerned about Vlad's troops who are fleeing from the battle?"

"No," Mallory replied. "It looked like most of them were Maroons. Spartacus predicted that they would take advantage of the first opportunity to abandon the army that conscripted them."

They were interrupted by the roar of cannons that belched fire and smoke from the ramparts of the Rock atop Skull Ridge. "That's Hammer's makeshift artillery squad," Mallory said. "What's left of Vlad's forces will almost certainly get obliterated in the gorge. If any survive Hammer's barrages, they'll run straight into the Remnant's archers. And if any survive that gauntlet, my special forces are waiting in reserve at the Rock to finish them off."

John's radio crackled to life again. "John here," he snapped, then listened briefly to a panicked voice on the other end. His face turned ashen.

"What's wrong?" Mallory asked.

"Everything," John said darkly. "We underestimated Vlad. He split his forces in two. Most of his untrained conscripts went up the gorge toward the Rock, like we expected. The rest turned to attack the other half of our pincer movement. They were Vlad's Palace

Guard, his best trained and most loyal troops. Our guys suffered massive casualties during the surprise assault. Jed and others were taken prisoner."

"Shit!" Mallory exclaimed. "I didn't expect that."

"No time for second-guessing," John said. "We need to move fast. Give me ten of your best men. Then radio your reserves at the Rock. It's time to bring them into the fight."

"What are you thinking?"

"I'll race with a small squad toward Jed's last known position to try to disrupt things. Your special forces will hustle from the Rock to back me up. Our men here will continue pushing Vlad's conscripts up the gorge. We can't let them escape our ambush."

Mallory nodded. "Not bad. Other than you may be on a suicide mission."

"I have no choice. Jed and I have been through desperate times together for decades. He's my last connection to my former life in Kansas. He embodies everyone I loved there. If he dies, that part of me dies. I refuse to let that happen. I'm going to rescue him."

"That's a big risk for just one prisoner," Mallory said.

"If we wish to live in a world filled with love rather than indifference, we must treat our loved ones as irreplaceable."

Mallory held John's gaze for a moment. Then he ordered Lieutenant Gonzalez to gather his best men. In seconds, Gonzalez and his grizzled soldiers were huddled around John, who explained the life-or-death urgency of their dangerous mission. The men kept their steely gazes without flinching. There was silent, palpable trust in his leadership and respect for his courage.

"Let's go!" John shouted.

The men double-timed toward Jed's last known position. It was a brutal trek. The jungle was a tangle of vines, the footing was treacherous, and occasional gunfire forced them to duck and cover. The slow progress agonized John, but he knew they were at the limits of their physical endurance. Sweat soaked his uniform. Blood oozed from scrapes and cuts. His ankles throbbed from the jolting terrain. He gasped for breath in the humidity. His throat ached for water. His heart pounded furiously.

After sliding down a muddy ravine and fording a shallow river, they came to a small clearing in the hilly jungle. This was where Jed was to have herded the Proletariat into the gorge. John could see that the encounter had turned to disaster. There was visceral evidence of a major gunfight. Corpses from both factions littered the clearing. The surrounding flora was charred from grenade and mortar explosions. The ground was pocked with smoking craters, and blood stained the earth.

John heard one of the Pathless Land casualties moan. He rushed over to the fallen soldier, knelt beside him, and dribbled water from his canteen onto the young man's lips. He noticed the crumpled white rose that was pinned to the lad's uniform. John's heart jolted. He forgot for a moment his dangerous mission as he stared directly into his greatest fear: people were sacrificing their lives in vain at his behest. But before that unlivable thought could devour his soul, the young soldier spoke.

"I'm sorry," the lad said in a hoarse whisper.

"No one is sorrier than I," John said as his eyes welled with tears. "Where are you wounded?"

"I can't feel my legs. Maybe I'm just hallucinating. Or maybe I'm already dead."

John dribbled more water on his lips. "We'll get you out of here. Hang on." He waved a frantic signal to two of his soldiers who were checking other bodies for signs of life. "What happened?" he asked the young man.

"We were supposed to surprise them. They surprised us instead." The youth paused, summoning some strength. "They captured some of our men. I played dead. I heard them say they were headed for the Caves of Despair. I'm really scared. . ."

"Shh. Rest now. You've been incredibly helpful. You're a hero." John sensed the shadow of his two companions hovering over him. "These men will get you to safety. What's your name, son? I'm going to hang a medal on your chest when this is over."

"Julio Cruz."

John nodded his thanks. "Godspeed, Julio."

John arose and gave instructions to the two deputed medics. Then he gathered the remaining men in his squad and unfolded a topographical map. "We're going to hightail it to the Caves of Despair on the other side of Skull Ridge. We've got some climbing to do. I don't know how far ahead of us the Palace Guards are, so we must be prepared for a firefight at any moment. I know you guys are tired. I am too. But I have a hunch that we're tracking some high-value targets. Wherever the Palace Guards are, the palace leaders are likely to be too."

The men started scrambling up the rocky incline of Skull Ridge. John radioed Mallory to tell him that their targets were heading toward the Caves of Despair. He instructed him to redirect his special forces there as fast as possible.

It took thirty minutes to reach the summit of Skull Ridge. Oddly, John had noticed a few discarded white roses along the way. He also saw several bodies that had succumbed to wounds inflicted during the earlier battle. This evidence gave him confidence about Julio's account that Jed's captors were heading toward the Caves of Despair.

John scanned the opposite slope of the ridge. It was apparent that a large group of marchers had shuttled down the slope toward the caves. Bushes were trampled, the ground was disturbed, and pieces of gear had been discarded to lighten loads. Something else caught John's eye though. Another white rose was slightly obscured by a thicket of ferns. It suddenly dawned on him that the captives were leaving breadcrumbs for their rescuers.

"Do you see anyone?" Lieutenant Gonzalez asked.

John shook his head. "Vlad's Palace Guards are likely the best of his best. It would be a mistake to expect sloppiness. It's possible that they can see us, but we can't see them. It's also possible that the riffraff they sent up the gorge to be ambushed were just part of a bigger ruse. Sacrificial animals, so to speak. Maybe we're the ones being led into a trap."

"Hmm," Gonzalez mused. "You just ordered Mallory to pull his special forces away from the Rock and come here instead . . ."

John turned ashen again for the second time today. "Damn! I

may have screwed things up by recklessly trying to save Jed and his mates."

"What's that noise?" Gonzalez asked abruptly. Both men swung their heads to their left. Some small rocks had just tumbled down the slope, dislodged by someone or something.

"Everybody down!" John shouted. Before his men could react, gunfire erupted. John watched in horror as several of his men dropped awkwardly to the ground, screaming in agony. The horrific sight lasted only a split second in his mind's eye as three bullets tore through his body. He collapsed into a heap, and everything went dark and silent.

35

EL MORRO

Le Clerc studied the imposing walls of El Morro as his landing craft cleaved through the breakers near the shore of la Habana harbor. The anxiety of his fellow boatmates was palpable now that the fortress loomed high above them.

Le Clerc swung his head back toward the sea, wondering if the planned bombardment from the *USS Comrade* had been delayed somehow. As if on cue, missiles flamed through the night sky and slammed into the fort. The explosions lit up the night like a holiday fireworks encore. Debris rained down, pelting the sea like hailstones. When the smoke from the blasts cleared, le Clerc admired the handiwork of the missiles, several of which had gashed a gaping hole in the twenty-five-foot-high exterior wall. He could see fires erupting inside the fort.

The timing was perfect. The two landing crafts plowed into the sandy beach. Their front ramparts dropped heavily to dry land. Camouflaged soldiers poured out from the bowels of the boats and dropped to their stomachs on the beach in firing positions, but no gunfire came from the fort. The disoriented defenders apparently weren't expecting an assault from the sea, and they were likely overwhelmed by sudden casualties and fires.

Le Clerc heard massive explosions come from the sea. He turned his head and saw the two cruisers on fire. One was in its death throe, listing to port and slowly settling into the black depths of the sea. The other was shuddering from internal explosions as its ammunition stores detonated.

Captain Anders had masterminded a two-pronged attack on the cruisers that were still loyal to the World Order. A barrage of missiles was fired at such close range by the renegade ships that the loyalists had no hope of countering them. The other prong was a series of explosives that were planted by Mallory's Seals under the waterlines of the two ships. Their detonations were timed to coincide with the blasts from the missiles. The two cruisers would never see another sunrise.

Le Clerc refocused on their amphibious assault. Since there was no gunfire coming from El Morro, he stood with Sergeant Brown and Olga. Orange light from the flames inside El Morro flickered across their grease-painted faces.

"What are we waiting for?" Le Clerc turned and began sprinting toward El Morro. Olga sprinted after him.

Sergeant Brown shouted to his men, "Battle's on, men! Follow me!" He and his invading brigade tore across the sand.

They zigzagged and kept low profiles to avoid potential gunfire, then arrived breathlessly at the large boulders that formed the base of the wall. They climbed the rocks to a massive pile of demolished masonry. Still no gunfire.

Le Clerc led a tortuous scramble over the jagged chunks of fractured masonry. He was the first to breach the hole in the wall. Peeking inside, he saw a scene straight out of hell. Fires raged everywhere. Black smoke billowed upward like a luminous cloud rising above an erupting volcano. A fine mixture of masonry dust and fire ash was settling over everything like a macabre snowfall. The smell of sulfur lingered in the air.

He waited for Sergeant Brown and Olga to catch up with him. "Let's split into three teams. Brown, take half of your special forces and clear Vlad's headquarters. If he's there, try to take him alive. Olga, take the rest of Brown's men and sweep the castle's perimeter.

Kill anyone who resists. I'll take Sinbad and my few pirates to break open the front entrance to the castle. That will make it easier when the rest of my men arrive from their fake attack at the Rock. Then my team will inspect the interior structures. Let's meet at the front gate in one hour to debrief."

Olga and Brown nodded. The three leaders organized their groups. When all were ready, le Clerc gave a signal. The teams poured through the giant hole in the castle's wall.

Le Clerc and his small band sprinted across the smoke-filled interior to the front gate. There were three elderly soldiers manning the entrance. One spied the advancing pirates and levelled his rifle, but he was cut down before he could pull the trigger. The other two men dropped their weapons, raised their arms, and fell to their knees.

Le Clerc put a pistol to the head of one of the cowering soldiers and said, "If you two want to survive, open the gates now!"

Both soldiers got the message and leapt to their feet. They lifted the heavy crossbeam that secured the entrance doors, unlocked the chains that were a secondary security measure, and winched the doors open. They looked back toward le Clerc with terrible fear in their eyes, believing that they were doomed despite complying with his orders.

"Run!" le Clerc shouted. "You're just pawns in an unholy chess match. Get lost in the jungle. Never come back."

The soldiers turned and ran from the castle like scared rabbits. Le Clerc pivoted toward the interior. He and his crew navigated by the surreal twilight cast by burning buildings. They were surprised by the stark absence of people. The small plazas in the fort were deserted. A few shadowy figures fled like rats toward the opened gate, but no one interfered with their escape.

Le Clerc spied a small group huddled in an alleyway away from the fires. They were hiding in one of many labyrinthic passages that snaked throughout the smoke-filled castle. The frightened people shrunk back into the shadows as le Clerc approached them. He saw in the gloom that there were three women and four children.

The alley was as dank and dismal as a dungeon. It smelled of garbage, dead rodents, and fetid water. Le Clerc studied the seven huddled proles. They had hollowed eyes, missing teeth, and sallow skin. Their skeletal bodies were clothed in tattered rags. The women appeared prematurely aged. Their eyes spoke of horrors that no human should abide. One of them coughed with the rasping sound of impending death. A malnourished child sobbed in fear.

Le Clerc was overcome with pity. He had long known that most of the ills of civilization were caused by a conspiracy of its self-enriching leaders. It was clear to him that the moneyed aristocracy was always going to beggar the common man. But seeing the physical manifestation of that in the form of these seven huddled victims stabbed his soul. He recalled his youth as a starving orphan in the dangerous alleys of Cairo. His circumstance then was no different than that of the seven tragic skeletons staring in fear at him now. His life had come full circle, which made its meaning startlingly clear.

"What can I do for you?" le Clerc asked them in a soft voice.

"Please, don't kill us!" a women begged pitifully.

"That might be the most merciful thing I could do," le Clerc replied gently. "But it would be the same as killing myself. Life is going to change on this island. Continue to hide here. In a few hours, I'll return to help you. I know that you don't believe anyone right now, but I beg you to believe just one thing. It's always darkest before the dawn. And I am the dawn."

There was no response. Terror was permanently etched on their faces. Le Clerc smiled anyway and then left to resume his inspection of the castle's interior. He explored the maze of ramshackle buildings, directing his team to examine the inside of each one they passed. They were all abandoned.

Then they came across a prison filled with prisoners who were near death. The suffocating air in their cells was worsened by smoke from the fires. They were skeletal from starvation and had only bare boards to sleep on. Their latrine was a channel cut into the stone floor that didn't run to a drain. Sawdust was strewn across the floor like cat litter. Most of the prisoners were too sickly to notice the newly arrived strangers. A few eyed le Clerc and his pirates as if they were loathsome apparitions from another dimension.

"What should we do with these vermin?" Sinbad asked.

Le Clerc thought for a moment. "If Vlad imprisoned them, they probably didn't deserve it. Break the locks on their cages. They may not all be physically able to flee, but let them know they're free to go. Their chances are better out in the jungle than in here."

Sinbad nodded and signaled to his men to begin the jailbreak. Le Clerc saw a prison guard crumpled on a chair in a corner who appeared to be in a deep slumber despite the missile blasts and the subsequent commotion. When le Clerc approached him, it was clear from the man's stench and the empty rum bottle on the floor that he was in a drunken stupor. Le Clerc kicked the chair out from under him. The drunkard fell hard and came to his senses in a sputtering fury, then sprang to his feet.

"Who the hell are you?" he asked with a ferocious scowl on his face. But when he saw le Clerc's gun aimed at his heart, his expression changed abruptly.

"I'm your worst nightmare," le Clerc replied. "If you want to live to get drunk another day, answer my questions."

The man nodded dumbly.

"Where is everybody?" le Clerc asked. "El Morro is nearly abandoned."

"Gone. The soldiers went to fight Pathless Land. Most of the peasants slipped into the jungle."

"Why are these men in prison?" le Clerc asked.

"Vlad says they're our enemy."

"Why are they near death?"

The drunkard didn't respond, but le Clerc could see in his guilty, frightened eyes the horrible confession that would have poured forth if he had spoken.

Le Clerc glanced back toward the cells where Sinbad and his crew were breaking the locks on the barred doors. He called his lieutenant.

Sinbad hustled to his side. "Sir!"

"Shackle this man to the bars of a cell. Tell the prisoners they can do with him as they wish. His fate will be in their hands."

Le Clerc studied the situation as Sinbad and his men finished their assignments. A few of the prisoners had enough strength to flee toward the jungle. The others lolled indolently, trying to fathom from within their delirium the meaning of this strange turn of events. The shackled prison guard, seeing the gradual stirring of the prisoners whom he had tormented for years, was filled with a rising terror that cut through his drunkenness. His future, short though it would be, was now brutally apparent to him. He began ranting incoherently.

Le Clerc and his band left the prison to finish reconnoitering the castle's interior. The rest of the buildings had been abandoned. Le Clerc ordered his men back to the prison to help the exodus of the freed prisoners. He headed toward the gate of El Morro because nearly an hour had elapsed.

He met Sergeant Brown and Olga there at the appointed time and began the debriefing. "There was one enemy casualty during the opening of the gate. Some people have fled the castle. We didn't find many others when we searched the interior buildings. Most of the remaining folks are unable to flee into the jungle. We opened all the jail cells in the prison. The prisoners are in rough shape and are not a threat to us. The weaker ones will probably get a visit from the Grim Reaper soon. Olga, what did you find around the perimeter?"

"Pretty much the same thing," she replied. "A few stragglers were on the ramparts pretending to defend El Morro, but they surrendered immediately when we accosted them. They were old and decrepit. It looks like the able-bodied men were marched off to fight at the Rock."

"Sergeant Brown, what did you find at Vlad's headquarters?"

"A ghost town," Brown replied. "There was an old clerk pretending to shuffle papers even as the castle burned. He said that Vlad left with his elite Palace Guards to fight at the Rock."

"This is bizarre," Olga said. "Why would Vlad abandon El Morro?"

"I can think of two reasons," le Clerc replied. "The first is that my ruse worked beyond my expectations. Vlad thought he had nothing to fear from the World Order ships in the harbor, so he didn't expect an assault from the sea. He also had assurances from

Cosimo that my pirates would march with his troops to assault the Rock. Since the Jackals were slaughtered weeks ago, there would be no other threat left in the area. He was recklessly overconfident."

"And the other reason?" Sergeant Brown asked.

"Something more ominous. While our cleverness may have gotten us the upper hand here at El Morro, perhaps Vlad is getting the upper hand at the Rock with his own cleverness. He's putting all his chips on the table by joining the battle personally with his Palace Guard. I fear a trap of some kind. He was probably going to double-cross my pirates during the battle for the Rock."

Their conversation was interrupted by a feminine shout that came from the edge of the jungle near the gate. The three spun their heads to see Benita galloping toward them on her lathered stallion.

"Olga!" Benita exclaimed breathlessly when she reached them. "Maria said I would find you here. The Council of Sages—what's left of them—sent me to bring you a message because I have the fastest horse. It's bad news."

Olga turned ashen. Perhaps le Clerc was right about a trap. "What is it?"

"Vlad split his forces in two," Benita explained as her chest heaved. "One half went up the gorge on Skull Ridge as we hoped. They're being slaughtered."

"What's the bad news?" Sergeant Brown asked impatiently.

"Vlad's Palace Guards surprised Jed's soldiers who were planning to trap them in a pincer movement. They slaughtered most of Jed's team and took him captive."

"That's terrible!" Olga cried. *The poor man was eternally fated to be a captive*, she thought.

"It gets worse," Benita said darkly. "John led a small squad to try to rescue Jed."

"And?" Olga asked, almost in a whisper.

"They were ambushed too. Mallory's special forces found John's companions dead near the top of Skull Ridge."

Olga's body became rigid, and her eyes widened with fear. "And John?"

"Missing."

36

———————

EXTORTION

John was curled in bed next to Mary. He stroked her bare leg while she slept in angelic peace. The sensual joy of her skin against his was electric. He reveled in the gentle, rhythmic heaving of her chest and the blessed whisper of her breath and inhaled the scent of her homemade lavender perfume. He nuzzled her neck, then kissed it again and again with greater urgency. If this was heaven, he was glad to be dead.

A sharp grating sound disturbed his reverie. He raised his head and listened carefully. It must have come from James in another room of their ranch in Kansas. He heard it again, this time louder and nearer. Dreamily, he became aware that his wrists were heavy and aching. Something was terribly wrong. He shot up in bed.

He awoke in an alien world of darkness and agony. His head hammered. The skin on his wrists and ankles burned from abrasion. Jolts of pain shot through his torso. His tongue was dry from thirst. He was desperately weak, more so than after being shot by Guzman months ago. His gut cramped from injury and a nauseating hunger.

He fought through his delirium to recall what happened and remembered standing on the summit of Skull Ridge, scanning the valley below for signs of the enemy. Then he remembered hearing gunfire. A last flash of memory scudded across his brain, an image of a companion's head exploding in crimson gore. And then his memory went blank.

He must have been shot.

But where was he? Hell? He scanned the gloom for clues. Dim candlelight flickered against angular outcroppings of rock. He was lying on a cold slab of stone. He rotated his head painfully to view his surroundings. There were candlelit walls of rock on all sides. The air was dank and stale like in a dungeon. *I must be in a cave*, he thought. *One of the Caves of Despair? But how did I get here?*

He tested his body. His arms and legs were pinioned by iron fetters that were chained to the rock wall behind him. He must have been transported here unconscious. One thing was now clear. He was a prisoner.

His shirt was saturated with blood, and he felt searing pain in his chest. His breath came in short, stinging gasps. He moaned, but little more than a rasping rattle came from his lungs. One or both must have been pierced by a bullet.

He heard footsteps scraping against the rocky ground outside. Someone was coming closer. He noticed an opening in the rock walls through which he could see the stars of the night sky. Then a husky silhouette loomed in the entrance.

"You're awake," the silhouette spoke in an authoritative voice that had an effeminate nuance.

John tried to speak, but his tongue was crusty, his lips were parched, and his lungs failed to deliver enough breath. A grunt was all he could muster.

The silhouette moved toward him. John watched warily in the flickering candlelight. "Try this," the stranger said. He pulled a flask from his pocket and gently tipped it into John's mouth. "It's rum mixed with honey."

The sweet liquid soothed John's parched mouth. He swished it around and then swallowed slowly. He felt a slight boost in energy. "Who are you?" he croaked.

The stranger bowed slightly. "Vladimir Lenin Sokolov, the leader of the Proletariat." He paused for effect. "And I know you to be John

Paine, the leader of Pathless Land. You can call me Vlad. I will call you Prisoner."

John heard the scratching of a match. Vlad lit a small oil lantern that he set on the stone floor of the cave, then lit a cigar. As he puffed it to a glow, his pallid face seemed to float bodiless in the gloom.

"How do you know who I am?" John croaked.

"*Comandante* Garcia identified you before I shot him."

John tried to shake the cobwebs out of his head. He recalled that Garcia had been assigned to Jed's team in the pincer strategy. He must have been captured along with Jed.

"Why did you shoot him?" John asked.

"I never forgave him for losing the Rock to you rebels. You'd have been proud of him at the end. With my gun to his head, I offered him a reprieve if he renounced his allegiance to Pathless land. He refused. He said that you and someone named the Carpenter had opened his eyes. Then he insulted me. So I pulled the trigger."

"Why not kill me too?" John asked in a rough voice.

Vlad drew heavily on his cigar. John fought back the urge to retch from the noxious cloud he exhaled. "I'll get to my reason for not killing you," Vlad said. "But first, tell me what happened with my Benita."

John's memory went blank for a moment, then he recalled that Benita was the beautiful woman who had fled El Morro and expressed her love for Spartacus.

"I'll tell you," John replied haltingly. "But first I need to know if a man named Jed is still alive. I was trying to rescue him."

"You're a shrewd negotiator, Prisoner. The man Garcia identified as Jed is still alive. Garcia told me you and Jed are best friends." He paused. "I may have a role for Jed as a courier. Now tell me what happened with Benita."

"She followed her heart."

"To whom?" Vlad asked morosely.

"Spartacus."

"I see." Vlad drew heavily on his cigar again. John saw a malevolent leer on his face. Benita's betrayal clearly agitated him. John wondered how long it would be before the vile man jabbed the lit end of the cigar into his defenseless skin as retribution.

"She's happy now," John said. "And no longer your concern."

"Ah, but she *is* my concern," Vlad countered. "Everyone is my concern. Isn't that what our two factions are fighting about?"

John was surprised by Vlad's insight. "Yes," he grunted. "I believe we each own ourselves." He paused to catch his breath. "But men like you want to own others too. Hence eons of political violence."

"Ah, but I do own you! And you're on the losing side of that violence, Prisoner." Surprisingly, he offered John another sip of honeyed rum.

"Maybe we're both on the losing side," John replied. He felt his pain ease and his strength grow as the honeyed rum took effect. "A hidden force in this world has set everyone against each other."

Vlad grunted a laugh. "Is that so? For what purpose?"

"So we don't all fight the real enemy."

"Who's that?" Vlad asked.

"The Syndicate," John grunted. "You should fear Cosimo. Everyone should."

"He's my ally," Vlad replied haughtily. "He ordered the World Order to support my attack on the Rock and bribed le Clerc to join me in the battle."

"Did any missiles hit the Rock? Why did le Clerc's men disappear? Maybe I'm not the only prisoner in this cave."

Vlad fell silent. The expression on his face changed.

"You're a fool," Vlad finally muttered, "because you're rebelling against all of history."

John smirked. "While not making a whore of my soul."

"Are you suggesting I am?"

"The price for power over others *is* your soul."

"You're a hypocrite!" Vlad exclaimed. "Aren't you selling your soul by leading the people of Pathless Land to fight against me?"

"We're defending against violence," John replied. "You're initiating it."

Vlad snorted. "I remind you I have the power of life and death over you here."

"That's my point," John replied. "But despite your power, you're just a pawn too. Some other villain holds your life in his hands."

"What the hell are you talking about?" Vlad sputtered.

"Why was the Syndicate so eager to help you attack the Rock?"

"Because they support my socialism!" Vlad replied.

"And you called me a fool!" John chided. "Your power is an illusion. You're a useful idiot because you're so willing to sell your soul. Cosimo embraces you only because your political philosophy serves his purposes."

John coughed brutally and spat out a gob of bloody phlegm. Vlad offered him another swig of honeyed rum.

"You're wrong," Vlad replied. "I'm more than a useful idiot. The ruler must rule so that the weak can be protected. The warriors must fight so that the ruler can rule. The proles must obey, or else there will be chaos. It has always been thus. That's the nature of man and society!"

"That's the greatest lie in human history. Rulers use their power to serve themselves and their secretive masters. The warriors all die. The proles are always beasts of burden," John declared.

Vlad tossed his cigar to the stone floor of the cave, then dropped his head into his hands. "It's maddening," he mumbled through his manicured fingers. "A couple of days ago my power and prestige were secure. But now . . ."

"But now . . . ?" John prodded.

Vlad threw his arms up in frustration. "Benita left me. My soldiers are deserting. And I lied to you about support from the World Order. I just received a terrifying message from one of my couriers. I've been betrayed. The World Order ships are fighting each other in the harbor, and some are on fire. Missiles struck El Morro. Le Clerc's men aren't supporting my attack on Pathless Land; they're ransacking my headquarters. Now I'm holed up in the Caves of Despair."

John was stunned by Vlad's revelations. He pondered the implications of le Clerc's deceit against Vlad and the Syndicate. He wondered what desperate move Vlad would make next.

"Maybe the Syndicate is removing you from their chessboard," John speculated.

"I don't believe that!" Vlad's shout echoed eerily in the cave. "Why would they abandon me at this pivotal moment?"

The question clouded John's own efforts to understand what was happening. Up until today, he feared that the World Order would be a decisive wild card in the battle between the Proletariat and Pathless Land. Now it seemed that le Clerc was the wild card, with the aid of Olga and the resources she borrowed from Mallory. But why? Maybe le Clerc had always been the wild card. He had betrayed the Remnant, captured Morgan's treasure, slaughtered the Jackals, and bamboozled Vlad and Cosimo. Now he was in command of El Morro and had Olga in his grasp.

And then John remembered something even more puzzling.

"Why haven't you killed me?" he asked Vlad, repeating a question that went unanswered earlier. Oddly, Vlad hadn't tortured him. He had even comforted him with rum.

"Because I have only two options left now that El Morro has fallen. One of which is to take back the Rock and set up my headquarters there."

"You'll never take the Rock!" John boasted. "You've already failed once. Pathless Land has only gotten stronger. The Proletariat has gotten weaker. Your allies have abandoned you. And our Rangers are headed here."

"None of that matters now," Vlad said.

John looked at him quizzically.

"You haven't figured it out yet?" Vlad asked. "As my prisoner, you're a valuable bargaining chip. You're worth nothing to me dead but everything alive."

"What if others don't consider me a bargaining chip?" John countered.

"That's where your friend Jed's role as a courier comes in. He'll deliver my ransom demand to Pathless land. Your life in exchange for the Rock. If he can't convince them to make that trade to save his best friend, then I'll kill you and resort to my last option."

"Which is?"

Vlad unleashed an unholy grin. "Using a couple of devilish artifacts the Soviet Union stashed in these caves almost a hundred years ago to hide them from Kennedy and the old United Nations. Not even Cosimo knows about them. My scientists have moved the missiles and their warheads to a lab where they've made them operational again. The threat of nukes will terrify everyone on this island into submitting to my demands."

37

RESCUE

"Olga, you must come with me now!" Benita begged. "Mallory summoned the Council of Sages to an emergency meeting at the Rock." The two women were standing beside le Clerc and Sergeant Brown amid the smoldering ruins of El Morro. Benita's plea followed her news that Jed and John had been ambushed near the Caves of Despair, resulting in Jed's capture and John's disappearance.

Olga turned to le Clerc. "I'm going!"

Le Clerc looked at her with surprise. He recalled that she was a prisoner of sorts by orders of Captain Mallory. "You can't go!"

She shot him a withering glare. "You have no right to decide that for me!"

Le Clerc gave her a gentlemanly nod. "So noted. However, it was Sergeant Brown who declared you to be his prisoner. His orders from Mallory were to never let you out of his sight."

"And Mallory has summoned me back to the Rock," Olga said, then turned her attention to Sergeant Brown. "John's in trouble. I'm going to move heaven and earth to help him."

Sergeant Brown nodded his approval. Le Clerc's heart sank. He had deluded himself into believing that Olga would choose to be with him while the future of Outcast Island was decided. He chastised himself for his weakness and lack of focus. He was on a sacred personal mission that didn't require her involvement.

"Very well," he said to Olga. "Go to him. He jousts with windmills while I slay dragons."

A virulent anger rose inside Olga, but she measured her words carefully. "Come with me to help him, Dragon Slayer. He may not be an audacious pirate like you, but he has a vision for the future of this island—and for the future of the world."

"I have a vision too," le Clerc replied. His breathing was labored from his own rising anger and his lips were pursed. "I'm now in command of what will be the new capital of Outcast Island. John is missing in action and perhaps already dead. But you have chosen. Besides, I have an important mission here that includes attending to some destitute women and children whom I promised to help."

Le Clerc bowed slightly and then turned his back to her. He began shouting orders at Sinbad as if Olga, Benita, and Sergeant Brown had evaporated from his world.

"Follow me," Benita said urgently. Olga took one last fleeting look at le Clerc, then turned and ran behind her through the gate of El Morro.

The two women mounted Benita's horse. After a hair-raising jaunt through the jungle, they arrived at the Rock. They found the Council already assembled in John's eerily vacated office. Mallory, Spartacus, the Carpenter, Maria, and the Monk were all wearing white roses and somber looks on their faces. To Olga's surprise, she saw that Jed was there too.

"Jed, I heard you were captured," Olga said.

"It's good to see you too," Jed replied with a touch of acid. "Vlad's using me as a courier to deliver an ultimatum to Pathless Land."

"I-I don't understand . . ." Olga stammered.

Mallory jumped in. "This is late-breaking information. Jed arrived here with shocking news after Benita left to summon you. John is being held hostage as a bargaining chip by Vlad. He's been wounded by gunshots."

The color washed out of Olga's face. "How bad is he hurt?"

"We don't know," Mallory replied. "But time is of the essence. There are seventeen hours left in the deadline Vlad imposed for our response to his demands. We have decisions to make."

"What's he demanding?"

"He wants to trade John for the Rock," Jed replied. "He intends to make it his new headquarters because he's lost El Morro. As part of his proposal, we must evacuate the Rock and move somewhere else. If we don't, John will be killed, and then he'll threaten us with something even more terrifying."

"We can't let him kill John!" Olga exclaimed.

"Of course not," Mallory affirmed. "We've all agreed on that. But we're also unwilling to surrender the Rock."

"We could trade the Rock for El Morro," Olga offered. "Le Clerc has captured Vlad's headquarters with the help of Sergeant Brown's men and some missiles from the World Order ships. Vlad can move into the Rock, and we can move into El Morro."

The group paused to ponder Olga's proposal. Mallory broke the tense silence. "Absolutely not! We've fought too hard for the Rock. It's not in my character to surrender a position we can clearly defend. And I don't trust le Clerc to play along. I'm sure Vlad wouldn't either, since le Clerc betrayed him."

Olga threw her arms up. "Then what the hell are we going to do?"

The room fell deathly still. Finally, the Carpenter spoke. "Let me take Farmer John's place as a hostage."

They stared at him in confusion. "How does that solve our problem?"

"After I take his place, you'll refuse to negotiate any further with Vlad," the Carpenter replied softly. "Pathless Land gets John back and keeps the Rock too."

"That's a suicide mission!" Maria exclaimed.

The Carpenter looked at her with a peaceful expression. In his white robe and shawl, he looked like a shepherd tending his flock rather than a besieged rebel in a corrupt land. "Maybe they'll kill me. But there's no greater love than laying down your life for that of a friend. Farmer John is a beacon of hope for the peace on

Earth that I fervently desire. I'm willing to sacrifice my life to support his vision. A world with Vlad, the World Order, and the Syndicate in charge is not one that I can condone. The meek would never inherit such a world because they'd always be human chattel."

Mallory shook his head. "There must be a better solution. Vlad will murder you when he realizes he's been double-crossed."

The Carpenter smiled serenely. "*Sí*. I'm likely to be executed. But my sacrifice is intended to save the rest of you. Each of you is sacred and worthy of salvation."

"I've been Vlad's prisoner a couple of times," Jed interjected. "His henchmen are ruthless. He's also not a fool. Who are you to him? Why would he accept you as a substitute for John as a hostage?"

The Carpenter looked at him with sad eyes. "I can no longer participate in the deceptions of this world. If Vlad doesn't consider me a worthy substitute for John, then so be it. He must drink from his cup, and I must drink from mine."

"I admire your courage," Mallory said. "But Vlad won't buy it."

"Captain Mallory, I have the perfect solution," Benita interjected.

A flash of hope jolted Olga's heart. It dawned on her that Benita knew Vlad better than anyone else. "What is it?" Olga pleaded.

"I'm Vlad's Achilles' heel," Benita replied. "His desperate love for me makes him irrational. He would do anything to get me back."

"What are you saying?" Spartacus asked. A look of concern spread over his usually stoic face.

"I'll join the Carpenter to take John's place in Vlad's captivity," Benita replied. "It'll be a two-for-one trade."

"I won't allow it!" Spartacus shouted, spittle flying from his lips. "You can't go back to that vile man!"

"I love you more than anything," Benita soothed. "But my life belongs to me, so I'll take my own risks. I escaped from Vlad once in El Morro. I'm sure I can escape his clutches in the Caves of Despair. I refuse to let him extort us. My ancestors were abused for centuries on this island. I want the next generation of Cubanos to live in a world that promises freedom and peace. I wish that for *our* children, if we're so fortunate. Therefore this is what I must do."

Spartacus fell silent, but his agony remained etched on his face. Benita's determination to risk everything to save those she cared about was one reason he loved her. But the game she was about to play had colossal stakes, including a gamble with her own life. The giant man was filled with anxiety, but he acquiesced.

Mallory jumped in. "There's a spark of brilliance in your plan, Benita. But how confident are you that Vlad will agree to such a deal? Jed already pointed out that Vlad won't consider the Carpenter a worthy exchange for John."

"Perhaps that's true," Benita replied. "But a chance to get me back will cloud Vlad's judgment. To seal the deal, we must convince him that the Carpenter is a vital part of Pathless Land's leadership team. Maybe we portray him as the spiritual leader of our society, the only one who can hold it together. Vlad may be so enthralled by the chance to have me again that he'll willingly believe the Carpenter is irreplaceable."

"There's some truth to your view of the Carpenter," Olga interjected. "John told me many times that the wisdom of both the Carpenter and the Monk have kept him from spiraling into a dark place."

"There's another reason Vlad might fall for this," Jed said. "If the trade of a hostage for the Rock falls through, I've heard that he has a terrifying fallback plan. It's so terrifying for everyone that he probably doesn't want our negotiations to collapse and leave that as his only option."

"Any specifics?" Mallory asked.

"Not many. When I was a captive in the Caves of Despair, my drunken guards shared more information than they should have, probably because they thought I was about to be executed."

"What did you hear?"

"They said that the Proletariat found two Soviet nukes hidden in the Caves of Despair years ago. The weapons were taken to a secret place where Vlad's scientists have been working to make them operational again. They said Vlad's fallback plan is to use the old North

Korean tactic of threatening to blow everybody up unless his demands are met."

"Holy shit!" Mallory exclaimed. "Any clue about where the nukes are now?"

Jed hung his head. "No."

"I have an idea where they might be," Benita said. "Vlad slipped away from El Morro many times to visit his 'lab.' It was in a town called Bauta between here and la Habana. I didn't know why he visited so often. I guessed he was keeping another woman there. But maybe there's a real lab and that's where the nukes are."

"That's not a lot to go on," Olga said. "But we're out of time and options. Mallory, here's my idea. Take Pathless Land's best commandos and technicians and head immediately to Bauta. Be prepared to either destroy the nukes or blow the lab to smithereens. But wait until you hear from me that the trade for John has been successfully executed before you act. We don't want Vlad to realize his plan B no longer exists—if it exists at all."

"Agreed," Mallory said. "But we still have a loose end to our plan. Vlad will wonder why we're bothering to trade one high-value prisoner for another. It weakens our argument that the Carpenter is important to us."

"Here's a thought," Jed said. "John is wounded and perhaps dying. Let's argue that we need to get him to our clinic at the Rock immediately. We can't wait for the time it will take to evacuate all our people and equipment out of the Rock. Vlad will realize that if John dies before a trade for the Rock is consummated, he loses all his leverage. A dead hostage is a worthless hostage. The Carpenter has the advantage of being healthy. It's a win-win. We save John's life, and Vlad still has a high-value hostage, plus Benita."

"Not bad," Mallory said. "Benita, will it work?"

"I think so. As soon as he sees me in person, his perspective will be blurred anyway."

Mallory looked at Jed. "Vlad picked you as the go-between for this trade. Are you up for going back and selling our proposal?"

Jed nodded somberly. "I'll do anything for John."

"Good man," Mallory said. "I think we have a plan. Everyone agree?"

Everyone nodded except the Monk. Mallory eyed him with concern. "You've been silent during this discussion. What's on your mind?"

The Monk's eyes welled with tears. "I've learned to love the Carpenter as a kindred spirit. We come from different worlds, but his perspectives and mine align, and both of ours align with John's. Individual salvation requires individual responsibility, which requires individual freedom. Those who teach such truths to others are the true heroes of the world. I cry for him because I don't want him to sacrifice his life. But it's his choice, so I must accept it. I'm not obliged to encourage it though."

"But do you agree with our plan?" Mallory persisted.

The Monk looked at him with reddened eyes. "John has convinced me that the sun never shined on a cause greater than Pathless Land's. We must all do what we can to achieve it. I support the plan."

Mallory nodded. "Then let's go. Jed, head to the Caves of Despair and deliver our answer to Vlad. You must go alone. Wave a white flag when you arrive so you're not seen as a threat before you can even start negotiating."

"Got it," Jed replied.

Mallory put his hand on the Carpenter's shoulder. "Your sacrifice is generous beyond measure. If you wish to change your mind, this is your last chance."

"I've finished my work here," the Carpenter replied. "As an Outcast, Farmer John was the rough stone that the elitist builders rejected. But with our help, he will become the cornerstone of the future. Therefore I must save him. And now I must go pray."

Mallory studied him carefully. "Because your sacrifice is God's will?"

"God does not will our actions," the Carpenter replied. "He judges them. We are each endowed with free will. It's up to us to act."

38

———————

GALLANTRY

"**D**anger!" Merlin squawked.

The screech from the irascible bird caught Sinbad's attention. He turned his head and saw le Clerc entering El Morro with Merlin riding haughtily on his shoulder. Le Clerc sidled up to Sinbad, looking more troubled than Sinbad had ever seen him.

"You all right, boss? You disappeared for hours while the rest of us were getting this castle back into shape. Not that I'm complaining," Sinbad added adroitly.

"Slacker!" Merlin squawked, staring with beady eyes at Sinbad.

Le Clerc playfully slapped Merlin's beak and said, "Behave!" then directed his words to Sinbad. "I took a stroll on the beach to clear my head."

Sinbad glared at Merlin with clenched fists. "Sir, how has that awful creature survived all the dangers you've faced in your life?"

"I suppose he wonders the same thing about me," le Clerc mused.

Sinbad shook his head in frustration. "Did you clear your head?"

"Not completely. But taking action is the best medicine for the soul. Gather your bravest men and round up some horses. We're going on an excursion."

Sinbad looked at him agape. "Sir, you told us that the most important thing right now is to transform El Morro into our base of operations. We've just started! And now you want us to go on a lark somewhere?"

"During my sojourn on the beach, I learned that El Morro isn't the most important thing to me right now."

Sinbad threw up his arms. "We just hijacked a navy and captured an enemy castle. What could be more important than solidifying our hold on those?"

"We're going to the Caves of Despair to free the leader of Pathless Land, and then we're going to kill Vlad, his captor."

"Sir, you've lost your mind. How does that reckless plan help us?"

"It doesn't. It helps Olga."

Sinbad rolled his eyes. "You want to risk our men to impress your woman? How many times has she jilted you? She left you after you abandoned the Remnant when they attacked the Rock. She left you after you rescued her from the Jackals. And she left you yesterday when she heard that John was missing in action. Do you enjoy rejection?"

Le Clerc glared at him. "No! That's exactly the point. It's not in my character to give up. The most chivalrous thing I can do now is to rescue the man she professes to love. Perhaps then she will see that my love for her is sincere and selfless, and that my skill and daring are unequaled on this island."

"Danger!" Merlin squawked again.

Despite Sinbad's distaste for the hateful bird, he had to agree with Merlin in this case. His boss was risking everything to win the fleeting affection of an exquisite though mercurial woman. That mistake had befouled many an adventurer.

"Love is fickle, boss. It can never be counted on, unlike gold coins and bottles of rum."

Le Clerc shook his head. "Two hours ago, I would've agreed with you. But sometimes, in the harrowing stillness of being alone, you encounter something surprising deep within your soul, something so different about yourself that you become reborn as a new person.

Just because gold coins can be counted doesn't mean they're all that counts, and just because love is immeasurable doesn't mean it's worthless."

"This is a rare moment when that stupid bird seems smarter than you," Sinbad replied. "But you're the boss, and my loyalty is unflinching." His left eye developed a tic as he spoke. "I'll keep a skeleton crew at El Morro to continue our rebuilding. I'm sure Sergeant Brown's men will gladly help our best pirates rescue John. Our expeditionary force will be ready to go in one hour."

"Perfect," le Clerc said. "That gives me one hour to figure out what the hell we're going to do when we get to the Caves of Despair."

Their ride to Skull Ridge revealed gut-wrenching evidence of the battles that had been fought between Pathless Land and the Proletariat. Most of the carcasses were the ill-trained and unwilling misfits whom Vlad had conscripted. Their lives were brutally swept away by tidal forces beyond their ken, whereas the deserters who had slipped like ghosts into the anonymous jungle were still alive somewhere.

When they neared the summit of Skull Ridge, le Clerc and Sinbad dismounted and crept uphill on their bellies until they could see the Caves of Despair in the distance.

Le Clerc put his telescope to his eye. "It's pretty clear which caves Vlad and John are in," he observed. "Each have a squadron positioned outside to stand guard. Which way is the wind blowing?"

Sinbad raised a wetted finger to the wind. "Exactly the direction we hoped. And it's even gustier than we expected. Maybe a hurricane is bearing down on us."

Le Clerc examined the grasses, brush, and small trees that lined the face of Skull Ridge. They were bending in the rising wind. "It hasn't rained for a while here. Everything is dry, like tinder."

"Do you think our tactic will work?" Sinbad wondered.

"I dread the alternative," le Clerc replied. "Attacking an enemy who's hiding in caves is usually suicidal. You got the matches?"

"Check."

"And the kerosene?"

"We collected every drop from El Morro."

"Tell our men to stay low and out of sight," le Clerc instructed. "We need Vlad's soldiers to think the fire is a natural disaster. With luck, he'll assume it was caused by lightning strikes from the looming storm. Split your men into two groups and have them ready to advance on our signal. You lead one group; I'll lead the other. Memorize the locations of the two guarded caves. Finding them in the smoke and chaos will be a matter of life and death when all hell breaks loose."

"Will do," Sinbad replied. "We gotta move fast once the fire starts. This grass and brush will burn out quickly. We'll have a very tight window to pull this off."

Le Clerc and Sinbad crawled back to where their men were waiting just below the crest of the ridge and unpacked the jarred Molotov cocktails they had stashed in the saddlebags of their horses. They distributed them to ten strong-armed men who then crept to the top of the ridge. On le Clerc's signal, they lit their cocktails and heaved them down the opposite flank.

They heard glass breaking at the same moment they saw orange flames leap skyward. There were deep harrumphs from flash ignitions of the exploding cocktails, then a wave of heat washed over them. The wind whipped the flames and smoke toward Vlad's forces guarding the caves below.

Le Clerc and Sinbad crawled to the top of the ridge and peered down. The effect of their wind-aided arson was astonishing. The wildfire spread rapidly, consuming the dry tinder in a frightful rush. Le Clerc looked through his telescope. The soldiers below had spotted the advancing flames and were running helter-skelter in confusion.

Le Clerc nodded to Sinbad with a satisfied grin. Even Vlad's elite Palace Guards were unprepared for such an emergency. Their undisciplined reaction was exactly what he hoped for.

They studied the rate at which the flames were dying out behind the advancing wall of fire. When the flames nearest them had burned out, leaving ash and charred tinder in their wake, le Clerc said, "It's time."

Sinbad turned and waved a frantic signal to the mounted troops behind them. The men had already formed the two squads they had been assigned. Sinbad and le Clerc leapt onto their horses and assumed the lead positions of their squads.

"Let's go!" Sinbad shouted.

The horses crested the ridge and poured down the other side. Their thundering hooves made a resounding din, but it was lost in the crackling roar of the wildfire spreading down the mountainside. The smoke from the fire hid the attacking riders from the eyes of the scattering enemies. It was a moving blind that le Clerc's men could advance behind until they were near their targets.

The horsemen slowed their advance to match the pace at which the flames ahead of them were dying out. They could feel the heat rising from the smoldering embers on the ground. Some of the horses skittered nervously as they pranced through the ashes and the tendrils of lingering smoke.

Le Clerc realized with some foreboding that the moving wall of fire and smoke now blinded both sides in the incipient battle. The defenders couldn't see the attackers bearing down on them, and the attackers could no longer see the defenders through the opaque cloud. But hesitation was out of the question. Their opportunity for a successful mission was limited to the narrow window of blind panic when the wildfire swept past the two critical cave entrances. He and Sinbad had to trust their memories of the locations of the caves. His anxiety rose with each additional minute that the smoke obscured his view.

He knew, however, that they were getting close to their targets. They had already passed three of the four landmarks he had memorized. Suddenly, a strong gust of wind blew a gap in the rolling wall of smoke. The fourth marker materialized. They were less than a hundred yards away from the first cave entrance with no sign of enemy resistance.

Le Clerc caught Sinbad's eye and nodded. Both men signaled a halt to their squads. Everyone dismounted so they could cover the remaining distance on foot. Sinbad's team sprinted ahead first. They had the most dangerous assignment, which was to dash past the first cave to the second cave as quickly as possible. That would draw the attention of any defenders at the first cave. When they got to the second cave, they would eliminate its guards and then search the interior.

After giving Sinbad's crew enough time to sprint ahead, Le Clerc's squad began sprinting toward the entrance of the first cave. Le Clerc cringed when he heard gunfire on the other side of the wall of smoke. Sinbad must have encountered some resistance at the second cave, he reasoned. But there was no time to check. If John was in the first cave, his team had to get there before the defenders could recover from the surprise of Sinbad's sprint. Le Clerc was also concerned that John might die of asphyxiation if smoke was pouring into his cave.

Le Clerc's squad arrived at the entrance to the first cave. He saw three dead enemies splayed on the ground, casualties of Sinbad's gun-blazing rush past it. He heard more gunfire in the opaque distance, then he saw movement just inside the cave entrance.

He instinctively rolled to the ground and fired his pistol. Enemy bullets whizzed above his tumbling body. Answering gunshots erupted from the pirates behind him. He peered through the haze from his prone position. There were now two more dead soldiers on the ground by the cave entrance. But how many more were inside?

There was at least one. A soldier stumbled out of the cave, coughing violently from smoke inhalation. He fired his gun indiscriminately to cover his escape, taking a few hopeless steps before a fusillade of bullets shredded his torso.

It was now obvious to le Clerc that the cave was filled with deadly smoke. It was now or never. He arose and began a reckless sprint toward the entrance. His fellow pirates sprinted close on his heels, and he dashed headlong into the cave.

The sudden transition into smoky darkness blinded him momentarily. A shot rang out. A staggering blow to his left shoulder spun him around. He fell to the floor of the cave, writhing in pain. Shots came from behind him, aimed at where the muzzle flash of his assailant was seen. A scream born of mortal agony echoed hauntingly in the cavern, followed by the thud of an unseen body crumpling to the ground.

Le Clerc fought though his pain and shock and rose to his knees. He was lifted to his feet from behind by unseen hands. He heard a horrific fit of coughing nearby, followed by a wheezing death rattle. As his eyes adjusted to the dimness of the cave, he saw the blurred orange glow of tallow candles mounted on the walls. Their faint light outlined the silhouette of a man lying on a slab just ahead. Le Clerc heard the rattle of chains, then a low, raspy voice that seemed on its way to a grave.

"Who's there?" the dying silhouette rasped.

"John, is that you?" le Clerc asked. His shoulder screamed with pain, and he wondered if he would soon be facing the Grim Reaper too.

"Who's asking?"

"François le Clerc." His words carried a touch of arrogance that belied the grim circumstances and transcended his pain.

There was silence. Le Clerc wondered if the man had heard him or if he had simply died.

Finally, some more brutal coughing. The silhouette croaked, "I'm John. If you're here to kill me, you'll have to stand in line."

"I'm here to save you," le Clerc answered.

Silence, then more coughing. "Why?"

Le Clerc felt his knees wobble from the trauma of his own injury. The pirates behind him steadied him. "We have two things in common," he replied. "We're injured. And we both have a passion that consumes us."

"Your passion is gold," John corrected. "There's none here."

"Gold *was* my passion," le Clerc admitted. "Now I desire something priceless. I'm certain you understand."

There was a longer, deathly silence. "I see. You've come to claim Olga?"

"She can't be claimed," le Clerc replied. "Her affection can only be earned."

"If you save me, it'll put her in a terrible predicament," John said.

"Life itself is a terrible predicament, from birth to death. There's no alternative but to do what one must and then hope for the best. I must save you. If I kill you, my intended gallantry will instead be villainy."

"Then bring me back to the Rock," John moaned through his spiraling delirium. "We have doctors there. I see you're bleeding too."

Le Clerc turned to the two men steadying him. "We must go now! Free John however you can. Shoot through his chains if necessary. Then carry him to my horse. Everything depends on keeping him alive."

The pirates carefully ported John to le Clerc's horse. He was now unconscious, so they gently draped his body across the mount. They tied him to the saddle to secure him, a task made easier by the manacles still on his wrists and ankles. Le Clerc mounted a horse occupied by a fellow pirate and wrapped his good arm around his mate. His wounded arm hung bleeding and limp. John's horse was roped to the one le Clerc was riding.

As they rode, the jolt of each stride sent lightning bolts of pain through le Clerc's torso. They travelled through the smoldering ashes of the dying wildfire as they climbed the slope leading to the summit of Skull Ridge. When they crested it, le Clerc's riding mate reined their horse to a sudden halt. "What the hell?" his mate exclaimed.

Le Clerc, surprised by the sudden stop, peered around the broad shoulder of his companion. "What the hell?" he echoed. Riding toward them at full gallop up the opposite slope of Skull Ridge was a lone horseman. The mysterious stranger appeared to be unarmed. He, too, reined suddenly after spying the pirates.

Everyone froze in place. Then le Clerc heard a ruckus below them on the slope they had just climbed. He cried out in pain as he twisted around to see what was happening. "What the hell?" he exclaimed again.

Hundreds of Vlad's Palace Guard were kicking up a grey cloud of ash as they galloped toward the rear of the pirates. Le Clerc's heart sank to his toes. What had happened to Sinbad at the second cave? He recalled hearing shots. Was his beloved lieutenant lying dead somewhere? With terrible foreboding, it dawned on him that they might have blundered into a trap.

Two nightmarish questions raced through his head. Was his gallantry all for naught? And who was the mysterious rider coming from the other direction?

The malevolent forces on the island seemed darker than ever.

39

SUMMIT

The stranger galloped toward le Clerc's forces, waving a white flag. He reined his horse as he drew near. Le Clerc told his riding companion to dismount, then he shimmied forward in the saddle, grabbed the reins with his good arm, and cantered over to the stranger.

"Who are you?" le Clerc demanded.

"Jed Starnes."

Le Clerc was stunned. Jed Starnes was the man who had stolen the map to Morgan's treasure from him, although he looked like he had aged twenty years since then. But this was not the time to settle old grievances. "What insanity leads you to the Caves of Despair?"

"I'm going to meet with Vlad to negotiate the release of Pathless Land's leader, John Paine," Jed replied.

Le Clerc laughed. "Vlad is thundering toward us as we speak." Then he gestured toward the horse trailing his. "John Paine is the inert body draped over that saddle."

"Dear God!" The color washed out of Jed's face. The bloody body was indeed wearing John's familiar clothes. He dismounted and went to him. "Is he dead?"

"Nearly," le Clerc replied.

"John's your prisoner now?" Jed asked, confused by the deepening mysteries atop Skull Ridge.

"He's not a prisoner."

Jed looked askance at le Clerc as he felt for John's pulse. "What did you offer Vlad in exchange for him?"

"Pirates don't negotiate. We snatched him from Vlad." Le Clerc pointed to the onrushing Proletariat forces who were now within a hundred yards. "I might have pissed them off."

Jed's mind raced. The plan Pathless Land had concocted was already in shambles. John was comatose and near death. Le Clerc had hijacked him for unknown reasons. Vlad was bearing down on them in a murderous mood. Jed quickly estimated that Vlad's forces outnumbered le Clerc's by at least five to one. If there was to be a battle, Jed and John were on the wrong side of the match.

Jed ignored le Clerc's inquiring gaze and climbed back onto his horse. He spurred it and headed directly toward Vlad's army in a mad rush, then stopped when he was midway between the two opposing forces, who were now less than fifty yards apart.

Vlad had forgotten in his furious pursuit of le Clerc that Jed was due to return with a reply to his ultimatum. He reined his horse to a sudden stop as his mind raced. What negotiation was possible now? Were Jed and le Clerc working together? He congratulated himself for having sent Leon to Bauta with clear instructions. It was getting more likely that his back-up plan would have to be executed.

Vlad rode up to Jed. "What is Pathless Land's response?" he demanded.

Jed pointed to John's bloody body. "I don't owe you one anymore."

Vlad sputtered something unintelligible and then fell silent, gritting his teeth in frustration. While he stewed, le Clerc nudged his horse to join the two men. The three adversaries glared at each other. The treacherous impasse needed to be broken, but all options seemed fraught with peril, including the possibility of mutual slaughter.

Vlad pointed a shaking finger at le Clerc. "Return my prisoner to me!"

"No."

Vlad's lips trembled and his face contorted. "You're vastly outnumbered. If you don't return my prisoner, I'll slaughter you all!"

Jed positioned his horse alongside le Clerc's, although he felt no compulsion to ally with him. He was simply looking for a way to extricate John from this showdown. "I've been negotiating with Vlad," he explained to the pirate. "I'm delivering a counteroffer, but it means nothing if you keep John. We need to finish our transaction for the sake of everyone on this island."

"Pirates don't negotiate!" le Clerc repeated loudly.

Vlad ignored le Clerc but snarled at Jed, "I wasn't waiting for a counteroffer from Pathless Land. I insist on complete capitulation."

Jed measured his words. "Things are more complicated now. First, John may die while we argue here. A dead hostage is a worthless hostage. We must take him to our clinic at the Rock. Second, le Clerc has possession of John, so your negotiating position is much weaker now. Third, we're willing to offer Benita and Pathless Land's spiritual leader as hostages in exchange for John to give us time to evacuate the Rock."

"Damn you!" le Clerc swore at Jed. "I said I don't negotiate, and yet you offer my prisoner in a foolish trade that I gain no benefit from!"

Jed eyed le Clerc. "What benefit were you expecting by snatching John? The clear benefit you'll get now is that you'll live to see another day if we can settle this peacefully. You're missing a key bit of information. Vlad has two Russian nukes at Bauta. If we don't make a deal that satisfies him, Outcast Island will be made twice the hell it is already."

Le Clerc's jaw dropped. He silently pondered this awful news.

"I'm impressed," Vlad said to Jed. "Your spies are cleverer than I thought. Tell me more about your counteroffer."

Jed breathed a sigh of relief. He sensed from the softening of Vlad's body language that the opportunity to get Benita back was an emotional game-changer. "We give you Benita and the Carpenter as replacement hostages, and we take John to the Rock for emergency treatment. You give us seven days to evacuate our people from the Rock, then you release the hostages and take control of the Rock."

Vlad shook his head. "What leverage does that give me? If you renege on the deal, I have no wish to kill Benita, and I see no value in your carpenter."

"The man we call the Carpenter is Pathless Land's spiritual leader. He's the real inspiration for our new society. He's as valuable to us as you presume John to be. We know you won't kill Benita. Offering her is a show of good faith on our part."

Vlad considered this, then he shook his head more violently. "I know nothing of this carpenter. It smells like a trick. Benita is priceless to me, but she's useless as a hostage."

"Then what deal can we strike?" Jed asked. "Wasting more time will just mean John dies. Killing each other here won't get you the Rock back. Blowing up Outcast Island will devastate everyone."

"Here's my new demand," Vlad declared. "Ride as fast as you can to the Rock. The rest of us will remain here until you return. Bring Benita and the Carpenter back with you."

"I thought you said that wasn't sufficient . . ."

"It's not!" Vlad barked. "I'll release John in exchange for Benita, the Carpenter, and . . ." He paused for effect, then pointed. "François Le Clerc. He seems to be thick as thieves with Pathless Land, and the bastard stole El Morro from me. Then you'll have your seven days to evacuate the Rock." A wily smile creased his limpid face.

Le Clerc was stunned. His first instinct was to be angry that he was being made a bargaining chip, but then he saw an opportunity. Since Pathless Land's leaders were already willing to trade away the Rock to get John back, his daring rescue had lost much of its luster. The emotional impact it would make on Olga was greatly diminished. But now he had another way to win her heart. She would hopefully see that him sacrificing himself as Vlad's hostage to free John was a profound expression of his love for her.

"I'll do it," le Clerc said calmly. "I'll join Benita and the Carpenter as your prisoner."

Vlad was suspicious of the wounded pirate's quick acquiescence.

Maybe le Clerc was more involved with Pathless Land than he suspected.

"I expected more resistance," he said warily. "You, the grand conqueror of Guzman and the Jackals? You, the thief who stole Morgan's gold and then captured El Morro? And now you're willing to be my hostage? There must be a woman involved."

Le Clerc nodded. "We both suffer from the same glorious affliction."

"No one is worth sacrificing your own life," Vlad replied.

"I'll be the judge of what my life is worth. I'm willing to risk everything for the woman I love."

Jed fidgeted with the white rose on his uniform while the two antagonists jousted. He didn't care what le Clerc's motivation was because the pirate's willingness to become a hostage would seal the deal that Jed had come to make with Vlad. He also knew that Pathless Land was going to renege on the deal, which would mean the death of le Clerc and the end of Vlad's tyranny. That would remove the biggest threats to Pathless Land on Outcast Island.

"It appears we have a deal," Jed announced. "Everyone agree?"

Le Clerc didn't hesitate. "I'm all in."

Vlad hesitated. The situation was shifting too fast. He had no one he could trust for counsel, and the fate of the Proletariat and perhaps his own life hung in the balance. But if le Clerc loved a woman enough to risk his life for her, maybe she loved him equally and would hold the Pathless Land leaders to their bargain. Vlad's own unyielding passion for Benita was confounding him to the point of irrationality once again. Besides, if all else failed, he had a devastating ace in the hole in Bauta.

"It's a deal," Vlad said shakily. "But know that Leon, my lieutenant, has been dispatched to Bauta. His instructions are very clear. If I don't send a messenger to him soon reporting that all is well, he must execute our plan for Armageddon. So if you double-cross me, he'll trigger the Soviet R-12 missiles."

"Then it's settled," Jed declared. He wasted no more time on formalities. John's life was at stake, and the wind was growing stronger. Ominous cyclonic clouds darkened the horizon. He spun his horse around and headed toward the Rock.

But after he rode for a few miles, it dawned on him that le Clerc was still a wild card, as he always was. What foolishness would he attempt on Skull Ridge while waiting for Jed and the substitute hostages to return? The pirate had volunteered his own liberty much too easily. He had also backstabbed Cosimo, who was the most dangerous man within a thousand miles of Outcast Island. That meant le Clerc was reckless enough to do anything. And Cosimo was powerful enough to do anything in response.

Also, John was dying. The man who had saved his life several times in the past. The man who was his best friend in the world. The man who was his last connection to a life in Kansas that no longer existed. A sense of dread washed over him. The darkest human impulses were on full display on Skull Ridge. It seemed to him that hell must be empty of its devils because they were all plying their demonic trade on Outcast Island now.

Fighting back a tsunami of fear, Jed whipped his horse into a frothing gallop.

40

BAUTA

Mallory threw his radio to the ground. "Damn it, Nicolai!" What's wrong with our radios?"

Nicolai shrank from his furious commander. He was a technical wizard, not a warrior. He felt out of place among the battle-hardened special forces who were hunkered down in the woods outside the lab near Bauta. The exhausting march to get here had already frazzled him, and now a critical resource that he was responsible for was malfunctioning. Soon he would have to help deal with Vlad's two nuclear weapons. He was unprepared for such pressure.

He glanced at Mallory timidly. "Captain, none of our radios are working. The base station at the Rock must be malfunctioning."

"I want solutions, not excuses!" Mallory barked.

Nicolai shrugged his narrow shoulders. "The only solution is for me to hike back to the Rock to fix it."

Mallory tempered his fury. He knew that an emotionally unstable leader was a dangerous one. Pausing to evaluate their situation, he reasoned that his team had a solid battle plan, but three things had destabilized it. First, the rising storm was getting worse. The wind whistled in his ears. Dark, moisture-laden clouds tumbled over the landscape. Second, there were far more soldiers stationed at the lab than anticipated. His men would have to face greater danger, and the presence of such a strong force suggested that the nukes weren't a myth. Third, without their radios, they had no way to get the anticipated signal from the Rock that John was safe and that their attack could begin.

The lack of a signal was a huge problem. If Mallory attacked the lab before John was safely out of Vlad's clutches, Vlad might get word of the assault and realize that Pathless Land was double-crossing him. Then he would kill John. If Mallory waited too long to attack the lab, Vlad would know that Pathless Land was reneging on their deal after he released John during the prisoner swap. Then Vlad would authorize the detonation of the nukes in retaliation.

He shook his head in frustration. Beads of sweat broke out on his forehead.

A fellow Ranger ran up to Mallory. "Sir, we apprehended a man who was riding through the woods toward the lab. I think you should interrogate him immediately."

"Who is he?"

"He's wearing a Proletariat uniform. He calls himself Leon."

Mallory's jaw dropped. Based on intel from Benita, he knew Leon to be Vlad's most trusted lieutenant. What was the meaning of his lone journey toward Bauta? Then it struck him. Vlad undoubtedly had his own signaling protocol in this tense standoff. Maybe Leon was carrying the dreaded signal. Maybe the whole situation had come off the rails and Vlad was now executing his backup threat. Mallory and the Ranger sprinted toward Leon.

When they arrived, Leon was under guard. He looked frightened and angry. His hair was disheveled, and his face was bruised. Mallory surmised that his Rangers had already tried to extract information from him.

"Why are you headed to that lab, Leon?" Mallory asked.

"Who are you?" Leon asked haughtily.

"Name's Mallory. I'm Pathless Land's military leader. I hold your life in my hands, so I'll ask the questions."

"I hold everyone's lives in my hands," Leon replied. "If I don't make it to the lab in less than six hours, the unthinkable will happen."

Mallory paused. It seemed like every step in this intrigue was ending in a standoff. "Then I have five hours to torture you before we proceed with *our* plan. Is that how you want to play this?"

Leon laughed grimly. "Torture? That's how Pathless Land treats their prisoners?"

"Sometimes," Mallory replied. "No one is obliged to play nice if it leads to their demise. Those who attack us will always pay a heavy price. Self-defense is the first law of nature and the most basic human right. All constraints evaporate when one's life hangs in the balance. And the lives of everyone on this island are threatened by your Proletariat right now. I'm your judge and jury. And your executioner, if you don't cooperate."

Leon lifted his chin in defiance. "I've committed my life to our utopia. I'll never betray it."

"Utopia?" Mallory scoffed. "Your society is merely a regression to the primitive politics of Neanderthals." Mallory gestured to a Ranger standing guard. "Get me a pair of pliers."

The Ranger scrounged in his backpack and extracted pliers from his tool kit. He handed them to Mallory. In anticipation of Mallory's next step, he wrapped his arms around Leon to restrain him.

"I'm going to speak the only language you Neanderthals understand," Mallory said. He grabbed Leon's left hand and held the prisoner's fingers in his iron grip, then clasped the pliers onto a fingernail and pulled with sudden brutality. The nail was ripped from Leon's finger like an eggshell being peeled. Leon screamed in agony as blood dropped from his torn flesh.

"We know there are nuclear weapons in that lab," Mallory barked. "How do we stop them from being detonated?"

"You must not interfere!" Leon sobbed. "Collectivism is the salvation of humankind, as long as everyone complies with our well-meaning dictates."

Mallory shut him up by jamming one hand into his mouth to pry it open. With his other hand he clamped the pliers onto a tooth. He pulled so violently that Leon's head snapped forward. The

Ranger restraining Leon let him go. Leon dropped to his knees and pawed at his face. Blood seeped between his fingers from his mouth.

Mallory waved the bloody tooth in front of Leon. "I'm happy to yank out the rest. How do we stop the nukes from being detonated?"

Leon shook his head violently. Despite being wracked by pain, he was still intoxicated by a fervent desire to carry out Vlad's commands, being a true believer. His stubborn resolve in the throes of brutal torture cemented Mallory's belief that ideological zombies like him were a mortal threat to everyone.

"Give it up, Leon!" Mallory shouted at his kneeling prisoner. "Everything you believe is a lie! You're just a tool of others more powerful than you. Save yourself! Save everyone!"

Something broke inside Leon. Mallory could see it in the sudden sag of his shoulders, the softening of his facial features, and the tears filling his eyes. "I'm just following orders," he sobbed in broken syllables. "Please, no more torture. Mercy!"

"Mercy?" Mallory exclaimed. "The biggest cowards are those who take moral refuge in following orders. That's how evil overwhelms entire societies. That's how Stalin starved millions and Hitler incinerated the Jews."

Mallory pulled out his pistol, aimed it at Leon, and pulled the trigger. The bullet ripped through Leon's right arm. He recoiled from the impact and fell on his side, writhing in pain and shaking violently. He whimpered incoherently. Mallory gestured to some nearby Rangers.

"Put a tourniquet on his arm. He's coming with us when we assault the lab. There'll be more hell in store for him if he doesn't stop this madness."

Mallory went to study the lab as darkness fell. He lay on his stomach at the edge of the woods, examining the compound through his binoculars. A new detail grabbed his attention. There were two low-slung concrete pillboxes covered with large metal lids.

"Damn!" he swore under his breath. Until now, he assumed that the nuclear devices would be detonated in place, which would essentially be suicide for the collapsing Proletariat and murder for every innocent person in range. But the pillboxes looked like the hardened covers over missile silos.

If Vlad's technicians had resurrected the Soviet missiles that carry the nuclear payloads aloft, then their intention must be to fire the missiles at targeted locations. If so, they weren't intending to commit suicide; they were planning genocide of their enemies.

Then he wondered what the likely targets would be. The two most strategic spots on Outcast Island were the former Proletariat headquarters at El Morro and the Pathless Land headquarters at the Rock. The rest of the island was a wasteland of evacuated cities, impoverished villages, nests of gangs in the mountains, and isolated hermitages. A shiver ran up his spine. His mission took on a new urgency.

Mallory swallowed hard while he considered his dwindling options. He was incommunicado with Pathless Land, Vlad had sent Leon to Bauta with a deadline, and nuclear missiles were staged in launch silos inside the compound. Assaulting the lab now had its risks, but failing to act had greater risks. He decided it was better to destroy evil before it destroyed everyone else.

He turned and shouted, "Plan B!" to his troops. His men fanned out in two directions. One squad headed toward the rear of the fenced complex. A second squad, led by Mallory, surreptitiously crept toward the front gate with Leon in tow. He had been gagged to prevent him from alerting the guards.

The first squad intentionally made a lot of noise when they neared the rear of the complex. When they were fifty yards from the electrified fencing, they launched flares that arced with pyrotechnic brilliance above the compound. They tossed grenades over the fence, then fired their rifles at anyone who moved inside the compound.

Mallory's squad patiently studied how the defenders reacted to the decoy. Predictably, guards left their positions near the front gate and rushed in alarm toward the commotion at the rear of the compound. Search lights came to life and scanned the fields and woods where the first squad was creating havoc. Heavy gunfire was exchanged. More explosions erupted. Fires broke out. The strong winds fanned the flames and blew a heavy blanket of sulfurous smoke toward the front of the compound.

Mallory waited until the smoke formed an opaque wall between his squad and the front gate. He was taking a calculated risk by waiting. The danger was that someone inside the lab might panic in the chaos and trigger the nukes. However, he gambled that the lab was under strict orders to wait for instructions from Leon, who was safely in his clutches.

A thunderous explosion rent the air and lit up the night sky. That was the cue for Mallory's squad to attack the complex. Mallory rose and began sprinting, followed by his troops. He tossed a grenade at the front barricades. The troops behind him fired into the smoky darkness to give him cover. The men dashed through the demolished opening, firing in patterns to keep any enemies at bay.

Sporadic gunshots came from darkened buildings that were silhouetted by firelight. Mallory and his team returned fire toward the muzzle flashes. Mallory heard screams behind him but ignored them. He focused instead on a bigger problem: he had no idea which building to infiltrate. He dashed to the rear of his squad where Leon was being dragged along like a bloody rag doll.

Leon was delirious with pain. Mallory slapped him hard. Leon opened his eyes and blinked several times to orient himself.

"Which building is the control center in?" Mallory screamed.

Leon moaned but said nothing. His head lolled to one side. Mallory couldn't tell if he was incapacitated or obstinate. There was no time to decide. He put the barrel of his pistol between Leon's eyes so he couldn't mistake his intentions. "Where's the control center?" he repeated.

Leon hesitated, then moaned, "Building C."

Mallory kept the pistol jabbed between Leon's eyes. "It's too dark to read signs!" he barked.

"Antenna," Leon grunted, then his head fell to his shoulder.

Mallory scanned the compound. He spotted a large building that had the silhouette of an antenna on top. "Let's go!" he shouted to his men and began running. He heard continuous gunfire from the raging battle at the rear of the compound, but he remained focused on his own mission.

He stopped short of the heavy doors to Building C. "Down!" he yelled to his team. He lobbed a grenade at the doors. A deafening explosion erupted, followed by shrapnel whizzing overhead. The Rangers leapt to their feet and poured through the smoking wreckage of the entrance, guns levelled.

There was no resistance. Mallory saw through the smoky haze that the white-coated technicians inside had scrambled for any cover they could find. Banks of untended electronic consoles and displays glowed and flickered in the smoke-filled room.

Mallory waited until Leon was dragged into the room, then put his pistol to Leon's temple. "I've brought your messenger to you!" he declared to the bewildered technicians. "Who's in charge here?"

No one moved from their hiding spots. "Step forward, or I'll put a bullet through Leon's head!"

A tall, gaunt technician with graying hair emerged shakily from his makeshift shelter. He stared in horror at the battered, near-death figure of Leon slumped in front of the phalanx of armed soldiers who were adorned with white roses on their uniforms. The technician was certain his life was in grave danger. He was a true believer, too, but the thing he believed in most was his own survival.

Suddenly, Leon stirred from his stupor. He couldn't remember much in his delirium, but he knew that the dream of the Proletariat was slipping away, along with his own life. He saw the gaunt technician waiting wide-eyed for direction.

"Launch the warheads," Leon muttered in a voice so low and garbled that it was almost inaudible.

Mallory fired his gun. Leon's head exploded in a crimson mist that settled on the nearby consoles. It also splattered the face and the white coat of the graying technician, who doubled over and retched.

"He delivered the wrong message," Mallory said grimly. He hoped that Leon's gory murder would destabilize the technicians enough to bend to his authority.

Nobody moved, except for the technician who continued to convulse with nausea. Mallory debated whether to shoot everyone in the room preemptively, but then he considered that the launch of the warheads might be set to a timer. He recalled Leon mentioning that if he didn't arrive at the lab by a certain time, Armageddon would be set in motion automatically.

Mallory turned his pistol to the nauseated technician. "This is your chance to be a hero or a villain. Shut everything down. Now!"

The technician raised his arms submissively but shook his head. He began trembling in a frightened palsy. "I . . . I can't. The computer program that controls everything is locked, and only a secret code can unlock it."

"Does that mean a timer is running that can't be stopped?"

"The secret code can stop it," the technician replied. "Vlad didn't want any traitors to circumvent his plans."

"Who has the code?" Mallory demanded, aiming his pistol directly at the face of the technician.

"T-two people," the technician stammered forlornly. "And you just k-killed one of them."

"Who's the other?"

"Vladimir Sokolov."

Mallory's blood turned to ice. He shivered. "How much time is left before launch?"

The technician glanced at a control panel. "Four hours and forty-nine minutes."

41

TERMINATION

Cosimo sat glumly in a darkened underground chamber outside Rome, one of many secure bunkers maintained by the Syndicate around the world. He had been waiting nervously for an hour for Six to make his appearance. Part of him wished his boss would hurry so that the dreadful wait would be over. The other part of him wished the inscrutable member of the Syndicate's Deka would never show.

A door to the chamber creaked open. Cosimo heard the familiar shuffle of unsteady feet ambling toward him in the shadows. He heard a chair being pulled up to the other end of the long table and then a faint grunt as his boss sat down. He must be getting old, Cosimo thought, although he knew little of the personal particulars of the faceless man who held his life in his hands.

Cosimo heard a metallic clank. Six had plopped something heavy on the table separating the two men. Cosimo's heart lurched at the jarring sound. He squinted in the near darkness to see the object Six had set down. He saw the vague outline of a pistol.

Cosimo expected this meeting to be unpleasant, but he didn't expect it to be terminal for him. Upon further reflection in the nerve-wracking silence, he realized that the stakes in the Syndicate's game were so high that the cost of failure was unavoidably dire.

So this was going to be it for him. He sighed heavily. He considered lunging for the gun and shooting Six, but he knew he would never leave the chamber alive if he murdered one of the ten most powerful people in the world. Besides, he would get no satisfaction from killing Six because Six had never failed him. The fault was entirely his. An honorable exit was all that could be salvaged now. He supposed Six knew this too.

"You orchestrated many failures during your apprenticeship," Six judged bluntly, breaking the grueling silence.

Cosimo's throat became constricted. He couldn't utter a syllable. He nodded his understanding instead, then realized that nodding was pointless in the near darkness.

"Here's your scorecard," Six continued. "A wannabe pirate bamboozled you. A tin-pot dictator failed to carry out your orders. A rebel named John is creating an alliance with other renegade outcasts despite your divisive tactics. You caused two World Order warships to be sunk after selling another to the pirate for your own personal gain. And the island may become a nuclear wasteland. I summoned you here to end your apprenticeship as a Centurion."

"Of course," Cosimo croaked. There was no point in arguing his case. Honor required him to accept the awful verdict. Six's judgment was all that counted in the Syndicate's unforgiving code of justice.

Six's shadowed arm reached for the gun. Cosimo's entire body tensed, his bowels churned, and he broke out in a cold sweat. While fighting to keep his legs from jittering, he became lightheaded and dizzy. He was ashamed that fear was going to be his final emotion because a real Centurion would never die in fear.

Cosimo heard a metallic click. He flinched reflexively, but nothing happened. A drawer opened, then a clunk sounded from the drawer before it was slammed shut.

"You passed the first of today's tests," Six announced. "Complete accountability is necessary for aspiring Centurions. You accepted yours today while staring down the barrel of a gun."

Cosimo exhaled a heavy sigh of relief. He didn't know what to say or to expect now. He focused on keeping his sphincter closed.

Six uncharacteristically chuckled at Cosimo's discomfort. "I'm not ending your apprenticeship by killing you. I'm making you a full-fledged Centurion."

Cosimo was shocked and remained speechless.

"If you could pick your first assignment, what would it be?" Six continued.

Cosimo experienced a bizarre twist of emotion. One minute he was about to die; the next minute he was discussing his future. But that was always the way with Six. Unpredictability was part of the aura of his power. Even the simple question posed by Six was destabilizing. The Deka dictated assignments to their Centurions, and they expected unquestioning compliance. They did not solicit opinions or wishes because they cared nothing about them.

The question disoriented Cosimo so much that he blurted an emotional rather than a rational response. "I want to kill the three men who undermined my strategies on Outcast Island."

Six didn't respond. Cosimo feared that his irrational outburst was a failure of whatever test his boss was administering now. The Syndicate relied on cold-hearted executioners and tacticians, not maudlin reactionaries.

"Only two of those men are worthy of murderous revenge," Six began. "Vlad is a spineless apparatchik who will inevitably be killed by those around him. Maybe he'll even blow himself up with his own nukes. But your instinct to kill François le Clerc and John Paine is very sound. It shows you understand that renegades are intolerable to us. The only people the Syndicate can rely on are those we can manipulate. That includes world leaders who can be bought with money and whose egos can be assuaged with illusions of power. It also includes the timid sheep who are willing to sacrifice their freedom in exchange for sustenance and the illusion of hope at the ends of their hopeless rainbows. But heretics like Paine and le Clerc threaten our ascendency. It's impossible to rule them and they can't be bought. You've passed the second test."

"Then Paine and le Clerc will be killed within a week," Cosimo declared.

"I admire your enthusiasm," Six snapped. "But that's not your highest priority."

Cosimo did a double take. As always, he was being played by Six. A seed of doubt sprouted in his head. He aspired to be a grandmaster in the ultimate chess match of power politics, but was he destined to be just another pawn in someone else's scheme?

"We've decided to abandon Outcast Island," Six continued. "It's become a waste of the Syndicate's time and resources. It was useful to us as your training ground, but the factions will eventually kill each other. It'll devolve into a barbarous muddle of anarchy of its own accord. We have far more pressing concerns. The biggest obstacle to our complete ascendency is America, the birthplace of the scourge called individual sovereignty."

"Didn't the Syndicate instigate a civil war there?" Cosimo asked.

"Yes, we started it in 2053. Our strategy was to manipulate the Jackals, the Caliphate, the Rebels, the Blessed, and the Elites to devour each other. But the rebels are proving to be stubborn adversaries, and Regis, the leader of the Elites, is more of a fool than we expected. He reminds me of Vlad. Your new mission is to finish destroying America. Your failures on Outcast Island were the price we were willing to pay for your training, but no more mistakes will be tolerated. You must resolve the threat of independent thinkers in America by their submission or their death."

Cosimo contemplated his new marching orders. It was a grand assignment, perhaps one of the most desirable for any Centurion. This was a surprising change in fortune for him. Just moments ago, he was prepared for a bullet between his eyes; now he was being given great responsibility.

"Your Excellency, since you're ending my apprenticeship, I'd like to close it out by getting better clarity about the tactics that are critical to my success, and therefore the Syndicate's success."

"I'm heartened you recognize that the Syndicate's success is paramount," Six replied. "Here are the three guiding lights for the rest of your career.

"First, you must commit yourself to our unyielding agenda. We're a small aristocracy pursuing control over the world. Our goal is to be like the gods on Mount Olympus, administering world affairs to our advantage. As such, we are subject to no laws, and we exempt ourselves from any moral judgment.

"Second, you must use politicians to preserve our anonymity and to keep us separated from the filthy proles. Select leaders who will do our bidding, and remove them when they fail to do so. We don't care whether they have integrity or not, and their ideology is irrelevant to us. They must be able to serve us while at the same time conning their subjects into believing they're being served instead. Bribe these narcissistic politicians to use their bureaucrats, media sycophants, cultural influencers, educators, secret police, and military forces to keep the proles bamboozled and unwilling to resist.

"Third, keep the proles ignorant and at each other's throats. Use our hired politicians to mystify them with lies and errant dogmas so that the truth is unrecognizable. Sow division and hatred—race against race, gender against gender, young against old, ideology against ideology, country against country, humans against nature—so that the proles fight each other or fight imaginary bogeymen. We don't care which factions win; we only care that their rage isn't focused on us. Make the proles so intoxicated with discontent that they're unable to perceive the real cause of their damnation."

Six fell silent, so Cosimo surmised that his lesson was over. "A very concise and helpful outline, Your Excellency," he patronized. He paused, knowing that he was about to stretch the limits of his boss's rare graciousness. "But I have one last question."

"My explanation was complete. There's nothing else to know."

"Then please excuse my unforgivable ignorance," Cosimo said. "You said that the Syndicate doesn't care who wins the ideological conflicts, and yet I notice that in practice the Syndicate prefers socialism."

Six sighed heavily from his shadow. "The reason is obvious. We care nothing about any ideology. However, there are times when we must assert heavy-handed control over a society. Socialism breeds submissive populations and totalitarian governments. It's essentially an elitist monopoly on everything because the proles own nothing and decide nothing. They're simply the means to our selfish ends. That's why I suggested that you support Vlad on Outcast Island."

"But Vlad is failing miserably."

"Socialism always fails," Six retorted. "It's inherently nihilistic and irrational. It destroys but never creates. It implodes after colliding with human nature. The trick is to use it to the Syndicate's advantage before it implodes. I don't hold Vlad's failures against you. Otherwise, the janitors would be squeegeeing your blood from the floor right now."

"Thank you for that reprieve, Your Excellency."

"Don't become complacent," Six admonished. "I have little patience, and I expect extraordinary results. Your new assignment is simple but vital. America must collapse, completely and spectacularly. It's the only remaining obstacle to the full unfolding of our world hegemony."

"I won't fail, Your Excellency. But I repeat my request for your blessing to terminate François Le Clerc and John Paine in my spare time. It's personal for me."

"Happy hunting," Six grunted. He knew it was important to throw an eager young Centurion a bone every now and then. "But as with everything, you'll no longer be forgiven for failure."

Cosimo heard Six's chair scrape against the floor. Then he heard the shuffling of his boss's feet as he walked away. A door closed, and Cosimo was alone in the darkness with no conscience to keep him company.

42

SERMON

Vlad experienced a strange blend of euphoria and confusion.

He was ecstatic seeing Benita among the mounted contingent that had just arrived on Skull Ridge. Her lustrous brown skin, dark eyes, and black hair tossing in the rising wind sent shivers down his spine. She caught his adoring, lust-filled gaze and smiled. Another shiver.

He was confused, though, because the contingent from the Rock was much larger than anticipated. He had ordered Jed to fetch Benita and the Carpenter as part of a trade for John. But hundreds more Pathless Landers had accompanied them. Most of them were Maroons with white roses pinned to their uniforms and guns at their sides. They were clustered around Benita like a swarm of bees protecting their queen.

A statuesque blonde woman spurred her horse to the front of the arrivals. "I'm Olga Kozlowski," she announced to Vlad with an authority that rivaled her beauty. "Jed told me that a swap of prisoners has been arranged to save John's life."

Vlad was momentarily paralyzed by the sight of the sculpted Valkyrie who presumed herself to be his equal in this parley. Her stunning beauty and her unexpected presence unsettled him. He turned to Jed. "I ordered you to bring me two prisoners, but in addition you bring an army led by a woman?"

"There's a method to my madness," Jed replied.

"I only see madness," Vlad countered.

"Shut up and listen!" Olga snapped. Vlad recoiled as if slapped. "You will negotiate with me and no one else. I'm the senior officer of Pathless Land in the absence of John, our leader, and Mallory, our military commander. Before joining Pathless Land, I was the leader of the Remnant, the faction that captured the Rock from you."

"On your second attempt and with some help," Vlad countered feebly. He felt a bolt of shame from being diminished by a domineering woman while Benita looked on. Benita was the only woman he permitted to treat him this way.

"We brought Benita and the Carpenter," Olga said. "We also brought two medics to treat John. Where is he?"

Vlad gestured to his left. His soldiers parted ranks to reveal a limp, bloodied body curled in the fetal position on the ground. A tall, dark man with long, flowing hair and a bleeding shoulder was kneeling beside John and tending to him. The Samaritan's back was toward Olga. He turned to look at her.

Her heart skipped a beat. The last man on Earth she expected to see tending to John was François le Clerc. Was John still alive?

Le Clerc nodded in the affirmative, reading the unspoken fear etched on her face. Olga held his imploring gaze briefly, then signaled to Doc and his aide.

"Tend to John now!" Olga commanded without waiting for Vlad's approval. The two medics dismounted, grabbed their kits, and rushed to where John lay under the threatening sky.

Vlad watched in dismay as this unfolded. "Why did you bring hundreds of warriors with you?" he demanded of Olga, fearing that violence might unfold.

Olga waved another rider forward. He was so massive and muscular that Vlad instinctively scooched back in his saddle.

"I am Spartacus!" the warrior bellowed. "My Maroons are here for two reasons. If you attempt any treachery, we'll slay you and your

Palace Guards. And I'm delivering a personal warning. If you harm even a hair on Benita's head, I'll hunt you to the ends of the Earth."

Vlad felt a rising terror. This encounter was not what he planned it to be. Then Olga destabilized it even more by dismounting and running toward John.

When she neared John's prone body, le Clerc arose and faced her. To everyone's shock, she fell into an intimate embrace with him, despite the bloodied arm hanging limp at his side. Vlad was stunned but then remembered le Clerc was sacrificing himself for the love of a woman. Olga kissed le Clerc with such urgency that Vlad smiled with satisfaction. He had been uncertain about le Clerc's value as a hostage, but his value was now abundantly clear. He was a tool who could be used to manipulate Olga.

After their kiss, Olga nestled her head on le Clerc's good shoulder. "Thank you, Ammon," she whispered into his ear. "Jed told me you volunteered to be a hostage in John's place. I don't know what the future holds, but I'm eternally indebted to you. For now, we must maintain the appearance that we're desperately in love. You're a dead man if Vlad doubts that."

"There can never be any doubt about my love for you, now or ever."

"Are you hurt badly?" Olga asked.

"My physical wounds are not as grave as my spiritual ones."

Olga slipped from his embrace to inspect Doc's ministrations of John. "Prognosis?" she asked, her heart in her throat for more than one reason. She glanced down at le Clerc's blood smeared on her clothing. It reminded her of a blood oath they had taken long ago.

"Grim," Doc replied bluntly. "He's still alive, but his vital signs are perilously weak. We'd be burying a lesser man right now. We must get him to our clinic at the Rock immediately."

Olga nodded, then ran back toward Vlad. "We're taking John now!" she shouted. "Our negotiations mean nothing if he dies. You have no choice in the matter!"

Vlad froze, fuming inwardly. Why was he letting this brazen woman shout orders? She had just declared she was taking his prized hostage right out from under his nose.

"I have every choice in the matter," Vlad declared finally. "John isn't leaving here until the hostages you've agreed to swap for him are released to me. That includes Benita, the pirate, and the man you call the Carpenter, whom I wish to interrogate before we complete our deal. I need to verify he's a worthy hostage and not just a stooge you're tricking me with. Where is he?"

The Carpenter nudged his horse to the fore while Olga silently cursed this deadly delay. He stopped near Vlad's horse. "I am he," he announced firmly.

Vlad's suspicion rose. The Hispanic man had long dark hair and was dressed in a white robe that was eerily bright in the gloom of the rising storm. He was adorned with a leather belt, sandals, and a shawl that covered his shoulders. He was attractive but didn't exude an aura of power or consequence. He seemed rather meek, with an aura of serenity.

"So you're the grand inspiration for Pathless Land?" Vlad sneered. "The animating spirit behind their attempted conquest of Outcast Island?"

"No, *señor*, I do not wish to conquer but to save," the Carpenter replied.

Vlad smirked. "Prove to me that your wisdom makes you a worthy hostage."

The Carpenter smiled pastorally. "I'll start with the very foundation of morality. Every human life is sacred. Each person owns themself and their own soul. That's why your profane philosophy will always fail. Individual sanctity is negated by your class conflicts, your culture of victimhood, your denial of personal responsibility, and your subjugation of some to others."

"Your ideas are archaic!" Vlad scoffed. "The collective is the new deity of humankind. All must submit to it for their own good. Our goal is a perfectly ordered society where selfish greed withers away. Personal conscience and individual salvation are nothing compared to collective conscience and class salvation."

"There's no such thing as class salvation or collective morality," the Carpenter replied serenely. "We will all be judged as individuals.

By our fruits alone we shall be known. Only individuals make choices. Societies have neither brains nor consciences."

Jed spurred his horse to the Carpenter's side. He knew it was vital that Vlad recognize the Carpenter as a critical cog in the leadership of Pathless Land.

"The Carpenter has given us a clear vision of how to achieve peace and justice," Jed said. "We've all rallied around him. He's the guiding light of our society."

Vlad glared at Jed and then squinted at the Carpenter. Doubt still clouded his face. "So you're the savior of the world?"

"Those are your words," the Carpenter replied. "My message is simple. The price of free will is personal responsibility. Everyone has an obligation to take care of themselves and to pursue their own happiness. From there arise all other moral ideals, including the reciprocity that underlies the Golden Rule. The last six of the Ten Commandments point out why collectivism always ends in a shattering collision with ethics and reality."

A shout from Olga interrupted Vlad's interrogation. "If John dies before we get him to the Rock, I'll order my warriors to attack immediately, damn the consequences! We're taking him now. We'll leave the hostages we've agreed to swap. Within one week, we'll evacuate the Rock and turn it over to you in exchange for the hostages."

Vlad abandoned his interrogation of the Carpenter. The stubborn Valkyrie was right. If John died now, his leverage in these negotiations plummeted to zero. But he hated being forced to make rash decisions. He glared at Olga.

"I'm not convinced that the Carpenter is a worthy trade for John," Vlad declared. "I'll take him as a hostage, though, just to be safe. But I want one more."

"In addition to the Carpenter, Benita, and le Clerc?" Olga asked with exasperation.

"That is my final demand," Vlad replied obstinately.

All that could be heard for a moment was ominous thunder in the distance and the gusting wind. "Who do you want?" Olga asked.

Vlad pointed at Jed. "Him. I've learned that he and John are like brothers."

Olga looked wide-eyed at Jed, who didn't hesitate. Instead, he leapt down from his horse, crossed the imaginary line separating the factions, and stood before Vlad with his arms raised in surrender.

"I'm yours!" Jed declared.

Le Clerc took his cue from Jed and left his vigil beside John, strode over to where Jed had planted himself, and surrendered to Vlad too.

Olga breathed a heavy sigh of relief. "Your move, Vlad," she challenged. "You have Jed and le Clerc. Release John to us, and then we'll complete the deal by giving you Benita and the Carpenter. It must happen now, or we'll attack."

Vlad hesitated. Olga raised her arm as if to signal a start to hostilities. Vlad glanced over at Benita, then capitulated. He ordered two of his men to help Doc and the other medic carry John's unconscious body to Olga. She checked John's feeble pulse, then directed her team to put him on the makeshift stretcher they had brought from the Rock. She nodded somberly toward the Carpenter and to Benita.

"It's time," Olga said. "We'll return here in precisely one week to retrieve both of you, along with Jed and François."

Every hostage but le Clerc knew that she had spoken a lie just for show. Olga looked at him one last time. She pointed to her own heart where her clothes were stained with the blood from his wounded shoulder, then pointed to him. She mounted her horse and tucked her head to hide the tears tracing lines down her dusty face.

Suddenly, Vlad shouted a question to her. "Why are you acting as leader of Pathless Land? Where's Mallory?"

Olga's heart dropped to her toes. How should she parry this damning question? They finally had John in their possession, which was the first critical step in their plan. But she had no way to get a signal to Mallory at Bauta to execute the next step. She didn't even know if he was still alive. And she certainly didn't want to tell Vlad where he was.

She decided to answer with a pointed query of her own. "Where's Leon?"

A feeling of dread came over Vlad. Why hadn't he heard from

Leon or anyone else at Bauta? Only a few hours remained until the planned triggering of Armageddon. He and Leon were the only ones who could deactivate the launch sequence. And if Leon was dead . . .

But at least he had valuable hostages, and he had enough time to get to Bauta to intervene if necessary. He needed everyone to survive for at least a week until the final trade for the Rock could be made. Then he would have his new headquarters, his beloved Benita by his side, and fresh momentum for his conquest of Outcast Island.

He ignored Olga's disturbing question about Leon and forgot his own question about Mallory. He spurred his horse to lead his faction toward Bauta with his prisoners in tow. But as soon as the jaunt began, he was haunted by thoughts that were even more troubling than Olga's question. Why had the World Order ships fired missiles at El Morro? Why had Cosimo reneged on his promise to help Vlad subjugate the island? Why had le Clerc been able to defy Cosimo with impunity?

He suddenly felt very much alone, despite the presence of Benita in his contingent. A chilly wind was blowing across the land, and an even colder one was blowing through his soul.

43

FRENZY

Mallory aimed his pistol at the gaunt lab technician, who trembled with fear. "There must be a way to shut this monstrosity down without the secret code!" he bellowed. "Try anything! Kill the power!"

The technician shook his head. "The launch software is programmed to detect disruptions to the equipment. If I cut the main power, the generators will kick on. If I kill the generators, the battery packs will take over. In the meantime, the software will assume that sabotage is occurring and automatically initiate the launch sequence of the missiles."

"Where are the missiles targeted?" Mallory asked.

"One is aimed at la Habana, the other at the Rock."

Mallory looked at his watch. "Shit! We've got four hours left! Someone must have an idea about how to stop this." He waved his pistol in an erratic arc around the lab, sowing the impression that he was a madman. A brutal idea popped into his head.

"I'm going to randomly shoot one of you every thirty minutes until the launch is terminated," Mallory warned.

The gaunt technician turned ashen. He rushed to a bank of

computer screens and gestured wildly for his aides to gather around him. A hubbub of frenzied discussion erupted, interrupted periodically by nervous glances at Mallory.

Mallory saw Nicolai still trying to resuscitate one of the dead radios. "Any luck?" he asked, although the answer was apparent from the deep frustration etched onto Nicolai's face.

"Nothing," Nicolai grunted. "But I'll keep trying."

Mallory shook his head. "Don't bother. Even if you fix them, no communication will save us now. We're on our own. Organize your team to assess the situation here. Vlad's techs may be lying to us. Can we cut the power without triggering a launch? Can the software be reprogrammed? Can we crack the secret code? Newton is a chemist. Maybe he has some ideas."

Nicolai's shoulders sagged. "Sir, I'll do whatever you ask. Newton is indeed very clever, and we've brought along some aerospace engineers who were banished to Outcast Island. But we're starting from scratch. We know nothing about anything here."

"Start with the power situation," Mallory said. "Study the main feed, the generator, and the battery packs. How are they interlocked? Can we safely cut power to the missile launch system regardless of the interlocks? Go!"

Nicolai saluted clumsily and then signaled to his companions. They scrambled out of the lab into the darkness outside.

Mallory hated the dilemma he was in. He was well-trained to deal with unexpected situations, but he had no idea what to do. He glanced at his watch again. Grimly, he found himself looking forward to the expiration of the first thirty-minute deadline. It would at least give him something familiar to do. He began to wonder about his own sanity.

Olga was paralyzed by indecision. She stood on Skull Ridge watching Doc and a few soldiers begin John's emergency jaunt to the Rock. She wondered if John would survive the arduous trip. She also wondered if there was sufficient medical talent at the Rock to treat him. She knew she should ride along with him, yet she was frozen in place.

The stark reality was that there was nothing she could do to help him. His fate lay with the army medics. She was now experiencing a powerful desire to try to rescue le Clerc instead. Even though the plan was always to sacrifice the hostages, le Clerc was never intended to be one of those casualties. He was unaware of his dismal fate. Despite their tumultuous relationship over the years, she felt obliged to help the man who had risked his life to save John and who volunteered to be a hostage so that John could get medical care. Those acts of selfless chivalry were wildly out of character for the pirate. He deserved a better fate.

Spartacus broke her confused reverie. "You have to pick one path or the other," he said as softly as a massive warrior could.

Olga looked at him in surprise. How did he sense the dilemma she was wrestling with? "What would you do?"

"I'm not hesitating," Spartacus replied. "My beloved Benita has fallen once again into the clutches of the tyrant who abused her for years. Even though she volunteered, her courage makes me love her even more. I'm going to pursue Vlad and rescue her."

"What's your plan when you catch up to them?"

"I don't have one yet," Spartacus mused. "The chase will give me time to think."

"Attacking Vlad may trigger Armageddon," Olga cautioned.

Spartacus's face grew rigid, and his whole body tensed. "I must do what I must do. I have faith that Mallory will succeed in his mission. I couldn't live with myself if I didn't try to rescue Benita. My Maroons have already agreed to join in the chase. They too are moved by her heroism and her love for her fellow Cubanos. Now you must decide what you're going to do."

Before Olga could answer, Sergeant Brown joined them and saluted. "I've heard nothing from Captain Mallory at Bauta, so I'm awaiting orders. Should my Rangers escort John to the Rock? Follow Vlad to observe his movements? Race ahead to Bauta to assist Captain Mallory in whatever predicament he's in?"

The plea for clarity jolted Olga out of her indecision. "Tell your men to get ready to ride hard," she ordered, then turned to Spartacus. "Your wisdom is appreciated. I couldn't live with myself either if I let François die in vain. We're coming with you and your Maroons. Together, we'll figure out how to save all the hostages."

～

Vlad's four hostages rode together, surrounded by hundreds of Palace Guards on the horseback trek to Bauta. The ground still smoldered from the wildfire set by le Clerc. The rising wind blew the lingering smoke and ash sideways. The hostages silently contemplated their fates.

Finally, Jed spoke. "It's time to fill you in on the bad news, le Clerc. All four of us are marked for death."

The pirate looked at him quizzically. "Not if Pathless Land makes the trade they've agreed to."

Jed shook his head, then looked around to see if any soldiers were within earshot amid the thundering din of horses. "There won't be a trade. The plan was always for Pathless Land to renege on the deal once John was released from captivity."

Le Clerc spun his head toward the Carpenter and Benita, who were riding on his other flank. "Do you two know you're being sacrificed to die?"

"*Sí*. We volunteered," the Carpenter replied evenly. "Benita believes she can bedazzle Vlad until she figures out how to escape. I'm prepared to be executed."

Le Clerc's eyes grew wide with shock. He glared at Jed. "Why didn't you tell me sooner?"

"I don't negotiate with pirates."

"Touché." Le Clerc fell silent as he pondered his dilemma. His wounded shoulder throbbed. His shirt was stiff from dried blood. It felt like little vermin were crawling around his wound. "Why did you volunteer at the last minute to die?" he asked Jed.

"To close the deal with Vlad so that John and his vision could be saved. I'm a tired old rancher from Kansas. This is my chance to ride off into an eternal sunset with my head held high and no regrets."

"Maybe that's a storybook ending for you," le Clerc reasoned. "But I don't intend to leave this world without a fight."

Jed scanned the hundreds of Palace Guards arrayed around them. "What fight do you think you can win here?"

"The Palace Guards didn't search me when I surrendered to Vlad. I have a knife tucked inside my boot."

"How many of these armed guards can you stab before the rest shoot you dead?"

Le Clerc stared pointedly at Benita. "What does Vlad cherish most?" he asked Jed conspiratorially.

The answer hit Jed like a thunderbolt. "Benita."

"Exactly! She's riding near us. I'll take her hostage with a knife to her throat. My demand would be the release of you, me, and the Carpenter."

Jed turned ashen. "You're willing to kill her in cold blood?"

Le Clerc hesitated. "I'm gambling that Vlad isn't willing to let her die."

Mallory skulked behind the gaunt technician. He looked at his watch, counted a few more seconds, then tapped on the tech's shoulder. The startled man turned around.

"Well?" Mallory asked.

"We're exploring the source code that controls the interlocks," the technician replied. "It's complicated. We're diagramming the logic trees."

Mallory shook his head. "You'll have to do that with one less person." A programmer looked up in horror at these words. Mallory considered him to have self-selected. He raised his pistol and shot him. The programmer fell grotesquely, his limp arms sweeping bloodied papers from the console to the floor as he collapsed.

The gaunt technician staggered backward in shock. He looked at Mallory like he was seeing the devil fresh from hell. "That . . . that was evil!"

"No, it was necessary," Mallory replied. "Thousands are going to die if you don't solve this problem. I'm making sure you know I mean business. Get back to work." Mallory waved his pistol toward the bank of computers.

Suddenly, an enormous crash on the roof shook the lab. All eyes looked to the ceiling, fearing an imminent collapse. "What the hell was that?" Mallory shouted.

The gaunt technician looked at him grimly. "Probably our antenna. It had several purposes, one of which was to track storms with radar. We've been watching a hurricane gather strength off the coast. The winds have been rising all day. The antenna must have snapped loose from its moorings. That's not a good sign, because I expect the storm to get worse."

Terrible thoughts raced through Mallory's head. He had paid the gathering storm little attention, but now he was worried about the wind roaring outside and the debris banging against the walls of the lab. "Can the missiles be fired without the antenna?"

"They can be launched but guiding them is harder. Their trajectories would be entirely dependent on their onboard computers and gyroscopes."

"Can they be launched in the middle of a hurricane?"

The technician looked at him somberly. "These missiles are over ninety years old. We've never tested them. I don't know how they'll perform in normal weather, much less a hurricane. But you're worried about the wrong thing."

Mallory looked at him quizzically.

The tech continued. "If the hurricane knocks out the electricity, and then if it damages the generators, the interlocks in the launch program will interpret the natural disaster as intentional sabotage and trigger the launch sequence for the missiles."

Mallory scowled. Just then, a door banged open, startling everyone. Wind and rain whipped in. Nicolai braced himself in the doorway, grasping the jamb with both arms to steady himself. "Captain Mallory! We found something!"

～

"I heard you plotting against me," Benita said to le Clerc. "We Cubanos have been conditioned for decades to eavesdrop discreetely on our overlords. It's been a matter of survival for us."

Le Clerc didn't reply. Rain was now falling in torrents, making a misery of their ride and turning the ash-covered ground into a slippery quagmire. He was focused on the hunched figure of Vlad riding toward them from the front of the column. He wondered what the tyrant was up to and used the distraction to avoid replying to Benita.

"Le Clerc!" Benita shouted. She, too, had spotted Vlad heading toward them. "Your idea is brilliant! Take me hostage!"

Le Clerc was stunned. He looked at her beseechingly to judge the sincerity of her intentions. Her pleading eyes bore the telltale trauma of years of abuse. Then he gauged the pace of Vlad's approach. There was little time left.

Le Clerc steered his horse alongside Benita's. He yanked the knife from his boot and slipped it into his mouth, then leaned over and grabbed her with his good arm. It was a dangerous maneuver given the treacherous conditions. His horse bolted, so they both fell to the mud with his good hand locked onto her clothing. She screamed, and he cushioned her fall as best he could with his body. The penalty was a crushing tumble on his wounded shoulder that nearly blinded him with pain and almost jostled the knife from his mouth.

Benita's scream got Vlad's attention. He had been wading into the ranks of the soldiers to extract her from among the other prisoners and cover her with blankets. Panicked by the commotion, he ordered those gathered around the tumbled prisoners to move aside. When his horse came upon Benita and le Clerc tangled together, he dismounted.

But le Clerc was faster. He scrambled to his feet, pulled Benita upright, grabbed the knife from his mouth with his good arm, and put it to her throat. Vlad froze just yards away and stared in horror. The love of his life was covered in muddy ash and had a sharp blade pressed against her delicate neck. Her eyes pleaded with him for rescue. The nearby Palace Guards aimed their rifles at le Clerc, waiting for an order from Vlad.

"You've been doubled-crossed," le Clerc shouted to Vlad above the storm. "Pathless Land has no intention of trading the Rock for your prisoners. They've all volunteered for a suicide mission—except for me."

Vlad shook his head in disbelief as the sideways rain pelted his face. His hat blew off his round, balding head in the tempest. "Benita, is this true?"

"It's true for Jed and the Carpenter," she shouted. "I wanted to be with you again. Please, save me from this madman!" She struggled violently against le Clerc. In the staged fracas, the knife nicked her throat. Blood oozed from the shallow wound, mixing with the rain into pink rivulets that stained her blouse. She screamed again.

"What do you want?" Vlad shouted at le Clerc. He couldn't tell how serious Benita's injury was, and he couldn't bear her plaintive wail.

"Let the three of us go!" le Clerc shouted. "Then you can do what you wish with Benita."

Vlad was lost in confusion. "Why do you care about Jed and the Carpenter?"

"I don't!" le Clerc replied. "I'm just like you. The only person I care about is the woman I love. But she'll never forgive me if I let them die."

"But . . . what about the Rock?" Vlad was nearly blubbering in his addled state.

"You fool!" le Clerc replied. "You were never going to get the Rock back. Your only hope now is to save Benita and then do what you must at Bauta."

"But thousands will die . . ."

"You and Benita will live," le Clerc reasoned. "So will I. The other two hostages and I will ride with Benita to the top of the ridge. Once we're safely up there, we'll let her go. Then we'll gallop down the opposite side and disappear. We get our freedom and you get your lover."

"And if you don't let her go?"

"Hunt us down and kill us. You outnumber us by hundreds. But that will delay you from your important business at Bauta. I assure you, though, that I have no interest in keeping Benita. She's nothing to me or to Olga. Her only value is to ensure my flight to safety."

A guard rushed to Vlad's side, frantically beseeching his attention. "Sir, we've spotted horsemen pursuing us. Hundreds of them. The Pathless Landers must have decided to attack us rather than return to the Rock."

Vlad sank deeper into a murky sea of treachery. The clock was ticking at Bauta, enemy soldiers were bearing down on him, and le Clerc had a knife to Benita's bleeding throat.

"Go!" he shouted to le Clerc. "But if you betray me, I'll hunt you to your death. Without Benita, I am nothing."

Jed and the Carpenter helped le Clerc and Benita onto a single mount. The pirate's knife was never far from her jugular. They spurred their horses into a treacherous climb up the slope to the top of the ridge.

Halfway up, le Clerc halted and looked back toward the Proletariat. He heard faint shouts from Vlad, who was trying to get his forces organized. Then he looked toward the oncoming pursuers. It was hard to see through the squalls of rain, but at the front of the attackers the massive figure of Spartacus was unmistakable. And the blonde-haired Valkyrie riding next to him could only be Olga.

His heart leapt. She was coming for him, just as Spartacus was coming for Benita.

There was yet another tidal shift in Vlad's sea of treachery. Two harried Proletariat horsemen galloped from the direction of Bauta and pulled up near him. "Sir!" one of them shouted. He was nearly out of breath and drenched by the relentless storm. "Bauta is under attack! Leon's been killed!"

Vlad lost the last vestige of his composure. The Pathless Landers had no intention of honoring any deal. They had stolen John from him, they had conned him out of Benita, they had murdered his trusted lieutenant, and they were attacking the lab that housed his precious missiles.

He had an apocalyptic decision to make. He could race to Bauta just ahead of the pursuing Pathless Land forces to stop the assault on the lab and cancel the launch of the missiles, being that he was the only person left with the secret code now that Leon was dead. But there were overwhelming reasons not to do this. It would mean abandoning Benita to her own fate. It would mean abandoning El Morro to le Clerc. And it would mean abandoning the Rock to Pathless Land.

The alternative was for Vlad to stand and fight his pursuers. Let the missiles fly. What did he care now if El Morro and the Rock were destroyed by nukes? If he could defeat the Pathless Landers on this battlefield, he could hunt down the four fleeing hostages and rescue Benita. He would have to escape with her to the mountains in Eastern Cuba, but at least they would be alive, and together they could restart their utopian empire.

During his indecision, the Pathless Land army split into two columns. One was formed by a band of Rangers led by Olga; the other was formed by a band of Maroons led by Spartacus. Olga's Rangers circled rapidly to the right of Vlad, uphill from him on the ridge. Spartacus's Maroons circled to the left, downhill from him on the slope. It was a classic pincer maneuver designed to force Vlad to fight and to prevent him from fleeing to Bauta.

As Olga's horse climbed the slope of the ridge, she spied four familiar faces waving to her from a grotto that was sheltering them from the wind and the rain. She was exhilarated to see that le Clerc, Benita, Jed, and the Carpenter had somehow escaped. The serendipitous encounter meant that she and Spartacus didn't have to restrain themselves in their attack on Vlad for fear of harming them.

She shouted at them with the blood-stirring enthusiasm of a warrior. "The battle's on! Follow me!" Then she turned her attention back to her prey below. Jed and le Clerc heeded her call, mounted their horses, and charged to her side. Benita and the Carpenter remained in the grotto.

Olga reached into her saddlebag and tossed le Clerc a pistol, the same one that he had tossed her when she fled his captivity outside Sinaloa. He caught it deftly with his good hand. Their eyes met, and it felt like old times between them.

~

Mallory spun to face Nicolai. The electronics wizard was gripping the lab's door jamb to keep his balance against the savage wind. "What did you find?"

Nicolai gestured for him to follow. Mallory did, but first he instructed a Ranger to shoot another technician on the thirty-minute mark if he wasn't back by then.

The two men shouted back and forth as they ran in the rain and the near darkness. "Newton thought of a solution," Nicolai said.

"What's his idea?"

"Computer programs are one thing. But missiles aren't propelled by electrons. They run on fuel."

"So?"

"I'll show you." Nicolai waved Mallory into the vestibule of a missile silo. An elevator door was inside. He pressed a button on the control panel. When the elevator door opened, they stepped over the bloody carcass of a Palace Guard sprawled on the floor. "We ran into a few obstacles," Nicolai said. The door closed and they descended.

The elevator opened onto a grated platform inside the underground silo. Mallory's eyes adjusted to the relative darkness haloed by some sparse emergency lights. Directly in front of him was the giant booster stage of a Soviet-era nuclear ballistic missile. Nearby were four large tanks connected to the missile with hoses.

Nicolai pointed to the tanks. "The fuel is still in storage. Newton said the liquid propellant isn't transferred to the missiles until shortly before launch. The kerosene and the liquid oxygen become highly unstable once they're blended. The mixture is quite explosive."

Mallory scanned the equipment and nodded. "What's your plan?"

Nicolai shrugged his shoulders. "Blow everything up here. No need to worry about secret passwords and such."

"Blow it up with what?"

"Sir, you're standing next to some of the most explosive chemicals on Earth. There's enough flammable material in those four tanks to blow the whole lab and most of Bauta into oblivion."

"If you blow up everything up, won't the two nuclear warheads detonate?"

Nicolai hesitated. "Probably not," he replied with less conviction than Mallory hoped. "According to Newton, there's a complex set of mechanical steps required to detonate the warheads. It's unlikely that our giant bonfire will trigger a nuclear chain reaction. It is likely, however, that the radioactive material inside the warheads will be spread far and wide, especially with these hurricane winds. Bauta and its surroundings will be a radiation hazard for years."

"How long will it take to rig up a timed detonation of the fuel tanks?" Mallory asked. "I'm assuming we'll want to be far away when everything blows."

"We're scavenging for materials to use as a timer and a detonator. I can't predict when we'll find what we need. When we do, it'll take a half hour to assemble and wire the triggers. Then we'll have to run like hell. How much time is left before the missiles are scheduled to launch?"

Mallory looked at his watch. "About three hours. Which means there should be another gunshot inside the lab shortly."

Vlad assessed the threat posed by Pathless Land's pincer maneuver. A couple of oddities caught his attention.

He saw Olga perched on her horse with her forces near the top of the ridge. Le Clerc and Jed were alongside her. The implications of this rocked him. It meant that Benita no longer had le Clerc's blade to her throat. She was either dead or incapacitated. Or perhaps she had never really been a hostage in the first place. This last thought caused him more despair than if she were dead.

On the slope below Vlad, Spartacus dismounted his horse. He left his troops behind and jogged on foot directly toward Vlad. He carried a white flag aloft, so his intention was clearly to parley. *But about what?* Vlad wondered. There was such a confusing swirl of intrigues in this unfolding disaster that he couldn't fathom what there was to talk about. In his mind, the only path forward was a decisive battle.

The scene fell deathly still when Spartacus ran up to Vlad. The dictator felt like he was standing in the shadow of a mountain as he looked up at Spartacus's menacing sneer, his storm-twisted dreadlocks, and his fierce, penetrating eyes. He wondered if the giant was going to smite him on the spot. Instead, Spartacus roared, "Where's Benita?"

Vlad shivered from the cold rain, from fear of his antagonist, and from the realization that all hope of a life with Benita was gone. His lips trembled so violently that he couldn't respond with words. He raised his arm and pointed dejectedly toward the top of the ridge where le Clerc and the other hostages had fled earlier.

Spartacus peered in that direction but saw no sign of Benita in the raging storm. He could see Olga, however. To his surprise, Jed and le Clerc were beside her. As if reading his mind, they gave him a thumbs-up signal. He interpreted their gesture as confirmation that the hostages had escaped from Vlad and that Benita was safe somewhere.

Vlad finally recovered the ability to speak. "What do you want?" he demanded, craning his head upward at his adversary.

"I want to avoid a battle and save lives. You're surrounded and outgunned. I wish to address your soldiers to explain their predicament."

"Why should I let you?" Vlad asked petulantly.

"Because you shouldn't want yourself or your troops to die."

Vlad didn't answer. His mind had shut down. Spartacus ignored him. He turned to face the mounted Palace Guards, who were numbed by the weather and the surrealistic developments.

"Fellow residents of Outcast Island," Spartacus boomed. "Today marks the end of the Proletariat. El Morro has fallen to the pirates. Vlad's attempt to save himself using hostages has failed. The Rock is firmly in the hands of Pathless Land. Bauta is under assault by our Rangers. Vlad's allies in the World Order have abandoned him, and their navy in la Habana harbor is gone. You are surrounded by well-armed and well-trained fighters. But I don't want you to die on behalf of a tyrant or a flawed philosophy."

He paused to assess the sea of desperate faces in front of him. He clearly had their attention, so he continued.

"The choices before you are unavoidable. You must either drop your weapons, dismount from your horses, and begin marching down Central Highway toward the east end of the island, or you must prepare your souls for slaughter. In other words, retreat or die. We don't want to kill you, nor do we want our soldiers to die fighting you. Our sacred wish is for peace and prosperity to spread across this troubled island."

He paused again. "Any questions?"

There was a long silence, then a lone voice called out, "What will happen to Vlad?"

"Justice will be administered. Any more questions?"

There were none. "You have five minutes to decide," Spartacus announced. He turned and jogged back toward his fellow Maroons. Vlad remained frozen in place, mourning for a world that no longer existed for him.

The emergency lights went dark in the missile silo. In a few seconds they flashed back to life when the generators automatically switched on. Deep inside the silo, Mallory could hear the howling storm become even more ferocious. If the generators went out next, two very bad things would happen. The fail-safes in the software powered by backup batteries would trigger the launch sequence, and the elevator in the silo would stop working.

He hailed a Ranger who was helping Nicolai's team. "Go up the elevator to the lab now! Tell our team that if the generators go out, they should immediately head to the Caves of Despair as fast as they can."

The Ranger gave him a quizzical look, saluted, and dashed to the elevator.

Mallory's sense of impending doom lightened a bit when Nicolai brought him some encouraging news. "We've found materials for making a timer and a detonator, and we have enough explosives to set the fuel tanks ablaze. We need thirty minutes to get ready. Then we can evacuate."

Mallory nodded. "Move fast. If the generators go out, everyone's in deep shit."

Nicolai saluted. "If the lights go out, we have enough combustible material to start a fire to illuminate our work." He left to help his team wire the detonator.

Mallory fretted all alone. He debated whether to ascend the elevator and return to the laboratory. But he knew he would be of no more help to the technicians working on the software above than to the technicians working on the detonation wiring below. He felt claustrophobic in the dim underground silo standing next to a weapon of mass destruction. But he decided to remain below because the detonation strategy seemed more viable than a software fix. He wanted to be where the action was; it was in his nature as a warrior.

The emergency lights went out again. They didn't come back on. Mallory heard pumps activating, presumably powered by battery packs. He could tell from the sounds that the pumps were now moving fuel and catalyzer to the rocket's boosters from the four storage tanks. The launch sequence had begun.

Vlad didn't wait for his Palace Guards to decide their futures. He knew deep in his soul what their decision would be. He turned his back on his own men, spurred his horse violently, and began a mad dash toward Bauta.

His desperate escape lasted mere seconds. Several Palace Guards raised their rifles and fired at him. His bullet-riddled body fell from his horse like a sack of meat. It splashed into the muddy ash and tumbled grotesquely. His riderless horse continued galloping. Lightened of its load and frightened by the gunshots, it wished only to survive.

From the grotto high on the ridge, Benita watched Vlad's final act unfold as if in slow motion. She knew she should rue the death of a human being, even one as revolting as Vlad, but an overwhelming sense of relief swept over her. She was lightened of an immense emotional load that she had carried for years and fell instinctively into the Carpenter's embrace.

"Peace be with you," he whispered knowingly. And it was.

Vlad's Palace Guards knew that a point of no return had been reached. The regicide they committed was the final cleft in their attachment to their prior lives. Almost in unison, they dismounted, laid down their weapons, and began a long sojourn toward Central Highway. No words were spoken. No salutes were offered. No loyalty was left. Like the riderless horse that had bolted, their load was lightened, and they wished only to survive. The funereal silence, broken only by the howling wind of nature's ineffable force, was a fitting end to the legacy of the Proletariat.

Mallory saw that Nicolai's team had started a small fire on the metal grating near the missile. The flames cast haunting shadows of the team members in their various poses on the curved walls of the silo. Mallory scrambled in the near darkness to join them. "Status?" he asked Nicolai.

"The wiring will take ten more minutes. Newton estimates that it'll take thirty minutes for the pumps to transfer the fuel and catalyzer to the rockets' tanks. That should leave us time to get out of here."

Mallory nodded, then a look of dread washed over his face. He rushed back to the elevator shaft, felt around in the darkness for the control panel, and madly pushed buttons. There was no response.

He felt around the walls nearby, searching for a door to a stairwell or at least a ladder running up the silo to the hatch above.

His hand found the rung of a ladder. He breathed a heavy sigh of relief and began climbing as fast as he could. His sweaty palms made his grip tenuous. When he got to the top of the ladder, he clambered onto a grated platform, probing the wall with his hands. There was another control panel, presumably to operate the hatch. In the darkness, he pounded on the buttons, but there was no response. His hands found the frame of the hatch, but after a frantic hand-sweep, he didn't find a handle or wheel with which to open it manually. There was no way for his men to escape the silo.

Mallory banged his head against the hatch. He recoiled from the pain, then felt a rivulet of blood dripping down his forehead and into his eyes. He wiped the blood away with his sleeve, then climbed back down the ladder.

He saw the men working beside the fire and joined them. They saw the blood on his forehead and the despair in his eyes. "Nothing works, does it?" Nicolai asked insightfully. "Except for the pumps feeding the missile."

"We're trapped," Mallory replied somberly.

"Should we stop working and make peace with ourselves?" Nicolai asked.

"Rangers never give up," Mallory snapped. "We have an island to save. And maybe ourselves. Courage, my friend. Are you ready with your detonator?"

Nicolai nodded.

"Do you have any explosives left over?"

"Not much."

"Enough to blow a hatch open?"

"Depends on the hatch. Is that our last hope then?"

"Set the timer on the detonator to blow the fuel tanks in fifteen minutes," Mallory instructed. "Then have your men follow me with your leftover explosives."

"Do you think we'll get out of here alive, sir?" Nicolai's voice had the naïve, hopeful tone of a young boy believing his father knew the way through a dark forest as wolves howled in the distance.

Mallory hesitated, then put a consoling hand on Nicolai's frail shoulder. "No one leaves this planet alive. Treasure every second you have left. If nothing else, we'll meet again in Valhalla."

~

Olga, François, Jed, and Spartacus met on horseback on the rain-drenched battlefield that the Palace Guards had just fled. Spartacus was roundly congratulated for his courage in confronting Vlad, and for the effect that his speech had on the Proletariat soldiers. They discussed their next steps while they waited for the Carpenter and Benita to join them from the grotto above.

"We should send a squad to follow the Palace Guards on their march down the Central Highway," Jed suggested. "Let's make sure they've truly exited this region so that François can stabilize his hold on El Morro and Pathless Land can safely expand around the Rock."

"Good idea," Spartacus replied. "We also need to send a squad to Bauta. We've heard nothing from Mallory."

"Agreed," Olga said. "And we need to get François to the Rock's clinic to fix his wounded shoulder—if he's willing." Her eyes spoke of hope and invitation.

Le Clerc nodded appreciatively. "I'll take you up on that."

Suddenly, a searing flash of brilliant light shattered the gloom of the storm. It was followed seconds later by the sound of a thunderous explosion, which was then followed by a small quake that shook the ground they stood on.

An ominous column of black smoke rose in the distance where Bauta lay. The underbelly of the cloud was illuminated by a staccato series of smaller explosions. The storm clouds and the burgeoning mushroom cloud took on a pulsating orange hue.

"Dear God!" Olga exclaimed. "Is that what a nuclear explosion looks like?"

"I don't know," Jed replied. "But given its magnitude, I don't think it matters to anyone in Bauta whether the blast was nuclear or conventional."

More explosions lit the sky. In the strobing flashes of light, Spartacus saw riders coming toward them from Bauta wearing Pathless Land uniforms.

He pointed them out to the team. A wave of relief washed over them until they realized that there were far fewer riders than had originally set out for Bauta.

44

____

DECISIONS

John awoke and blinked his eyes to adjust to the bright lights of the clinic. He was in dreadful pain and felt an overwhelming sense of exhaustion. His addled mind began to recall things. Unpleasant things.

He assessed the condition of his traumatized body. He wiggled his fingers and toes. He moved his arms and legs. Everything functioned, but the pain in his torso was brutal. He ran his hand gingerly across his bandages to probe his wounds. It was obvious from the sharp, stinging sensations where his surgically repaired gunshot injuries were.

He glanced at the clock on the wall. It was 3:00 p.m., but then he realized the time of day meant nothing. He needed a calendar. He looked around in the recovery room and noticed that he wasn't alone. It took him a dazed moment to realize that his roommate was François le Clerc.

"Welcome to the land of the living," le Clerc chided. "You're tougher than I gave you credit for. You'd make a good second-in-command as a pirate, no matter what Merlin might say."

John looked at him in confusion but chalked his muddle up to his groggy awakening. "Was I out long?" he asked.

"Hard to say. I was moved here from surgery yesterday."

"What did I miss?"

Le Clerc sighed. "The world's been turned upside down."

John tried a deep breath, then winced at the sharp pain. "Tell me the bad news first," he groaned.

Le Clerc nodded. He would have wanted the same. "There was a deadly explosion at Bauta. Conventional, not nuclear. It destroyed the lab, the two missiles, and much of the town."

John looked at him with more confusion. "The lab? Missiles? Bauta?"

"Vlad had two nukes at a lab in Bauta. He threatened to blow everyone up unless you were traded for the Rock. Mallory led a team of Rangers and technicians to assault Bauta."

John's eyes grew wide with apprehension. A wave of nausea and lightheadedness swept over him.

"Many men were killed," le Clerc continued. "But they demolished the missiles before they could be launched. They would have been good pirates too."

John was devastated. It was likely that many of those men were his friends and original shipmates. "Mallory?" he asked feebly. He choked on his own question. His throat was now dry and constricted.

"Presumed dead," le Clerc replied bluntly. "There's too much radiation to search for survivors. There's no hope anyway because Bauta was wiped out. Every missing Pathless Lander is presumed dead."

John's hand shook as he reached for a glass of water on his bedstand. He ignored the jolting pain from the effort and took a sip to wet his throat.

"I also suffered terrible losses," le Clerc continued. "Sinbad, my faithful lieutenant, was killed when we attacked the Caves of Despair to rescue you. Many of my pirates died with him."

John now remembered the reason le Clerc had risked everything to save him. "I appreciate their sacrifice," he murmured. "And yours." There was an awkward pause. "And Olga?" John dreaded the answer.

"She survived. She showed once again why I love her. She was fearless and heroic. She and Spartacus vanquished what was left of the Proletariat. Vlad was killed by his own soldiers. The surviving Palace Guards fled on foot toward the eastern end of the Island."

John was relieved beyond measure that Olga was still alive, but he was equally haunted by not knowing what her future held. That intrigue would have to wait. "Tell me everything that happened after I passed out in the Caves of Despair."

Le Clerc recounted the tales of those who volunteered to trade themselves for John's release. John was elated to hear that the substitute hostages survived the ordeal, although once again le Clerc's courage and cleverness were at the root of it. With the help of le Clerc and his pirates, John had been rescued, the Rock had been saved, and the Proletariat was destroyed.

Le Clerc's exploits, along with his avowed passion for Olga, made John acutely aware of the tense irony of lying next to him in the recovery room. The two men were never friends. Their two factions were never allies. He and le Clerc were competing for Olga's affection. The pirates had become an even stronger force than Pathless Land because they controlled El Morro, had five warships, and owned half of Morgan's treasure. In recent days, le Clerc had demonstrated his selfless bravery and cunning in many ways.

John didn't know where Olga's loyalty lay now. He feared she was slipping through his fingers. That also meant he didn't know where the loyalty of the Remnant lay. And with Mallory dead, he had lost his military commander. He had also lost two of his key technical advisors, if Nicolai and Newton were among those killed at Bauta. His mental anguish had become more acute than his physical suffering.

"What's your next move?" John asked, baiting his competing suitor to show his hand.

"A pirate's life is never dull," le Clerc replied. "My first order of business is to find Merlin. I'm hoping he flew to safety during the mayhem. Then I have to finish converting El Morro into my headquarters. After that, I'll explore the Caribbean coastlines with our new ships. I haven't lost my lust for adventure and treasure." He paused. "And my most important order of business is quite personal."

"I see," John replied coolly. He fully understood the oblique reference to Olga. He also understood the importance of keeping friends close and enemies closer. His desire to keep le Clerc very close triggered a sudden brainstorm.

"How would you like to be the admiral of Pathless Land's navy and the head of our military?" he asked. The idea of having le Clerc under his command seemed brilliant.

Le Clerc raised an eyebrow in surprise. "That's unexpected." He paused to reflect on the proposal. "Your offer is peculiar. Pathless Land doesn't have a navy. You don't know me well enough to entrust me with your military. I have a nasty habit of stabbing people in the back. Besides, we pirates prefer to gallivant around."

"Fair points," John conceded. Maybe his brainstorm wasn't so brilliant after all, but he persisted. "Pathless Land doesn't have a navy yet, but you do. Combined, we can create a secure society on Outcast Island. And I want someone to gallivant around the world. My ambitions are far greater than just civilizing Outcast Island. I intend to spread a vision for freedom and prosperity everywhere. The next step will be to share it around the Caribbean basin."

"And the step after that?" le Clerc asked with tepid interest.

John took a long sip of water. "Someday, we'll invade Florida in order to liberate America. Let me show you a couple of things." He pointed to the insignia of Pathless Land's military that was hanging on the clinic wall. It depicted a ferocious eagle with a white rose clenched in its beak, clutching a lightning bolt in one talon and an olive branch in the other. The raptor seemed to be challenging adversaries to choose one or the other, although its head was pointed toward the olive branch. Then John pointed to Pathless Land's flag hanging beside the insignia. The flag had a background of faint red, blue, and purple stripes, almost like watermarks on a legal document. Hundreds of brightly colored and wildly diverse stars were randomly superimposed over the stripes, representing a society of free individuals. The creative chaos of the stars was lightly bound together by the tri-colored stripes that represented the moral, philosophical, and political principles of Pathless Land.

"Picture that insignia on your ships and that flag fluttering above them," he said to le Clerc. "You could be the standard-bearer for our vision around the world."

"You don't know me well," Clerc replied. "I can't be the standard-bearer for others. I'm ungovernable, which is why the pirate's life is for me. I could never wear the uniform of Pathless Land nor salute its flag. The same is true of any uniform or flag. Except the Jolly Roger, of course. It's the banner of the ungovernable."

John shook his head. "Pathless Land's libertarian vision should appeal to the ungovernable. The only difference between your perspective and mine is that Pathless Land believes freedom is an illusion if it can't be defended. People enter into society because some structure is needed to keep coercion and violence at bay. I'm inviting you to help establish that structure."

Before le Clerc could reply, the door to the infirmary swung open. The brown-robed Monk glided in on noiseless feet. His face registered pleasant surprise that John was conscious. He bowed politely to the two patients. "How are you today, gentlemen?"

"In pain and trying to figure out what to do next," John replied.

The Monk nodded knowingly. "That's the story of all humankind. Suffering is unavoidable, but without it you can't grow, just as your muscles can't grow without being stressed. What we must learn from our pain is how precious those moments are when it isn't present. Don't be imprisoned by your suffering, or else you'll miss paradise."

"Paradise?" John scoffed. "I've got three bullet holes."

"The universe is always trying to kill us, and it always succeeds in the end," the Monk replied. "We can't change that. We can only change how we approach the days and years that we're blessed with."

John thought for a moment. "I see some truth in that. I've learned that things are never as bad as we fear. I used to be terrified of being shot. The idea of a bullet plowing through my flesh and bones and ripping apart my vital organs once horrified me. But now that I've been shot twice, I realize it's survivable. That gives me the courage to confront other dangers that the universe will throw my way."

"That's a good example of suffering making you stronger," the Monk said. "But it's not enough to be strong. You must also know how to use the remaining days of your life to the greatest advantage."

"That's what the pirate and I were discussing," John replied. "Any words of wisdom?"

"Obvious ones," the Monk said. "Use your natural talents to rationally accomplish what you value. As you achieve successes, you'll experience satisfaction. Over time, you'll progress from satisfying the needs of your body to satisfying the needs of your heart and mind. Eventually, you'll understand that things are neither right nor wrong, but instead beneficial or not beneficial in the deepest and most comprehensive sense. From there, the path to a state of joy becomes much clearer."

"That's all there is to it?" le Clerc asked sardonically.

"Of course not," the Monk replied. "Don't confuse the raft with the shore. The raft is the proper way of thinking that I just described. Your unique vision for your life is the shore. What connects the two is action. The shore can only be reached by rowing your raft with great enthusiasm. Deep thoughts are helpful but not sufficient. Prayer is helpful but not sufficient. Meditation is helpful but not sufficient. Wishes are helpful but not sufficient. The shore will never come to you. You must always paddle to it."

The Monk paused to sip his tea, then continued. "Paddling your raft toward your chosen shore is your responsibility alone. Life requires unceasing effort by each person. As you expend that effort, you must make choices. A lifetime of good choices leads to joy, peace, knowledge, and success. A lifetime of bad choices leads to failure, rage, impotence, and loneliness. Each pull on the oars moves you in one direction or the other. Paddle wisely. You alone choose your vision, your thoughts, and your actions, and you alone will be responsible for the consequences. Life is purely karmic."

He took another sip of tea. "And finally, the most important point. To live, people must think and choose. To think and choose, they must be free. If you can't choose your thoughts or actions, your life has no meaning. You're simply the biological tool of someone else's meaning. Putting it all together, the universe gives you a certain amount of time to live, and freedom gives you the opportunity to make the best of it. The rest is up to you."

"Yes, of course! I agree!" John exclaimed.

Le Clerc looked at John with surprise. "Why?"

"Because he described my vision for my life. Freedom is my highest value. That's why I came to Outcast Island. The chaos here was the perfect opportunity to wipe the slate clean and to rekindle the fire of liberty. We're going to build a civilization where we don't hurt each other or take each other's stuff. We will neither coerce nor be coerced."

Le Clerc chuckled. "I agreed with the Monk, too, but for a very different reason. He made me realize that there's a vast difference between fighting *for* freedom and *being* free. I want to live the life of a pirate, unconstrained by others, beholden to no one, and free to do whatever I choose. John, I admire your passion for rescuing this awful world, but I don't want to follow laws that others make nor conform to norms I don't agree with. I don't want to be the biological tool of anyone. Not even you. The world treated me terribly when I was an orphan in Egypt, so I owe the world nothing now."

John understood what le Clerc meant. He and Mary discussed this issue many times. Was it wiser to fight the political battles of the day at the cost of burdening your own life or even risking death? Or was it better to seek refuge from the political tumult and live life in blissful ignorance until the wolf was at your own door?

His answer had driven his decision to come to Outcast Island. Fighting for liberty gave him purpose and satisfaction, despite the danger and sacrifices involved. Mary not only accepted his choice; it also made him a hero in her eyes. During his subsequent ordeals, he took refuge knowing that a free person dies only once, but a submissive person dies every hour of every day.

He nodded to le Clerc. "You're locked into your vision, just as I am to mine. Enjoy your adventures. I wish you fair winds and following seas." Then he turned to the Monk. "So how is it that we both agreed with your wisdom yet ended up embracing radically different paths?"

The Monk finished his tea while gathering his thoughts. "In many ways, all humans are alike. We all prefer life over death. We prefer ease over burden. We prefer cooperation over conflict. We want to love and be loved. We want to thrive. We want to be seen, heard, and approved of. But despite our commonalities, we are each unique and wish to choose our own paths. We differ in our desires, aptitudes, and conditioning. No two people will ever see existence the same way, nor wish to live their lives the same way. That's why freedom is so vital for human fulfillment."

Le Clerc smiled ruefully. "Well said, Monk." Then he looked at John. "You and I have charted our own courses. But one important person hasn't."

John's heart sank. He, too, wondered what direction Olga would choose for her life.

The Monk saw John's distress. He walked over to him, placed a gentle hand on his shoulder, and smiled serenely. "We all long for permanence and attachment, John. But everything is impermanent, and attachment is a waste of your life force. Things always change. Then they all pass."

"That's hard to swallow when the subject is a person you love deeply," John replied.

Le Clerc nodded. "We agree on that."

"Of course," the Monk said. "But you can't love and imprison at the same time. Those we love are like a breeze that must waft freely if they are to refresh and invigorate us. If you put the breeze into a container, it becomes stale air. Setting others free is the only path to setting yourself free. It takes two to imprison: the prisoner and the jailor."

The door to the infirmary swung open, ushering in a rush of fresh air. Olga strutted in with Merlin perched on her shoulder. An awkward silence followed her dramatic entrance.

Undaunted, she walked over to le Clerc's bed and gently touched his wounded shoulder. "I found Merlin moping outside the clinic. Maybe he'll cheer you up. Are you healing well, Ammon?"

"Danger!" Merlin squawked.

John closed his eyes to block out the shock of Olga's doting concern for le Clerc. He felt like he was back in the Caves of Despair.

45

———

DESTINY

John looked to the heavens as he lounged on a bench near the Rock, basking in the glorious sunshine that was consecrating another blessed day in Pathless Land. The sky was a cloudless azure. An intoxicating breeze wafted over the island, carrying aloft the alluring scent of tropical flowers in bloom.

"Looking good!" a farmer tilling a field shouted to John. John waved and nodded. He was indeed feeling strong again, although Doc warned him there would be some permanent damage from his gunshot wounds. It had been six months since his brush with death in the Caves of Despair.

John was pleased with the progress of Pathless Land. Its population continued to grow as refugees from the outlying regions of Outcast Island flocked to it, drawn by the hope for security, freedom, and prosperity. Other new arrivals came via the ships that regularly disgorged misfits and rebels onto the island from countries around the world.

To aid the shipborne diaspora, Pathless Land formed a brigade of volunteer rescuers equipped with boats and lifesaving equipment. They were on call to race to the shoreline whenever lookouts spotted ships dumping outcasts into the ocean. The survivors were endeared to Pathless Land for this assistance.

Every new arrival to the Rock was homesteaded a parcel of land in the surrounding region. This gave each person property that belonged to them alone, fueling a spirit of pride, responsibility, self-sufficiency, and ambition. The free-market philosophy of Pathless Land ignited a burst of productivity. Technology was enhanced by the engineers and craftsmen who had been banished to the island. Hammer and the Carpenter collaborated on constructing a shipyard for building boats. Hammer's new sailboat would be the first off its production line.

The laws of Pathless Land were simple and understood by all. They were founded on four key imperatives: Don't initiate aggression. Interact only by mutual consent. Honor all contracts. Steal nothing. The well-trained volunteer militia of Pathless Land discouraged the rogue elements on the island from disturbing the peace.

John's pleasant reverie was interrupted by a familiar voice.

"Hello, sweetheart!" Olga said as she approached him from behind.

She had come to join him for their daily homage to Pathless Land's fallen heroes. They strolled hand in hand to the cemetery they had named Arlington. The pristinely kept plot was a sobering counterpoint to the growing success of Pathless Land and a morbid reminder that everything comes with a price. Many brave people had made the ultimate sacrifice to enable the peace and prosperity now enjoyed by their new society.

There were nearly a hundred tombstones in Arlington now, each with a white rose bush planted beside it. Many graves didn't contain a body because the deceased heroes had died in brutal circumstances. The explosion at Bauta was the worst. The bodies of the men killed there would never be recovered. The women of the Remnant who died while in captivity at the Rock were also memorialized with empty caskets.

The couple paused their stroll when they arrived at the adjacent tombstones of Nicolai and Newton. John bowed his head and whispered a short ode of thanks to the two scientists. They were his shipmates on the harrowing transit to Outcast Island. Their expertise had blessed Pathless Land with vital technology, including radios, generators, windmills, explosives, and refurbished drones. Most importantly, they had sacrificed their lives at Bauta to help avert a nuclear apocalypse that saved countless other lives. "Rest in peace," he consoled them. "It's because of heroes like you that we survivors can live a better life."

Their next stop was Mallory's grave. They both were awed by the selfless courage of the military commander. In every major conflict that Pathless Land endured, Mallory had devised the tactics, trained their raw troops, worked with Hammer to develop weaponry, and fearlessly led the team into battle. He was as courageous a warrior as anyone who ever walked the Earth. John put a hand on Mallory's headstone and bowed his head. He gazed at the epitaph: "The Wolf is always at the door, so Freedom must always be defended." It saddened him that Mallory's body was lost at Bauta, and it horrified him to ponder the heroic man's awful final moments. He never had a chance to properly thank him.

In this dismal moment, John reflected once again on Pathless Land's progress. Many people had contributed to it in countless ways, but those who were buried in Arlington had contributed something beyond comprehension to him. He felt small in their ghostly presence. The cemetery was a reminder that life should never be taken for granted, and the men and women who protect life should be placed on the highest pedestals of honor. Pathless Land was indebted to its deceased warriors in a way that could never be repaid but would always be remembered.

Next, they came to the grave of Julio Cruz. Julio had died enroute from Skull Ridge to the Rock's clinic after the Proletariat ambush. His final words to John helped point the forces of Pathless Land toward Vlad's refuge in the Caves of Despair. The young man's courage and his forlorn final words were permanently etched on John's soul. They reminded him that too often the renowned leaders are the ones who are honored for their heroism, even though the greatest acts of valor are usually performed by anonymous soldiers who place their lives in harm's way to protect those they love from predation. Those nameless and faceless heroes are usually forgotten, while the beneficiaries of their sacrificial valor live on.

John would never forget. The body of Julio Cruz was buried under the largest monument in Arlington. John kept his promise to the dying soldier that he would give him a medal for his valor, even though it was posthumous. He commissioned Hammer to craft an ornate plaque made of gold gifted by Spartacus. The plaque was prominently mounted on Julio's stone monument and engraved with the words, "My name is Julio Cruz, and I gave all." John bowed his head. "Thank you again, Julio. Godspeed," he whispered.

As they left the cemetery, Olga sensed that John was particularly despondent from today's homage. She gently took his hand.

"Don't be so sad," she said. "There's more reason for joy than you know." She led him to a bench situated on their plot of land where his cherished white roses and lavender grew. They sat down. Olga put her arm around him and leaned her head against his shoulder.

"John, I received a note from François today."

John cringed at this unwelcome news. Even though he and Olga were informally married now, John had never conquered his insecurity about the pirate. The mention of a note from his competing suitor spoiled the solemnity of their morning.

"That's reason for joy?" John grumbled.

Olga could see from his reddening face that she had once again touched a sensitive nerve that might never heal. "John!" she exclaimed. "You don't have to react this way every time I mention le Clerc. Surely you know by now that I'm committed to your vision of Pathless Land and that I'll be by your side until I die."

John nodded but avoided her eyes. "You broke my heart the day you entered the clinic with that annoying parrot on your shoulder. You went directly to le Clerc's bed to console him."

"He had to be the first to hear of my decision," Olga explained. "I owed him that much. I also had to bring Merlin to him. That creature is like a homing pigeon."

John continued to look away.

Olga glared at him. "Let's resolve this once and for all. I admit I loved Ammon. That was his given name. But he's no longer Ammon.

He became François le Clerc, the invincible pirate seeking revenge against the world. You're a greater man who wants to make the world a better place. I was drawn to you from the moment you came to the Remnant camp after your rogue soldiers attacked us. Le Clerc would never have done that. Instead, he broke our blood oath. You kept our blood oath sacred, despite everything."

"What did his note say?" John asked.

"He has sailed to the major ports around the Caribbean and seen the same anarchy in all those places as we had in Outcast Island. The people live in fear and destitution. But the region has lots of natural resources, and everyone is desperate for hope. He wrote that the time is right for Pathless Land to begin sharing its vision with them. He said your idea to establish a Caribbean Federation that can eventually challenge the World Order is possible."

"What else?" John asked.

"He mentioned that there's a price on your head and his. Several assassins have attempted to kill him while he was exploring. One of the assassins confessed under torture about the ten-million-dollar bounties being offered. He advised you to trust no one outside of Pathless Land."

"That would include him," John observed. "Anything else? Anything personal?"

Olga sighed. "His travels are making him fabulously rich, although it's not clear if that's from trading or pirating." She paused to put a gentle hand on John's arm. "He says he's rich enough now to build me the palace of my dreams."

"I see," John muttered. "He'll never give up, will he?"

Olga felt his muscular forearm stiffen under her touch. She took his hand and placed it on her abdomen. This puzzled him until the reason struck him like a lightning bolt. He had noticed some extra weight around her midsection but wisely never mentioned it. He looked at her wide-eyed. His hand shook with excitement.

"We're going to have a baby!" Olga cried. "The Rock is the palace of my dreams, and I want nothing more than to raise a child with you."

John leaned over and kissed her more passionately than ever

before. When their lips parted, he gazed into her eyes. They were always mesmerizing to him, but now they glowed with a radiance that was otherworldly. The onset of motherhood was elevating her spirit to something magnificent.

"What do you wish most for our child?" Olga asked, brimming with motherly enthusiasm.

"Freedom," John replied. He paused to study the matronly swelling of her belly. The news about the conception of their child changed everything for him. A blessed peace came over him. But it only lasted for mere seconds because he was struck by a troubling thought.

"We have to discuss our child's surname," John said.

Olga flashed a quizzical look.

"It must be Kozlowski," John declared.

"What's wrong with Paine?"

"It's attached to me," John replied. "I'll eventually be the most hunted man in the world. Anyone named Paine will be at risk when the Elites seek retribution. I want to avoid exposing our child."

"Aren't you at risk too?" Olga asked. "Maybe *you* should have an alias."

John smiled coyly. "Just before I was apprehended in Kansas, I signed off my journal for last time with the initial *J*. I intended to hide my identity behind that cryptic letter. That idea got lost in the ensuing chaos. An alias seemed pointless in the anarchy of Outcast Island. But now that Pathless Land is preparing to engage the rest of the world, I'm going to use the initial *J* in any formal communications or records. It'll be my permanent alias."

"That's wise."

John frowned. "Maybe. But my life's mission is dangerous to everyone I love. You'll be exposed to the risks too. And you may pay a high price. Are you willing, given the new addition to our family?" He caressed her belly.

"What a ridiculous question!" Olga pulled up her sleeve to bare her ferocious Polish eagle tattoo. "I'll be sidelined during my pregnancy, but then I intend to face the same risks as you and pursue the same dreams for the future of our society. I'm willing to pay any price."

"Spoken like a true warrior," John replied. He fumbled with the white rose that was pinned to his shirt, then removed it and placed it gently on her belly. "I need you by my side, Olga. Dark days are ahead."

"What do you mean?" she asked.

"Our challenges have just begun, even though we've been through hell already. Achieving our vision will be grueling and dangerous, and it'll take time. Probably more time than I have left in my abused body. Doc said there's less sand left in my personal hourglass than normal. A couple of decades at most. One of the bullets nicked my heart, and there isn't much he can do about it with the limited resources he has."

Olga's eyes reddened. She held his hand again and nestled her head on his shoulder. "That saddens me more than I can put into words."

"Ditto," John said. "But the truth of our existence is that none of us will live to see the end of all our stories or the realization of all our dreams. But we must work toward something, even if we'll never arrive at the destination. Without that sense of purpose, what is there? We need something to do, something to hope for, and people to love. Those three treasures will keep our fire burning during the difficult road ahead. I want freedom for everyone I love, and for everyone they will love, and so on. If I don't work toward that future, then everyone who lies buried in Arlington died in vain."

"So we have purpose, love, and hope," Olga replied. "What do we do next?"

"What humans should do. We build a safe and prosperous society. We defend ourselves from enemies within and without. And we prepare for the storm that we're going to unleash to liberate the rest of the world."

"Isn't it enough to create a peaceful society here?" Olga asked. "Why must we be storm-bringers who cast thunder and lightning in other lands? Especially since you're running out of sand in your hourglass."

"Because the cause of Pathless Land is the cause of all humankind. There's a Goldilocks Zone between the extremes of anarchy and totalitarianism. That Zone is the narrow political heaven where there's enough government to protect life and freedom, but not so much that it suffocates them. Once each person is safe in their lives, their property, and their contracts, then peace for the entire society naturally follows. Pathless Land will refine the recipe for that Goldilocks Zone on Outcast Island, and then we'll share it everywhere. Until the whole world learns to peacefully coexist in the Goldilocks Zone, there will always be storm clouds of anarchy or totalitarianism looming on the horizon, threatening to engulf the world in tyranny."

"Who's behind that perpetual threat of tyranny?"

"An enemy I don't fully understand yet," John replied. "A sinister, secretive organization of money changers who are nearly invisible, yet their shadow is cast everywhere. I know how to fight real enemies like narco-terrorists and dictators, but how do you fight ghosts like that?"

"That's an awful paradox for humankind," Olga said. "Money is the lifeblood of civilization, and yet it's the weapon that the puppet masters use to manipulate common people and to turn their governments into Trojan Horses."

"Money itself isn't bad," John replied. "It's necessary for widespread collaboration in a free and productive society. But it isn't without risks. Who creates it? Who controls it? Who are the gilded aristocrats who profit by manipulating it rather than by trading goods and services? How is it that a small cartel of financial marauders can plunder entire nations?"

Olga fell silent. She had no answers. It was clear to her, though, that John was zeroing in on the root cause of most of humankind's political distress.

A young man rushed up to them. "John!" he cried anxiously. "It's time for your broadcast."

The young man was one of a bevy of skilled technicians who had scavenged old electrical components from abandoned warehouses in la Habana. From the scraps, they fabricated a crude radio transmitter, and Hammer's craftsmen erected a crude radio tower. And now they were manufacturing radio receivers that were being distributed around the island.

"Gotta go," John said to Olga. He kissed her cheek tenderly.

"What are you broadcasting?" She was mildly perturbed that he had kept this project a secret from her, but then she remembered she had kept her pregnancy a secret from him for a while.

"I wanted to surprise you," John replied with impish enthusiasm. "It's the premiere episode of an educational series."

"What's it called?" Olga asked.

"The Voice of America."

She gave him a puzzled look. "But you were exiled from America. Our new society is called Pathless Land."

"I was exiled from a geographical entity called America that was hijacked by the Elites. But America is an ideal that's unbounded by time or geography. Our vision of Pathless Land is an enrichment of the original American principles, honed by the lessons learned since 1776. To help connect the old and the new, I've decided that the formal name of our new nation will be Pathless Land of America."

Olga frowned. "Won't a public airing of such ideas put a bigger target on your back for any enemy within range of your radio signals?"

"That's the bargain I've chosen to make with life," John replied. "As Plato put it, the price good people pay for indifference to public affairs is to be ruled by evil people. I refuse to be ruled by evil people. That means I must be willing to pay a different price."

"The price may be every grain left in your hourglass," Olga warned.

"Then so be it. Outcast Island gave us an opportunity to begin the world over again. I can think of no greater purpose for my life, and no greater contribution I can make to posterity. Someday, there will be peace on Earth, a peace that began here. We will create a world without coercion where people are free to disagree while not harming each other. It is only a world without coercion where the playing field can be leveled between the Elites and everyone else. I will achieve that vision or die trying."

46

THE SWORD OF DAMOCLES

Cosimo abandoned the last vestige of his well-practiced self-control. He hurled his half-empty glass of sambuca at the ornate stone fireplace in his posh Washington, DC, hotel. It shattered in a spectacular eruption of shards and bright-red liquid, but the violence of it gave him no satisfaction. He did, however, pause to admire the bloodstain-like splotches it left in his suite.

He was alone. He had ripped off his Italian suit jacket and tossed his silk tie onto the floor. Sweat soiled his pressed shirt. His normally well-coiffed hair was a tangled pomade mess. His fists were clenched, and his bloodshot eyes blazed with Luciferian rage.

His great consternation was caused by several documents that littered his writing desk. Six had couriered the offending paperwork to him. The documents represented Cosimo's first report card as a full-fledged Centurion in the Syndicate. Judgment from Six was his worst and only nightmare. Goosebumps spread across his cold, clammy skin, and a sense of impending doom hung over him.

He grabbed Six's pithy cover note and reread it.

Still waiting for a progress report on your new mission in America. In the meantime, enclosed is my assessment of your self-chosen assignment to kill your two antagonists from Outcast Island. It appears that those men were more consequential than I originally judged. Unfortunately, the enclosed documents indicate abject failure on your part. The Syndicate will not tolerate failure now that your apprenticeship is over. Ours is a world without mercy.

Cosimo grabbed the open bottle of sambuca and took a long swig, then slammed it down on the desk. The liquid courage coursing his veins numbed his reluctance to read Six's dire enclosures. The first was a report from Giovanni, one of Six's nine other Centurions and thus Cosimo's peer. The note was addressed to Six, but the notations on the envelope made it clear the subject was Cosimo. The spying of Centurion against Centurion was one of Six's Machiavellian methods for keeping tabs on all his lieutenants. Cosimo closed his eyes for a moment, then opened Giovanni's report.

Your Excellency, per your instructions, I have assessed the progress of Cosimo's assignment to terminate François le Clerc and John Paine. The situation is more serious than you or I previously believed. Here's my report.

Cosimo has circulated a bounty offer throughout our network of hired killers guaranteeing $10 million in gold bars to any assassin who eliminates either of the two targets. This is standard protocol.

There have been several attempts on le Clerc's life as he sailed with his pirated navy around the Caribbean. All failed. Le Clerc is quite clever, and he's surrounded by a phalanx of loyal pirates who've either killed or captured his potential assassins. There have been no further attempts on his life in the last two months, simply because no sane assassin deems the $10 million bounty worth the risk now.

No attempt has been made on Paine's life. There's no practical way to reach Outcast Island since le Clerc eliminated the World Order's naval quarantine. No opportunity will be coming soon either. The World Order is unable to provide more ships because almost every nation is embroiled in civil or international strife.

Cosimo paused and imagined Six's furious reaction when his boss got this note from Giovanni. He recalled their last meeting in Rome when Six began their discussion by placing a gun on the table between them. The Syndicate's code of justice was unforgiving. He took another long swig from the bottle of sambuca and continued reading:

My concerns grew about Outcast Island when satellite photos revealed that the Pathless Land rebels are constructing a shipyard near la Habana. The ships it can produce are small (for now), but it shows the rebels have ambitions of extending their reach beyond the island. Since the World Order is unable to redirect naval resources to the Caribbean, there's nothing impeding the creation of a crude Pathless Land navy. This situation could get worse if le Clerc and Paine join forces, which they don't appear to have done (yet).

Cosimo grimly recalled his foolish move to sell a World Order destroyer to le Clerc in exchange for half of Morgan's treasure. It was a regrettable decision that led to the dismantling of the fleet that was quarantining Outcast Island. Cosimo knew Six would never forget that. He opened another bottle of sambuca, took a long swig, and returned to Giovanni's assessment:

Your Excellency, the Voice of America broadcasts originating from Outcast Island are an even bigger concern. They're presumably voiced by Paine, although they are enigmatically attributed to a person calling himself J. Pathless Land's radio signal is powerful enough to reach the entire Caribbean basin, including the shorelines of Central and South America. The rhetoric that J (Paine?) broadcasts is exactly the kind of inflammatory swill that can incite the proles. The Syndicate has spent centuries trying to squelch such incendiary speech. The world is on a razor's edge right now, and his fiery words could spark events that threaten our dominion. His broadcasts are weapons more powerful than missiles or bombs because they're as contagious as a virus and can move hearts and minds.

I won't trouble you with the detailed transcripts of his speeches, but here's a brief summary that will make your blood boil. He claims his philosophy can politically unify all the proles in both the East and the West. His rallying cry is that all political turmoil in the world is an outgrowth of an eternal conflict between the Elites and everyone else. Freedom is his highest political ideal, which can only be secured by governments limited to protecting life, liberty, and property. Most egregiously, he claims that people everywhere retain an inalienable right of revolution in order to resist, alter, or abolish tyrannical governments and institutions.

We both know that such heresies must be expunged from the face of the Earth, along with those who utter them. It's impossible for the Syndicate to survive a world of unified proles who've identified us as their common enemy and who feel empowered to expose and resist our coercive influence in world affairs. We're outnumbered a million to one.

My final point is a sensitive one, so please indulge me. I offer it as your humble and respectful Centurion. I know that you were using Outcast Island as a training ground for Cosimo. I also know that you believed the island was an insignificant speck on the globe that would likely cannibalize itself in brutal anarchy. And I know that you believed any mistakes Cosimo made during his training were therefore of little consequence.

Your Excellency, with great reluctance I must observe that you were mistaken on all counts. The island is not falling further into anarchy. Under the banner of Pathless Land, it is organizing itself into a functional society that is independent of the Syndicate's influence. It's conceivable that a rebellious Caribbean Federation could emerge someday. Cosimo's failure to terminate François le Clerc and John Paine is exposing the Syndicate to immense danger. In their separate ways, they are metastasizing a deadly cancer that could spread everywhere and disrupt the benevolent serfdom that is our ideal world. We can't allow common people to think of themselves as anything but subjects and ciphers.

As always, it will be up to you to decide how to deal with Cosimo. I know that you've invested a great deal of effort training him. Perhaps it's worthwhile to give him one final opportunity to rectify his shortcomings. But there can be no more forgiveness after this. He must be made to understand that the Sword of Damocles hangs over his head with every decision he makes.

Hopefully he'll realize that he must poise an even more devastating Sword of Damocles above the head of every enemy he's assigned to kill. Starting with le Clerc and Paine.

Cosimo spread out the two photographs Six had enclosed in the envelope with the note from Giovanni. One was a grainy portrait of John Paine, the other of François le Clerc. Both were taken from a time when the World Order was still operating drones above Outcast Island. He stared at them, absorbing every grainy detail, focusing every bit of his fierce attention on his two adversaries. It didn't take long to bring his hatred to a boil. He felt it in every fiber of his being. It crowded out every thought. His whole body shook with emotion.

He stood up and carefully stacked the two pictures on top of each other, with Paine's being the uppermost.

He pulled his hunting knife out of his briefcase, gripped it with both hands, raised it high above his head, then plunged it through the pictures.

He did this with such force that the tip of the blade buried deep into the wooden surface of the desk. One of his hands slipped from the hilt onto the blade, gashing three of his fingers. The pain was exquisite. The sight of his blood dripping from his whitened knuckles onto Paine's grainy face was exhilarating.

It became a kind of blood oath, a death pact with himself. John Paine and François le Clerc would die, even if he had to spill the last drop of his own blood and spend the last sovereign of Morgan's treasure to do it.

He realized that Six had always been right. The biggest threat to the Syndicate wasn't marching armies or popular political movements. It was those few renegades who were uncorruptible.

He was going to rain hellfire upon his two antagonists. His greatest desire now was to see their caskets being lowered into the ground in mute witness to the ineffable power of the Syndicate.

ACKNOWLEDGMENTS

Perhaps the only task more daunting than writing a novel is to properly acknowledge all the wonderful people who helped breathe life into these pages. This book would not have been possible without the contributions and support of many talented and patient collaborators. This is my wholly inadequate attempt to recognize and thank them.

I am deeply indebted to my beautiful and talented wife, Audrey. Not only did she manage our household while I was immersed in writing, but she also invested countless hours helping to improve this book. She read, edited, and critiqued the manuscript at least five times, which was a heroic feat of patience and endurance. She was my toughest critic and my greatest supporter, which is a tough combination to artfully navigate. The novel in its final form was heavily influenced by her steady stream of ideas and suggestions.

I am indebted to Erin Schade, Jimmy Keena, Colleen Hahn, Katie Keena, Maureen Carmody, Ella Keena, Peggy Lothschutz, Karen Byrne, Sharon Lollio, Caleb Byrne, and Andy Brandt for their assistance with reading and critiquing the beta version of this novel. I thoroughly appreciate their willingness to bravely slog through my imperfect draft and to offer ideas and suggestions that made the book more vibrant and coherent.

I am indebted to Illumify Media Global for their tireless and often brilliant efforts to bring the final product to the marketplace. Mike Klassen, Geoff Stone, Karen Bouchard, Jenna Love-Schrader, Melissa Carter, and Illumify's network of support resources were consummate professionals in this endeavor. Their creativity, their hard work, and their dedication to this project polished the rough edges off the novel and made it glitter.

I am indebted to my close friends who regularly engage with Audrey and me in discussion and debate about political, economic, and philosophical issues pressing on our society. Their intellectual insights have honed and shaped my perspectives and have left an indelible mark on the concepts woven into the tapestry of this novel. I appreciate every enriching thought and insightful challenge put forth by Terry Hughes, Angie and Patrick Colbeck, and Sharon and Marco Lollio, and I will forever cherish our lively monthly dinners together.

Finally, and most importantly, I am indebted to all of the brave men and women who have ever served in the American armed forces. Without their courage and sacrifice over the centuries, our freedom would be nothing but a forlorn and distant memory. There are no words sufficient to thank them. While I cannot match their sacrifice, I can offer the power of my pen to complement the might of their swords in defense of our liberty.

ABOUT THE AUTHOR

James Keena is an author of critically acclaimed books and commentaries. A popular radio guest, he has also been a featured speaker at political and educational events throughout the Midwest. He is the author of *2084: American Apocalypse, Insurrection Resurrection*, a novel of political and religious satire, and a nonfiction work entitled *We've Been Had: How Obama and the Radicals Conned Middle Class America*. James has eight children and twenty-one grandchildren.

Visit him at: www.jameskeena.com

www.ingramcontent.com/pod-product-compliance
Lightning Source LLC
Chambersburg PA
CBHW031843310726
48972CB00005B/1381